not

Lemn Sissay, Booker Prize judge

'Soulful, urgent… Cook is adept at matter-of-factly deploying unadorned detail to deadpanning, gut-plummeting effect… Supremely well-crafted.'

Observer

'Riveting… Bleakly compelling, and leavened by wry, sparkling humour that Cook combines seamlessly with existential dread.'

Daily Telegraph

'Cook's propulsive tale is moved along as much by the engrossingly complex mother-daughter relationship that develops as by the Community's grim attempts to survive… *The New Wilderness* is a well-formed and powerful piece of writing.'

The Times

'Cook leavens her satire with sly wit and real wisdom, expertly deconstructing the borderline separating human beings and other anim

sy Books, 2020

'*The New Wilderness* is Diane Cook's debut novel that brings to life a wildly imaginative and terrifying dystopian story of a mother's battle to save her daughter from a world ravaged by climate change. Touching on humanity and our contempt for nature, this is a timely and compelling novel.'

Independent

'A visceral, elemental performance... Dense with believable detail.'

The Sunday Times

'5 of 5 stars. [A] gripping, fierce, terrifying examination of what people are capable of when they want to survive in both the best and worst ways. Loved this.'

Roxane Gay

'This...novel's driving questions—who will live and who will die? And which kind of leadership will triumph along the way?—remind us, in a compelling fashion, why we read at all: to learn how better to survive.'

New Statesman

'A dazzling debut... The unease between mother and daughter as they navigate disparate understandings of self, belonging, society and each other is the beating heart of the novel... Cook takes command of a fast-paced, thrilling story to ask stomach-turning questions in a moment when it would benefit every soul to have their stomach turned by the prospect of the future she envisions.'

Téa Obreht, author of *The Tiger's Wife*

'*The New Wilderness* is a virtuosic debut, brutal and beautiful in equal measure.'

Emily St. John Mandel, author of *Station Eleven*

'This gut-wrenching story of survival, danger, power, control and, most importantly, love is one you won't want to put down.'

CNN

'Wonderfully imagined and written, this is a tense future-shock novel that's also a tender exploration of a mother-daughter relationship under extreme pressure.'

Booker Prize judges

'Gripping and provoking... Violence, death, tribalism, lust, love, betrayals, wonder, genius, and courage—all are enacted in this stunningly incisive and complexly suspenseful tale akin to dystopian novels by Margaret Atwood and Claire Vaye Watkins. When Cook finally widens the lens on her characters' increasingly desperate predicament, the exposure of malignant greed, deceit, and injustice resonates with devastating impact.'

Booklist, starred review

'An absolutely riveting and propulsive novel. Terrifying, and as real as can be. Epic in scale and story; granular and recognisable in people and place. *The New Wilderness* is surely an instant classic in our stories of survival, sovereignty and adaptation. Cook's writing is so sure-footed, prescient and trustworthy, it's all the reader can do to follow her. For fans of Ling Ma's *Severance* and Hernan Diaz's *In the Distance*, and many, many readers in between.'

Caoilinn Hughes, author of *The Wild Laughter*

'*The New Wilderness* left me as stunned as a deer in headlights. Gut-wrenching and heart-wrecking, this is a book that demands to be read, and urgently. With beauty and compassion, Diane Cook writes about the precariousness of life on this planet, about the things that make us human—foremost the love between mothers and daughters, at once complex and elemental. Cook observes humanity as a zoologist might—seeing us exactly as the strange animals we really are.'

Rachel Khong, author of *Goodbye, Vitamin*

'A deft portrait of human nature.'

Mail on Sunday

'A wry, speculative debut novel... Cook's unsettling, darkly humorous tale explores maternal love and man's disdain for nature with impressive results.'

Publishers Weekly, starred review

'Diane Cook upends old tropes of autonomy, survival, and civilization to reveal startling new life teeming beneath, giving a glimpse into the ways the world we think we know could come unstuck and come to life in the care of the women and girls of the future. This is not just a thrilling, curious, vibrant book—but an essential one, a compass to guide us into the future.'

Alexandra Kleeman,
author of *You Too Can Have A Body Like Mine*

'Expertly plotted... Highly seductive writing... It is the anthropological acuity in Cook's writing that makes it so persuasive... The chief power of *The New Wilderness*, and what distinguishes it from less successful environmental dystopian fiction, is Cook's talent for world-building.'

Times Literary Supplement

'*The New Wilderness* strips us of our veneer of civilisation and exposes us for what we are: driven to survive, capable of shocking cruelty and profound, fierce love. This story of what a mother does to save her daughter is unflinching, horrifying, forgiving, deeply moving, and filled with truth that stayed with this mother long after the final page.'

Helen Sedgwick, author of *The Comet Seekers*
and *When the Dead Come Calling*

'Precise, beautiful and matter-of-fact... Cook's rendering of the numberless threats her characters face—both from too much nature and too little—makes *The New Wilderness* a tense and absorbing read, while her attention to the complicated intensity of human relationships gives the work its power.'

Literary Review

'The push-pull of ambivalent but powerful love between mother and daughter centers the novel… Cook also raises uncomfortable questions: How far will a person go to survive, and what sacrifices will she or won't she make for those she loves? This ecological horror story (particularly horrifying now) explores painful regions of the human heart.'

Kirkus, starred review

'The emotional core of the story is the relationship between Bea and Agnes, whose perspectives drive the narrative. It's a damning piece of horror cli-fi, but it's also a gripping and profound examination of love and sacrifice.'

Buzzfeed

'Cook has a keen eye for the relentless weigh-ups of parenthood… The tale of a hazardously self-denying lifestyle pursued on health grounds, it has uncanny resonance.'

Metro

'An imaginative, dystopian look at what our world could become… I was gripped by how vivid the story was, how expertly Diane Cook got into the dynamics of a group of strangers surviving in the wild, and their relationship with those in power.'

Hey Alma, 'Favourite Books for Summer'

'The novel tackles the deepest of human emotions—as well as big ideas about the planet—in satisfying ways. Also, it's a page-turner!'

LitHub

'Urgent and inventive… People who switch off when they hear the phrase "climate change" should read it. And so should everyone else.'

Irish Times

'Her writing is deceptively simple, beautifully corporeal.'

San Francisco Chronicle

'[The] meditation on mother-daughter relationships (and by extension, humanity's relationship with Mother Nature)…provides the emotional heft in this thrilling, allegorical tale.'

Irish Independent

'In this beautiful novel, the United States has become largely unliveable and so Bea takes her ailing daughter Agnes to live in one of the last patches of wilderness… In that possibility Cook finds humour, incredible heart and something like hope.'

NPR

'I absolutely fell in love with *The New Wilderness* by Diane Cook, as it so deftly weaves environmental concern with familial bonds, and looks to answer the question of how far we would go for our children… Beautiful, and also a stark reminder to reconsider what we value in our short times on this earth, and to be conscious of what we leave behind.'

NB Magazine, Best Books of 2020

'This debut novel erupts with a ferocity that barely falters.'

South Australia Weekend

'Diane Cook's *The New Wilderness*, shortlisted for the 2020 Booker prize, is another powerful climate-change novel.'

Canberra Times

'More than timely, the novel feels timeless, solid, like a forgotten classic recently resurfaced—a brutal, beguiling fairy tale about humanity. But at its core, *The New Wilderness* is about motherhood, and about the world we make (or unmake) for our children.'

Washington Post

PRAISE FOR
MAN V. NATURE

Shortlisted for the *Guardian* First Book Award, 2015
Shortlisted for the *LA Times* Book Prize, 2015

'Exhilarating… Cook's is a fresh and vivid voice; it's unsurprising the likes of Miranda July and Roxane Gay are fans.'

Observer

'*Man V. Nature* is a knockout… Every single story could make a great movie.'

New York Times Book Review

'Masterly.'

New York Times

'A deeply original collection…deliciously unsettling…uncomfortably resonant.'

Independent

'Makes for compulsive reading… These tales dizzy and trick.'

New Statesman

'Astonishing… The stories are surreal, with the sharpest edge and in one way or another, each story reveals something raw and powerful about being human in a world where so little is in our control.'

Roxane Gay

'Sharply written and imaginative… Cook is an accomplished writer with a darkly comic touch [with] echoes of Margaret Atwood.'

Irish Times

'These are grimly funny stories; dark, but dizzyingly alive.'

Sunday Express

THE NEW
WILDERNESS

DIANE COOK

ONEWORLD

A Oneworld Book

First published in Great Britain, Ireland and Australia
by Oneworld Publications, 2020
This paperback edition published 2021

ISBN 978-0-86154-001-3
ISBN 978-1-78607-822-3 (eBook)

Title page illustration by Avychai Chinwan / Shutterstock, Inc.

Printed and bound in Great Britain by Clays Ltd, Elcograf S.p.A.

Oneworld Publications
10 Bloomsbury Street
London WC1B 3SR
England

Stay up to date with the latest books,
special offers, and exclusive content from
Oneworld with our newsletter

Sign up on our website
oneworld-publications.com

MIX
Paper from
responsible sources
FSC® C018072

For my mother, Linda, and my daughter, Cazadora
And for Jorge

. . . I am glad I shall never be young without wild country to be young in. Of what avail are forty freedoms without a blank spot on the map?

—ALDO LEOPOLD

Get me out of here, get me out of here
I hate it here, get me out of here

—ALEX CHILTON

Part I

THE BALLAD OF BEATRICE

THE BABY EMERGED from Bea the color of a bruise. Bea burned the cord somewhere between them and uncoiled it from the girl's slight neck and, though she knew it was useless, swept her daughter up into her hands, tapped on her soft chest, and blew a few shallow breaths into her slimy mouth.

Around her, the singular song of crickets expanded. Bea's skin prickled from heat. Sweat dried on her back and face. The sun had crested and would, more quickly than seemed right, fall again. From where Bea knelt, she saw their Valley, its secret grasses and sage. In the distance were lonely buttes and, closer, mud mounds that looked like cairns marking the way somewhere. The Caldera stood sharp and white on the horizon.

Bea dug into the hard earth with a stick, then a stone, then hollowed and smoothed it with her hands. She scooped the placenta into it. Then the girl. The hole was shallow and her baby's belly jutted from it. Wet from birth, the little body held on to coarse sand and tiny golden buds brittled from their stems by the heat of the sun. She sprinkled more dust onto the baby's forehead, pulled from her deer-hide bag several wilted green leaves, and laid them over the girl. She broke off craggy branches from the surrounding sage, laid them over the distended belly, the absurdly small shoulders. The baby was a misshapen mound of plant green, rust-red blood, a dull violet map of veins under wet tissue skin.

Now, the animals, who had sensed it, were converging. In the sky, a cyclone of buzzards lowered as if to check on the progress, then uplifted on a thermal. She heard the soft tread of coyotes. They wove through the bloomy sage. A mother and three skinny kits appeared under jaggedly thrown shade. Bea heard whines ease from their impassive yawns. They would wait.

A wind stirred and she breathed in the dusty heat. She missed the stagnant scent of the hospital room where she'd given birth to Agnes what must have been eight years ago now. The way the scratchy gown had stretched across her chest and gotten tangled up when she tried to roll to either side. How the cool air blew around her hips, between her legs, where her doctor and nurses stared, prodded, and pulled Agnes from her. She'd hated the feeling. So exposed, used, animal-like. But here, it was all dust and hot air. Here, she had needed to guide the small body—had she been five months pregnant? Six? Seven?—out with one hand while with the other she'd had to block a diving magpie. She had wanted to be alone for this. But what she wouldn't have given for a probing gloved hand, stale recirculated air, humming machines, fresh sheets under her rather than desert dust. Some sterile comfort.

What she wouldn't have given for her mother.

Bea hissed at the coyotes. "Scram," she said, pitching the dirt and pebbles she'd just dug at them. But they only slid their ears back, the mother sinking to her haunches and the kits nipping at her snout, irritating her. She probably snuck off from the rest of the pack to get her young something extra, or to let them practice scavenging, to practice surviving. It's what mothers did.

Bea shooed a fly from near the baby's eyes, which at first had looked startled over having not made it, but now seemed accusatory. The truth was Bea hadn't wanted the baby. Not here. It would have been wrong to bring her into this world. That's what she'd felt all along. But what if the girl had sensed Bea's dread and died from not being wanted?

Bea choked. "This is for the best," she told her. The girl's eyes clouded over with the clouds that rolled overhead.

During one nightwalk, back when she'd had a flashlight and still carried batteries to make it glow, she'd caught two eyes gleaming in her beam. She clapped her hands to scare the eyes, but they just dipped down. The animal was tall but crouching, sitting perhaps, and Bea feared it was stalking her. Her heart sped up and she waited for the cold dread that she'd felt a couple of times by then. Her inner sense of being in danger. But the feeling never came. She walked closer. Again the eyes dipped down, supplicant, like a dog obeying, but it was not a dog. She had to get closer before she could see that it was a deer with its sloped back, the peaked ears, the resigned flick of the tail. Then Bea saw another eye in the light, small, not looking at her, but quivering, unsteady. The deer heaved up and then the quivering eye wobbled up too. It was a small glistening fawn, on shaky, toothpick legs. Bea had unknowingly witnessed a birth. Quiet in the dark. Bea had come stealthily upon the mother like a predator. And the mother could do nothing in that moment but lower her head as though asking to be spared.

There were few things Bea let herself regret these days, these unpredictable days full of survival so plain and brute. But she wished she had walked another way that night, not found their eyes in her light, so that the doe could have had her birth, nuzzled and licked her baby clean, could have had the chance to give her baby a first unblemished night before the work of survival began. Instead the doe lumbered away, exhausted, the fawn stumbling after her, disoriented, and that was the beginning of their life together. It's why, days ago, when Bea no longer felt the kicks and hiccups and flutters and knew the baby had died, she knew she'd want to be alone for the birth. It was the only moment they would have together. She did not want to share that. She did not want someone watching her own complicated version of grief.

Bea peered at the coyote mother. "You understand, don't you?"

The coyote pranced impatiently and licked her yellow teeth.

From a far low ridge, some foothills of foothills to come, she heard a joyless howl; some watching wolf had seen the carrion birds, was signaling prey.

She had to leave. The sun was going. And now the wolves knew. She'd tracked her shadow becoming long and thin, a sight that always made her sad, as though she were seeing her own death by starvation. She stood, stretched out her sand-pocked knees, wiped the desert off her skin and ragged tunic. She felt foolish that she'd tried to resuscitate what she knew to be dead. She thought the Wilderness had cast all sentimentality from her. She would not tell anyone about that moment. Not Glen, who she thought wanted a child of his own more than he would ever admit. She wouldn't tell Agnes, even though she thought Agnes would want to know about this sister who never materialized, would want to understand the secret particulars of her mother. No, she would stick to the simple story. The baby did not survive. So many others hadn't. So we move on.

She turned without another look at this girl she had wanted to name Madeline. She gave that mother coyote a sharp kick, landing it against her visible ribs. The dog yelped, slunk, then snarled, but she had more pressing concerns than engaging a human insult.

Bea heard the scuffle and yips behind her. And though the dogs' rising excitement resembled a newborn's cry, Bea knew it was just the sound of hunger.

* * *

AN UNMISTAKABLE SHADOW of a path led toward the camp. It was hard to know if it was from the Community's own impact, animals making their own animal trails, or a remnant of all the things the land had been before it became the Wilderness State. Maybe it was Bea alone who had blazed the trail. She visited that place as often as she could, whenever they migrated through the Valley. It was the reason she'd chosen it for Madeline. There was something subtle in that view. It seemed like a hidden valley. The depression of verdant grasses and coarse bushes lay slightly lower than the land around it so that it had a secret view toward the horizon and the inky hump of mountains there. All the land in view formed a mosaic of blurred, muted colors. It was pretty and quiet and private, she thought. A place someone wouldn't want to leave. Again, Bea felt a fleeting relief to have Madeline poised there, instead of facing an unknowable landscape with her, a mother who felt incapable of maneuvering it with grace.

Bea could hear the voices of the others in camp. They carried across the even, empty land and dropped at her feet. But she did not want to return to them and their questions or, possibly worse, their silence. She shifted away and scrambled up boulders toward the shallow cave where her family liked to spend time. Their secret perch. She saw her husband, Glen, and daughter, Agnes, above her, kneeling in the dirt, waiting for her.

Bea saw Glen's brow furrowing in concentration as he spun a leaf by its stem, peering at it from every vantage, pointing to something on its green spine so Agnes could see, asking her to notice some remarkable detail in its common shape. They both leaned closer to the leaf, as though it were telling them its secret, their faces breaking into delight.

When Glen saw her approaching, he waved her toward them. Agnes did the same, a generous and awkward sweep of her arm, smiling with her newly jagged tooth, chipped against a boulder. *Why couldn't it have been a baby tooth?* Bea had thought, her daughter's head in her hands, inspecting the damage under her bright, bloody lip. Agnes had held still and quiet, one tear squeezing from her eye and trailing through the dirt on her face. It was the only way Bea knew the accident had fazed her. Like an animal, Agnes froze when fearful and bolted when endangered. Bea imagined that as Agnes grew up this would change. She might feel less like prey and more like a predator.

It was something in her daughter's smile, some unnameable knowledge. It was the smile of a girl biding her time.

"This one is alder," Glen was saying when Bea reached them. He took her hand, kissed it gently, lingering until she pulled it back to her side. She saw him glance at her stomach and wince.

He had prepared hot water in the brutish wood bowl, but now it was the temperature of the air. She squatted next to them, lifted her tunic, spread her knees. She scooped water under her skirt and gently washed between her legs, her stretched, worn folds, her splattered thighs. She felt raw, but she could tell she had not torn.

Agnes assumed the same position, her slight and toady legs splayed, splashing imaginary water on herself, eyeing Bea carefully. She seemed intent on not looking at where the baby had been.

Agnes was in some kind of mimicry stage. Bea saw it in animals. She'd seen it in other children. But in Agnes something about it disarmed her. She'd understood Agnes up until recently. Around the time the leaves last turned color, Agnes had become strange to her. She didn't know if this fissure was just something parents went through with their children, or mothers went through with daughters, or if it was just some special hardship she and Agnes would have to endure. Out here, it was hard for Bea to dismiss things as simply normal because every aspect of their lives here was anything but normal. Was Agnes behaving normally for her age, or was it possible she believed she was a wolf?

Agnes had just turned eight but didn't know it. They no longer marked birthdays because they no longer marked days. But Bea had taken notice of certain blooms when they'd first arrived. Then, Agnes had just turned five years old. It was April on the calendar. Bea had noted a field of violets during their first several days of walking. When she saw violets again, it seemed likely a year had passed— they'd felt the heat of summer, they'd seen leaves turn color, and they'd shivered in the snowy mountains. The snow had gone. She'd seen violets four times. Four birthdays. She knew Agnes's eighth birthday had happened sometime since the last full moon, when she had seen violets in a patch of grass near their last camp. When they'd first arrived, Agnes had been so gravely ill, Bea hadn't been sure she would see violets again with her daughter. But there they were, Agnes bounding through them.

Bea crept toward the back of the shallow cave. From behind a boulder, in a divot she'd hollowed out on their first time making camp here, she pulled a throw pillow and a design and architecture magazine that had featured one of her decorating remodels. It was a national magazine and the spread had been a turning point in her career, though not long after it published, she left for the Wilderness. These were her secret treasures she'd smuggled in from the City, and rather than carry them place to place, facing scorn from the others and damage from the elements, she hid them, blatantly disregarding the rules laid out in the Manual. When they passed through the Valley, which they had a few times each year, she dug out her treasures so she could feel a little more like herself.

She sat next to Glen and hugged her pillow. Then she thumbed through the pages of her spread, remembering the choices she'd made and why. Remembering what it felt like to have a home.

"If the Rangers find those, we'll get in trouble," Glen said, as he always said when she dug out her treasures, always so concerned with the rules.

She scowled. "What are they going to do? Kick us out for a pillow?"

"Maybe." Glen shrugged.

"Relax," she said. "They'll never find them. And I need them. I need to remember what pillows are like."

"Aren't I a good enough pillow?" He said this so sweetly.

Bea looked at him. He was all bones. They both were. Even her belly, which had barely jutted with the baby, seemed to have immediately sunken. When she looked up at him, he was offering a small broken smile. She nodded. He nodded back. Then he staged a long, loud, languid yawn, eyeing Agnes. Agnes's yawn followed with a big, fisted stretch.

"Big day tomorrow," he said. "We start our trip to Middle Post. And we get to cross your favorite river on the way."

"Can we swim?" Agnes asked.

"We've got to get in it to cross it, so you bet."

"When?"

"Probably be there in a few days."

"How much is a few?"

Glen shrugged. "Five? Ten? Several?"

Agnes huffed. "That's not an answer!"

Glen poked her and laughed. "We'll get there when we get there." Agnes's scowl was just like Bea's scowl.

"Is everything packed?" Bea asked.

"Mostly. You don't have to worry."

Bea gave the pillow in her lap a tight squeeze. It was moist and smelled bitter, but she didn't care. She buried her face in it, imagining she could transfer love to her small baby. She sighed and looked up.

Agnes was watching her, hugging the air, pretending to have her own pillow, or perhaps her own baby, and smiling the same sad smile Bea had no doubt just displayed.

The bustling and hoot-filled evening quieted as they passed through it.

At camp, a few of the other Community members were still at the fire, but most were breathing lightly in the circle where everyone slept. Bea and Glen eased down under the elk pelt they used as bedding. Agnes arranged herself, as she always did, at their feet. Her hand curled around Bea's ankle like a vine.

"Maybe there will be some good packages at Post," Glen murmured. "Maybe some good chocolate or something like that."

Bea *hmm*ed, but really she couldn't eat things like that anymore without becoming ill, her body overwhelmed by what it used to crave in their old life.

Instead of chocolate, she wished instead Glen would mention the child she'd just buried. Or she thought she wished for that. What would she say? What could she say that he didn't already know? And did she really want to talk about it? No, she didn't. And he knew that too.

She looked at Glen, and in the firelight saw a look of hope play on his face. He knew chocolate couldn't soothe such bewilderment, but maybe the suggestion could do what the chocolate was supposed to. She fit herself into his arms. "Yes, some chocolate would be nice," she lied.

All around them, Bea heard the sounds of the wild world bedding down. Ground owls cooed, and something else screeched; shadows of night fliers skimmed between the sky and the stars. As the campfire hissed itself to sleep, she heard the last of the Community walking cautious and blind from the fire to the beds and nestling down. Someone said, "Good night, everyone."

Against her ankle, Bea could feel Agnes's blood pulsing through her hot clutching hand. She breathed in and out to its rhythm, and it focused her. *I have a daughter*, she thought, *and no time for brooding*. She was needed here, and now, by someone. She vowed to move on quickly. She wanted to. She had to. It was how they lived now.

RIVER 9 MOVED fast and swelled against its banks, and to the Community it looked like a wholly different river from the one they were familiar with. So different that they had consulted the map again, trying to match the symbols with what was now there and what their memory insisted ought to be there. They had crossed the river many times since they first arrived in the Wilderness State. From their encounters with it elsewhere, they had even considered it a lazy river, the way it turned tightly back and forth through rocks and dirt from the foothills down across the sagebrush plain. They had a usual crossing spot that they considered safe, or as safe as a river crossing could be. But it looked as though a storm had altered the bank and submerged the patch of island where they used to regroup before attempting the far bank. It was a very helpful little island. But it was gone now and they could no longer be sure where that fording spot was. Perhaps the same storm that had kept them on the other side of the mountains since last summer had also remade this river.

They lowered themselves and then the children down a small ledge to the almost nonexistent bank where greens grew, a color found almost exclusively next to rivers. The grasses, mosses, the striving trees, so thin they could be snapped between two fingers, their new spring leaves quivers of creamy green. They handed down their bedding rolls, the pouches of smoked meat, jerky, pemmican, the harvested pine nuts, precious acorns, wild rice, einkorn, a handful of wild onions, the disassembled smoking tent, their personal satchels, the hunting bows and arrows, the bag of hollowed wooden meal bowls and the chips of wood and stone they used as utensils, the precious box of precious knives, the Book Bag, the Cast Iron, the Manual, and the bags of their garbage they carried with them to be weighed and disposed of by the Rangers at Post.

In the water, a loose log, stripped naked of its bark and limbs, bobbed and rolled past even though the nearby landscape was treeless. The log must have traveled from the foothills, the unusual torrent of water ushering it through. On a lazier river, or even a lazier part of this river, a log might have gathered farther upstream in an eddy or been nudged onto a bank. Here, it rolled in the rapids. Rapids they'd never even noticed in previous crossings, when the water was low and any whitewater was just a skimming thin hat the river rocks wore. They watched another log vault head over tail, after which Caroline took her first tentative step out into the water.

Caroline was their river-crossing scout. She was the most surefooted. Had the lowest center of gravity. Her toes could grip like fingers. Beautiful toes wasted for years crammed into shoes in the City. She had learned the most about how water behaved. She was good at making sense of things that seemed erratic.

"Okay," Caroline yelled over the rumble, her feet firm in the first foot of water, testing its pull, deciding whether to continue. "Rope."

Carl and Juan handed her one end of the rope, which she secured around herself and they looped once around each of their waists, Carl behind Juan, and then held the rope in front of them. The children and the other adults stood as far back as they could.

They had already tried to ford two other spots, but Caroline, either feet out from the bank or waist deep in water, returned to the shore each time. "It's too deep," or "It's too fast," or "See that lip? There's a pock somewhere under the water that will take us down."

On this, the third spot, Caroline waded out halfway. From the bank, things looked promising. She paused, her head cocked slightly, like a coyote listening for the calls of the Wilderness—*friend or foe, friend or foe.* Her hands hovered over the whitewater, and it broke around her body and came together again behind her. Caroline turned her head toward them, her shoulders following, a hand turned palm up, about to signal something. She opened her mouth to speak just as the tip of a log surfaced where she stood, and with a terrible thwack and splash, Caroline was gone.

Then the river, like an awakened bear, yanked the rope and Juan went down too. He tried to dig his heels in. He bellowed as the rope wrung his waist. Carl tried to pull on his rope section, not to help Juan but to slacken the rope to avoid the excruciating thing that was happening to Juan.

Bea stood back with the others, her hands crimped on Agnes's shoulders. She thought about how, long ago, they always had someone stand by the rope holders with a knife to cut the rope in case something like this happened. But nothing like this ever happened, and Carl and Juan decided they were strong enough for a catastrophe like this. Besides, no one really wanted to be the one to cut the rope anyway. Still, at each river, they would have a lengthy discussion about whether to require a rope cutter or not. When they inevitably decided they needed one, no one would volunteer, so they would have to draw for it and the person who lost would shit themselves the whole time. And when nothing ever went wrong, they begrudged all that worry and work for nothing. So finally, they had decided, not that long ago, in fact, to stop mandating there be a rope cutter.

Clearly that had been the wrong decision.

In a move, Bea grabbed Carl's personal knife from his belt, lunged, and cut the rope in front of Juan, releasing him to the bank, where he crumpled and howled in relief. Carl, cursing, catapulted back into the others, and then everyone was tumbled over and tangled in weeds. Caroline, presumably still on the rope and most certainly dead, rushed downriver.

Carl clambered to his feet. "Why did you do that?" he screamed.

"I had to," Bea said, replacing his knife in the holder tied to his belt.

"But I had it. I fucking had it."

"No, you didn't."

"Yes, I did."

"No, you didn't."

Carl sputtered, "But it was our best rope."

"We have others."

"Not like that one. It was our river rope!"

"We can get another one."

"Where?" Carl cried. He grabbed his hair in theatrical frustration, looking around at the empty Wilderness. But the feeling was real. He seethed.

Bea didn't answer. Maybe she could talk a Ranger into giving them something as good, as long and thick. But she wasn't going to promise that. She noted that while no one had sided with Carl, no one had defended her either. Everyone had busied themselves with some small task—inspecting their pouches, picking something out of another's hair, eating an ant—until the moment passed. Except Agnes, who watched with unnerving neutrality.

Bea helped Juan to his feet, and Dr. Harold hurried forward to put a salve on the rope cuts around Juan's waist and hands. It wouldn't do much. None of Dr. Harold's salves did much.

Debra and Val ran along the bank to see if Caroline resurfaced. She had, a few hundred feet downriver, her hair tangled in the branches of another log, her face submerged, her body limp. Her body and the log were snagged on something for a moment, and then were freed, speeding again down the river. There was no way to retrieve the rope. And not much to do for Caroline.

They took a moment to regroup, drink water, pass a pouch of jerky. Debra said a nice thing about Caroline and how being their river scout had been essential to their survival here and that she would be missed. "She taught me so much about water," Debra said, looking quite shook. She and Caroline had been close. Bea looked around at the faces of the group, working their feelings out. Personally, Bea thought Caroline had been aloof, though she kept that feeling to herself. She chewed on a knuckle impatiently while she waited for the ritualized silent moment to end.

After all that, they argued about Caroline's last intention. She'd turned and opened her mouth to tell them something about the crossing. But tell them what? Had her hand begun to signal a thumbs-up or thumbs-down before the log smacked her? What had her facial expression been before she'd grimaced in painful surprise? In the end they decided the spot was still the most promising place to cross, despite Caroline's demise. Juan took over as the river scout and ventured in without a rope. Close to the middle, he turned and gave a thumbs-up. Single file they carefully shuffled out, children clinging to the backs of adults. It turned out to be quite a good spot to cross, and if it hadn't been for that log, they all would have gotten to the opposite bank easily. Poor Caroline. She had bad luck, Bea decided.

With the children across, the adults formed a chain over the river and passed the heavy and cumbersome items across, the Manual, the Cast Iron, the Book Bag, the garbage, the bedding, the disassembled smoker, the food pouches, the wooden bowls and slabs of utensils, then all the individual packs, one item after the other, bank to bank. And once they'd hoisted and tied and strapped back on all their gear, they started walking again. The sun dried them instantly. They spit out the silty earth kicked up by their feet. Their skin became dusted and slippery with it. Covering one nostril, they rocketed snot out their noses into the dust and trudged through the sagebrush plain that unfurled around them like a sea.

*   *   *

WHEN THEIR WAY became lit by moonlight they stopped for the night. A small fire was built, and they lay on the ground around it. No skins were unrolled, no pelts unbundled. The sleep wouldn't be worth the effort. They would be moving with the dawn. When they wanted to move fast, this is how they went.

On the horizon Bea saw the pinprick glow from an outdoor light that burned at Middle Post. They were close.

Juan said, "Just a quick story or two," and, yawning, began one of his favorites from the *Book of Fables*, which they used to carry in the Book Bag but which had been lost to a flash flood some time ago. All stories had been told so often now, they came from memory.

The children were asleep in little mounds at the foot of the fire. Except for Agnes, who insisted that as the eldest child of the Community she ought to stay up with the adults and report on decisions made that might affect the youngest ones. There were never any such decisions made at night around the fire. She just liked staying up. Bea didn't argue. She reveled in Agnes's restlessness. She couldn't forget when Agnes had been a frail, failing little girl too sick to hold her eyes open.

Bea squatted next to Glen, who grunted up from his task.

"How are those arrows coming along?" she asked, jostling his shoulder.

"Arrowheads," he mumbled. "Good." He was distracted, trying so hard to make a good point. She peered over his shoulder. They would be useless. He'd overflaked them. Bea smiled encouragingly. Glen was a terrible hunter. He knew it. She knew it disappointed him. Carl was the true hunter of the Community and provided much of their meat. So Glen was trying to master making tools, wanting to be of use in a way he had always dreamed of being. Of course, Carl was also a master arrow flaker and they were rich in perfect arrowheads already. But she wasn't going to point that out to him.

Bea watched Glen's brow furrowing in desperate concentration. Despite his shortcomings, he was having the time of his life here. All he read, as a boy, were tales of primitive life. The caveman stories of his youth were all he'd ever really been interested in. Now he was a professor, expert in how people evolved from the first upright steps to the first wheel. He knew the most basic nature of humanity, and he knew the how and why behind the onslaught of civilization. But when it came to living primitively, he was surprisingly hapless.

They had met in the City. Bea had been hired to decorate the University apartment Glen moved into after his first marriage ended. It was shockingly large as apartments went, and she understood that he must be an important person there. As she showed him samples and talked about the placement of pieces, he told her the origin of every object she'd chosen for his home. It made her work feel important, like she was a steward of history, of usefulness. They married. He was fatherly toward Agnes, whose real father had been a worker on a weekend furlough from the vast Manufacturing Zone outside the City. Bea had liked the men on leave because they had good hands and they didn't stick around, and she liked her life and her job as they were. And she loved Agnes fiercely, though motherhood felt like a heavy coat she was compelled to put on each day no matter the weather.

Glen had been a nice change. She was ready for him at the time he came along. She had hoped he would change her life in surprising ways, but she never could have imagined just how much of it he could change.

Glen was the one who knew about the study, putting people in the Wilderness State. When things worsened in the City and Agnes's health cratered, like so many children's had, Glen was the one who offered his help to the researchers in exchange for three spots—for him, Bea, and Agnes. Bea's hunch had been right—Glen was important at the University, and the researchers agreed without hesitation.

It still took almost a year of working and waiting to get the permission to place humans into what was essentially a refuge for wildlife, the last wilderness area left, to gather the funding needed, and to find other participants. They had wanted twenty skilled volunteers with knowledge of flora and fauna and biology and meteorology. A real doctor or nurse, not just an amateur herbalist. Even a chef would have been nice, but they eventually had to pad out the group with people who were simply willing to go. It sounded risky, people said. It was risky. It was uncomfortably unknown. It was an extreme idea and an even more extreme reality. More extreme than suicide, Bea remembered a mother from her building arguing. It had been a hard sell. Meanwhile, Agnes got sicker.

During that time, when Bea cradled her sleeping daughter, she'd sometimes wonder what she would do if Glen's plan didn't work, or worked too late. She could think of no other options for how to save Agnes. The medicines weren't strong enough anymore. Each cough was pink with blood. "What this child needs," the doctor had said ruefully, "is different air." Since there was no other air, she recommended palliative care, and Bea found herself wholly dependent on Glen and his stupid idea. Toward the end of the wait, right before they got permission—she hadn't and wouldn't ever tell anyone this— she had started to think ahead, to a life after Agnes. She'd begun to say goodbye. There was a terrible comfort in reaching that point. And then, with very little time to prepare, the study and the group of twenty were approved, and trying on army-issue gear, seeing doctors, providing urine samples, doing intake interviews, packing up their belongings, tying up loose ends, and then, without fanfare, leaving. Bea was stunned by the turnaround and the change, unsure whether this all was real, even as the first cold nights in the Wilderness descended on them and she found herself scrambling to protect Agnes in a new way.

It had seemed like such a game, even on that first evening when the sun set on them before they had a fire. Even as their stomachs knotted from coarse food or, soon, not enough food. Even when their camp was first ransacked by a hungry bear. Then the first person perished, from hypothermia. Another after misidentifying a mushroom. And another from wounds sustained from a cougar. And then a climbing accident. It felt as though they'd escaped one monster by hiding in a closet, only to find another there among the hangers, claws unsheathed. They couldn't possibly stay here, could they? It felt unreal. Some kind of terrible trick.

At any moment she imagined Glen taking her by the wrist, turning her around, and marching her and Agnes back to the border fence, back to civilization. But that never happened. Eventually it dawned on Bea that the ground they trudged wearily upon day after day would be endless. And if they found an end, a border, a fence, a granite wall, she realized, they would just turn around. How could they ever return to the City? Agnes was like a colt, bounding, curious. And healthy for the first time in her short life. For the first time, Bea let herself believe Agnes *would* be long for this earth. And Bea was surviving when others had perished, others stronger than herself. It soothed her anxiety, stroked her ego. She might actually be good at this survival thing. *Maybe this was the right decision. Maybe this will all be fine. Maybe we aren't insane.* It was her mantra. She thought it almost daily. She thought it now.

Bea looked around the circle at the faces deranged by the dancing firelight. She thought there was a heaviness to the group since River 9. Since the rope. Since Caroline. No one would look at her. The jerky bag had been passed to her without comment, and taken from her too quickly. The heaviness seemed directed at her. Which she thought was absurd. People had certainly lost important things before and they weren't shunned for it.

There was the teacup they'd used during ceremonial moments for rituals they had made up early on for the different milestones of their new life.

The teacup had belonged to Caroline, passed to her through a line of family members who were early settlers in the New World. It was a ridiculous thing to bring into the Wilderness, but it was fine and pretty with a chipped gold rim and a colorful coat of arms from the place those relatives had fled. It had its own carrying box of wood, lined with old crumbling velvet, where it sat snug until needed. Ridiculous, but they cherished it. In it, they might pour a tea of blossoms, or roots, or bone, depending on the ritual or the season, and they'd pass it around the fire. It felt lovely in their hands and though there were many things in the Wilderness that looked delicate, really, nothing was. Hollow bird bones? Gossamer spiderwebs? Filigree-like lichen? They're tough, hardy. The teacup, though, was truly a delicate thing, and it would make each of them delicate when it passed into their possession. And that feeling is a kind of gift when they had to otherwise be hard.

It had been lost in the climbing accident. They were heading into the mountains for the winter because winter in the lowlands was too harsh and empty of food, while the caves and mounds of mountain snow made for good dwellings that in spring melted away any sign of them, which was like disappearing without a trace. Thomas was carrying the teacup in his pouch. As they climbed, he lost his footing and fell backwards off a ledge that everyone else had managed just fine. He tumbled down, and the bag's contents scattered across the rocks below. When they saw the box fly and open against a rock, they had gasped, though no one had gasped when Thomas had begun falling, or as he continued to fall. No one was that close to him, except Caroline, his wife. He'd never taken to the group. He wasn't a joiner, he'd explained pleasantly when they all first met.

The teacup flew out into the air from its safe velvet bed, the gold rim glinting in the sun, and some of them who were close enough tried to reach out to catch it. Even Thomas reached for it mid-tumble rather than reaching for a handhold that might stop his fall.

The cup came to rest in pieces, the porcelain dust settling like bone ash across the rock. Some gathered small shards and put them in a skin pouch as a new keepsake. But those shards cut them when they rummaged for anything, and eventually they were deposited discreetly across the landscape they walked, the shards small enough to disappear in the dirt.

Of course, poor Thomas had continued to fall, and presumably he had died. A couple of people climbed down partway, but they couldn't see him and he didn't respond to their shouts. So the Community took a moment to say some nice things about him and console Caroline, and then they walked on. They didn't perform many rituals anymore, in large part because the teacup was gone. It was true that rituals took time and effort, and the more time they spent in the Wilderness, the less they wanted to celebrate. At first, every river crossing had been notable, but now they barely wanted to mark the first of the year. Regardless, Bea knew that without the teacup there was simply no ceremonial feeling. They were just drinking tea. But still, no one spoke ill of Thomas afterward. If he'd survived, they wouldn't have given him the silent treatment around the fire. No one blamed him for losing the cup, at least not out loud. Bea wished they'd remember that now.

Across the fire she tried to catch Debra's eye, but Debra would not look at her. Her mouth was set, her gaze stern. She had Caroline's bag next to her and was fingering the soft hide strap. All at once Bea realized they must have been more than close. Debra had arrived with a much younger wife, and Caroline with a much older husband. Both of their spouses were gone now—one deserted, the other dead. The pairing made sense, Bea supposed. It had to have been something new. They slept next to each other in the sleep circle, but not together. Whatever had happened they'd kept private. No easy task in the Community.

Dr. Harold busied himself packing a new salve into a hollowed-out chunk of wood. Bea could see his cheeks blaze red even in the firelight as she stared at him, trying to be acknowledged. Carl couldn't help but look at her simply to snarl and show he was still sore about the rope. She didn't bother looking at Val, who she hated and who hated her. The surprising one was Juan, who looked at each person around the fire as he told the story, held their gaze a beat, and then moved to the next. But his eyes jumped anxiously, perhaps angrily, over Bea. *But I saved your life,* she wanted to yell.

The only person paying attention to her was Agnes, who watched her actions and irritatingly imitated each one. When Bea scratched her ankle, Agnes scratched her ankle. Bea mouthed *stop*, and Agnes mouthed *stop*. Bea shook her head and rolled her eyes. And so did Agnes, dramatically, as if to mock her. Then, as Bea's anger sparked, Agnes put a hand on Bea's knee as though an adult consoling another, and grinned with that broken tooth. Bea melted from her daughter's goofy smile and the warmth of her hand. Bea wanted someone to be kind to her. She wanted some unconditional love. She reached to embrace her, but skittish Agnes slipped through her arms. She tried a new tactic. Bea yawned so that Agnes would yawn. She stretched her arms so that Agnes would stretch her arms out. She leaned back, trying to pull Agnes down with her to sleep. But Agnes wouldn't be tricked. She didn't want to sleep. She pulled her arms into her chest, stifled a real yawn, and scooted to Glen, pressing a curious fingertip into the flint shavings at his feet. Bea, dejected, stood up, shivering to be even that far from the fire. She did not want to sleep in the same circle as these people. Far off, behind some butte, coyotes yodeled to one another, *friend, friend, friend*, and Bea felt bereft at the sound of such communion.

What she could see was from starlight and from smell. She sniffed and found Glen's bag with their bedding. Their scent was all over it. She laid it out on the ground some distance from the fire. She heard a crunch behind her and tensed for a moment before she felt Glen's hands on her shoulders, kneading them.

"Tough day," he murmured near her neck. She could tell he felt bad about ignoring her at the fire.

"You would have cut the rope, right?"

"Of course." She felt his cheeks lift to a smile as he put a small kiss to her temple.

"But . . . ?"

"I might have waited just a tad longer."

"Well, fuck, Glen. Did I just murder Caroline?"

"Oh no, no, no," he said patiently, pulling her down to their bedding. "Caroline was dead the second that log attacked her."

"Then what does the timing matter?"

Glen shrugged. "I guess it doesn't. But if she was already dead, then what was the rush?"

"But Juan."

Glen waved his hand. "Juan was always going to be fine."

She stamped her foot, and Glen put his hands back on her shoulders. "Look, Juan was fine. Caroline was lost. But that rope wasn't. Not until you cut it. People just need a minute." He paused, then shrugged. "It was a really good rope."

Agnes slunk up at that moment as Bea and Glen went silent naturally at the end of their conversation. But Agnes took it personally. "You don't have to stop talking," she lisped angrily. "I know a lot. I'm mature."

Glen grabbed Agnes around the waist and flipped her. "We were already done talking," he sang, dangling her an inch above the ground until her huffs and puffs became reluctant laughs, then shrieks of glee. Glen eased her down to the bed, and she arranged herself, as she always did, at their feet.

Glen and Bea nestled down, and in the ensuing silence Bea's mind drifted to the sky that had shone white-hot above her when she had Madeline and she was grateful for the distraction when Agnes, from the bottom of the bed, cooed, "I'm sad about Caroline."

"You are?" Bea couldn't keep her surprise in, and she could tell from Agnes's sharp breath that she was surprised by her mother's surprise.

"Yeah," Agnes said, though now she phrased it more as a question.

"Well," Bea said, "Caroline was always nice to you." If Bea were being completely honest, she thought Caroline was more aloof than Thomas and really hadn't liked her at all. It wasn't that she was glad she was dead. She just wasn't that bothered to have lost her and felt uncomfortable about the level of mourning happening. It was bad enough to be blamed about the rope without everyone moping about Caroline too. She rolled her eyes in the dark. She was never sure what was better parenting—modeling compassion or just being honest. Agnes was so nice to everyone, even if she wasn't always very nice to her mother. So she kept her feelings about Caroline, once again, to herself. "She was a lot of fun," she said with a nod into the darkness.

"It's just," Agnes ventured, "I really wish we could have saved her."

Even her daughter thought she'd cut the rope too fast. "You too?" Bea barked. "I suppose you really miss the rope as well?"

"Okay, okay," Glen said, putting an arm around Bea and ruffling Agnes's hair. "We need to get to sleep." Bea saw Agnes's teeth in the dim dark smiling up at Glen and Bea, realized she was being toyed with. Of course Agnes had heard enough of their conversation to know, or want to know, how that comment would sound to Bea. It was something Agnes was playing with lately—pointed comments, knowing looks. Testing boundaries like she had as a toddler, but now with a sharpness, a tartness to her. Agnes was playing at a lot of things lately, and Bea felt she could hardly keep up.

Agnes scrunched down under the skins, and her hand clasped around Bea's ankle like it did every night. Bea fought the urge to pull it away. Bea tried to fit herself into Glen's arms, but her blood was revving and she felt tied by them instead of embraced.

Agnes fell immediately into an unworried sleep, her breaths sounding like heavy drapes shuffling against the floor. Of course she had heard, Bea thought. Agnes was always listening. And she was right. She did seem to know everything. And she did seem older, more mature, than she was. Bea had fully lost sight of the baby Agnes had been. Found it hard to believe she'd ever been anything but this complicated person at her feet. She was short but she was solid, as though already fully formed. Much more solid than the other children. Glen always gave her more meat than he gave himself. As if on cue, Glen joined Agnes with his own sleep sounds. Bea stared wide-eyed into the dark night.

*   *   *

IN THE MORNING, a truck raced toward them, spewing dust. Far behind it the sun glinted against the roof of Middle Post. As the truck pulled to a stop, they saw it was Ranger Gabe. He was the son of someone very high up in the Administration, he had told them once, as though it were a threat. He was not well liked.

Some Rangers enjoyed being outdoors and conversing with the Community. But not Ranger Gabe. He seemed skeptical of them and of the dirt he walked upon. His uniform was always crisp and spotless, and he moved carefully, as though he hated to get it dirty.

He shut off his truck, sat a moment, then leaned long on the horn. The birds previously hidden in bushes dispersed in a cloud. The horn's bleat echoed back to them from a faraway butte.

The Community, packed and ready to leave, gathered around his truck.

"You've got new Manual pages at Lower Post."

"But we've almost reached Middle Post," Bea explained. "That's where we were told there were pages."

"And mail," Debra said. She'd been very vocal about not having received a letter from her aged mother for a long while. She was unsure what it meant that she'd heard nothing.

"Well," he drawled, his heel pumping the sideboard, "I don't know what to tell you. All I know is there's nothing for you at Middle. Nothing. You've got to go to Lower." He squinted at the horizon like an explorer.

"But Middle Post is right there," Bea said, pointing to the roof roasting under the sun.

"There's nothing there for you."

"But—"

"You've got to head to Lower. And you know where I mean, right? Even though it's Lower, it's not just lower."

They looked at him blankly.

He scowled and pulled out a roughly drawn map of all the Post locations. Pointed to where he meant, an X at the very bottom of the map.

Carl growled, "Lower Middle? Why all the way down there?"

"Not Lower Middle. Lower."

"But it's right in the middle here"—Carl pointed—"*and it's lower.*"

"Look, this one's called Lower Post. And you've got to go there. That's all that matters."

"But why?"

"Why?" Ranger Gabe mockingly scratched his head. "*Why?* Because you left your last camp a total shithole, that's why."

"No, we didn't," said Bea. They did their micro trash sweeps. They'd found as much micro trash as they found after any time they spent anywhere.

"It looked like you'd been there forever. The vegetation was destroyed. It'll take years, maybe even a lifetime for it to bounce back. If it bounces back at all." Spittle had collected in Ranger Gabe's beard.

Bea saw Carl getting vexed. She smiled ingratiatingly. "I'm so surprised to hear this. I feel like we barely unpacked we were there such a short time." This was a lie. They'd been there much longer than they should have. Everyone knew it. Ranger Gabe knew it. This was a common dance between the Rangers and the Community. Bea figured they'd been there about half a season—an obscene amount of time to stay in one place—and the only reason they'd begun moving was because she'd wanted some distraction from thinking of Madeline. And people wanted their mail. They were supposed to stop only when they needed to hunt, gather, and then process what they had. They were limited to seven days in one place as stated in the Manual. But they almost never followed this. It was hard to start moving once they'd stopped. To pack everything up in such a way that would be relatively easy to carry for the foreseeable future. That smoker was delicate and tricky, and right after a hunt they were weighed down with meat. A good thing overall, but a lot more weight to drag around.

"Oh, please," Ranger Gabe said. "Even around here is a mess. How long have you been here?"

"One night."

He shook his head. "Incredible," he said. "Well, maybe it's just not possible to avoid impact when you're a group this large. I've always felt that way. I've always said there is no reason for this. For a group to be here. I said they shouldn't let you in. Have I ever mentioned that?"

"You have," said Bea.

"Well, I'm not the only one who feels that way." He spoke through a crooked, satisfied smile.

"If it's any consolation, we're about half the size we used to be," Bea said feigning graciousness, thinking of the dead.

He glared.

She mostly liked the Rangers, even the mean ones. They were fun to banter with which is why she had volunteered to be the Community's liaison. She found that a small smile easily disarmed them. They were young and always seemed new no matter how long they'd been there. To her they would always be soft-eared cubs. Except Ranger Bob at Middle Post, who was older, gray filling in the temples and his mustache. He was a peer. She would go so far as to call him a friend. A good one, even. But these boys were fun for her.

"Let me also add that you've been at that camp too many times," Ranger Gabe said flatly. He could not let it go. Carl was pacing, panting. He would break soon.

"I thought the rules only covered duration of time," Bea said coyly.

"No. It's a whole presence thing. You're impeding wildlife opportunities by repeatedly returning and overstaying. No animal wants to call this home while you're stomping around."

"It's not about presence," Carl exploded, and rummaged furiously for the Manual to prove his point.

The Ranger smiled and Bea sighed. She felt she'd been winning their unspecified game, but now Carl had ruined it.

Ranger Gabe laid a heavy hand on Carl's shoulder. "Don't bother, sir. I saw all I needed to see. What matters is impact. And yours is severe. I've already catalogued it extensively in my report and I will send it up the chain, stamped *URGENT*. Infractions like this can get you kicked out." His eyes were as stern as his unwavering voice. There was no generosity here. "What you need to do is start walking in the direction of Lower Post." He pointed somewhere in the distance, in a direction they'd never been. "As ordered."

They'd been rerouted before, twice to be exact. Once due to a controlled burn (if it had been a natural fire, the Ranger made sure to point out, they would not have been rerouted, as per the Manual). Another time it was due to a septic tank overflow at Upper Post. They were moved to the next most convenient Post to tend to business. But this felt unnecessary, a task meant to endanger them. They looked at the map. Lower Post was farther away than anywhere they'd ever been. It was meant as punishment. An invitation to a forced march.

Glen eased Carl back, away from Ranger Gabe's hand and out of reach in case Carl decided to throw a punch.

"You know," Glen said, "we thought we'd done a good job with micro trash and re-wilding, but we will be certain to give it more attention next time."

"If there's a next time," the Ranger snapped. Then he slumped slightly. He knew the encounter was wrapping up and seemed regretful. Perhaps Bea had misjudged. Having the Community here might give the Rangers something to do.

"Well, duly noted," Glen said. "Now, it's Lower Post, you say?"

"Yeah."

"Great. We'll repack today—you have to pack right for a trek like that—but then we'll head there first thing."

The Community sighed.

Glen smiled. "Gang, I personally cannot wait. Who knows what wonders we'll see?"

Only Agnes cheered.

"That's my girl," Glen said, beaming at her gratefully.

Agnes beamed back.

Ranger Gabe got back into his truck and drove, squinting at them in his rearview. Glen smiled and smiled until the truck crested a mellow hill and disappeared. Then Glen's face slackened. He massaged his cheeks.

"Well," said Debra, hoisting her pack, "I'm not turning around. Not when we're this close to Middle Post." She took a few steps toward the glinting roof.

Glen put his hand up. "Wait."

"Don't tell me we have to discuss this," said Juan.

"Of course we have to discuss it. We need consensus," said Glen.

Everyone groaned.

"We're barely a mile away," said Debra, her feet dancing toward Post.

"Well, some of us don't like to go to Post and would prefer to avoid it whenever possible," said Val. She was only saying that to please Carl, who hated having to go to Post.

"But our mail," cried Debra.

"Debra, our mail won't even be there," snapped Carl.

Debra flapped her arm in the direction of Post. "But it's right there."

"First, Debra, consensus is your dumb thing, so don't complain," said Carl.

Debra scowled. She loved consensus usually. She was the one who'd brought the idea to the Community.

"Second, you realize they're doing this so we will disobey and they can write another report and then maybe they can get us kicked out," Carl warned.

"Since when are you so concerned with the rules?" spat Debra.

Carl blushed angrily. He hated the rules, especially when his desires aligned with them.

"Listen, gang, they're doing it to get us to go somewhere else. They're saying we've been lazy," said Glen. "I think it's a valid criticism."

The allure of following the same route each year they'd been in the Wilderness State was great. If they knew the route, they knew what to expect. These plants grew at this time and they grew here. Those berries come in beyond that ridge, there. They had learned to read the land and decide where a ptarmigan had moved its burrow after they found the first one. They learned how animals thought and so they made better hunters. They'd learned how to survive in this quadrant of the map. Would what they learned allow them to survive elsewhere? Anywhere? They'd already passed through all the hardship of learning in the early days and come out on the other side, alive. They did not want to go through it all again.

"But what if we're not meant to return?" Dr. Harold had broken away from the group and was pacing. He was so far away that his question was almost inaudible. A whisper, a secret only to himself.

"Don't get paranoid, Doc," Glen said kindly, and Dr. Harold seemed startled to be the focus of attention.

"I'm not. But look." He pulled out the map and pointed. "Lower Post isn't even the next Post. It's just a place, a place very far from here, over a new range of mountains. These are dunes. These are dry lakes. And here"—he trailed his finger along—"is the only river I see."

"Oh no," Debra said.

"I don't mean there aren't *any*," he said quickly, "but we don't know. We don't know what will make sense when we get there. Maybe where we end up, it won't make sense to ever come back."

They sobered at the thought of not returning.

Val said tentatively, "Well, maybe we should check in at Middle Post just to be sure."

A few more murmured agreements rose.

"Maybe we should check with Ranger Bob."

"Maybe Ranger Gabe is wrong."

Dr. Harold from outside the circle suddenly cried, "Who *is* this Ranger Gabe anyway?"

"Okay, okay," Glen interrupted. "We're getting worked up about something as silly as the unknown. Don't forget, it's all just land."

Carl interrupted. "And we're people who live on the land. We travel land. We *know* land. We go where we want, when we want. And we can come back here whenever it suits us. There's nothing to be worried about. So, I say let's head somewhere new. Let's go to Lower Post."

"But this is where we first arrived," said Juan. "Who knows when we'll be back?"

Carl slapped his forehead. "We'll be back when we want to be back. Didn't you just hear me say that? We are sovereign over our experience. So let's turn around."

It hadn't occurred to Bea that they might never return here. It didn't seem possible. She didn't know how to live in the Wilderness without their lovely hidden Valley and trips to Middle Post. It was one thing not to know what animal might stalk them tomorrow. It was another not to know which cave to hide in when it did. A fear crept up her throat so that she croaked when she said, "I'd like to say goodbye to Bob."

Carl threw his hands up. "No one is listening to me." Val tried to pat his shoulder, but he jerked away.

Glen smiled at Bea and nodded. "Then let's go to Middle Post." He nodded around the circle until each of the adults nodded back. Carl, the last, stared angrily at him before giving a curt nod. "Good work, everyone." Glen looked to the horizon again to see that Ranger Gabe was truly gone, and the dust from his tires settled. Then he whistled and twirled his finger and they started to walk.

*   *   *

THEY ARRIVED AT Middle Post just as the sun began to drop. The pink light glanced off the roof, the numerous windows, and Ranger Bob's pickup truck, which Ranger Bob was just climbing into.

He jumped back out when he saw them. "Well, all right," he said, grinning. "You are not supposed to be here, but I'm sure glad to see you."

Some of them smiled. Bea beamed. Agnes waved shyly from behind her mother. Carl sauntered to the small, neat building and pissed high against the wall.

Ranger Bob pivoted toward Bea, his arms outstretched as though to embrace her. Then he brought them together in a loud clap, his smile wide under his bushy mustache. He was a kind of cowboy, but not a wild one. More like one who'd be hired for a child's party.

"You know the drill," he said. "Weigh your trash, and get your stories straight. I'll wait for ya inside."

Ranger Bob turned and high-fived Glen, who seemed startled by the instinctual high five he returned, and Ranger Bob jogged inside. As he flicked light switches, Bea could hear the new fluorescent hum over the lower hum of desert crickets.

Val, and two of the children, Sister and Brother, weighed the garbage, and then others sorted. The Cast Iron and other vessels were rinsed in the spigot, which jutted from the little beige building. Debra slipped out of her busted moccasins and luxuriated in the patchy grass that formed a green perimeter around the building. She scrunched her toes in and out of the blades.

The fluorescents blinded Bea momentarily as she walked in. She covered her eyes with her hands and slowly spread her fingers apart until she could handle looking at Ranger Bob behind his gleaming counter.

"We missed you this spring," he said.

"We got caught on the other side of the mountains by that storm. It just made more sense to work those foothills. On that side it was so calm."

"Yeah, freak early storm. Getting earlier."

"Yeah. Then, you know, it's spring, the game is good, the bulbs are hard to pass up."

"Of course." He smoothed his mustache thoughtfully. "But I don't need to tell you how important it is for you to get to Post when you're supposed to."

"I know. I'm sorry. We just couldn't."

Ranger Bob smiled. "Well, hopefully next time you will."

He never threatened them. It was one of the many things Bea liked about him. Still, there was a seriousness to his words that she was cautioned by. "We will," she said. "I promise."

Ranger Bob cleared his throat. "You know you were supposed to get along to Lower Post, right?"

Her heart skipped. She felt like they were doing everything wrong. "We heard. But we were so close. It didn't make sense to turn around. And we worried it might have been a mistake . . . " She trailed off.

"It's not a mistake," he said, again with a sternness that surprised her. "Granted, Ranger Gabe should have caught up with you earlier. But there were some unexpected events that needed handling."

"Like what?"

"Well. Hmm." He screwed his mouth. "That's classified."

"Really?" Bea didn't know why, but she felt incredulous to think there were things she couldn't know about this place where they ate, drank, slept, and shat.

"It's a big place. You're not going to know about everything that goes on." He winked. His lightness returned. "Anyway, really important to set out for Lower Post first thing in the morning. But we might as well take care of whatever business we can since you're here. How many in the group?"

"Eleven. Lost four, gained one."

He opened a binder labeled *Wilderness State Study Subject Log.* "Okay, gains. Name?"

"Pinecone."

"That's an interesting one. Season of birth?"

"Last spring."

"So maybe last year, right about now?"

Bea shrugged.

He jotted some notes. "Okay. Mother?"

"Becky."

"Father?"

"Dan."

"That's nice. Just the one addition, right?"

Bea nodded, thinking of Madeline.

"Okay, now for the part I hate. Losses. Names and causes?"

"Becky. Cougar maul."

Ranger Bob *tsk*ed as he scribbled into the ledger. "That's too bad," he said. "Next?"

"Dan. Rock slide."

"And he died?"

"His pelvis was crushed."

"And he died."

"We assume." Bea paused. "I mean, we had to leave him behind."

She saw Ranger Bob raise his eyebrows as he stared intently at the paper before him. He didn't say anything. But she could see how hard he pressed his pen into the log. She hoped it was just to capture the information in triplicate. Ranger Bob was one of the more sympathetic of the Rangers they dealt with. She didn't know what she would do if he started to judge them too. They had seen a lot of death. They had become hardened to it. Not just the Community members who had perished in grisly or mundane ways. But around them everything died openly. Dying was as common as living. They worried about one another, of course, but when one of them ceased surviving for whatever reason, they closed ranks and put their energy into what remained alive. This was an unanticipated outcome of living in the Wilderness, but it had happened quickly and cleanly. There used to be a cultural belief, in an era before she was born, that having close ties to nature made one a better person. And when they first arrived in the Wilderness, they imagined living there might make them more sympathetic, better, more attuned people. But they came to understand there'd been a great misunderstanding about what *better* meant. It's possible it simply meant better at being human, and left the definition of the word *human* up for interpretation. It might have only meant better at surviving, anywhere, by any means. Bea thought living in the Wilderness wasn't all that different than living in the City in that respect.

Ranger Bob coughed and said, "Well, jeez. That's too bad for"—he looked back over his form—"Pinecone. Who's taking care of him?"

"We are," Bea said, snapping a bit. Heat rose to her cheeks. She couldn't tell if it was shame or anger.

Ranger Bob looked up. "Well, of course you are." He smiled. "Who else?"

"Caroline. We lost her in River 9."

"When?"

"Yesterday."

His pen stopped. "Now you're sure? Because she could just be zipping along not far from here."

"We're sure."

"Because River 9's fast right now but not too cold. And below here it gets slow again."

"It was a log. She's definitely gone."

"Ah, that's too bad. I liked her."

Bea couldn't believe she had to hear about Caroline again. She hit the counter angrily. "Seriously?"

Ranger Bob took a step back, startled. "What?"

"I'm so sick of hearing about Caroline," she grunted.

Ranger Bob's jaw dropped.

"I mean, why are we still talking about her?" She chewed on a finger distractedly. She shook her head in disgust. *Caroline?* Honestly, fuck Caroline.

Ranger Bob regarded her like a wild animal. He said cautiously, "Well, she just died . . . yesterday, you said?" He might as well have been saying, *Hey, bear, hey, bear* to calm a beast.

Bea blinked and tried to swallow her rage. "Yes, of course." She straightened. "She did just die yesterday." She exhaled slowly. "I'm sorry for losing my temper." The heat rose back into her cheeks.

"Well, I hope you'll forgive me, but I liked Caroline and I'll miss her," he said, smirking.

She hid her face. She didn't want to see how she blushed. "I'm sorry."

He held up a hand as though he understood. He was so good at seeming to understand everything. She thought again about Lower Post and felt truly sad. What would she do without Ranger Bob? Would he miss her too?

Ranger Bob leaned in. "I guess I won't be ruining her secret anymore, but I used to let her use the commode back here. My wife puts a little bowl of potpourri in there. Caroline said she liked the smell." He chuckled. "It's the little things. Okay, moving on from Caroline, may she rest in peace. How much garbage?"

"Wait," Bea croaked. "One more. Madeline. Stillborn." Her face blazed. She stammered, "I didn't know if it counted."

Ranger Bob gazed at her for a moment, then looked at his form, flipping it over and back. "Well, seems like it doesn't count. Good to know. So let's just call it three, shall we?" He scratched out the 4 in the column for *Total Deaths*, smiling a mayor's smile, tight, all lip.

Bea sputtered in agreement so she wouldn't whimper. Her little unfinished girl was not quite finished enough to count. Was there some kind of comfort there, or did it make the loss more devastating? All at once she felt nothing.

"How much garbage?" he asked again.

"Twenty pounds," she whispered.

Ranger Bob whistled. "Wowsers. That much?"

Bea wanted to crumple to the floor. How monstrous they must sound. A dead baby and now too much trash.

She said, "On account of our missed trip to Post."

"Ah, ah," he said, nodding. "Makes sense. How many bags is that now?"

"Three of those bags we picked up here last time."

"Oh, those bags are awful."

"Just awful. I can't believe they didn't bust open."

"Well, because you made those ingenious covers for them."

"Debra made those."

"She's quite a seamstress."

"Quite."

He perused a checklist. "Well, I can give you the new Manual pages, but I can't promise I have the newest versions. And we might as well fill out questionnaires since you're all here. They might appreciate having some new data. Since it's been a while."

"Blood and urine too?"

"No, we sent the equipment to the Lower Post." He peered at her again. "Because you were supposed to go there."

"We're going."

"Of course you are. You'll want to— I already sent all your mail down there," he said, winking again. But again, his tone turned weary. "But also, you *have* to go."

Bea leaned in. "Bob, I get it," she cooed and thrilled when a blush rose to the apples of his cheeks.

"Okay, okay," he said, sheepishly.

"We've never been to Lower Post." She tried to sound excited, but she heard her dread.

"Well, I'd be surprised if you had. It's not easy to get to," he said, counting out questionnaires. A look of concern passed over his face, but he erased it with a small toss of his head. "So, think of it as an adventure." He handed the papers over. "I've got to be on my way so the missus won't get mad. So just drop these in the mail slot when they're done."

She nodded, took them, and then he boyishly thrust his hand out.

"So? Good luck to you then!"

She shook it. "I hope we see you again soon."

Their hands lingered, as though they might not.

Bea turned toward the door and tried to memorize what she could. The particular stale chemical smell of the place, the light buzzing at a high pitch, the quiet whir of some machine that was always on here but never at Upper Middle Post, where they sometimes stopped midwinter. Ranger Bob wore a women's deodorant—she was sure of it. Or perhaps he put baby powder in his socks so he wouldn't get blisters. Her mother had done that sometimes, when she put on her nice shoes, which pinched her feet. But Ranger Bob wore regulation sturdy sensible shoes. What was his excuse? She imagined it kept his feet soft, and that he and his wife would rub feet in bed, under clean white sheets, nudging the warm and loyal dog that lay at the foot. She felt a yearning to be in that bed, that domesticity. She looked at Ranger Bob's wedding band glinting under the fluorescents and briefly hated Mrs. Ranger Bob, whoever she was.

She stopped short. "Oh, hey, I almost forgot. Do you have any good thick rope you could give us?"

Ranger Bob frowned. "Bea, you know I can't supply things like that."

Bea nodded, embarrassed and irritated that she'd asked at all. Fuck everyone and their rope.

"But," Ranger Bob continued, "I shouldn't, but—" He brandished a vibrant green lollipop. "Give this to your darling girl," he said. "I know how much she loves them. But don't tell." Then he cocked his head, brandished another sucker with a sly smile. "This one's for you. You look like you could use it," he said, his smile disappearing.

*   *   *

THE ROUTE THEY chose to Lower Post purposefully swung back through the Valley they'd just been told never to return to. They'd hoped Ranger Bob would tell them this was all a mistake and to walk the route they wished to walk, wherever that took them. Now that they were sure they must head to Lower Post, they wanted to say goodbye to the place. Just in case.

They found their old camp cordoned off with yellow tape and sticks. *Re-vegetation in Progress* signs were posted all around the perimeter.

"Who is this sign for?" Carl said, kicking uselessly at some of the tape. It gaped and hung.

"Us," said Bea.

"The only impact here is by Rangers," he complained.

"Say your goodbyes, everyone," Glen said with a hint of melancholy.

"And hey," Carl said, "if you left anything behind, you better retrieve it." Carl looked right at Bea when he said it, his lip curling.

Bea looked around, trying to feign ignorance, as if to say, *Who is he talking about?* She caught Dr. Harold's eye and nodded sympathetically. He looked down in shame. She'd meant to deflect, but perhaps she'd uncovered a secret. The doc hid things too! She looked around, and a number of them stared at their feet, or off into the distance at a stand of trees or other small outcroppings, perfect places to tuck secret belongings. Carl stood haughty, his arms crossed. Of course Carl wouldn't have hidden anything. But she saw Val alternate between indignant and sheepish looks, and when they scattered, Bea saw her slink off. Carl could fume at the Community's tenacious hold on the past, on its secrets, but Bea was enlivened by the idea that each of these people who she'd shat, pissed, and nearly starved with, who she'd heard fucking, who she'd had endless Community meetings with, might still have managed to keep something private. The Wilderness, and the people in it, seemed interesting again.

Bea returned to her cave and chomped through both lollipops. The last thing Agnes needed was to remember what sugar was. Bea watched the others secret off to their own favorite spots. How stupid to think she had been the only one attached to the past.

Bea's blood revved from the green sugar. Her heart flitted. She felt like she could run for miles. She giddily skipped back to her hiding spot and discovered her pillow and magazine were gone, replaced with yellow re-vegetation tape. The delight from the sugar was instantly replaced by a headache. The yellow tape felt like a slap. How could they have found her stash? She felt watched. She squatted tightly at the mouth of the cave and held her knees hard, trying to quiet herself so that she could match the landscape. It was a form of protection to be like the land and animals that hid there. Were the others quietly mourning their losses? Were they feeling as trapped as she felt?

From her stoop in the cave entrance, she watched Glen swiftly moving toward the place where Madeline had lain. In camp, she spotted Agnes circling Carl with a length of the re-vegetation tape, torn from the stakes. They stood in the middle of the cordoned-off patch. Agnes stomped and shrieked, and Carl pretended to be tied to a pole, death by execution a certain future for him. His pleas for his life lilted up to Bea, small whispers in her ear, and she turned again to Glen.

He stood gazing down, toed something, knelt to inspect. Then stayed squat, running his hands over bushes, over the dirt, looking out at the view Bea had chosen for Madeline. She hadn't thought the spot was visible from the cave. She wondered if he was in the wrong place, hadn't gone far enough. Or, she thought, perhaps she *herself* had not gone far enough to be out of view. Maybe Glen had watched her bury their daughter, while she thought that it had been a private act.

Bea looked back toward camp, searching for Agnes. Her little survivor. Her strange, vibrant daughter. She was lunging at Carl with a stick. He groaned, clutched his stomach, pretending to be stabbed. With her last lunge, he fell to his knees.

"I'm dying," he cried, overacting, his voice a ghost's moan, his hands raising, swaying.

Agnes tilted her head at this eager, jolly, dying man. She became still before yelling, "Then die!" She spit on the ground in front of him.

Carl roared, fell over, and died.

Agnes giggled with delight as she pantomimed slicing his abdomen open and pulling out his entrails.

Bea's eyes darted back to the horizon, looking for Glen, but she couldn't find him. He didn't have anything hidden, she was sure.

Bea noticed she was anxiously digging fingernails into the dirt, and now the tips were raw, slippery with fine dust. She sucked them clean and then spit brown. Before she knew it, they were right back scraping the dirt.

The Community had been on long walks before, walks they thought would never be matched. One walk in their first year had prompted someone to leave. But even though they walked almost every day, day after day, they'd never strayed into other quadrants. They'd only visited three Posts, the three that lined the map's eastern border.

They were given their first map just after Orientation had ended, when they were packing up for their official entry into the Wilderness. Ranger Corey had driven up and tossed it from his truck window. It was a strange document that seemed to lack any sense of scale. It was covered in symbols that made it look like a child had dreamed it up.

"What are these black circles?" they'd asked him.

"Places not to go," Ranger Corey had said with a smirk. His affect was steely and amused, but his face was young and inexperienced.

They pointed to a flat-topped mountain and an orange flag, messy and colored out of the lines. It was a Post. "How far is this?" they asked.

Ranger Corey smiled. "Dunno, haven't figured that out yet." He dug into his pocket and pulled out a silver disk the size of his palm. "Who's the leader here?"

"Well, we're not going to have a leader," Glen had said proudly.

Ranger Corey's eyes rolled skyward. Then he surveyed their faces. "You," he said, holding the disk out to Carl.

Carl took it and stood taller, alert, happy to be identified as a leader.

"What do I get to do with this?" Carl asked, turning it around in his hand. He pressed a button along the side and it clicked. He pushed again. *Click*. Push. *Click*.

"Tell us how many paces from here to Post," Ranger Corey said. "One click per step."

Carl's face instantly raged. "Are you fucking serious?"

Ranger Corey acted surprised, but he wasn't. "Oh, yeah," he said. "I'm fucking serious. Do you have a problem with that? Because you could also tell me how many paces to the nearest exit."

Carl squeezed the clicker, trying to crush it, and lunged at the Ranger. But Ranger Corey ducked his head back into his truck and rolled the window up till it was open just a crack. "A click a step," he cried, revving the engine and peeling away.

No doubt the Rangers had far better ways to determine distances. This was busywork, a way to turn a nice walk into a slog. To make their lives slightly less free than the Ranger assumed they wanted.

They picked a direction and walked, and within days found themselves in vast grasslands full of antelope, sitting with their legs daintily tucked beneath them or wrapped back. Some places the grass got so deep Bea could only see their ears pricked up and pivoting above the undulating expanse. There were a few hawks in trees, not riding the nice breeze on what was an unusually warm and sunny day. A few energized antelope rose up to run in frantic circles, as though chased by regret. The Community just kept walking. They were new enough then that they hadn't understood: These were warnings. Something was about to happen. Had they turned around they would have seen the grasses flatten and reach forward, as though each blade was trying to run for its life. Once they were exposed in the middle of the parched plain, the hail and wind hit them suddenly, as though the weather had been straining behind a door that had just been opened.

They hunkered in place, flung their packs over their heads and clung to one another and to the ground, mimicking the flattened grass. Spiderwebs glistened in front of their noses, lightly wafting as though in a gentle breeze because these human bodies blocked the worst of the wind.

Around them they heard the pathetic whines of the antelope signaling to one another above the roar, until they were drowned out by the storm. And they heard the crack and crash of some reedy cottonwoods nearby splitting.

The hail was brief, but the wind lingered. The sun had begun its descent. They knew the worst was over when the hawks took flight again, whipping across the sky, their flat wings straining in the gusts. It was a game. They were showing off for a future mate or daring a rival. They flew shakily against the strong wind, then caught it and zipped away. Then they'd stop and hover as though painted there, while on the ground, Bea could barely stand up against the wind.

It was their first big storm. Spooked, they stayed put for so long a Ranger drone eventually arrived to coax them out. They trudged, disoriented and bleary-eyed, scared of putting one foot in front of the other. At their destination, Carl stomped on the clicker in front of the desk Ranger, shattering it, but not before reporting the steps, which he had begrudgingly collected.

This had happened in the first year, when many of them still had shoes, sleeping bags, when to some it still felt like one of those camping trips they'd heard grandparents talk about, something they would soon return home from, something they could shower off. It was their first storm but also their first long walk in the Wilderness. They talked about it in epic terms around the fire for seasons afterward. It was their origin story, how they'd finally come to be a part of this land. It had felt like they'd accomplished something impossible. Like they had discovered a new world. Bea remembered looking at her family, at her blisters, the toenail she'd lost, and feeling proud. In total, the journey had taken almost eight weeks. Some of them still had watches that told the time and date. Back then they felt awed that they could head in one direction for that long and not run into a dead end. They didn't understand yet just how much land there was to roam.

Now, hunched in the cave, Bea pictured the map in her head. This walk would be much, much longer than that walk. There were three lines of upside-down Ws to cross. Three mountain ranges. A feeling of dread turned her toes and fingers prickly cold. She scratched at the back of her neck, trying to dispel the anxiety.

She saw that most of the Community had come back together. They mingled among the yellow tape. They would want to leave soon. She heard a foot slide against loose rock, and then she heard a grunt and saw the top of Glen's head appear below her, then his face, half smiling, and then his hands and arms scrambling the rocks to reach her.

"Where have you been, stranger?" she asked even though she knew.

"Had a look around, saying goodbye to this place. In case we don't come back."

She smiled. "You know, we can always just head back to Middle Post."

"We can?" Glen sank beside her, slightly perplexed, thinking she was serious.

"Of course! Ranger Bob has a guest room. He invited us to stay there whenever."

"He did?" He scratched his head.

"No." Bea sighed. She was pretending. It was one of the ways she got through a day under the relentless sky. "Not really," she said. She expected that would end her game—Glen shooting her a quizzical look—but surprisingly, he laughed.

"Oh, okay, sure, I get it," he said. "Hey, Ranger Bob! Mrs. Ranger Bob!"

Bea sat up straight. "Hey, do you think we could use your shower?"

"We'd need some towels. Oh, and soap. Oh, and I'd love a shave. Hey, Bob—can I call you Bob?—have you got an extra razor?"

"Hey there, Mrs. Bob, what's good on the Screen?"

"Oooh, are those pretzels?"

They were giggling, their shoulders shaking together. Glen never fantasized about, or even seemed to miss, the coziness of their old life, of any kind of civilization. She was grateful not to have to be alone with the sour, lonely ache she now felt for it all.

"You know, I've been thinking," she said, "maybe we should have gone to the Private Lands instead." She was trying to keep the joke going, but her voice fell and she could not laugh at the suggestion like she'd meant to. It was a good joke because the Private Lands were a make-believe place as far as Bea was concerned. A fantastical place that people had talked about for as long as she could remember. A place where the living was better, easy and nice, as it had supposedly been in the past. A secret place for the wealthy and powerful, where they could have their own land and do as they wished. The Private Lands were the opposite of the City and had all the freedoms the City could no longer offer, and you either believed in it or you didn't. It had always seemed to Bea that the number of people who believed was proportional to how bad the City was becoming. One of her aunts believed now, and still sometimes mailed her newspaper clippings about its existence, secret maps of where it could be found. Her mother had always told Bea to toss such things. "You cannot just believe what someone tells you," her mother said. "Not without a good reason." Her aunt's husband had convinced her to believe and now she was dour and anxious. Before that she'd been sweet and fun. Very close with Bea's mother. "Oh, she was a laugh before," her mother would sigh.

Glen hooked his arm around her neck and pulled her close. "Now, now," he murmured. "This will be fun."

She knew that a big part of Glen believed this. But no part of Bea did. She pictured the map in her head again and saw all that unknown land, that beige parchment, all that nothing. They would be changed on the other side of it, that much she knew. Not knowing how was only one of the things that scared her.

Part II

IN THE BEGINNING

IN THE BEGINNING, there were twenty. Officially, these twenty were in the Wilderness State as part of an experiment to see how people interacted with nature, because, with all land now being used for resources—oil, gas, minerals, water, wood, food—or storage—trash, servers, toxic waste—such interactions had become lost to history.

But most of the twenty didn't know much about science, and many of them didn't even care about nature. These twenty had the same reasons people have always had for turning their backs on everything they'd known and venturing to an unfamiliar place. They went to the Wilderness State because there was no other place they could go.

They had wanted to flee the City, where the air was poison to children, the streets were crowded, filthy, where rows of high-rises sprawled to the horizon and beyond. And because all land that hadn't been subsumed by the City was now being used to support the City, it seemed everyone now lived in the City. Whether they wanted to or not. So while a couple of those twenty had gone to the Wilderness for adventure, and a couple for knowledge, most fled there because they believed in some way their lives depended on it.

In the beginning, they had shoes, and army-issue sleeping bags, tents, lightweight titanium cookware, ergonomic backpacks, tarps, ropes, rifles, bullets, headlamps, salt, eggs, flour, and more. They walked into the Wilderness State, made camp, and on their first morning made pancakes. They sprinkled sugar on them. They flavored their early stews with bacon. None of that stuff lasted long, though. That first day felt like a vacation in a wondrous new place. That feeling didn't last long either.

In the beginning, their skin coloring matched that of wood pulp, riverbed sand, wet tree roots, the rich underside of mosses. Their eyes were brown. Their hair was dark. They had all ten fingers and toes. Their skin was unscarred. The dangers of the City had never been from scrapes and cuts.

In the beginning, they were written about and reported on back in the City. A group of people who had forsaken civilization to live in the wild? Why would anyone do that? Op-eds wondered what would happen to them. Mainstream journalists wondered what they were running from. Alternative publications wondered if they knew something everyone else didn't. Regular people sent them care packages of homemade cookies, coffee, hot dogs, generally inedible by the time they opened them. Batteries, toothbrushes, pens. Useless items for people attempting to live primitively. Someone sent them a forty-pound cast-iron pot. It was a family heirloom. It had been in his closet for years, he wrote on a card. He couldn't bear to throw it out. He hoped they would have use for it. The Ranger took a picture of them pretending to struggle to lift it. They were smiling or making pained faces. They sent the picture as a thank-you of sorts. But also as a way to tell the sender what a ridiculous gift it was for people who walk every day and carry what they own. With little discussion they voted to leave it behind. It was an obvious decision. But that night they cooked in it. And they'd been carrying the Cast Iron ever since.

In the beginning, they acquiesced to finger pricks, cheek swabs, urine samples, blood pressure readings, filled out questionnaires each time they went to Post, to see how they were impacting nature and how nature was impacting them. Their days were data to someone, though they never believed the data could be all that important.

In the beginning, they followed all the rules in the Manual, the written rule of the Wilderness State, for fear they'd be sent home. They never camped in the same place twice. They picked up all their trash, and even trash they couldn't imagine being theirs. They buried their bones. They measured out their pit toilets to the right depth, the right length from water. They restored their fire rings to look like virgin land. Where they walked, one would hardly know twenty people had passed through. They left no trace. They drank bad water because they couldn't always find good water, and they paid the price for that.

But that was all in the beginning.

Over time, the guns and tents and sleeping bags were wrecked. So they learned to tan skins, sew with sinew, hunt with handmade bows, sleep comfortably on the ground and in the open. The salt was the thing that lasted the longest. And after it was gone they discovered that real food tastes like dirt, water, and exertion.

Over time, they became sunbaked, darkening the way anything darkens when it soaks up rain. Their dark hair bronzed. Their eyes were still brown, but they were dry, crusty, and sunburnt too.

Over time, they learned when to hide by listening to birds. They learned to be cautious by watching deer. They thought they learned to be bold by watching a wolf pack take down a healthy moose. But then they learned how to see the almost imperceptible limp that a healthy-seeming moose was hiding. They learned to know seasons not by their watches, broken in the first few months, or by the calendar they burned early when a cold snap threatened fingers, but by what hatched, what was small and how long it took to get bigger. They learned to tell age not by size, but by the color and sheen of an animal's coat. They learned to head for the foothills when they heard the elk's mating bugle. And when they saw a female looking as wide as it did long, even if the snow was still high, they knew it was spring and time to trudge back to the plains. They knew the different flavors of leaves depending on the season; knew the secret sweetness of the red-tipped grasses in the fall, and the bitterness of last season's grass, buried in winter snow but somehow still green, like how poisonous mushrooms have alluring colors. Those colors only beckon the foolish. Colors are warnings. They learned that too. They learned what to eat by watching the animals eat.

Over time, they all came to know of some hair elastic, fork tine, frayed rope, or lonesome earring that had fallen and not been recovered in a micro trash sweep. They dug pit toilets in the wrong places and not deep enough. They camped in the same places again and again because those places felt like home. And they discovered spigots that rose out of wells or aquifers below. Spigots the Rangers might have installed to fight fires. Spigots they were not supposed to use. They took their water from these whenever they could because it was clean and they didn't have to worry like they had worried in the beginning.

Even the study seemed to stall over time. They began to miss their seasonal Post visits because of storms. And when they would finally arrive, the equipment wasn't working. Or the nurse wasn't there. The questionnaires hadn't been updated. The scientists were unreachable. Maybe they were simply studying some other aspect that didn't require blood work, they hoped. Or maybe the scientists had ended the study and forgotten to tell anyone. What would happen to them if it had? Would they have to leave? But always at the peak of their anxiety, a nurse would appear at Post with gloves and needles, and the questionnaires would be too invasive and personal again, and everything would return to normal. Or as normal as was possible.

Over time, the media and the people in the City turned on them. After the news of the first death (Tim to hypothermia) finally reached the City, the op-eds called them selfish, heathens, even murderers, and hoped they would perish. The Rangers told them, and were not pleased with the optics. They wanted the Community to do damage control. So Juan wrote a letter to the editor to explain what their life was like and what they had learned about death. In it he told a story about how one night, early in their first year, they'd stumbled upon a runty deer curled up tight under a cluster of trees, its slender head resting on its gleaming black hooves. By morning it was gone. Three different nights they encountered it. It never ran. It would only look up at them and then rest its head again. They assumed its mother had placed it there to wait for her to return, as deer do. But on the fourth night they saw it coming out of the grasses, wobbling on unsure legs, toward the trees. Alone.

A large herd of deer spent its evenings nearby in the grasses. And though this small, orphaned deer stayed close to them, it never joined them. It did not belong with the herd for reasons only they knew. But still, it stayed close, its instinct for preservation at odds with the one for social order.

That fourth night, the temperatures dipped, and in the morning the Community woke to the grasses sparkling with frost. Some rushed to the tree and were relieved to see the small deer was gone. But then they saw it in the first tall grasses beyond the tree. It lay frozen, its neck elongated as though straining to breathe, its front legs bent as though it had knelt first in exhaustion before it collapsed. Blood pooled in its graceful ear. The other deer, some just a few yards away from the dead fawn, licked the frost off the grass tips dumbly. The Community were enraged and sickened. They threw stones at the deer. "Why didn't you take care of this one?" some yelled. "It was a deer too."

It wasn't until they lost Tim to that bitter cold night that they understood. Of course, they were different from deer. But not as different as they had always imagined. That night, they knew he was suffering, but everyone was suffering. And in that moment something innate kicked in. It surprised them how easy it was to misunderstand a cry for help. Even to ignore one.

When the letter was published, people in the City were disgusted. And soon after, all the op-eds outlined the terrible deaths they wished upon the Community in the Wilderness State—burned to death in a forest fire, mauled by a cougar, wasted away from uncontrollable diarrhea. The Rangers told them about all these, gleefully it seemed. And actually, that is how a few of them died. Eventually, their numbers would dwindle to eleven. It's not that those losses weren't difficult. It's just that loss was now a part of their daily life, as so many new things were.

That's why it heartened them to see an elder animal, say, an elk, with gray in its muzzle and a slight limp, a limp that would be more pronounced if it hadn't learned to hide it. It had survived. A good mother and herd had protected it when it was vulnerable. Hardships had been weathered by the herd. Fires flying across the plain. Floods and rock slides. Disease that jumped from elk to elk. Droughts or population explosions that meant a fight for all necessary food. Pleasures had been discovered. Bucking and kicking down a hill in its youth with other calves. The otherworldly buoyancy of its first swim. The first snows on its hooves would have been a miraculous new feeling. Only later would it have noticed the anxiety of the herd snuffling their noses beneath the soft powder, looking for food.

If the elk was male, battles had taken place. How many harems had he defended? How many bloody lashes became scars on its formidable body? If it was female, calves had been reared. Had she watched them amble off happy and healthy? Or did she have to witness the weakest succumb to a wolf pack, mewing for her plaintively? If she was the dominant, the matriarch, did she ever worry her decisions were wrong? Or feel ill-equipped to lead the herd?

And yet, each night, that animal bedded down beneath whispering trees, on dead leaves, or in grasses under the moon and stars, listening to the chatter of the owls, the cautious step of the night animals, a whole new world relatively unknown to it except in these still moments, no comfort but the comfort of the group and of having lived through one more day. No guarantees for tomorrow.

It wasn't that different for the Community. They were living the same wild life. Of course, they could always outwit the animals.

Well, almost always. The drive for survival is strong. Even the most brute creature can be clever if it means another morning under the cool light of the sun in the Wilderness State, which was the last wilderness.

Of course, now it's gone. But let's not talk about that yet.

Part III

THE BIG WALK

THEY CAME TO call it the Big Walk because they walked for the duration of a whole season and a portion of the next before they even reached foothills for the very first of the three mountain ranges they were meant to cross.

On the Big Walk they passed through entirely new landscapes. Tumbled into grasslands that smelled of nutmeg after a rain. Bugling elk crowded valleys with sounds of a lost world. The animal equivalent of a haunting, lonesome whistle from the Refineries outside the City. They passed into regions of low, strange mountains, a mix of jagged licking peaks and mellow, rolling red-capped hills. From far away, some hills stood like tiered wedding cakes. Up close they were only once-solid things crumbling to pieces. Between them lay swaths of grass dotted with juniper and pinyon.

The stars at night vibrated so closely together, their cloud of light covered the whole of the sky. So much more comforting than the narrow embrace of the Milky Way.

They crossed new sage seas where all it did was rain. They didn't know if it was the season or the climate. The wet sage smelled like its best self. Better even than its sunbaked self. It smelled clean and soapy and left the air sticky. The deer they met ran and ran and ran and ran, then stopped and looked. And after seeing them still, the deer ran and ran and ran some more. The horizon was unreachable.

They found the true desert, or it seemed to them. The soft alkali sands where they lost their tracks as the sun moved overhead,

changing the texture of the land with its light. The loamy dry lake-
beds, playas, smelled of mushrooms, of dark body crevices. The hot
horizon floated in front of their eyes like a river of gold.

They walked for days through knee-high plants and by alkali lakes,
dried and white and glazed and crackled. Up long, low slopes, then
down, and the sight was always the same: another expanse of tossed
brown and green sagebrush, tufted white grass, each plant distinct
and curling into itself and only itself. They could walk between each
bush without touching one. It was a lonely landscape.

Sometimes a tree stood stunted but conspicuous, and Bea thought,
Poor thing.

The slopes they walked upon looked as though a giant had lifted
the front edge of earth. Plates of land sloped up and dropped off at the
end. At the zenith edge of each of them, the walkers scrambled down
the escarpment to another valley floor that seemed flat as a sheet of
paper. Not until their calves strained would they realize they were
climbing again.

Sometimes the escarpment was high and they might climb, slide,
or stumble down stories of rough land; sometimes it was just a few
hundred feet, but it seemed in that drop they must be losing whatever
height they'd just gained. A zero-sum landscape. But each night the
air became more chilled in that high-elevation way, and so they knew
that, slowly, they were rising into new mountains.

They walked mostly in silence, made uneasy by the uncertainty
of where they were heading and the strangeness of the land leading
them there. They saw less and less vegetation with each slope they
put behind them, and Bea, rather than feeling as though the landscape was changing, felt more that it was simply disappearing from
under her, and that soon she'd be walking on nothing, near nothing.
The sage and grasses thinned out and the sand became loose, shifting
in the wind. From the top of each rise, the whole valley floor below
would seem to move as though full of ghost snakes slithering between the plants. In the immensity of the land, their faulty eyes saw

movement rather than the stillness that was there. At night, when they camped, they slept poorly under the light-pricked, energetic sky.

*   *   *

AT THE END of one long day of a gradual climb, they reached the top and looked out over the next valley. Far off to the right they saw a trail of dust hanging in the air. At the head of the cloud were horses, maybe a dozen or so, running fast and together over the valley floor.

"Must be water," said Glen.

"Let's wait here and see if they stop," said Carl. "We always need water, but we don't need to walk seven days in the wrong direction for it."

They sat. Some dangled their feet over cliff edges; others lay in between the sage. Hawk cries came from above, whining, *Go away, go away.* Carl and Glen stood, hands shielding their eyes, watching the horses' progress.

Just before the edge of where they could see, the dust stopped and the cloud settled. Carl lifted the scope to his eye and looked through the cracked lens. "It's green," he said. He pointed to a spot on the horizon where the shadows seemed slightly darker than the rest of the land. "That's not too far," he said, passing the scope to Glen.

Once down in the valley they followed the animals' trail and a day later found a compact marsh circling a trickling spring. Bea had wanted desperately to hear the horses whinny or watch them be rambunctious with one another, or even have them look upon her with that disdainful gaze specific to horses, but the horses were gone now. Where they had stood, the tender stunted grasses were bent or kicked up. The ground held onto the impression of their wild hooves.

"Only take from the mouth of the spring," Val warned. "Those dumb horses shit all over the place." She scowled.

Bea only saw the droppings of one horse, on dry land well away from water. She watched Val angrily kicking aside clods of dirt as though they were turds.

She took Agnes by the hand and led her to the other side of the small but striving marsh. They stepped over the thin rivulets that were trying to get somewhere new but drying before they arrived. A frog jumped out of their way, and they both laughed in surprise.

"A frog," Bea called to the others, but no one heard. It splashed forward, croaking for the companionship of another, then became lost in the marsh that was verdant on its edges and blue with mirrored sky at its core.

"Where did it come from?" asked Agnes.

Bea looked out across the bunchgrasses and sagebrush, unruly and unwelcoming.

"I think it must have always been here," she said.

The Community waded through ankle-deep mud, browning the water in their wake, and passed forward personal bottles, skins, and a few large bladders and jugs they carried for the Community to fill at the mouth of the spring. They drank, refilled, and then harvested watercress growing wild around the edge. The sudden moisture made them feel waterlogged and dreamy, and soon they bedded down just a few hundred yards away.

In the night, Bea heard a parade of animals. The scamper of rodents. The light pad of coyote paw and the soft grind of antelope hoof against dirt. Bea was sure some antelope had stepped into their camp and then reeled back in surprise. She heard the soft push of water from snouts and tongues reaching in. She sat up and could see shapes and the faint glow of eyes around the water that shimmered in the scattered light the night brought. A crescent moon was rising, and it cast a road of light across the floor of the plain. A fire-bright sliver. It seemed impossible to illuminate so much. But she could see animals moving toward the water, could even see some of the markings on their coats.

Then she heard a taut snap behind her, a whiz next to her ear, and a second later the antelopes stampeded away from her, returning to the shadows. She turned and saw Carl, sitting up, lowering his hunting bow.

He turned to Bea and said, thick-tongued and sleepy, "Am I dreaming?"

"You almost hit me," she hissed, touching her ear and second-guessing if he had.

Carl rubbed his eyes and peered into the dark. "Did I get one?"

"Of course not," she snapped.

"Oh, relax," he said, shaking off his grogginess. "You're fine."

Bea felt Agnes stir at her feet. She was awake. Probably Agnes had been awake this whole time because it seemed like Agnes was always awake, attentive, watching. Bea nudged her hard with her foot. "Even animals sleep, you little spy," she said under the covers. Agnes played dead. Bea lay down again and curled up, withdrawing from her daughter, from Glen, who'd slept through everything.

She heard Carl whisper, "I'm going to see if I got one."

She heard his tread toward the water. She heard him return, whistling.

He rustled back into his bed. "Hey, Bea," he hissed. "I didn't get one." When she didn't answer, he hissed again, "Did you hear me—"

"Shut up."

He chuckled, pleased to have irritated her.

At her feet, Agnes squirmed to a place where some part of her was again touching her mother.

Bea closed her eyes. She heard the hum of insects, alive now in the safety of the dark. She listened for the footsteps of more animals returning to the watering hole, but she heard none. Against her eyelids, the crescent moon shone. A shadow passed quickly over her eyes, and the insects got quiet, and she knew the shadow wasn't some wayward cloud, but was from a night flier out hunting whose presence had been exposed by moonlight. She pictured the moon in some kind of pact with all the would-be prey on the plain, and all the prey of the plain offering thanks and small sacrifices to their guardian moon. Then she pictured the night flier, alone on the wing, cursing the moon and the light and the thankful creatures below, and vowing revenge on them all.

*   *   *

AFTER DAYS OF walking into this increasingly barren landscape, they crested a slope near sunset. Beyond the valley below lay a playa, a vast dried-white lakebed, its ends reaching farther than they could see. And its far side was rimmed by a high ridge dusted with snow. The ridge was a series of bulbous mounds, cleanly rounded in the way Bea rarely saw in natural landscapes. In shade now, the mounds themselves were black as coal, and probably in daylight too. But the fine cover of snow took the severe edge from them, and as Bea looked, she thought they resembled old pictures she'd seen of whale backs arcing up just before diving into ocean depths.

"This must be where the Post is," Glen said.

But they could see no building or structure.

"In the morning, we'll catch the sun on the roof and we'll know," said Juan.

"Let's get a fire going and eat, then sleep. Then we can wake up and be done with this awful trek," Val said.

They swept up whatever blowdown they could, branches of sage broken off and dried, a strange orange lichen crusted on many of the smaller twigs, and mixed it with starter pieces they tried to carry with them. The fire smelled medicinal and smoked more than it flickered. They made acorn cakes and heated some smoked chunks of deer, which made the meat almost juicy.

As the last residue of sunlight vanished, Carl called everyone to the fire. He squatted and drew in the dirt with a stick. He said, "There might come a time when we have to split up."

"Why would we need to do that?" Bea asked.

"I mean it as a what-if question. I think it's good to think through all the possibilities," Carl said, whipping the stick into the fire, but it flew through to the other side and hit Dr. Harold.

"Ow," said Dr. Harold.

"Sorry," said Carl. "Bea, do you have objections to that?"

"Not necessarily."

"Good. We move as a group now, but we should have a buddy system like we had in the beginning."

"Can't we just have our buddies from the beginning?" Debra asked.

"Some of our buddies are dead," said Juan, whose buddy was dead.

"I'm also worried that different people have taken on different roles and that we each don't know how to take care of ourselves."

"Well, we are a group," said Glen. "So what's the harm in thinking like a group?"

"Because we might not always be a group," Carl said again. "And do we know how to take care of ourselves without the others? For example, Debra and Dr. Harold usually identify the poisonous stuff, plants, mushrooms, bugs, et cetera."

Dr. Harold said, "Carl, I really don't think—"

"What if you're on your own and starving? What if there's only this one plant you've never seen before? What if you come upon a water source—do you know how to tell if it's clean?"

No one answered. Not because they didn't know but because they didn't like Carl's tone. It was a scolding tone, and they were exhausted and wanted to sleep.

"How do you check the potability of a water source?" Val joined in, haughtily and impatiently, trying to mask that she herself probably had no idea.

"Ask the animals," said Agnes.

Some of the adults chuckled.

Debra crowed, "So cute."

Agnes frowned. "Ask the animals," she repeated, lowering her voice as if to create a sense of seriousness. "Ask, *Where do you drink from?* And then go to where they drink. I want to try a food, I give it to them first. They eat it, I eat it. They don't eat it, I don't eat it. Ask, *Where are you going?* And they'll tell by going there."

"It's a good start," Carl said to Agnes. "But it's just a general rule, not a way to live." Bea saw Agnes scowl at the correction.

Carl continued. "We have different needs and different tools from animals. We have fire, so we can eat more. We have thumbs, so we can hunt better. We have different microbes in our guts, so we can drink from more rivers."

"Actually," Glen said, "we can drink from fewer rivers because of our microbes."

"Well, *I* can drink from more rivers," Carl snapped, "so I don't know what's wrong with your microbes." Under the flickering firelight he appeared to be snarling.

Agnes sniffled as though she was crying, and Bea pulled her up and away from the circle. Glen shrugged at her as they went past.

They sat on their bed of skins.

"Are you upset?" Bea asked her daughter.

"No," Agnes said. "I had smoke in my nose."

That seemed as likely, if not more likely, than emotional tears, Bea thought. She found her brush in her pouch and ran it through Agnes's hair. "You've gotten very tangled. We need to do this more often."

"I don't like it."

"You'd like it if we did it more often. Most girls like getting their hair brushed." Agnes's hair was frilly and bronze. Fern hair.

"Can Carl really drink from more rivers?" Agnes asked.

"No."

"Why did he say he could?"

"Because sometimes Carl says things that aren't true."

"But even when Glen said he was wrong, he said no, he was right."

Bea said, "Don't listen to either of them." She paused. "Well, you should listen to Glen because he's family. And because he is a smart man."

"And Carl isn't?" Agnes asked, all innocence.

"Well," Bea said.

"I think they're both wrong."

"Oh?" Bea smiled in the dark.

"Yes. The animals are always right, and when I do what they do, nothing bad happens."

"Next time we're hungry, thirsty, or lost, I'll follow you."

"Okay." Agnes straightened. She seemed proud.

"We might need to cut your hair."

"No," Agnes said.

"Well, short hair doesn't tangle. And something has to be done about these tangles." Bea gripped a chunk of Agnes's hair at its base and then tried to pull the brush through to the bottom. "When in doubt, listen to Glen," she said. "The difference is Glen loves you and Carl doesn't."

"Carl loves me," Agnes said. "He says so."

A snag came free and Agnes's head snapped back.

"Ow," Agnes said. She touched her head near the loose snarl gingerly. "Carl says he loves me and he loves you," she continued.

"Well," Bea said. She didn't want to hear about who Carl loved. She wasn't sure Carl loved anyone but himself.

They were quiet.

"Do *you* love me?" Agnes asked.

"Of course."

"Even when you're angry?"

"I'm never angry," Bea lied. She didn't want Agnes to see her that way. And it was better if everything Bea did was labeled as love, wasn't it? Bea yanked the brush through again and Agnes whimpered, "Mama," and it was such a lonesome sound that Bea stopped. The top of Agnes's head was a soft smooth dome that ended in a nest of snarls.

Agnes picked up the brush and whimpered her way through her own tangles. "Maybe I could put lard in my hair and it would be easier?" she hoped out loud.

"Sure, you could do that, and the next thing you know the coyotes will be eating your hair."

Agnes smiled through the pain. "They wouldn't," she said almost shyly, and Bea watched Agnes's face contort, trying to imagine coyotes snuffling her hair.

"They might." Bea laughed. But she really did think they might.

Bea saw the adults rising, moving about, some putting out the fire. The meeting was over and soon everyone would bed down.

She yawned theatrically. "Time for sleep now." Agnes fought against her mirror yawn, but it slowly crawled out. They lay down, Agnes at the foot. Bea wished she'd come up and sleep in her arms like she had when she was young, but she wouldn't ask because she didn't want Agnes to say no. So she waited for the cold rush of air as Glen joined them in the bed, but she was asleep before she felt him arrive.

*   *   *

THEY COULD SEE that this dry landscape ended at the ridge, and like prisoners who'd grown used to a captive life, they began to fear not being in it, this place they'd wanted out of so badly. Bea was looking behind her as much as she was gazing at the towering bulbous ridge. She knew on the other side of it was a profoundly different world. She thought it must be the border with the Mines. The land was mostly in active use, the jobs automated, but she knew there was housing for the workers who were needed. The workers tended to be those who couldn't afford even the smallest apartments in the City. Who'd been pushed out, priced out generations ago. Now they had barracks or low-cost apartment complexes for their indebted lives. What happened outside of the City had always seemed kind of mysterious. One guy she'd fucked from the Manufacturing Zone told her he got free housing, which was almost impossible to believe. She'd been impressed. She thought he'd seemed proud.

A wild wind was just kicking up when they'd made it to the edge of the playa, so they camped for the night. They still couldn't see any sign of the Post or other structures. But they did see signs of civilization. Discarded scrap metal and a few wooden electrical poles, the wires long gone, where hawks perched to hunt. A picnic table overturned in the sage. It was weathered almost white and covered in rock tripe, which they peeled off and ate.

Bea sat on the edge of the playa and watched the fine sand of the dry lake kick up in short-lived swirling dust devils, at first excited and then dying down as though realizing there was nothing to be excited about. The ridge rose to her right, and in the far, flat distance tall banks of brown clouds hugged the horizon. Dust storms. They were so far away that she could distinguish the different storms from one another. Three in all. Their front ends curled out like snake tongues, hurriedly flicking to learn where they were. The back ends dragged across the land like sandbags.

Behind her she heard Agnes talking to the birds that were hiding in the sage. Agnes always talked to the hiding animals, even though Bea had explained that they were hiding from her because she was talking to them. "They want to think you don't know they're there," she would explain.

"But I want them to know I can see them. So they know they need to hide better."

It was not logic she could argue with.

She watched Agnes flitting about the bush, talking a blue streak and flapping her arms, while the birds, now trapped by her daughter's manic actions, complained back in a high pitch. Incredible. Bea remembered when Agnes could not lift her head off of her bloodstained pillow. Those many frantic trips to the private doctor who lived in the building, the one who took on emergencies for a steep price. All the nights she lay on the floor next to Agnes's bed, listening to each breath, her own heart stopping when there was a gasp. The number of times tears leapt to her eyes in the too-long pauses between her daughter's labored breaths. It had been untenable.

She'd never forget the feeling around her conversation with Glen.

Sitting at the small round dining table after another emergency visit, wineglasses half full, dinner mostly untouched, pasta still curled around her fork, lying where it had clattered to the table at that sound, "Mama," through that hacking. The music was still playing, low. Agnes was asleep. Safe. Glen giving his brief history lesson about the convalescence movement that was once common but had been utterly forgotten about. Of sanatoria, of people escaping to far-flung places to get well. To take in the good air. To find health away from the place that ailed them. "What does this have to do with anything?" she'd snapped, half listening, half tuned for sounds from Agnes's room. He and Bea weren't married yet, though they knew they would. He was already in love with Agnes. And when he explained fully about the study and his idea, Bea had said, "It seems crazy." "It is crazy," he said. "But if we stay, she'll die." It came out so flatly, so unequivocal, she felt like he'd slapped her. They stared at each other, not speaking. She thought hours might have passed. She wished that she'd had better thoughts running through her head. Thoughts like, *I don't even need to think—of course that's what we'll do.* Like, *Whatever it takes.* But really she thought, *So, we have to risk all our lives just to save hers? Is this the rule, or do I have a choice?* She looked at Glen and he had that resolute look. That *no other solution* look. And she knew her eyes were spinning, confused, everywhere. She was thinking of how much she'd looked forward to the three of them being a family here in this cozy apartment. She was thinking about the projects she had lined up and how she wouldn't be able to do them now. Big contracts that had come in after the magazine spread. A career shift. She was thinking of her own mother and how she would have to leave her. If they did this, Bea knew already her mother would never come. She needed her mother still. Didn't she? Did her needs not matter anymore? Bea shivered at her cold heart. She hit the side of her head to rattle her humanity loose. To think of her daughter first. She didn't realize she'd kept hitting herself until Glen gripped her wrist and brought her arm firmly to her side, held her, and she felt the bitter tears on her face for the first time. She choked sobs into his shoulder. *This is motherhood?* she thought, furious and brokenhearted as she tried to let go of her own self so she could free her arms to hold up Agnes.

The playa dust devils were dancing longer and higher now, and closer to where Bea sat. She smelled dirt in the air. When she breathed through her mouth to escape the smell, her mouth gritted with fine, stale-tasting sand. She looked around. They seemed to be in a fog cloud, or was it already dusk? She squinted, looking for the sun, and saw its hazy imprint high in the sky. She looked toward the far-flung dust storms, and now there was just one large one. The searching tongue had ballooned into a cloud hovering on the horizon. But now the horizon was the whole cloud and the horizon was very close.

Bea stood.

She heard tinkering behind her from Debra and Juan making dinner. The rest had spread out for more kindling and for water. She turned quickly to run toward the camp, and there was Agnes behind her, hypnotized by the cloud, her hands making fists at her sides. She ran to Agnes and grabbed her clenched fist, and dragged her along toward the camp. Agnes stumbled and Bea looked down at her daughter. Her mouth was open and moving, and Bea realized she could hear nothing but a roar that had started so soft and risen so gradually she had noticed nothing but an increasing pressure in her ears. She screamed at Debra and Juan, but she couldn't hear her own voice. They were already running. She slung Agnes by the arm up and onto her back, and ran in the direction where people had gone for water. She looked at nothing but right in front of her feet so she wouldn't fall and the bushes ripped into her legs as she ran through them. Agnes pushed her face into her neck, her mouth so close to her ear she could finally hear her. She was crying. Bea felt hot tears and saliva on her neck. And then Bea could see nothing and she could not stand up straight and her skin was on fire with the pricks of a thousand needles and the shuddering knocks from stones. She fell over a sagebrush and onto her knees and Agnes flew over her shoulders and her face was one hollow scream but there was no sound over the scream of the wind. Bea crawled, reaching blindly for her daughter until she felt her feet. She pulled Agnes to her and covered her curled, quaking body with her own.

Twigs and dirt and stone whipped against Bea, and the roar became muted so that she thought her ears must have filled with sand. She bent herself so her back would shield their heads, and it felt to her there was a mound of debris around her, blanketing her, as though because they stopped they would be buried alive. She curled tighter around Agnes and gnashed her teeth against the onslaught. And then, mercifully, she stopped feeling anything.

*   *   *

BEA HEARD THE muffled chirp of a bird near her head. She smelled stale urine from deep in her huddle with Agnes. One of them had wet themselves.

She peeled open a gooey eye. A towhee stood uneasily in front her, peering at her with a black inquisitive eye. It hopped and then puffed itself up, and a little halo of dust from its feathers escaped into the air. Bea lifted her head and groaned. The bird flew away.

Bea pushed upward and felt things tumble off of her. What must have been a wall of sand behind her collapsed. It had been a rare gift from the storm, something that stopped her from being pelted to death.

She felt Agnes squirming under her.

"You peed," the girl's muffled voice accused.

Bea rolled away to let her daughter up. Agnes scrambled up and dusted herself off. But when she looked up, her eyes widened and she froze.

Bea jumped to her feet in front of Agnes, assuming some threat was there, some herd of bison whipped into a stampede. But Agnes was looking at the land and sky.

The sun had sunk behind the ridge and the day's light was in fast retreat. Across the sky, a reclining half-moon rose lazily, pink and pearlescent. It appeared so big it looked as though it was half of another earth rising. Around them were piles of sand, through which sage branches reached desperately. The land before them, where the playa had been, where the dry craggy land of bushes had been, now looked more like the surface of the moon, a moon where tufted tips of sage lay across its surface like crowns. The new dunes muffled the sound of the world. They listened for the ping of the bugs of dusk, for the trill of a towhee, for the sound of any of their companions, but they heard nothing, not even the storm, the back of which Bea could see on the horizon, wagging its tail goodbye.

She checked Agnes through the girl's protests. Her daughter felt intact, while her own body felt pocked.

They walked the slow and exaggerated steps of moon walkers, their feet unsettling the sand. And when they reached ground that was hard dirt beyond the storm's reach, they shot forward with ease as though released from a captor's grip.

They walked past where Debra and Juan had been cooking and saw nothing but the turned-over Cast Iron, wooden bowls, ruined food.

Bea looked for the pond where people had gone, but she could see no evidence of it. Then, she saw two small shapes low in the sky and getting lower and then landing somewhere not too far in the distance. They flapped and reared and dropped their legs before they dropped from her sight, and she led Agnes toward where they'd landed, hoping to find the water.

They walked awhile before they heard the honk of a goose. And then they were upon it: a pond at the bottom of a shallow escarpment. It wasn't the pond they'd walked by. That one had merely been a bloated spring ringed with some reeds and milkweed. They never would have seen this pond; it was below the horizon. It was small, almost a perfect circle, murky and browned by mineral and decay, but there were two geese and two ducks and some grebes noodling on the surface. Bea could see the animal trails heading to and from the water's edge. It felt secret, protected, even though nothing in the Wilderness ever is.

She looked at Agnes.

"You're filthy," she said. Agnes's bronzed hair was now matted with dirt. Her skin shimmered as the fine sand that coated her caught the light.

Agnes smiled shyly to hide her laugh. "*You're* filthy." Her cracked tooth making her smile impossibly goofy, cracking Bea's heart.

"Let's get something for a fire and then take a dip before the sun leaves," Bea said and took Agnes's hand.

*   *   *

THEY WERE DRIPPING dry and shivering, and Bea admitted to herself that perhaps the swim was not her best idea. How stupid it would be to survive a violent dust storm only to bathe themselves to death.

They'd gathered stems and grass for a fire and now searched for something to cook over it. Bea wanted meat and fat to ward off the cold that she could now smell in the air. The geese were pecking around the pond, and she and Agnes crouched in the shore grasses with Bea's slingshot. Around them, frogs croaked, and worst case, Bea thought, they could catch some of them, roast them, and nibble their legs and around their gooey middles. Agnes was in a pensive mood, and so Bea just concentrated on the geese, getting to know them before she made any moves. They hadn't been scared off by the swim. A good sign. But if they spooked and flew now, she and Agnes would be hungry.

Agnes's head snapped to attention. Bea thought she must have heard something ominous, but Agnes's eyes widened and she asked, "Did Carl do this?"

"Did Carl do what?"

"Make the wind?"

"Honey, of course not. Why did you think that?"

"Because he told us that someday we'd have to split up. Now we're split up."

Amazing how earnest she seems, Bea thought, *as though she believes Carl has sway over dust.* Then, Bea got a chill. It wasn't an absurd thing to think, she realized. There was something unsettling in how much Carl was capable of. How useful he had made himself. To a child, someone like that might seem capable of anything.

"No, sweetheart," Bea said, "he didn't do this. It's just a coincidence."

"What's that?"

"Well," Bea said, "it's when things happen that seem related but aren't."

"That's weird. Isn't everything related?"

"Well, not everything."

Agnes said under her breath, "Yes, everything."

"Of course you would think that, because here everything does seem related. But trust me. Where I'm from, not everything is related. And sometimes things just happen." She nodded to finish the thought. But she felt rattled. The idea that something was happening that was bigger than them started to seep under her skin.

They were quiet, listening to two frogs find each other in the water.

"Did Nana live in a house?"

"When she was young."

"I wish I could live in a house."

Bea scrunched her face. "You do?"

"They're pretty," Agnes said. She said it boldly, asserting this new feeling of being right.

"How do you know?" She didn't think Agnes had ever seen a house. Maybe she thought Posts were houses? But they weren't very pretty.

"The magazine," she said, bold at having snooped at Bea's hidden things.

The magazine she had stashed away had new design trends and spreads of modern, styled apartments like hers, but what made it one of the most popular magazines in circulation were the vintage spreads it printed every month. Scenes from the archives. Of the old days. Old estates, sprawling penthouses, rustic-chic farms, front porches, lawns, and even sky blue pools, views of landscapes that were nice to look at, of attics, of homes in all sorts of weather. These were astonishing to look at now. Such things didn't exist anymore.

"You're right, those houses were very pretty. But they're gone."

"Why are they gone?"

"That is a big question."

"And?"

"They just are. Those places are all in the City now, and you remember, it doesn't look like that at all."

"But what was it like?"

"Where Nana lived?"

"Yeah, when she grew up."

Stories from her mother's childhood formed a dreamlike picture that entered her mind, a series of snapshots rather than movies. Bea clung to them, perhaps because they were so far away and strange. So unattainable. When her mother had grown up on an oak-lined street of single-family houses, the world had been a very different place. They had been in the middle of a timeline, rather than at the precipitous end of it. It allowed for the memories to seem sweet. They were benign fables. She tried not to indulge Agnes with stories of the City, even though her daughter asked often to be reminded of it. But Bea didn't want the City to become mythic. They lived here now, and Agnes shouldn't have to wonder about life elsewhere. But these descriptions of a house in a place that no longer had houses were like favorite bedtime stories, the colors worn and the pages frayed. Something for the imagination. Harmless, she thought.

She said, "Sit next to me."

Agnes crawled closer.

"Your nana used to tell me all about it. It was pretty, as you guessed. The houses were old and they had lots of lovely ornate things on the doors and the ceilings. They had these things called fireplaces, and that was a thing where you make a fire inside a house."

"That's weird."

"It is. But it was really nice. The houses had big front yards, and the people who lived there planted flowers and pretty bushes and trees and in spring everything smelled good. And birds and bees would come, and skunks would amble from the bushes and scare Nana, and squirrels would chatter at her when she walked by their tree."

"Like here." Agnes was amazed.

"A lot like here. Now this was a long time ago. But Nana used to go to a park down the street and there was a big pond and there were geese that lived there and she would watch them."

"Near where she slept?"

"Yes, just down the street from her house. And she would watch the geese and think how lucky they were to have such a lovely pond, so quiet. Sometimes in the early morning she'd go down and there'd be mist on the pond, the lily pads would look silver in the light." It was as if she were describing a picture, or something she herself had seen. Bea didn't know where her mother's memories ended and her own began.

"We've seen that here," Agnes said, an edge creeping in. Trying not to be impressed.

"We have. We've seen many beautiful things. That's my point. I look at the geese here, and I see the view they have. So dramatic, so unique. They must feel lucky. They must know other geese don't have it as good. Don't you think?"

"I don't know."

"Well, guess."

"Are there geese other places?"

Bea assumed there must be geese elsewhere, just not in the City. But now she didn't know. And what of those other lands in heavy use? The cities of greenhouses, the rolling landfills, the sea of windmills, the Woodlots, the Server Farms. What of the lands that had long ago been abandoned? The Heat Belt, the Fallow Lands, the New Coast. Was it possible they were dramatic and unique? Many of them had been at one time. It was hard to believe they still could be. She hated to think about all those places, what they once were, what they were now. Bea shrugged. "I only know about the geese right here," she said, pointing. "And the only difference is that the geese on Nana's pond were safe. They were stupid in their behaviors. Waddling on people's lawns, in the road. Leading goslings across the road. Trucks would have to stop for them. They weren't scared. Where she lived, there were no predators, and people tended to protect animals. I think the geese knew that. Here, the geese are cautious because they have predators and we're one of them."

"What happened to the pond?"

"The pond was filled in and the geese left and Nana left soon after."

"Before you were born?"

"Long before I was born."

"Where did the geese go?"

"I don't know. Nowhere. There wasn't anywhere to go. Maybe here. Maybe that's them."

"They'd be old."

"Maybe."

"I wonder if Nana could recognize them if she were here."

Bea felt a flash of anger at her mother for not being here. Something she had not felt before. *Mothers ought to be with their children*, a voice in her head argued. Yes, she was an adult, but what else did they have but one another, the family, this line of women? It had destroyed her mother that her grandmother had not come with her to the City at first. That sharing a life in the City had seemed to be a life not worth living for her grandmother. Here she was with Agnes. It wasn't what she wanted to do, but she was doing it. Her mother, Bea thought for the first time, her jaw set, should be here.

Bea raised the sling and placed a good stone in the band. The two geese were so enamored with their view and with each other they didn't even hear it snap. It wasn't until it landed in a poof of feathers that the other leapt into the air honking out a distressed call, now alone.

Agnes waded out into the water to get the bird.

"Will you make me a pillow?" she asked when she returned, smoothing the feathers, smearing the blood around.

Bea took the bird from her, slit the throat to make sure it was dead, and drained the blood there.

"I'll make you the softest pillow, my love."

*   *   *

AS THEY LICKED their fingers clean, Bea saw Agnes shiver. It was going to be a cold night, and Bea didn't have all the skins they usually slept with in her bag. The bulk of their gear was carried by Glen. The fire wasn't keeping the cold at bay any longer.

Bea said, "Maybe we should try to find the others?"

Agnes shook her head. "I like it here with you."

Bea's heart leapt. She searched for some sizable stones and put them into the fire to warm them for bed.

"Why did we live in the City if it's so bad?"

"Because it's where everyone lived."

"Except your nana."

"Well, my grandma lived there when she was forced to leave her house. She lived with us for a little while. Until she died."

The first star blinked in the sky. The moon crawled farther out of its den.

"Do you like the City?" asked Agnes.

"Sometimes," Bea said.

"What do you like about it?"

"Oh, the fun parts."

"Like?"

"Well, the food. Food is different in the City. It's more for pleasure than for fuel. Of course now, all that's changing, but when I was your age, food was the ultimate pleasure."

Agnes looked down at her hands and Bea realized the girl might not even know what pleasure was. Or she knew it but hadn't the language for it. So much of what they did day-to-day was simply life. They put no words to it.

"You know what pleasure is." She pulled her close and rubbed her back. Agnes closed her eyes. "See how nice that feels? I bet you feel warm and safe. That is a kind of pleasure." Bea slowly moved her hand under Agnes's arm and tickled. Agnes shrieked, playfully dove into Bea, laughing. "That silly feeling is also pleasure."

Agnes kept her face buried in Bea's belly and slid her skinny arms around her waist. Bea felt her shallow hot breaths through her clothing and on her skin. "There are all kinds of pleasure between comfort and thrill," she said, squeezing her daughter. "Food can be either."

"What food did you like best?"

"Well, I guess it depends. If you'd asked me when I was your age I would have said pizza. Do you remember pizza?"

Agnes shook her head.

"It's big and round, warm, chewy bread and stringy cheese? Do you remember cheese? And a paste made from tomatoes? Do you remember tomatoes?"

Agnes smiled. Now she remembered those things.

"But now, I think I miss vegetables."

"Which vegetables?"

"All of them. We've found wild greens and wild tubers. But you can't imagine the vegetables we used to have. All sorts of colors, but I miss the green ones most. I'd love just a plate of vegetables right now."

"Me too."

"And some fried potatoes. And anything creamy. I miss cream. I miss milk. I'd love a glass of milk. You used to love milk. Do you remember?"

"Yes. I loved ice milk."

"You love ice cream."

Agnes bit her lip and fell silent again. "Why don't we live there?" she finally asked, struggling to remember.

"Living there made you sick."

"I'm not sick anymore."

"That's true."

"Is that the only reason we live here?"

"No."

"Why else?"

"Well, Glen really wanted to be here. The whole thing was his idea."

"Did you want to be here?"

Bea laughed without meaning to.

"Why are you laughing?"

"Because that is a big question."

"Are there small questions?"

"There are big questions and small questions. And big answers and small answers. And that is a big question with a big answer."

"Does that mean you won't tell me?"

Bea smiled. *My perceptive daughter,* she thought. "You needed to be here, and I need to be with you," she said. "And so, I'm here." That was her small answer. And the big answer was more complicated. And probably unimportant.

Agnes frowned. "But since I'm better, does that mean you're going to leave?"

Bea frowned back. "Of course not."

"But don't you miss the City?" Agnes asked again.

"I told you, sometimes." Bea knew this was unsatisfying, but what more could she say? "Do *you* want to live *there*?" Bea asked her daughter.

Agnes shrugged. It was such an honest gesture. How could she begin to have an opinion about it?

"What do you like about living here?" Bea asked.

Agnes shrugged again, but this time it was less honest. She had answers to this but no way to begin to explain them.

"Let's try this. What *don't* you like about living here?"

Agnes thought. "I didn't like the cougar."

"I didn't like the cougar either."

"And I don't like snakes," she added.

"All of them or just the rattlesnakes?"

Agnes frowned. "All of them," she whispered, as though afraid they'd hear.

"Well, there are no snakes in the City," Bea said and then wondered how that could possibly be true. How unlikely it seemed that a place could be devoid of snakes now that she knew all the secret places where snakes lived.

Agnes didn't seem moved by this information. She knew snakes were a small answer to a big question.

"I think we should sleep," Bea said. "It's so cold and you're shivering."

Agnes nodded. "I'm cold."

Bea took the stones from the fire and wrapped them in two pouches she emptied. "Hot," she said.

They squirmed under the only skin they had and Bea curled around Agnes and each of them held a hot stone to her chest.

Bea woke several times in the night as the moon took up new positions in the sky. It seemed to be calling down, wanting her to notice it. *Look, I'm over here now.*

In the midst of her fitful sleep, her eyes snapped open and she became awake and alert. She listened and then heard again clearly what she'd heard from under her broken sleep. Something moving nearby. Something big. She thought, *Bear maybe. That's bad. Cougar. Even worse, but I wouldn't hear a cougar, would I? If it's a bison, at least it won't try to eat us, but it could trample us. It's tall, whatever it is.* It stepped again and she thought, *Not so big. Wolf perhaps? Elk?*

She tensed in preparation to grab Agnes and run, or fling herself over the sleeping girl.

Then she heard a snap and then, "Ow."

"Who is that?" she whispered.

"Bea?"

"Carl?"

He stumbled toward them and all at once was nearly stepping into the ash of their fire.

"Here," she said, and held her hand up to stop him from stepping on her. He grasped her hand, leaned in, and peered.

"It *is* you," he said, relieved.

"Did you think I'd be a bear who knew your name?"

"After today—" he began, but he didn't finish the statement. Bea understood.

She could see now that he had his pack. She got up and took it off him. Inside was a larger, warmer skin. "Oh, thank you." She laid it over Agnes.

"I don't have food," he said, and she caught in his voice utter weariness.

"Why didn't you bed down somewhere?"

"I ran into some trouble."

"What trouble?"

"I'm not sure, but I knew something was on my trail."

"And so you came here?" Her voice rose and she instinctively crouched again by Agnes.

"It's fine now, but I had to keep moving and then I just didn't know where to go. I saw a goose fly up overhead and so I tried to find where it had come from."

Carl sat with a groan.

"Are you hurt?"

"Not really, but I think I'm cut up from stumbling in the dark."

"Where's Val?"

"I don't know. I told her to stay by my side, but of course she didn't."

He broke a twig into small bits and tossed them into the fire circle, and in a moment little flares erupted where the pieces met with the hidden heat of the coals.

"Well, I'm sure she meant to," Bea said.

He laughed a short sharp laugh. "Yeah, she *meant* to, but couldn't quite manage it." He shook his head, and Bea snorted in surprise that he'd take a swipe—and such an apt one—at his ally. She covered her mouth and glanced at Agnes, who really did seem to be asleep, her breathing relaxed in her throat. That was the first time she'd thought of Carl and Val like that. They were a couple, sure, but more, they were allies, and the distinction felt important.

"What a crazy thing that was," Carl said, sounding frightened of what they'd seen.

"I was terrified."

"Bea, I was too. I was never so scared in my life," he said, a catch in his breath. "But then, it was so incredible. The landscape was utterly changed."

The moon broke from the clouds.

Bea peered at Carl's silver-lit face. He had two bloody lashes across his forehead. She resisted the urge to reach out to them, touch them, tend to them. "Someone must be injured," she said. "Or worse."

He nodded. "Are you worried about Glen?" he asked.

"I am. Are you worried about Val?"

He sat up straight. "Not really." And Bea thought that could mean any number of things.

They were quiet. Bea listened to the frog's throaty bellows at the pond's edge. It seemed to gloat of its size, each croak bigger than the next. Its mate from earlier had vanished.

"You know, Agnes thought you'd caused it."

"Caused what?"

"Caused the dust storm. Because you'd told us to be prepared to split up and then we had to split up."

Carl laughed a delighted laugh. "I hope you told her I did."

Bea chuckled.

Then he made his voice serious. "I didn't, of course," he clarified.

"I know."

More ducks landed on the pond, and Bea pictured their landing V splitting open the water's surface.

"Bea?"

"Yes?"

"You don't like me very much, do you?" He sounded concerned and wounded at the thought, but also certain.

What could she say? She didn't like him very much. And she was sure he didn't like her either. There was something sly about him normally, but tonight that felt put aside. Tonight, things felt different, like there were new rules, or, rather, no rules. She breathed, preparing to speak.

"How about don't answer that," he interrupted. "I just want you to know that whatever you think, or how about whatever I've done, I'm not a bad guy."

"I don't think you're a bad guy," she said. He wasn't a bad guy. He was a child, a bully, dim in everything except survival, and so here he was a king because survival was king. It irritated her that different people thrived in different places. It irritated her that Glen, who romanticized this life and knew its history, was not particularly good at living it. If he were easier to disappoint, he might give up on it. Agnes wasn't sick anymore. So they might go home. If home even seemed like a good idea anymore. Good ideas were so relative and hard to discern in the dark, with goose blood gurgling in her gut, an animal skin warming her own.

"Well, I'm glad. I admire you and what you're doing out here with your daughter. You're very important here."

"I don't know about that." She chuckled.

"Well, I do." His sincerity silenced her.

The moon had moved and was now tipping its contents into the sky. The stars pouring from it.

"It is damn cold, though," Carl said, finishing a conversation aloud that he'd been having in his head.

She looked down at Agnes and thought of the warmth her small, thrumming body was creating beneath the new blanket.

"We should sleep," Bea said. "On that tree, we've hung some goose we caught and cooked up. There should be some good chunks of meat there for you."

"See, you're the best one out here," he said, his voice thick with false flattery. This was the Carl she took lightly. The one always seeming to be angling for something. The one who wanted her vote in some imaginary election.

She lay down and listened to him step carefully to the tree. The sound of his footsteps now so unmistakable. *How stupid to think he was some animal coming to eat us*, she thought. The steps were so obviously human. Funny that out here that's a comfort. She tried to imagine waking in the City to the sound of some uninvited human creeping near where she slept. How relative terror was.

The clouds overhead stretched thin in the air, crossing one another haphazardly like a mess of power lines.

Carl returned and crawled under the skin he'd brought that lay over them all. It was big, and he was able to be covered by it without touching Bea.

She heard his chattering teeth, and she could tell that he was trying to calm them so as not to be heard. But his shivering trembled the skins. And then she felt the creeping warmth he was adding to their world under the skins and she felt a little soothed. She turned from Agnes just enough to take Carl's arm and rope him toward her. He scooted quickly to her and wrapped one arm around her and Agnes and cradled Bea's head with the other, protective and tender. She felt his fingers there and thought he might thread them intimately through her hair, but he didn't. They just cradled her head like a pillow. They smelled of goose fat and of Carl.

"It was damn cold." He sighed into her hair. And they lay there like that, building heat under the blanket, like a little lost family. She couldn't remember the last time she'd felt as warm.

*   *   *

WHEN BEA OPENED her eyes in the morning, Agnes was staring at her, full of contempt and a mix of other less obvious emotions. Carl's arms were still around Bea, but because Agnes was up, the scene that had felt sweet last night now looked unseemly. But Agnes's scorn wasn't that easy. Bea wished it were. The look was something that made her stomach do loops, and for a moment she thought she must be guilty of something worse. Much worse.

Carl, lost to a dream, squeezed her tighter and nuzzled into her neck. It was so warm under the blanket that they were now both sweating, and she felt stuck to him. She disengaged as quickly as she could.

"Did you hear Carl stumble into camp last night," she asked Agnes, too brightly.

Agnes squinted. "No." But Bea could tell she was lying.

"Well, he did and he had this warm pelt, so we all slept under it."

"Is this one of those coincidences?"

"Excuse me?"

Agnes kicked a stone and stayed silent.

"Don't get surly with me, young lady."

"What's surly?"

"It's being a brat," Bea said, and even though she never said such things to her daughter, Agnes winced and so Bea knew her flash of anger had been noticed. The message had been clear. She felt the lovely spell of their night together broken, and resentment that Carl had come at all curdled her memory.

"Good morning," he sang out, stretching happily under the skin. "Did you hear me come in last night, Agnes? I must have made a racket. And your mom and I talked and talked—"

Agnes walked away.

"Stop," Bea said to him.

"What?" Carl drooped his face like his feelings were hurt. Or maybe he was mocking her. Didn't he know precisely the trouble his arrival had caused? The thought was as paranoid as it was potentially true.

Bea heard a birdlike chirp from above the lake. A birdlike chirp that sounded like it came from a man. Then one from a woman. The Community was signaling. From a plateau above their pond, a reflector glinted, the cracked mirror they used when hunting, that was to come in handy for times they got separated, which had never happened before now. Bea chirped back, and then behind her, Agnes howled, "*Dad*," like she was being kidnapped. She usually called him Glen.

"Agnes?" his alarmed voice yelled back.

"She's fine!" Bea yelled, to stomp any budding drama of the reunion.

"Bea!" Glen yelled, relieved.

"Water down here," Carl yelled.

"Carl?" Glen yelled, his rising tone laying a string of question marks.

Bea saw him appear at the edge. He was standing tall until he spotted them; then he slumped and scratched his head. She waved up ecstatically.

"We're here for water," she cried excitedly, hoping to seed in his mind some narrative of how she'd just arrived, found water and Carl, and so there was nothing to be concerned about, all with her flailing arm and her shrill voice.

He waved from the elbow, which stayed glued to his side.

Val appeared next to him and shielded her eyes to peer at them. Bea could see her face squish at the sight of the three of them together, and she turned to Glen, who shrugged. The rest of the Community appeared at the ridge then and cheered.

"Water," they cried and scrambled down.

Once reunited, Glen's hugs were tense, and after several unsatisfactory ones she led him off, away from the Community, to a spot behind a large eruption of grasses, laid him down and fondled him. He started off sullen, swatting her away. But he kept his legs loose so she would have no trouble reaching between them when he wasn't defending himself, and soon there were long stretches between his defenses. He squeezed his eyes shut as though indifferent to what her hand was doing, would scowl to stifle a rising moan, and then swat again. It was a game and it was his reward, and she kept reaching as a kind of penance for something they would never discuss, until finally he was hard and smiling and pulling her onto him. And then she rocked astride him until he was relaxed and she was too.

"You must have a guilty conscience," he said, but he was happy and she heard no edge or accusation.

"I don't, actually," she said. "But you have a tender one."

She did feel guilty, but not toward Glen. Nothing had happened. It was just survival. It was Agnes she felt unsettled by. She would have thought Agnes understood survival more. Would Agnes be so full of disgust if the situation had been different? What if they'd been hungry, cold, without any bedding, and happened to come upon Carl? What if Carl hadn't been feeling very generous? Though he'd never acted on his lecherous air, there was nothing Bea would put past him. What if she had to do something she didn't want to do in order to care for her daughter, for herself? She was doing that right now, under the empty sky in a far-flung land, wasn't she?

They decided to camp by the pond that night. Carl, Glen, and Juan went back toward the ridge hoping to scare up some meat. Bea watched the men go, saw Glen keep his distance from Carl, speak with Juan, who would then speak to Carl. But when they came back with three jackrabbits, each man swinging one of the animals easily as they walked, Glen and Carl were laughing boisterously, and Bea couldn't remember the last time she'd seen them laugh together. Out here she often forgot that Glen had been Carl's mentor once upon a time. He so often seemed to resent people's appreciation of Glen. But not now, she thought as she watched Carl clap Glen on the back, laughing maniacally at something Glen had said. Glen beamed back at him, almost as though he were the student looking for assurance and so pleased to have found it. They sat and laid their rabbits at Carl's feet. Bea felt a tingle along her spine, and her eyes narrowed to slits, just as Carl looked up and found her eyes. Still chuckling, he gave her a wink, pulled a blade from somewhere behind his back, and sliced his rabbit shallow and long.

They dressed the rabbits while Debra and Val built a fire, and they spit-roasted the meat. It wasn't a lot, but it felt good to eat fresh, hot rabbit, and they ate jerky to fill their stomachs the rest of the way.

They searched the spot where the dust storm had hit them and found the Cast Iron and other kitchen items. People had managed to hold on to their personal belongings, their beds and skins, the things that had remained on their backs. A few minutes of hunting and the Book Bag was discovered and dug out. The Manual too. The trash bags they'd been filling since Middle Post were gone.

"If those dunes ever clear, we're going to get a big fine for that garbage," said Debra. She tsked, as though someone were to blame.

"Maybe the sand will bury it forever," said Dr. Harold.

"In a hundred years some scientist is going to be exploring these dunes and he'll wonder, *What amazing civilization was here?*" Val's eyes widened crazily, as though imagining herself there to see it.

"As if this will be here in a hundred years," said Bea, and then clamped her mouth. She hadn't meant to sound so bitter. Across the loose circle, Agnes squatted, always wanting to be a part of the discussion. Her little mouth dropped open in surprise and Bea felt bad. *Don't ruin this place for her*, she scolded herself.

"Bea," Val said, her face empty and confused. "What do you mean by that?"

Stupid Val. Her ignorance made Bea feel as cynical as she'd ever felt, and she quickly forgot about Agnes's presence. "This is a Wilderness State *now*," Bea said. "Before this, it was a collection of small towns and farms that grew alfalfa. Before that, it was ranch land. And before that—you want me to keep going? It's going to be something else. Just wait." It wasn't something she'd thought much about. But suddenly, the notion of this place existing well past their own deaths, she knew in her gut it would not happen. She thought this place lasting *until* her own death was an absurd idea. Assuming her death was not imminent.

"That's ridiculous. This is the last wilderness. There are serious laws about this land," said Val.

"Don't you think there were laws about those other wildernesses? How do you think this got to be the *last* one?"

"There are laws, but they can get rewritten," said Glen.

"Oh, shut up, Glen," said Carl. "*There are laws,*" he whined, trying to mimic Glen.

Glen looked pained. "I was just stating a fact that there have been laws—"

"There are serious laws and yet they let us in." Bea shrugged. "And now look, we just dumped our garbage everywhere. Do you think there's a law about that?"

"There's certainly a fucking rule about it," grumbled Carl.

Val looked a bit stricken. "Well," she yelped, but had no follow-through. No doubt the conversation had gone too fast for her, Bea thought. This moment had devolved quickly. They must all be tense from the storm, from being separated. They might not always like one another, but they generally worked well together.

"Oh, stop," interrupted Debra. "The point is, someday some scientist—or maybe it'll be some construction worker, Bea—is going to dig up a bunch of our trash."

"And when he sorts through them, he's gonna find Val's used tampons," said Juan. They laughed, glad to have stepped away from an argument.

Val scowled. "I told you I can't use anything else."

"I can't believe you still get your period," Debra said.

"I'm young," Val shrieked.

Debra raised her eyebrows.

"I vote we make Val pay the fine if they ever find our garbage," Carl said.

Everyone waited for him to laugh, capping the joke, but he didn't. His gaze was angry and fixed on the fire.

"Carl," Val whined quietly, as if trying to keep the rift private.

"What?" Carl snapped. "If you can't adapt, there should be consequences."

Val's jaw dropped. Bea winced for Val. This was a definite betrayal.

Val roused herself up and walked away from the fire, haughty, angry, and expecting to be followed by Carl. But he remained seated. Bea watched Val disappear beyond the circle of firelight. Her shape shifted from color to shade to gray dots, and then she was gone in the darkness. Bea looked back to Carl and saw that he was watching her. He smirked at Bea over the fire as though sharing the joke with her. When his smirk dissolved, he stared at her until Bea had to look away. She reached for Glen's hand in the dark, and though they were near the fire his hand felt cold in her grip. She looked for Agnes, but the girl was no longer there. She'd snuck off. Again, Bea felt bad for her cynicism. She hoped she hadn't alarmed Agnes. She deserved to think of this place as protected. Though Bea thought of it, she realized then, as more of a theme park. That would probably eventually become a landfill or some other necessary thing.

No one went after Val. They gathered warmth by the fire and then, one by one, family by family, went to their beds. Eventually Val stormed back as the fire was being doused by Dr. Harold's piss. He was usually the last one up because he had no one to bed down with.

"She returns," he announced, shaking his penis off, tucking it into his pants.

Val beelined into the middle of the circle of bedding each person or family had laid out, past where Bea and Glen had just lain down to bed. She marched straight to where Carl lay, on top of his bedding, his arm tucked behind his head, looking up at the stars in performed reverie. Everyone braced for an argument, for Val's screech and Carl's smug, terse retorts, maybe some kicks to his ribs. Their usual spar with Carl feigning the high road and Val taking cheap shots. But instead Val pulled up her tunic and straddled him in one swift movement that reminded Bea of a big cat pouncing. Val strangled Carl as she also began to fuck him. She screamed obscenities while he gurgled and growled. After a moment he tore her hands from his throat and grabbed her hair, snapping her head back so hard that around the bed circle they heard her xylophone vertebra aligning and her shocked, excited gasp. Then Carl's hands groped at her hips and he thrust her back and forth, grunting angrily, while she clawed at his chest. Their sex was so loud and aggressive that Bea reached for Agnes, to cover her ears, and was relieved to remember that Agnes had slunk off, and was, as far as she knew, not witnessing this.

Everyone under the starlight tried to look at something other than Carl and Val's glowing shapes fucking vigorously, to listen to something other than their animal grunts and screams. But it was hard to ignore. Bea heard some others trying to stay silent as they touched themselves. Glen reached for Bea and pressed his erection against her, but she pushed him away even though she herself was throbbing. Disappointed, he cupped himself and shrank from her. They both lay awake, uneasy under the stars.

* * *

THEY SUPPOSED THE Post was on the other side of the playa, which was now dune-covered. But the playa was large. Larger than they'd thought. They had to stumble through the loose sand. They made slow progress.

After a day they believed they saw buildings. And they had been passing more human debris, the kind of things left by the wayside when a person is nearing home and getting careless: the foil from a piece of gum, a once-blue plastic pen cap that had yellowed. They were certain they saw rooftops glinting ahead.

After the sun slipped fully behind the ridge, they stopped walking and prepared dinner and prepared for darkness. The mountains turned stone-colored.

A line formed at the Cast Iron, but Val cut to the front and exclaimed, "I need more food because I'm eating for two!"

Debra and Juan, stirring the pot, looked at each other quizzically, then around at the others who waited for their portion. Then to Carl, who nodded. They gave her more. Bea shook her head. Val often thought she was pregnant. Bea was grateful she never turned out to be right. Carl and Val individually were difficult to stomach. She was sure Val wanted a child to solidify that union and that power. They enjoyed being at the top too much. Every chance they had, they tried to subvert a Community decision to follow their own idea, and were gleeful when it worked. Leaders shouldn't enjoy leadership, she told herself. Like Glen said, it should be a role one takes because one feels obligated.

With her hollowed-wood bowl full of stewed rabbit parts, Bea looked for where to sit or stand. Glen was nowhere to be found. Agnes sat close to Val on a log. So close that on the small log there was room for Bea to sit. Agnes, listening to Val prattle on, looked up and saw Bea eyeing the seat next to her. Agnes inched away from Val and widened her knees to try to occupy the empty space. Bea had to swallow a laugh at how childishly cruel her child could be.

Juan walked in circles a few hundred feet from them. He seemed to be talking to himself, gesturing in an orating manner with one hand while holding his bowl of food in the other. Dr. Harold sat in the dirt morosely watching Debra, who was eating with Pinecone and Sister and Brother.

Bea's eyes eventually rested on Carl, who was already watching her. He sat alone on a log, and when he caught her eye, he patted the space next to him. Where was Glen?

Bea didn't want to sit next to Carl. She couldn't stop thinking about their evening huddled together. Actions that she had told herself were essential had become a cringe-worthy offense. But there was no way to refuse a seat next to him now. Where would she go? Sit alone in a sand dune? A refusal would be obvious. He was watching her for glimmers of shame. She would not show him any. She strode over.

"Hello," she said cordially.

He nodded, his mouth full. He did not say more. Why had she thought sitting next to Carl would mean something? He had merely motioned for her to sit where there was an empty seat. She sat feeling vaguely humiliated and unsure why.

Across the fire, Agnes slouched now and looked bored as Val made some kind of soliloquy, her hand on her belly and her other hand fondling Agnes's hair, something Bea knew Agnes hated, and she hated to see Agnes allowing it. She wondered when Agnes would cease to be mercurial. Would she ever be a spritely girl, game and smiling again like when she was very young, before she got sick? Or when they'd first arrived here, when she'd rebounded, eyes dancing, feet running. Making up for the lost bedridden time. She wasn't that young girl anymore, though, in sickness or in health.

Bea thought about all their original reasons for coming to this strange Wilderness. Had everyone altered their reason for being here by now, or were they still clinging to adventure, health, opportunity? Opportunity for what? Had she? Looking at her daughter's scowl made Bea laugh at her reason: *To keep my daughter well.* This was an overture of love to a girl who now seemed to loathe such overtures. She wondered if it was a martyr's overture too. One couldn't live like this for unselfish reasons alone. But nothing she landed on felt true anymore. Was fear for her daughter enough?

She wished she could talk to her mother about it. She would write a letter and mail it at Post. Though it was exactly the kind of question her mother would relish. Her answer would no doubt be, *No! So come home!* But Bea thought she could word it so that her message was clear. Her mother knew when to be practical, but she also knew how to be kind, even if it meant not being entirely honest. It was not something Bea had inherited.

In her youth, her own mother was an uneasy caretaker in a changed world that had become almost unrecognizable to her. In Bea's early womanhood, her mother had been a bemused friend, questioning Bea's choices though they were often the choices she herself had made. And now, her mother was most like a mother. At an age when she might have thought she didn't need a mother, Bea craved hers more than ever. In every letter, even the ones where her mother seemed to have embraced Bea's mission, she still begged for her return. *We've become so close, it makes me miss you all the more.*

She'd been staring at Agnes and Agnes at her when Agnes's gaze darted to the ridge above them. But Bea saw nothing. When Agnes turned back, Bea felt a primal chill and she looked back up on the ridge to see what up there might have its gaze fixed on them. Where was Glen? she wondered and began to worry. She stood up reflexively, searching the ridge. When she looked back across the fire, Agnes was gone. Bea spotted her walking toward where the sleeping circle had been. There was Glen shaking out the bedding. Agnes arrived and helped him. *My weird family,* Bea thought, and watched them, her heart light with love but heavy with regret for whatever it was that made people keep one another at arm's length. It was a deep, human, instinctual regret. But it was also personal.

As the Community cleaned up and set up bed, they were surprised to see a light blink on in the distance. The light seemed to be moving. Carl cupped his ear toward it.

"It's a truck," he said, and the suggestion translated for them the strange alien hum that had broken their desert silence.

"A Ranger truck?" asked Val.

"No, a truck truck."

"We must be near the Boundary Road," Glen said, pulling out the map.

Supposedly a raw and frost-heaved road ringed the Wilderness State, connecting the Posts and allowing the Rangers access to different regions without having to disrupt the remote and wild middle. They'd only ever seen the part that stretched between the Posts farther east. There was never anyone on that road, but out here, where it felt emptier, they saw another set of headlights flick on. And then farther ahead another emerged. Then the red tail of a vehicle heading in the opposite direction.

Bea walked deeper into the playa and stood. It wasn't as though they never saw other people or structures. There were check-ins at Post. They met Rangers in the woods, in the plains. Rangers even drove up to them in trucks. But these cars and lights dazzled her, and she felt just how lonely she had become. Who were all these people, and where were they going? Was there somewhere to go to not far from here? Her heart galloped at the thought.

She heard footsteps behind her, a soft crunch, somewhat stealthy. But definitely biped. She didn't turn around.

Carl appeared beside her.

"Got to spend some time with Glen the other day," he said.

"Yes, you did."

"It's been a while since we just talked."

"Yep."

"Great guy."

"Great guy?"

"Yeah," Carl said, looking surprised. "He's a great guy."

"You've lived with him, slept next to him, shat in the same hole he shat into for years. And before that he was your mentor. And you just figured out he's a great guy?"

Carl scowled. "No, I know he's a great guy. I'm just saying it. It's been a while since I said it. Can't I just say it?"

Her knee began to bounce, a nervous tic she hadn't felt the need for in years. She sighed. "Of course. He is a great guy," she agreed.

"He handles the Rangers well," Carl noted.

"He respects them."

"I don't know how," Carl said, his signature irritation creeping in.

"I think," Bea said, knowing she might be saying too much, "he wishes he were one."

Glen had told her once that the Rangers had it best. Freedom to roam, he'd said, and still a bed to sleep in, a warm house with electric lights to ward off the darkest darkness. They'd been lying under a skin one cold night in their first year. They had been encountering a lot that frightened them, but they were also feeling emboldened by having made it so far, especially when others hadn't. But that night Glen held her tighter and perhaps his weariness was making him honest.

He had whispered, "Imagine having the comforts of modern life but also having access to this vast, beautiful place. To know it like the back of your hand because you've walked across it for years and years and years and years . . ." He yawned and trailed off.

"But that's us now, isn't it?" Bea had asked.

"Yes and no. We'll never see it all, I fear."

Bea smiled, realizing this probably was an actual fear of his.

"But a Ranger will," Glen continued. "He'll see it all again and again."

"But he won't know it like we do."

"I'm not sure. I bet a Ranger could know it like we know it. I would if I were a Ranger." He sighed. "How did I not know about being a Ranger?" he whined. "I never saw it on those career lists, did you?"

"I don't think so. But maybe I got different lists." Bea wouldn't have wanted to be a Ranger, not when she was young and deciding such things, and she guessed that Glen wouldn't have either. The world had been different enough even then. Who could have imagined that the Rangers would be the lucky ones? "Maybe you didn't get the list with *Ranger* because you're old," she teased. "It probably wasn't such a good job back then. I bet they don't even like it."

"Of course they like it!" Glen had exclaimed.

"Shh. You don't know that. Sometimes they look beat and irritated."

"Because they're dealing with Carl."

They had both laughed.

Glen had hugged her hard then, and as he fell into sleep, his grip had relaxed little by little, reluctantly.

Far across the playa, a new car appeared. It seemed closer. From where Bea and Carl stood, its whine sounded at first like a young coyote calling from the ridge.

"Can I tell you a secret," Carl said.

Inside Bea groaned. She did not want to be a receptacle for Carl. She didn't think there was any benefit to being his confidante. She *hmm*ed quietly and let him translate that as he wished.

He barreled ahead. "I tried to be a Ranger once."

Bea snorted in surprise, but then realized she wasn't surprised at all. "Of course you did," she said and wondered if it had come across as snide as she felt. But Carl chuckled, pleased with himself and her reaction.

"I did. But I didn't have what it takes, they said."

"Did you apply again?"

"You can only apply once. I would have applied a million times. It's all I wanted."

"Do you know why?"

"Why what?"

"Why you weren't accepted?"

Carl twisted his face, thinking hard, as though he had never thought to wonder. "I mean, I assumed it was because I wasn't cozy with the idea of enforcing all their rules."

"That makes sense."

"The Rangers have always been real yes-men. They're just the police in green uniforms. I wanted to be a Ranger to access this place. That's all I cared about. I didn't care about enforcing rules."

"Let me guess, you told them that."

"Probably," Carl said, swallowing the acknowledgment, embarrassed.

She felt a familiarity creeping in like the feeling between them the other night. Like they were two people who could talk, could share things, even though she'd never believed it before.

She hugged her arms to herself, putting up a barrier. "So," she said, being chipper. "You finally got what you wanted. You must be happy."

"That's the thing, Bea," he said, casting his eyes to her briefly. "Now that I have what I wanted, I feel somehow freed up to want more. Free to want without hesitation. I think wanting is man's natural state. Now *want* is an insatiable thing in me. Painful almost how much I want what I want."

He stared hard at Bea.

She cleared her throat. "I think you just described what being a child is like." She smiled innocently, trying to deflect his energy.

He smiled at her comment, but his stare did not waver.

She laughed. "Why are you staring at me?"

Carl said, "You know why."

"Are you trying to tell me something?"

"I'm not *trying* to tell you something. I *am* telling you." His smile masked an edge in his voice. Like his wants were dangerous.

"Okay," she said.

"Okay what?" he asked.

"Okay," she spat. Now she felt like a child. She mumbled, "I get it. You want to fuck me." The word, in this context, felt like dirt in her mouth.

"Of course, but that's not it. I want to fuck everyone. It's just what this place does to me. Like I said, it frees me up."

"So then?"

"I'm going to stop playing nice someday," he said.

"Oh, you're playing nice?"

"You can't insult me, you know that right?"

She blinked. She did know that. His forthrightness was like a slap in the face.

"Bea, I think you're powerful. And I think we could be very powerful together."

"What about Val?"

"What *about* Val?"

Bea raised her eyebrows.

"Look, Val is Val," he said. "But Val is half the woman you are." He said it without flattery. Just stated it flatly, as though it were fact. Bea felt bad for Val, even as she hated her. "People follow you. You lead without even realizing you're leading."

"But Carl," Bea said, "none of us leads. We all make the decisions. Together."

Carl giggled. It was a boyish giggle designed to make her feel foolish, and it worked. "You don't think some people are influencing things to get their way? They're getting what they want and calling it consensus. And no one is the wiser. They're the ones leading."

"I suppose one of those people is you."

"Of course."

She nodded.

"And one of them, I think, is you."

"You're wrong."

"Maybe. Maybe not. Regardless, this stealth-style leadership won't last forever. And I'm telling you, if you're smart, you'll accept that we should be a team, you and me. Not whatever it is we are now," he said, sounding a bit mournful, a bit bitter. Impatient. He put his hand on her shoulder and she winced—at his touch, at the idea that he thought they were something, anything, together. "Do you understand what I'm telling you?"

"Not really," she said, dodging. But the space behind her eyes throbbed and her gaze unfixed itself so that the dark horizon became a void.

"Don't play dumb," he warned. "It's beneath you." Sharply he took her chin in his hand and snapped her to attention. She swallowed hard against his fingers on her jaw, her throat.

"One day you're going to need me," he said calmly. "Me. Not Juan. Not Debra." He paused. "Not Glen. You're going to need *me*. You're going to *want* me. And I will be there for you." Then his hand was gone, and she sensed he was gone. But she could still feel him lurking in the tension between her shoulders. Thought she could hear his breathing, his steps breaking the salt crust, she felt his eyes on her. She turned. He stood at the edge of camp facing her. Behind him, she saw Val watching too. And behind Val, like a child hiding behind a mother's skirt, was Agnes.

Bea turned back to the dark road.

In the course of a night, what had seemed an uncomplicated situation had become overwhelming and messy. For the first time, she wasn't sure who knew what or thought what about her, and this frightened her. These people she had lived so basely with for so long felt like strangers. She didn't like for things to shift between them. But she guessed they had been for some time. It made her feel out of control, and in that feeling she realized how in control she'd been since arriving. She'd been a person others deferred to or followed, and she hadn't even noticed. She hadn't noticed because she hadn't cared. Why hadn't she cared? Maybe because she hadn't cared about any of this, the experiment. It was a game. It made her wish to disappear, to regroup, to assess what her role here was. But thinking of going off alone made her shiver from fear.

So then, take Agnes and Glen, she thought. *Shake them awake in the night and steal away, back to Post, back to the City. Live that life again, with all the risk it holds.* But no, the fantasy was over before it began. They would never leave. The lump in her throat stopped her breath.

It's not like she hadn't seen Carl for what he was. But faced with it now, she could smell the rot, the bile. So she gathered that cold, fearful feeling into her gut and held it there, squeezing until it was hard and compact, a new part of her.

The moon was arcing toward the ridge, and so the depth of the foothills and the ridge face were glowing. *It's pretty*, Bea thought. The mountains were tall, and they were real mountains, fronted by a real craggy and proud ridgeline. She suspected the highest point of the ridge might rise a mile above them. If they began to climb, they'd find out how layered and deep the small foothills were. During the day, she'd hardly noticed any depth—in afternoon light it had looked like a flat wall. But now she realized it might be miles and miles of gradual walking before you got the final steep climb to the top. There were mountains to climb before that ridge.

She heard no more cars and saw no more lights. And in their absence that ridge became enormous. She felt its foreboding all at once. Now that she knew how vast everything was. Were they even near the Post? Her legs wobbled. She felt exhausted and wrecked. She wondered if she would freeze to death if she slept right here. She felt such dread in her heart she wasn't sure her feet would oblige and take her back to camp.

She heard "Psst" behind her.

"Hey, ladybug." It was Glen. He was there and wrapping a pelt around her shoulders. She felt then how deeply she'd been shivering. "Ladybug," he sang quietly, and swayed with her there in the blanket. "I didn't think ladybugs liked the cold," he whispered into her ear.

Her shivering subsided as he and the blanket warmed her. She realized he was holding her up. Her knees were loose and making circles above her feet.

"Would you like to come to bed?"

She nodded, and felt tears dislodge from the corners of her eyes.

"Would you like some help?"

She nodded again. She felt forgiven. "Take me home," she said, and he scooped her up and took her to their bed.

A DRIVER LAY on the horn as the car rolled slowly by. Palm to the center wheel, one long jeer. With the other hand he brandished his middle finger. The tires spun by, kicking up the remnants of a rare dump of rain collected in the grooves of the asphalt. After the car squealed past, its spent gas burned their nostrils. The children hacked as though they were back in the City with their faces in their pillows.

They'd awoken in puddles, the dry earth unaccustomed to soaking in any water. They couldn't remember the last time they'd felt rain and scowled that it had come while they slept and so they hadn't collected it or washed in it. Now their beds were wet. Their clothes stuck to their grimy bodies.

They walked on the road because the dirt shoulder was mud and so was the playa. "Car," they called up the line. "Car, car, car," and then a slosh through the mud until it was safe.

The clouds hung in the sky like dirty globes of cotton. An hour into the day's walk, it began to rain again.

The glinting roof they'd spied from a distance had been nothing but a collection of abandoned buildings, an old Post, inhabited now by a suspicious great horned owl and several families of irritable crows. An empty horse corral was scattered with dried pucks of shit, but no horses. A watering trough with nothing but a shriveled wood rat dead in its bottom. On the door of one of the buildings was nailed a splintery board of wood with a paint-scrawled note: *We've moved down the road!* An arrow pointed to their left. They trudged to the water spigot, and all that came out was a puff of rust. With shoulders slumped, they walked on.

They heard a loud roar behind them, as though a plane might swipe so close it would blow their hair around. When they looked, it was a truck, still miles down the road. As it got closer, it flashed its lights at them and they cleared the road. "Truck," they called out, and moved to the side.

The truck shook with effort. Its silver paint was muted with dirt and grime, caked on and not coming off anytime soon. It slowed and tooted its horn. It sounded friendly but still all the children except Agnes hid behind the adults.

Even though it was going slow, when the brake was applied the rig convulsed and the back swiveled, out of control briefly. "Whoa," the driver said as he stopped next to them. "This monster's not used to the rain." He smiled with impossibly white teeth. "Are you those folks I read about?" he asked.

Carl stepped in front of the Community, puffing his chest. "We are."

"Damn it all. Maureen is never going to believe me." He fumbled with something in his lap. "Let me take a picture," he said, producing a glimmering rectangle.

"We'd prefer you not," Carl said, but the man was already tapping it, saying, "Good, okay now, squeeze together," and they instinctively did what they were told. The camera shimmered just like the guns on the Rangers' belts and made a loud chirp like a robotic bird with every tap. Sister, Brother, and Pinecone started to cry, at first quietly, then loud and uncontrollably.

The man lowered the rectangle. "Hey now, why are they crying?" he asked.

"You scared them," said Debra. "They've never seen a camera."

"Oh," the man said, looking sincerely forlorn. "I feel bad," he said. His shoulders slumped and he stared intently into his lap. Then he brightened.

"Hey, I can make it up to them. Wanna lift?" He nodded to the flatbed of the truck, caged in steel rails to keep loads in. But there was no load. It was long, empty, and wet. "Won't keep you dry, but you'll be wet for less time. Please stop crying, little ones," he said, but they already had.

They all looked at one another, then closed into a huddle.

"Are we allowed?" Debra asked, voicing the Community's hesitation.

"Who cares if we are allowed," Carl said. "The question is, *Is this something we want to do?*"

"Well, I care if we are allowed because I don't want to get in trouble," Debra whispered as though worried someone other than them was listening.

"If we get in trouble, we get in trouble," said Carl.

"But this seems like a big rule to break if it's a rule at all. I worry we'd get kicked out."

"We won't get kicked out," said Carl.

"How do you know?" asked Dr. Harold.

"We won't get kicked out. It's not in the Manual."

"We can definitely get kicked out for breaking some rules."

"But this isn't one."

"Are you sure about that?" Dr. Harold said. "Are you sure it doesn't say that in the Manual?" He glanced at Debra eagerly. No doubt he was attempting to defend her.

Carl sighed. "I mean, yes, I guess so. I don't know." His shoulders and face drooped into a superior despair at having to field such inane questions.

The truck driver whistled, then called, "There's plenty of room for you all, if that's the problem."

"One second, sir," called Glen.

"When did you get so scared, Debra?" said Val, in a pitying tone. She touched her arm quickly, consolingly. But she was trying to make her feel foolish. Debra growled at Val, and Val smirked back.

Bea held her hand up. "I really don't remember there being any rule about rides, Debra." She paused.

And Carl erupted, "Exactly, this is stupid."

"I'm not finished, Carl," Bea said. Carl's face fell. He knew he'd been baited. Debra's face brightened. Bea continued, "But *of course* we can look in the Manual." She said it calmly, even though she thought this was an idiotic endeavor. *Just get in the fucking truck already*, she wanted to scream. But she hated Carl and Val's bullying ways more than she hated this time waste. If someone needed to look at the Manual to feel okay, then they looked at the Manual. It's how they'd always operated. Carl and Val were becoming more ill-tempered about other people's needs, and she wouldn't have it. "Is that okay with everyone?" she cooed.

Everyone nodded except Carl and Val and, Bea noted, Agnes, who was paying close attention to the proceedings rather than playing Shadow Tap with Sister and Brother.

Val was carrying the Manual, and for a brief moment, she held it tightly and sneered at them, showing her teeth in threat. But she finally pulled it out, and also the folder of all the addenda that had accumulated over their years of walking, the result of new rules sent down from the Administration, and ever narrowing interpretations of *wildness* and *wilderness*.

As she gripped the cover to open it, the truck driver called out, clearly irritated now, "Well, I didn't mean for it to be so hard. You want a ride or not? This ship has gotta go."

They all looked at one another, at the Manual that looked so large and unwieldy, then at Debra, who frowned and looked longingly at the truck. "I just don't want to get kicked out," she said, even as they all moved urgently toward the rig.

Then they were hoisting one another onto the tall bed and hauling up the food bags, bedding rolls, the smoker, the garbage, the Manual, the Cast Iron, the Book Bag, all of their belongings. They sat dazed as the truck cranked into motion. Bea leaned against the side and propped her feet up. She couldn't remember the last time she'd had her feet up. Everything in her body sloshed back and forth, settling into an unknown ease. The wind in their hair was so different from when the wind just blew in across the plain, from somewhere else. This wind was soft like careful fingers. Then, as they picked up speed, it got wild and they were trying to push their hair out of their eyes.

The driver cranked open the back window so he could talk to them. He used to work in the Manufacturing Zone, he told them. "But that's a lonely life," he said. *"Bleep. Bloop. Bleep. Bloop."* So he'd taken a job with the Shipping Districts, and now he sees a bit of this crazy country.

He seemed energized by the company. He barely breathed before launching into his next sentence, about a fish he caught in a river by the road. "Well, I didn't catch it exactly. It just kind of flopped out of the water and onto the road. The river was flooded, I guess. There was water in the road. It was flopping there. So I grabbed it."

They all looked at one another. What he was describing was against the rules, but they weren't going to tell him that. So they just nodded.

"Of course," the driver continued, "I didn't know the first thing about how to prepare it. You all probably would have feasted. But I just threw it back. Wow, did it feel weird in my hands. Slippery and sharp. It smelt too. And it looked scared to shit. Which is also part of why I put it back. I hate to scare anything." He rubbed at the scruff on his face. It made a sound Bea could hear over the roar of the engine. "I haven't seen a fish in, well—" he said. "A live one, never. It kind of disgusted me, to be honest."

He turned in his seat as the truck rumbled down the road. "Sorry again for scaring you, kiddos."

Bea winced, afraid the truck might hit something without his eyes on the road. But what was there to hit? The road melted into the playa.

"Are there always this many cars?" Bea yelled.

"Ha, what do you mean? I haven't seen any."

"We've seen a lot."

"Well," he said, and rubbed his scruff again, and it made Bea tense in some long-forgotten way, like chalk screeching. He said, "It's a holiday weekend. So maybe people are on the move. It would be mostly Ranger families, maybe a few from the Mines."

"Is there a big town nearby?"

"Nearby? Not exactly. Nearest? Yes."

"And so people in this town are allowed to just drive around this place?"

"Oh no, just this stretch of road. And you need permits. Place is a prison. Locked up tight."

The rain was now spittle. Out at the edge of the playa they could see the clouds breaking. A morning rain, not a full day's deluge. Steam rose off the playa, the mix of hot and cold and wet weaving a fine curtain in front of their eyes.

The driver peered at them using the rearview mirror. "Crazy what you're doing, you know," he said quietly, almost to himself. But Bea heard.

The driver cleared his throat. "Where you headed?"

"The next Post," said Carl.

"Oh, yeah? What'll you do there?"

Carl sighed and said nothing. His aim was mystery.

"Paperwork," said Bea.

The driver laughed hard until he coughed, and it seemed like a real laugh. But she couldn't be sure. "That's rich," he said, chuckling some more, repeating the word. "Paperwork."

Bea said, "Yeah, I guess everyone has to do it. Our paperwork, your permits for the road."

"Yep," the driver said, a little wistfully.

"Lots of rules to follow," she said. She was thoroughly enjoying this everyman conversation.

"For everyone but the Rangers," the driver said, laughing joylessly.

"Oh, come on. I'm sure they have some rules," Bea said. "Everyone has rules." She knew for a fact Rangers followed rules, because she and Ranger Bob had bonded over their interest in following rules.

"Not everyone and not the Rangers," the driver said, serious now. "No, the Rangers can pretty much do what they want, when they want, where they want. They're in charge around here."

Regret pulsed through Bea. Why did Glen have to be so old? If he'd been Carl's age, maybe he would have known about the Rangers. They didn't take Carl because he was a bastard, but wasn't Glen everything they'd be looking for? If Glen had been a Ranger, Agnes would never have gotten sick. They could have lived here in an actual house. A home. She sighed and realized she was really missing her bed. What an absurd thing to miss now, over five—six? seven?—years later, she thought. She looked at Glen. He was staring into the sky, a happy little smile on his face. Of course, she wouldn't have met Glen if he'd been a Ranger. She wouldn't have had Agnes if she'd been a Ranger's wife. She'd have some other kid. Bea looked at Carl and saw he'd been listening to her conversation with the driver. His jaw was set, red heat rising into his face. She could read his mind. A life without rules had evaded him, because somehow he'd not understood that people who enforce rules don't have to follow them. It was too much. How had this tragedy happened?

Bea groaned and lay down against the wooden flatbed. The vibration from the road and the might of the truck made her queasy.

Under the grime and the dirt of the truck bed, she could see streaks of purple paint that said something, possibly something important about this truck. Or something that had been important years ago. Perhaps it was nothing.

Agnes turned to her with wet eyes. She touched the truck bed.

"Isn't it pretty, Mama?" she said.

Bea watched Agnes lick the rusted metal of the truck grate, exploring it fully. She thought of the way Agnes ran after rabbits, or climbed trees when they came across them. Of course she wasn't sick anymore. That wasn't the problem. The problem was there was nothing for her in the City. Schools were training grounds for jobs that needed filling. Rooftops didn't have paths, flowers, gardens of vegetables. They had water-collection tanks, solar grids, cell towers, and barbed wire to guard it all. No one was ever outside unless they were going from one building to another. A few blocks from their building was one tree, gated so no one could touch it. Somehow, it still bloomed every spring and people came from all over to see its tissue-tender pink flowers. And when the petals later dropped, people crowded around the gate to try to catch those that drifted in the wind. The rest rotted around the trunk. It was one of ten trees left in the City. They were lucky to live near it.

The driver was saying something about buildings: "New buildings. All just built. It's the new Post after the old one didn't work."

"Why didn't it work?" Glen asked, always the seeker of knowledge. The driver didn't answer his question.

"This Post has hot springs. And the old cowboys built a little shack over it so it echoes."

"What old cowboys?"

The trucker barreled on. "Sometimes it's too hot. Like, it gets a surge of something awful from below. Can't go in it then. It'll burn your skin off. But I'm hoping to get a little soak in. My back. This seat."

"How do you know when it's too hot?" Debra asked.

"Ya throw some meat in it," the driver said.

Dr. Harold elbowed Debra. "We've done that," he stage-whispered to the group as though they didn't know. Debra turned away without comment.

"It's really nice," the driver said of Post. "You're going to love it."

When they reached the top of a rise they didn't know they'd been climbing, they saw Lower Post laid out ahead. Behind it a border ridge with a craggy surface that seemed impossible to fake. A carpet of sage lay all around the truck. They were finally past the playa.

The truck was hurtling down the road, their speed clear now that there was some visual landmark to gauge it. The Post would have seemed big, but it was dwarfed by everything: the expansive land, the endless sky, the humped shoulders of the border ridge. But Lower Post was man-made, and so, to Bea, it felt bigger than everything around it.

Of course, it was deserted.

"Remember, holiday weekend," the driver said, shifting the truck, slowing it to a stop in an empty parking lot. "Long weekend too. They won't open till Monday."

"What day is today?"

"It's Thursday. End of day. And you know what that means." He sang these words as he hopped out of the cab and whipped a towel around his neck. "Soak time," he sang again and jogged toward a shack set a ways off from the tight ring of Post buildings. The metal roof of the shack quivered against the horizon, steam shape-shifting it in front of their eyes.

They climbed down from the truck bed as awkwardly as they'd climbed up, asses in the air, feet dangling until the body shimmied over, clumsy handing off of heavy objects. Dinged fingers and a couple of broken grouse eggs.

This Post was the living version of the one they'd just passed. The buildings were whole and covered in fresh paint. The metal roofs gleamed. They were new, rust-free, admiral blue. Corrugated metal. Carl lobbed a rock and it clanged against the roof, hollow and bright, then slid down the pitch, falling back into his hand. He tossed the rock to Brother. The children played the new game in earnest.

The adults wandered the buildings.

Debra whistled. "This is a big fucking Post."

Three larger buildings hid behind the main semicircle of buildings. They looked the same, had the same layout of windows, some curtained with cloth that still held the fold creases and others frosted. Inside one, a fluorescent light zapped on and off. They must have been bunks or barracks.

The inner circle of buildings looked official, and were labeled, of-ficially. The Office, the Garage, the Horse Barn, the Arsenal. *The Ar-senal?* Bea thought.

Aside from the erratic light in what must have been a bunkhouse bathroom, the rest of the Post was in shadow, and it became darker as the sun set. Even now, after all these years, Bea was still surprised by nightfall. Days never felt like they would finish. The sky was too big and filled with light until the very bitterest end. Sometimes it was as though the sun blinked out as suddenly as a lamp turning off. But she had noticed, long ago, in the first year, that the key to nighttime was in the clouds, if the sky held any that day. When it was time, the bot-toms of the clouds turned black. They reflected the dark world below before Bea even registered that the darkness had arrived. The clouds revealed what everything else refused to accept. The clouds were the warning: *Get the fire built and hunker down. The night has come.* Above her, the bottoms of the clouds were dark as coal.

They unrolled skin tarps and beds. Some went for kindling, though the land was so manicured within the property that there wasn't much, and they had to walk far for some dead sage on the outskirts.

Carl and Val built a fire that smoked and hissed and snapped the tiny dried branches to ash. It smelled like everything their lives had become. Under hot sun or around the fire on a cold night, their world was sticky with sage.

As they were getting their eating implements out, they heard the truck turn over and the tires begin to grind. The driver's soak was over and now he was someone they would never see again. They watched his red taillights dissolve to pinpricks, then disappear. They looked down the road, hunting the horizon for more lights coming, but there were none. The traffic was gone. The holiday had begun, and they imagined no one would be coming by until Sunday. Bea counted on her fingers, naming the days of the week out loud for the first time in years, like they were words of a foreign language. Four days. Forlorn, she looked over at the campus of buildings and saw that life in the desert had already aged them. Anything in the middle of nowhere looked lonely, and all things lonely looked worn down.

"We'll hunt tomorrow," said Carl. "We'll stay until it's processed. By then we'll know why the fuck we're here."

They made acorn cakes and portioned out some meat. It was a moonless night so far, and unless they sat against the fire, they couldn't see their hands in front of them. In the distance they heard the sound of horses tremoloing their lips at the dark. Perhaps they were the horses of the Horse Barn, Bea thought and listened to their soft nibbles of grasses, the brush of their necks against one another. Bea noticed the darkness brought a quiet to the Community. They cleaned up. They went to bed. The silence was heavy, as though they were sullen and shaking off a fight.

* * *

IN THE MORNING, two horses stood in the corral in the middle of the buildings and watched the Community with what seemed like disdain. A hunting party left at dawn, and the rest of them timidly entered the steaming derelict shack for a soak. This felt ancient. A structure from long ago, somehow preserved even as the land was re-wilded.

Condensation dripped from the roof, the echo pinging between the water and the metal. The soft wood walls were etched with names and drawings. Taken out of context they seemed like ancient pictographs. An etched horse looked like a sign to communicate horses were nearby. But these were more recent history. From the days when local kids might have driven out here to hide from their parents, to imagine they were adult and free. Now, to the Community, it felt like salvation, as it probably had for everyone before them.

When Bea lowered herself into the warm water, it was almost too hot, and at first her skin cringed against the heat. But soon an ease she couldn't remember feeling before settled over her. They all wept a little before they laughed. The hot spring filled an old concrete tub about the size of the flatbed they'd been on. They needed a stroke or two to reach the other side. The mineralized water was slimy, syrupy, and they flailed into the middle, then returned to the side, venturing out again and again, thrashing back to the pocked concrete edge, like kids learning to swim. Bea went under the water and listened to her heartbeat. She bobbed her ears slowly under, then out, under, then out, alive, dead, alive, dead. The sulfur would stay on their skin for days. It felt like a tonic.

Bea looked around for Agnes and saw the girl gingerly stick a toe into the water, then pull it out. She repeated, wincing. It had been a long time since she'd had a warm bath. It had only been brisk mountain streams for most of her memory. Bea swam over to her and put her arms up for Agnes to take. Agnes shook her head, but Bea didn't lower her arms, and finally Agnes melted down into them and Bea carefully pulled her into the water, turning her around. Agnes was light in her arms, buoyed by the water's mineral heft. Agnes laid her head on her mother's shoulder and Bea felt her relax. The way her daughter clung to her, she was transported back to their apartment, desperately clinging to her daughter, who she was certain was about to take her last breath. Slipping back into that anxiety took mere seconds, and she felt her heart begin to pound beneath the water. *But no,* Bea reminded herself. *She is well. She's healthy. She's safe. Not only that, she is extraordinary. You did it.* She nodded to herself, but it only made her feel wistful.

The hunting party returned with a deer and two jackrabbits, and that night they built the fire big and broad and a smaller one next to it. It took the whole Community to prepare for that much butchering. Grass gatherers set out. Whole dead sage bushes were dragged back. The smoking tent was large, but a whole deer could only be done in halves. The deer was skinned, then split, and the first half butchered, strips of meat sliced long and thin and draped over the drying racks, made years ago from strips of a downed maple, and repaired as needed with the pliable strips of smaller green bushes and trees they'd encountered along the way. It was an almost daily job, to look for materials to keep the drying rack functional. But it was possibly the most important item they had. The maple had proved incredibly resilient, and it lent good flavor too. They'd never seen another maple in all their walking. It was as though the Rangers had put it there for them to find, to study what they did with it.

The butchering was an all-night job. They switched off tending to the smoker. The whole atmosphere felt like fire. They built a larger campfire to keep everything dry and hot so the small fire inside the tent could do its small work. Create smoke and just enough heat. It was how they had evolved the process.

Near dawn they'd done all they could, and many were laid out where they'd stood, sleeping lightly.

By their count it was Saturday.

People began to worry.

"Do you think they'll all come back in the morning?"

"Maybe they'll come back tonight to beat the traffic?"

"What traffic?"

"What's traffic?" the children asked.

"We tried all the doors, right?" Debra asked.

"Yes. Even the Garage. And the safety door to the Arsenal," said Dr. Harold.

"Why is there such a door on the Arsenal? Do they expect people to storm the Post and steal their weapons?" Val said. She kicked at some dirt.

"Why is there an arsenal at all?" Glen said.

"Maybe beyond that ridge there is a militia waiting to invade," offered Dr. Harold.

"It's absurd they let truck drivers in," Val pivoted. "He just had a permit. Probably got it for a bribe. Actually, it's probably a fake."

Carl shrugged. "Like I said, commerce is king."

Bea laughed. "When did you say that?" She rolled her eyes at Debra.

But Debra frowned back. Bea looked around and no one was looking at her. They were all looking at Carl, nodding their heads. Was everyone on Carl's side now? She looked for Glen. He had wandered off, was crouched and dusting away some loose earth, peering closely at something. A relic or fossil, she thought. It was so Glen of him. He was only interested in the past. She felt briefly furious at him.

"And we wait here. Waiting for what? Our keepers to give us our orders?" Val spit into the dirt she had just kicked.

"Yes, we should leave immediately," said Juan. He even got up from his squatted position, as though he would just walk away, but he only stood, stretching out his bad hip, which had never fully recovered from the tumble he took in a boulder field in their second winter.

"This is our land, is how I see it," Juan continued. "We've been invited here. We are guests, and our rude hosts aren't even here to give us a place to lay our heads or somewhere to clean up, take a shower."

Sister asked, "What's a shower?"

"They never do," said Debra. "Why is this Post any different?"

"Because it is," Carl interjected, with a fake professorial voice. He had never been a professor. "They told us to come here. For no reason. It's wrong of them to not be here." His calm facade melted to show his true agitation. "At least have someone here to let us into the fucking building to get our fucking mail."

"Well," Bea said, "they didn't exactly know when we'd show up. And it is a holiday . . ." She let her voice trail off. She didn't enjoy this game of Us Against the Rangers that Carl and Val and now Juan were trying to start. It made the situation they were in feel precarious. But she too wondered where the hell someone, anyone, was.

Carl shot Bea a stern look as he leapt up and strode petulantly to the Office.

Everyone followed him.

They peered in through the windowed door.

The Office was lit by the sun through the side windows. A playful ray danced over everything. The stapler, computer, *In* and *Out* mail bins that sat atop the front counter. Vinyl carpet in Ranger green. A flag with the emblem of the Wilderness State. They saw the desk that must belong to the Post's head Ranger because on it sat a mug that read, *Porque yo soy el jefe*. And on another desk sat a vellum box spilling over with mail. Packages sticking out the top. Letters stuffed into all crevices. They pressed their faces to the windows, straining to read the names written with that ancient cursive.

"Okay, what are we doing?" said Val.

"Debra," Carl said, in a sappy voice, "do you have any issues with me opening this door? There's probably a rule about it in the Manual."

"Oh, fuck the Manual," Debra said. She yanked on the doorknob. "I want my fucking mail," she screamed.

Carl covered his elbow with a pelt and bashed it into the center of the glass. Shards rained inside and out. He reached in to turn the door lock, but couldn't.

"One of the children," ordered Carl.

Debra put her arms out like branches and the children scooted behind them. "Absolutely not," she said, eyeing the glass shards.

Carl tried to punch them out to create a smooth edge, but they just became more jagged and the children stepped farther behind Debra.

Then they heard a loud smack and a grunt. Glen had thrown himself against the door. He reared back and yelled as he threw himself again. Then he kicked at the knob. His noises were guttural, incidental, as though they were just what happened when a body hit a door. He kept kicking at it until the knob hung off. And then, with a roar, he threw himself full force at it one more time and sailed through, splattering to the floor and skidding a few feet. Glen beamed up at them and then at Bea, who knelt beside him and stroked his hair.

"Good work, babe," said Bea.

They swarmed the mail table. Val and Debra wrestled for the box.

"Wait, wait," yelled Glen, and they all stopped and turned to him, Val and Debra holding the box between them.

Glen smiled at this victory. "We need a system," he said.

Carl groaned at the word *system*. But, Bea noted happily, no one gave Carl any attention. They just waited for Glen to explain.

His system, it turned out, was simple. Two people would sort. And no one would get their mail until the last piece was sorted. Debra and Val were chosen as the sorters, and Bea could see that Val relished the task. With the reading of each name she would stare thoughtfully at the person, then place it solemnly on their pile. They were deliberate and slow, and everyone was salivating watching the progress. The piles lay across the help counter. It was possibly the only action the help counter ever saw. Who came here for help ever? Other Rangers? There were no other people. The Office seemed equipped as a welcome center from some long-ago time. In the corner there was even an educational display about soil erosion.

Bea wandered the Office, opening doors, while the others hovered as close to the mail table as they were allowed.

She found a bathroom and giddily washed her hands. Then she pulled up her tunic, wet a handful of paper towels, and scrubbed her vagina. It left the brown paper towel even more brown. The paper pilled, and she unhappily realized she'd be leaving tiny balls of paper towel everywhere she peed for the next few days. Or the bits might entangle in her pubic hair, making it snarl and clump. She sat on the toilet lid and spread her legs, hunching to investigate. She felt around for them and picked them out one by one as though they were an infestation of something worse. The cool porcelain felt good against her skin. So smooth and clean. When she stood, she'd left a vaguely heart-shaped smudge in scum on the lid. She wiped it away with more paper towel. She washed her hands again and splashed water on her face until the water ran clean. Then she noticed a mirror hung on the door, partially hidden by an old stiff towel. She held her breath, closed her eyes as she removed the towel. Then opened them.

Her skin had wrinkled in the sun. Her eyes turned down, as did her mouth. She looked many years older than she should. She had freckles for the first time since she was a child. And she only remembered them because of pictures that proved they'd been there. She had no memory of her young face anymore. Except, occasionally, she saw something in Agnes that looked achingly familiar. And she thought it must be because it was something she'd looked at every day as a girl, studied as a girl, picked at as a girl. Or, other times, it was because Agnes made a face that her own mother made. Or laughed in a way her mother laughed. In those moments genetic lines seemed like the only thing that mattered in all of life. That proved anything. She thought of the way children were viewed in the City. There were simply too many people already. Making more wasn't encouraged. No one became an ob-gyn anymore. She'd been lucky to get in with a doctor at one of the last birthing hospitals with Agnes. Home births now. Hidden behind doors. With no help if something went wrong. No one specialized in new life.

No one specializes in old life either, she reminded herself, pushing the corners of her mouth up until they formed what could pass as a smile.

Her hair was sun-bronzed like Agnes's; the old charcoal tones had turned the color of wet sand. It looked as though someone had sprinkled acorn flour on her temples and in streaks from her scalp. She looked like a different person.

"No, you look like you," said Bea to her face in the mirror. "I just haven't seen you in a while." She stared a beat longer. She raised a rigid palm and swept it in an arc in front of her. "Hello, you," she said to her reflection, and forced a yearbook smile. The tendons of her neck popped and a thick vein throbbed across her brow. She frowned and covered the mirror again with the towel. No one needed to see this.

In the next room she found reams of paper, a neglected printer that seemed broken. Light bulbs on shelves. Sponges, paper towel packs. A bucket and mop, vacuum, other implements of cleaning, and she wondered who did that work. The Rangers? Or did some cleaning crew from elsewhere come in? Did someone's wife do it for extra money? Did Ranger households need extra money? Did they need money at all?

She'd never thought about it at any Post. She'd never seen the inner workings before. The idea of all those people milling around this office, tidying up, making it smell nice, sucking dust up from the flooring, made her sweat with longing. What she wouldn't give to be the cleaner here. A small, clean bunk that she could tightly make each morning, then ease under the nubby, overwashed sheet at the end of the day. She'd wander around picking things up, wiping them off, placing them back in the perfect place. She'd scrub the toilet with bleach. Her nose burned at the memory of the smell. But why waste time on memories, she thought. She pulled a jug of bleach down and opened it. She inhaled and doubled over into convulsive coughs, sloshing bleach onto her hands and the floor. She put a wet finger up to her mouth and tentatively touched it with her tongue. Her mouth watered.

In the next room, she found a table, a worn couch covered in stains. Along the sides of the room were counters, a microwave, a toaster oven, and a coffee maker whose glass carafe was crusted in burnt coffee. She sniffed the room. It smelled of rot. A mix of stagnant marsh and carrion on a hot day. It was beginning to seem that this Post was abandoned too.

The other side of the room had a refrigerator and a vending machine. Bea floated to the machine as though pulled by a magnet. It was half full. The good stuff was gone. Instead there were granola bars, fruit-shaped gummies, a potato chip brand she didn't recognize but whose flavor turned her stomach. Beef stew. But whose beef stew did it taste like? She thought of a dish her grandmother made. When people could still freely travel, her grandmother had picked up a taste for interesting spices. These chips couldn't possibly taste like her grandmother's beef stew.

Bea opened the fridge and found the origin of the smell. An

uncovered old turkey sandwich and, in the crisper drawer, a head of disintegrating romaine. What a surprising waste. Precious lettuce. How could the Rangers have just forgotten about it? She wondered if the life of a Ranger was even more glamorous than she or Glen had imagined. They worked for the Administration. Perhaps those in charge had other supplies, stores of food, different choices, cheaper prices, discounts. Discounts! That's what people claimed when they spread rumors about the Private Lands. That the people there had all the things you could ever want. All the things you used to take for granted. Like discounts. For some reason finding a stocked cleaning closet and wasted food made Bea more receptive to the idea of Private Lands than ever before.

Other items in the fridge: powdered milk and yogurt, a large block of lard, boxed rice, orange drink, some Meat™ wrapped in white butcher paper. She lifted it to smell. It smelled nothing like the meat she ate now, but she could tell what it was by the way she began salivating. Bacon. Where had Rangers found bacon? She tucked it under her arm. She needed an implement or some help to get into the vending machine. Juan was very good at snaking a wire and catching a treat. And bacon would blow their minds. She thought Carl might even cry. She smiled at how happy Carl would be. Then she scowled that feeling away.

Through the final door, she found a closet full of rags, for cleaning she supposed. Some electric cords. And two fifty-pound bags of sand. A catchall closet. Then a stack of blankets caught her eye. She pulled them down and nuzzled her cheek to one that she would have described, at some point in her life, as scratchy. But to her cheek now it felt like fluffy cotton. There were softer things in the world—hides, furs, new grass, moss—but that it was man-made made it seem careful, tender. She would sleep under this blanket tonight, she decided.

From the hallway window, Bea could see Sister and Brother outside tossing a rock in the air. Then she heard the clang of it on the metal roof. Again and again. They never got any mail, and their mother, when she was still alive, had never gotten any mail either. How awful it must have felt to not have anyone missing them. They kept throwing the rock. *Clang.* Bea felt bad. She barely registered the other children. Debra and Juan took care of them all.

The Community were now crowded so close to the help counter, their hands were almost touching their stacks of mail, and they shouldered one another to keep their positions. Pinecone careened around, pinging from one wall to another, and Agnes sat on the floor scratching shapes into the carpet with her fingers. Glen too held back, watching the proceedings with a smile, scolding those who attempted to touch their mail.

"Not yet," he said. "Not until every last piece—"

And that's when Val, after placing a piece with great reverence, looked up at the others.

"The mailbox is empty," Val announced.

They pounced.

Glen yelled, "Slow, slow, careful, careful," over the commotion of the Community lunging for their mail and scrambling to find a place to open it undisturbed, to feel their feelings and eat their stale cookies in peace.

Juan milled about, tapping a new set of paints to his chest and cooing "Mamá." When they were at rivers, he liked to paint the stones and then wash them off. *Leave no trace*, he would say and kiss the clean stone. He said it was how he expressed his artistic side.

Bea saw Agnes with a small box in front of her. And she saw her gnashing her teeth against something that looked like a brownie that was now rock hard from one of these pen pal projects some schools did. They sometimes got letters from stranger children, carefully written out, spelling checked by a parent, asking what nature was like and why they were there and needling to write back soon. They never wrote back anymore. At first, when mail, always precious, had been desperately so, some had written back. Now they limited their time in Post, and Post was where the pens and paper were. Time in

Post was spent writing to family. It had become an unofficial rule. But even those letters were waning.

They'd carried stationery and pens, but the paper got wet and the pens broke, leaking onto their hands. One Ranger fined them because he claimed to have found blue ink smeared on a boulder. An indelible mark, he'd said, though it washed away in the next rain.

It got hard to think of what to say when they were out walking. Hard to carve time to write something important. The letters they got felt essential and full of information. But what information could they impart to their families in the City? After all this time—how many more sunsets could they describe? And often, whatever they offered was met with hostility: *I don't understand a thing about where you are or frankly why you're there. Why don't you come home?*

Now they wrote letters at Post that were simple, noncontroversial: *Not much new to report. We're heading to the mountains before the snows come. Sending love.* They'd begun just using the postcards that all the Posts carried, that showed a pretty view of the Wilderness State. They sat out for visitors to take, but what visitors? The cards did a much better job of conveying something to people in the City. No one ever commented on the picture in response letters, though. It was as though they didn't even look at it, or imagined it was just a stock image unrelated to the life of the Community, and not the real thing they were sending letters to or getting letters from. But it was real. It was the canyon they'd spent part of their first year traversing. They'd lost Jane and Sam there. They'd perfected smoking their meat. They discovered that when the water was fast it was fine to drink without the iodine tablets they'd been using, thanks to their guinea pig Dr. Harold. They'd learned Dr. Harold liked being a guinea pig. They'd become better at navigating by stars, and in the canyon was where Debra began sewing their clothes from animal hides with Carl's sinew. The place was meaningful to them, but they couldn't convince the people they were writing to of that. It felt absurd to say, *Jane was swept away in a flash flood along with our best knife in this very canyon.* The people they were writing to would never get that, even though they'd been sad to lose Jane because she was a good singer, the thing they pined for to this day was that knife.

The picture was of the ragged red cliffs snaking toward the horizon, and of the green-leafed poplars that ran the length of the river, the river that ran cold and clean and sometimes shallowed itself over expanses of limestone so that for miles they could walk in the river and it only went up to their shins. Yes, they'd lost Jane and Sam there, but in the canyon they'd been happy.

She saw Glen with a stack of envelopes she recognized as being from the University, and she saw him getting agitated as he read. He still got the minutes from department meetings and the decisions they made in his absence drove him mad. "Don't read them," Bea had said once. "But it's mail," he'd responded, his nose in the pages.

She saw a small pile of unclaimed envelopes on the counter. They were probably from her mother, a backlog of newspaper clippings about oddities of life in the City, gossip from her bridge club, a tearstained note card begging her to return. She wasn't ready to read them yet.

She got Juan's attention and brought him to the vending machine. He made a snake of masking tape and the rolled card-stock packaging from the light bulbs and pulled chewy granola bars out as easily as if he were pulling them from a box with his hand.

"You're a magician," said Bea, gathering the granola bars in the pouch of her tunic.

Juan smiled. "Mamá would be proud," he said.

They distributed the granola bars to the Community. They had already ransacked a couple of care packages, and were slumped and clutching their stomachs from the rancid baked goods. Others who hadn't gotten packages grabbed several bars and aggressively stuffed them into their mouths. They were scattered all around the room, spent as though they'd all just fought or fucked.

"How are we going to hide that door?" Val asked through a mouth full of chewy bars.

They all looked at Glen, their fearless leader, at least for the day, the man who'd made this all possible.

Glen froze. "Uh," he began, "that's a great question. We should talk about it and come to a consensus." He sat up, poised to facilitate a discussion.

Carl rose. "We're not going to hide it," he said. "We're just going to explain what happened. That when we got here, it was this way. And what can they do about that?" Carl grinned.

"Yeah," yelled Debra, "fuck them and fuck their door."

"Exactly, Debra," Carl said. "Fuck them and fuck their door. And fuck their rules."

Everyone let out a lethargic *yay* from their slump.

The discussion was over. Carl had taken the reins to corral them and they'd gone happily. Bea saw Glen's chest cave.

* * *

THEY SORTED THE packaging and recycled according to number, filled their water bottles, used the bathroom, and then they left the Office. They headed back to their ring of beds. The horses from before were gone.

"I've decided those horses are assholes," Dr. Harold said, clutching his stomach. He had an ex-wife who faithfully sent him packages. But she made odd sweets—things like sunny macarons and palmiers. One time a flourless chocolate cake dusted with snowy sugar. They were beautiful sweets, intricate, professional-looking, like from old magazines Bea used to leaf through for inspiration. They must have taken whole days to make. But they did not keep well at all. He ate them anyway. Bea thought it odd that the woman would go to so much trouble for an ex. And she sometimes wondered if she really was an ex, or if Dr. Harold was playing a role—the lonely divorcé—to win some kind of attention from Debra. If he was, it certainly wasn't working. Whoever this woman was, she clearly still loved Dr. Harold.

So whether he left the marriage or merely left his wife behind, Bea had to wonder why. Here, he was not exactly appreciated. Perhaps he was the kind of man who thrived on heartache. Perhaps he hated her. Dr. Harold walked to the horses' trough and tipped it over, spilling the little water that was in there, water they'd offered up to the horses and which the horses didn't seem to need.

Debra clicked her tongue. "Why would you go and waste perfectly good water?"

Dr. Harold looked ashamed. "*They* were wasting it," he muttered, regretting his action. He'd probably been trying to impress Debra. She shook her head at him.

They milled around the sputtering fire, fueling it more, picking at their teeth, getting the sticky grains from the granola bars free from between them. Bea spread her blanket on the dirt ground near the horse corral. Agnes knelt beside her and smoothed her hands over the material.

"Scratchy," she said. But she kept smoothing it. Then she bent her head to it and smelled it, rubbed her cheek on it, then melted down, curling into a ball in a way she never did on a skin.

"Scratchy," Bea said, rubbing her daughter's back, her full hand lifting to fingertips when she ran out of room, then beginning again.

From the blanket, Agnes's muffled voice said, "Read your letters."

"I will," Bea said brightly, but she was dreading it. The top one was from her mother, and she could only imagine the guilt she would lay on Bea. And today, after rummaging through closets and eating City food, she was weakened in her resolve against her mother's wishes.

The last time she'd seen her mother, they had fought. Her mother had stopped over at her request. Bea told her they would leave for the Wilderness State that week. Agnes was at her side, serious, observant, her stuffed unicorn clutched in her hand. Her mother squinted, looked at the apartment, eyed the luggage. Eyed the beginnings of stacks of clothes. Her mother had been skeptical of the idea but had spoken respectfully about it. So it shocked Bea when she unleashed a tirade of anger and incredulity. She hadn't thought Bea would *really* go through with it. She hadn't thought Bea would *really* leave. *How stupid of me*, Bea thought, watching her mother's face contort with wild emotion. Her mother called the plan asinine. She threatened to steal Agnes away and hide her from Bea so she couldn't leave. She'd even tried to reach out for Agnes, weeping tears of anger and frustration, spitting her words out. "You're going to kill her," her mother screamed. Bea's heart turned to stone. How could her mother think such a thing? Bea was trying to save Agnes. Bea forced her mother into the hallway. In the doorway, her mother inhaled sharply and said bitterly, "You can't—" And Bea closed the door on her. Through the door's peephole, Bea watched her mother touch her forehead to the door to sob. Her mother's back was long through the fish-eye, projecting out into the hallway, shuddering and heaving. Bea left her there and scrambled to finish packing. She did not sleep. She left with Agnes the next day, to Glen's apartment, which he kept to store his papers, books, things that didn't fit in Bea's place. There they finalized everything and left without another word to anyone. It had been such an anomalous confrontation. She and her mother rarely fought. Bea was an only child, her father a stranger, just as Agnes's father had been. It wasn't exactly that they'd been so close, but it had been them, together.

The letter Bea received six months after that fight was tearstained and simple: *I'm so worried. I can't eat. I can't sleep. I found a real doctor for Agnes. I can promise she will be okay. Please come home!*

It had been the first mail Bea had received in the Wilderness State. She felt desperately lonely. And the image of her mother crying over her had almost made her sprint for the border. How could she have just left her? What had she been thinking? A terrible mistake had been made. These thoughts floated again into her head as she touched her mother's letter on the pile. They often did.

Bea's letter back to her mother had again explained her reasoning. And her mother's reply was swift and engaged, still argumentative, but Bea saw an honest attempt at understanding. They corresponded, then, like it was their job to. Multiple letters at each Post received and sent out. Thoughts on this place, on the City, but mostly on caring for Agnes. That was what this was all about, wasn't it? Her mother's commentary on Agnes's strangeness: *Sounds just like you at that age.* Her forgotten history opened back up to her.

Bea picked up this newest one. The return date was six months ago, and she imagined there must be another one on its way, if not already here, sitting at some other Post, unsorted, undelivered. The other envelope was from the law office that handled her finances and affairs while she was gone. She'd gotten many letters from them over the years and they were always updates on some kind of change in sublet fees for her apartment, or tax information, though she had no job for which to be taxed. It was the easier one to open. She eased her finger under the envelope lip and broke the seal.

We request that you be in attendance at the reading of your mother's will on March 17th of this year. Aspects of her estate concern you and need your attention.

   We hope you realize the importance of attending this reading.

Bea's cheeks burned. She heard the whoosh of a hard wind, but felt nothing on her skin but the hard sun.

"No," she whispered, tearing open the letter from her mother.

My Dear, Didn't you get my last letter? I also called and spoke with a nice Ranger man who said he would take a message. Didn't you get it? Well, I found someone who would treat me and I felt so lucky to get it, of course. But sadly, the treatment failed. The cancer is terminal. It is only a matter of time they tell me. So again, I'm

begging you, please come home so I can look at my beautiful daughter
once more. And bring your Agnes too. How wonderful it would be
to have us three together again. I'd like to see how she resembles you
now. Maybe she even resembles me? Love, Mom.

Her mother was dead.

Her mother had felt sick, been diagnosed, treatment had failed her,
and then she'd died, all without Bea knowing.

All the while wondering why Bea wasn't there.

Bea felt a warm, small, searching hand on her leg and heard,
"Mama." She looked up from the letter to see everyone staring at her
from around the fire, their arms slack. She realized then that she was
blubbering, not able to catch her breath. She tasted salty tears and
snot and knew she must have been crying for some time. It could
have been days later for all she knew.

Her arms dropped. The letter wavered uselessly in her grip. "My
mother is dead."

Glen made a truly sad face. Carl made a fake sad face. Val looked at
the men and tried to make any kind of sad face. Her hand reached for
Bea's shoulder, but Bea stepped back. None of these people knew her
mother. None of these people, she realized, really knew her. Not like
her mother had. She felt her expression morphing into disgust. The
faces around her looked away nervously.

Bea heard a whimper and looked down. Agnes had tears in her
eyes, but her whimper had been purposeful, performed. She was imitating her mother. Trying to access the feelings she saw there.

"Nana is dead," she announced to Bea, quivering her lip dramatically. And this enraged Bea, as though Agnes were trying to take
ownership of this pain, of this relationship. This important relationship that Bea had abandoned in order to care for her own daughter,
her own daughter who was strange and simpering there, her own
daughter who seemed not to know what love was, who had turned

too wild to know it, looking now for attention she rarely had desired before and did not deserve now.

Bea's heart stopped for a moment. Her burning cheeks turned icy. Leaning toward Agnes's face, with cold emphasis, she pointed to her own thumping chest and repeated, "*My* mother is dead. *Mine.*"

There. She felt her grief crawl back into her own arms and was so warmed and comforted by it, she almost smiled. Her mother was back with her, safe, where she belonged.

She tasted metal. She'd been biting her cheek and had drawn blood. She spit it onto the blanket. Agnes touched the glob with a finger as though testing if it was real, this bloody and tearful phlegm, and regarded Bea with curiosity and some fear.

A loud bellowing horn sounded, and Bea and Agnes both startled out of their trance.

Down the road a tanker truck was slowing, screeching. Bea saw that half the Community had already walked to the roadside to greet it. When had it appeared? It seemed like an apparition, but she saw the real dust it kicked in its wake. Seeing their shapes against the massiveness of the truck, Bea saw how truly hungry they looked. She felt how wildly their bodies moved. Perhaps they would ransack the truck's bounty. Perhaps they would cut the throat of the driver, hijack the truck, and drive it far away from here.

Bea straightened. Smoothed down her hair with what spit she mustered into her hand. "I have to go," she announced, and she moved toward it mechanically, automatically. As though it were a magnet attracting all her minerals and metals.

"Bea," she heard Glen say, his voice edged with a warning. But no, she would not look back.

The driver pulled up to the group and leaned toward the open window of the passenger side. "I'm supposed to tell you to stay and wait for instructions."

"Bea," she heard Glen call again. But no, she would not look back.

"What did you say?" Debra asked the driver.

"Wait here for instructions."

"What instructions?"

"I don't know, man," he said to Debra. "I'm just the messenger."

"Where are you going?"

"Gas to Middle Post."

Upon hearing *Middle Post*, Bea quickened her pace.

"When will we get instructions?"

The man shrugged wildly so that they could see him in the dark of his cab. "Stay here," he repeated, and revved the truck engine.

Bea began to run.

"Bea!" Glen yelled, his voice high-pitched and alarmed. She heard running behind her.

No, no, no, no, no, she would not stay.

The truck pulled away from those gathered, slowly gaining speed, and Bea arced her path to meet it. She leapt onto the runner.

"Hey," the driver yelled and slammed the brake.

Bea hung off the rig and opened the door.

"Get me"—she panted—"out of here."

He looked afraid of her, and she herself felt dangerous because in this moment she would do anything to leave this place.

He nodded, and in a daze she hauled herself up and over his body and into the passenger seat and slumped against the window. She heard him gag from her smell. She heard the yelling of her name, the calls for her to stop.

"Are you in trouble?" the driver whispered.

She shook her head. "Go, go, go," she yelled, pummeling the dash. She was under a spell. She rubbed her eyes, trying to wake from the fugue. The truck rumbled and began to move.

Only then did she regain her senses.

She looked out the window at the Community, some looking angry, some dumbfounded. She found Glen, a look of panic on his face. *He'll be fine*, she thought, a wave of relief washing over her. And then she saw that his hands clenched the shoulders of her daughter, who stood, mouth agape, confusion and fury dancing across her face as her mother drove away.

Bea couldn't breathe. She curled tightly into the hot vinyl seat and covered her face.

"Go, go, go, go, go."

Part IV

THE BALLAD OF AGNES

WHEN AGNES WOKE, she saw the prairie dog that had sung lullabies in her ear all night on its haunches, watching her with a question on its face.

She rubbed her eyes and the dog recoiled but kept asking the question.

"I'm Agnes," she answered. "And yes, I belong here."

The dog cocked its head. Wrinkled its snout.

"I do TOO belong here." Agnes flicked a stone with her bony fingers at the dog, whose face scrunched in protest before it disappeared into its hole.

The lullabies had been meant to haunt her dreams and scare her away, any dumb thing could figure that. Chittering and cooing to make a dreamer think her ear was being invaded by something awful. To feel unsafe. But they had soothed her. They were sounds she understood. They were a blanket to keep away thoughts of her mean mother who had run away. The meanest of them all. Perhaps she'd never been anything but a mean mother and every kiss had been cruel, meant to eventually cause pain with its absence. Agnes bolted from her bed. The camp was singing already.

Agnes hadn't believed her mother had gone. Not at first. Hadn't believed it as she watched her mother leap across that dumb driver, who screamed and acted as though a beast were clawing him. Had believed the truck, once it started rolling down the road, would stop, turn around, or maybe that the door would fling open and her mother would come running back on all fours, so frantic to return that she'd evolved into her true self. Sniffing and snorting into the air, trying to locate the scent of her family.

Agnes didn't believe her mother was gone until the dust from the truck settled and she saw that the road was empty. And it took a very long time for the dust to settle. She didn't know how long. Maybe it took days. The dust had made her lose time. And maybe some nights in her middle sleep, she thought she'd felt the blanket pull back on her at the foot of their bed and felt her mother warm the bed like no other could, sliding her foot to Agnes so Agnes could clutch it for safekeeping. Only to wake grasping at air.

Now, though, she knew her mother had left and was not coming back. And so what? Those were the words that came to her after she let in the word *gone*. There were other mothers to be had. They stepped in right away and gave her more mothering than her mean mother ever had. That's the way she thought about it at the time, at least.

That truck, though. That truck, silver-barreled, claw marks of black paint across it, headlights like the sun glinting off their best knife, the metal underbelly dull and hard like a bad storm coming. And its spew of dust. So much dust. That truck followed her in dreams. Just before she woke, that truck had run over the prairie dog singing in her ear. Guts across the broken asphalt. Carl scraping it up and feeding it to her and the other children as dinner. She'd liked the singing and so would not eat it. They tried to make her. But she woke up before they pushed a tiny drumstick past her clenched lips.

Breakfast was made by Debra, and she made the best breakfasts. Agnes found a bowl in the bowl bag. The bowl she liked to use because of the knot in the wood where she could hook her finger through. No one else used that bowl because they knew she liked it. She brought the bowl to Debra, who scooped mush into it and then, putting her finger to her lips—*Secret*—sprinkled something over it.

"Something special," she said.

There was nothing there. There never was. Debra always sprinkled nothing because there was nothing to sprinkle. Agnes knew that. But she also knew that if Debra didn't do that, it would not taste as good, even though the only thing she added was air and maybe some dirt from her hands. Agnes couldn't even imagine what there was to sprinkle, but Debra seemed to have an idea. Something from another time and place. Debra was oldest and had seen more ways of the world than any of them. She certainly had seen a sprinkle or two.

"Mmm," Agnes said as she took a bite. And Debra cackled as though she'd gotten away with something wicked.

Agnes squatted next to Glen and put her head on his knee quickly in greeting.

"Hey, kiddo," he said, his face briefly rounding as he smiled, then going long again. His eyes took in the horizon.

They would be leaving this place soon and she was glad. Soon the horizon Glen stared at would be new and he would not be looking for her mother. Glen didn't have a replacement for her mother like she had.

She wolfed her breakfast and licked her bowl and returned it to the bag. She sucked her spoon and put it in her sack. She rolled up their bed and tied it to Glen's sling. She pulled her own blanket out and tied it to her sling. Her mother and Glen usually carried everything together, but she would have to help now. She was glad. She could finally show how strong she was. She felt a lightning bolt of happiness that her mother was gone. Glen appeared behind her, his arms useless by his sides.

"I'll do it," she said, allowing him to just stand there. She brushed the ground, moved some stones around. Stood back a moment to take in the scene. She found a twig from a sage and tossed it into the middle of it all.

"Perfect," she said, clapping her hands together. The prairie dog popped its head out, offering an opinion before darting down again.

Agnes bent her face to the hole. "It IS perfect," she screamed.

Glen took her by the shoulders. "Okay, he heard you," Glen said, straightening her. She swung her sling across her torso. It was heavy, but she was determined not to show it. She watched Glen struggle under the weight of all their bedding, and made note to take on even more weight next time.

They congregated and re-wilded the fire and kitchen area. They buried charcoaled wood and ground what they could into powder to mix into the dust on the ground. Dr. Harold collected good bones to be carried along separate from anything that was pure garbage. He made a broth with them. Everyone hated his broth.

Carl lifted Agnes's sling a bit off her shoulder. "Whoa," he said. "Heavy load. What are you doing? Carrying all of Glen's gear?" He laughed, smirking at Glen.

Agnes jerked away, proud and mad that Carl had announced her secret. Glen's long face returned. She scurried ahead in the direction they needed to go, and the others followed. When she looked behind, Glen was small and just beginning to move his feet. He moved slowly as though he didn't want to leave. Agnes quickened her pace.

She couldn't wait to leave this place behind. She was so eager to be gone, she willed it gone from her memory. In her mind she watched the truck her mother escaped on explode in a fiery ball and disappear from the horizon. A thing she'd seen in a movie she'd sneaked one night when her mother was asleep, back in their apartment in the City. She'd seen a similar thing when lightning hit a parched tree dead center in its heart. She felt lucky to have seen fireballs twice in her short life. And now she could imagine her mother had been caught in one.

She clapped her hands. Done and done.

*   *   *

NO RANGER EVER showed up at Lower Post. It was as though the Community had been sent there for no reason other than to move them miles and miles and miles away from Middle Post, their lovely hidden Valley, the looming Caldera. After what could have been one week or eight, a new directive was airdropped by drone. Coordinates on a torn page of loose-leaf to a new Post on another far edge of their map, along with the words: *New Pickup Location*. Carl snarled, "Pick up what?" Another area they had never been to. Between where they had been and their new Post were seven upside-down Ws. Mountains. Lots of them.

There were plenty of other mountains on the map. They'd wintered in those. They'd summered in those. Mountains were nice areas for them to be. But looking at the map, they noticed the mountains they'd already spent time in were represented by two upside-down Ws, or four upside-down Vs. These seven new Ws were stacked on one another as though representing an endless expanse of them. The Community looked to the horizon but saw only flatness. Beyond these new mountains there was nothing drawn on the map until the Xs that marked the boundary of the Wilderness State. The rocky border ridges, the man-made berms, they assumed. Or perhaps another kind of boundary. But it was strange to see nothing in between.

The sun was low, but it was still hot on their faces until it was wholly gone from sight. After it disappeared, the sky blazed purple, a green glint just as the last glowing sliver sank, a trick of the eye or of the light. They'd seen it before, and Agnes had dubbed it the Wizard. Carl reminded her of that now. Agnes scowled.

"It's just light," she said. She wasn't that silly girl anymore.

Having no mother meant she was an adult now. She straightened her posture and hoped the others would notice that she was important. She led the Community across the flatlands and it was easy. She was fast and sure. Sometimes she got so far ahead they called for her to stop and wait.

At the fire that night, Val squatted next to her.

"I know you're an adult now and all that," Val said, "but you need to stay with the group."

Agnes blushed, and her heart skipped at this compliment and scold bundled together.

"It's not safe," Val continued. "And if something happened to you, we'd all be very upset."

"You're too slow."

"You're too fast," Val said. "Walk with me and we can walk the same speed."

"At the front?"

"Yes, we can walk at the front. I can ask Glen if he wants to walk with us."

"No," Agnes said, quickly enough that Val seemed surprised. "He wants to walk in the back. I know."

Val shrugged. "Okay, I trust you." She had said it casually, but Agnes heard it as an overture full of meaning. Because *trust* was an adult word. And nothing was casual out here.

They camped in place for a few sunrises and then packed up and carried on. Soon, the horizon looked muddled, no longer the sharp line they'd grown accustomed to. The brown landscape ahead morphed into white, gray, and black mounds that loomed more with each passing day. The ache in their calves grew, the sign that they were climbing.

The land turned from dust and silt to rocks and dirt clods that broke open under their feet. Agnes scooped them into her small hands as they walked and further cracked them open in her palm, feeling the cool dirt slide between her fingers and fall with heaviness to the ground. Nothing like the fine dust that hung in the air in the desert. She breathed lightly. Her shoulders became loose. The dust, she realized, had made her nervous. The dust storm they'd choked in. The one that turned her mother into a ghost. And then, in that truck, the dust was a curtain her mother had disappeared behind. With the dust behind Agnes now, she knew unwanted surprises were behind her too.

Soon stunted junipers appeared and so did evening rains that cooled off the land and turned the air herbal, sweet, sour, and sticky with the essence of those trees. Their evening fires were savory, and they carried the sap with them from their morning cleanup, clearing the burnt sticks, trying to crush them underfoot, only to get sap on moccasins or between fingers trying to fling the burnt sticks that instead stuck to their palms. The mix of heat and moisture made the trees weep, and brushing against one meant gluey clothes until enough debris matted the stickiness away.

During one evening, camped at the edge of a juniper forest, Agnes gathered the sap in her hands and stuck her hands to many parts of her body repeatedly until the stickiness died. She hugged the sticky junipers and then struggled to pull herself off.

As she writhed away from the tree, Sister and Brother and Pinecone walked up.

"What are you doing?" Sister asked.

"Playing Stickers."

"Can we play?"

Agnes looked at Sister and said yes. Then she looked at Brother and said yes. When she got to Pinecone, he looked so stupid in his little deer necktie he insisted on wearing, she couldn't help but pause.

Tears sprang to his eyes. "Why don't you like me?" he said in his warbled way.

"I don't not like you," Agnes lied.

"You don't want to play with me."

"I don't like your games."

"I don't have games."

"You always want to play Shopkeeper."

"No! I don't like Shopkeeper!"

"Don't lie, Pinecone," Sister and Brother said in unison.

Pinecone was born in the Wilderness, and yet he only ever wanted to pretend he was in a store working a cash register. He'd heard someone talking about it once. How they had bought something and the salesperson had been rude, long ago in their old City life. He'd then asked the whole Community to describe different stores and how a cash register worked. It was so stupid, but he put so much time into it that the adults had encouraged everyone to play the game with him. Even the adults had to pretend to shop for rocks and sage leaves.

"Shopkeeper is the only game you like to play."

"I play your games."

"But you don't like my games."

"Yes, I do."

"Okay, what about Bears and Coyotes."

Pinecone bit his lip.

"Or Stick Tag."

Pinecone shivered. "I don't like those games."

Agnes groaned. "See? Your name is Pinecone. You should want to play those games."

"Why because of my name?"

"It's Pinecone!"

"I know!"

"It's from this place. It's from your home. I wish my name was something wild like Raptor or Spotted Newt."

"But your name is Agnes."

"I know what my name is."

"What does it mean?"

"I don't know. It's a family name."

"It sounds like *agony*," said Sister.

"And what kind of name is *Sister*, Sister?"

"It's my name," Sister sniffed. Then she lifted her chin triumphantly. "Your name sounds like what you are." Her face scrunched up like she was in pain, her lips quivered, her eyes teared and danced in the back of her head. "*Agnes*," she snarled.

Agnes frowned. She didn't want to get into a fight with Sister or Brother. Or even Pinecone, really. She hated watching the adults argue. It was not the kind of adult she wanted to be. "Okay," she said. "All I meant is I wish I had a wild name. I'd kill for a name like Lightning or Condor. Or even Pinecone."

"Let's play Kill for a Name," said Pinecone.

"How do you play?"

"I don't know. Pretend to kill for our names?"

"Kill what?"

"Each other?"

Agnes shrugged. "Okay."

The game didn't last long, but it was fun, and after, Agnes felt a little kindlier toward Pinecone. He was learning. Someday she would steal that necktie he'd requested Debra make him. Where he'd ever seen a necktie was unclear. But he loved it, would hunch over and swing the weight of it back and forth like a tick-tock clock.

They went back to hugging the junipers. And then Agnes made up a new game that involved them pulling their hair back with the sap, then piling dirt clods on top to make it unstick. Agnes called it Wet Head, but for some reason the sap in the hair never unstuck, could not be coated enough to become unsticky again.

Debra gathered them together, their hair matted in odd angles, looking like mountain cats caught in a squall. She shook her head.

"I can cover your heads with dirt or I can cut your hair off. Your choice."

Around the fire that night, the children got blunt awkward haircuts and Agnes was shorn to the scalp.

Debra clicked her tongue. "It's even on your skin." She sprinkled dirt and patted the sticky spots until they were smoothed over. "What were you thinking?"

Agnes kept touching the sticky part of her head, finding short soft hairs left behind, or longer ones coiled against her scalp. She gathered the cut hair, banding it together with more sap into a great long tail.

"Are you going to save that for your mom?" Debra asked.

Agnes slapped the tail against her open palm, wincing at the surprising force of it. "Can't," she said.

"Why not?"

"She's dead," Agnes said, slapping the tail again. She jumped up and whipped her hair tail around her head, whooping, and the other children gathered their hair and tried to join her. But her hair had been the longest and her tail was the most dramatic, and so they just leapt around behind her, copying her moves. She was the oldest. Her new haircut the most severe. She knew that made her the leader. She pranced and slunk and watched the children fail to embody her uniqueness. But then, as she leapt around, she saw the adults exchanging looks she took to be displeasure, and so she abruptly stopped, knowing the children would stop too. She threw her tail into the fire and marched away to bed. The children followed. Their hair burned with the juniper sap, and the smell was so terrible everyone else went to bed too.

*   *   *

THE FOOTHILLS ROLLED into something more treacherous. Jagged, brittle rock that behaved more like hardened, sculpted dirt. It crumbled underfoot or in their hands as they scrambled higher. Then more rolling land, higher meadows where they would camp for a few nights and scout to get a sense of just what exactly they were heading toward.

In daytime excursions from camp for game or provisions, they found the animals were different. The squirrels were red, not gray or brown. The deer had bushy black tails that stood up two feet high when they ran from them. Their antler velvet was thick and black too. And they were small in comparison to the deer from the lowlands. The wolves were bigger, and the one bear she saw was brown, not black. And there were condors with wingspans as long as three people that blotted out the sun when they flew overhead. All the newness made the land feel newly dangerous.

And yet they had found ruts cut into the land that appeared to lead into the mountains. As though once, long ago, people and their wheels had passed through here for so long and with so much impact it could not be restored or re-wilded without tearing the whole mountainside out. It was like having the way forward whispered in their ears.

Agnes found the ruts. Early in the foothills, the Community had been following a stream, but Agnes had beelined away, and the group blindly followed. Soon they noticed their feet hugging the new grooved land.

"Had you seen them, Agnes?" Carl asked, trying to decipher if this was luck or mastery.

Agnes shook her head. "There will be more deer over here—see the trees?—and we want deer, so I took us here."

"But did you mean to follow these lines in the ground?"

Agnes didn't understand. "Why wouldn't we follow these? They are easier to walk."

At first the move had made some of them nervous. It was risky. Juan suggested returning to the stream. They always stayed by the stream when there was a stream to stay by.

But others sided with Agnes. Carl said, "We've got a burgeoning tracker on our hands."

At camp, they sent a party to follow the stream for a day and report what they found. The stream began farther up the mountain in an ice-blue pool. Snow-fed. Perhaps spring-fed too. A horseshoe cliff face surrounded it. No clear way through. The party returned with news of the dead end.

Agnes smiled shyly as people patted her shoulders. Val rubbed her scalp where new hair was sprouting in stumpy patches.

"Our fearless leader," Val said.

Agnes knew they felt bad for her. Motherless in the way she'd been made motherless. But Agnes had always paid attention to the small things here. The creatures. Agnes had noticed that a mother would only be a mother for so long before she wanted to be something else. No mother she'd ever watched here remained a mother forever. Agnes had been ready for this without knowing it. She hadn't cried once and that had to mean she was ready for it. She was not a bear cub any longer, but a juvenile on the lookout for her own place in the world. And so when Val called her a fearless leader, Agnes believed her. Val saw her for what she was now. An equal.

That night by the fire, Agnes scooted closer to adults as they discussed camp breakdown and the plan for the morning. The children yawned and squeezed juniper berries between their toes. Laughed and looked at Agnes to see if she was watching their antics. But she kept her gaze very steady on the grown-ups and tuned her ears to the conversation they were having so she would know exactly what was expected of her in the morning. She was their fearless leader after all. She'd found the trail into the mountains. And she had to make sure it would lead them to the other side.

* * *

BY FOLLOWING THE ruts, they avoided the white peaks that rose high above. Each time they arrived at a new threshold where the route seemed impossibly steep or rugged, the ruts led them through a gentler scene, bypassing the up-up-ups. Following rivers and streams. Sidestepping sheer rock face. There were some scrambles. There always would be. But they wondered if the Rangers knew of the ruts. If they'd wanted the Community to follow them on purpose. Or if they had simply lucked out by finding them. They wove in and around giant trees they couldn't even see the tops of. The bark changed color and texture. Smooth white with knotty eyes, orange and scaly, then dark, almost black, like the charcoal from a dead fire. Occasionally they moved through hardened snow, their moccasined feet breaking through the iced-over sheet, cleanly making a hole through to shallow powder. They walked days through a melting snowfield made eerie by a long-ago fire. What remained were black trunks naked of branches and sharp as blades, reaching out of the snow toward the colorless sky. Beyond the snowfields, the ruts directed them to a pass where they descended into forests of lean ponderosas with feet blackened by a ground fire that had never made gains. They moved on through this clean forest over the course of a mountain summer. Then the forest thickened, and soon it was shrouded, dark and dank. So dark and dank the tips of the coarse hairs of their hides collected dewdrops. The walking here was slow. The ground was knobby with thick roots hidden under carpets of mosses. Everything chilled. Gloom settled on the group.

Then at some point it seemed like it was all downhill. The ruts came and went from view or were covered under mosses, rock slides. But the path forward was obvious. The rushing sound of rivers multiplied until it seemed they were surrounded by falling water. The air changed from sharp to cool to wet, and their clothes never felt dry. Small spores of mold colonized their clothing.

As they walked, the hum of water became a howl, then the roar of what must have been a large, epic river just out of view. They called it the Invisible River because it sounded as though it ran right under their feet, but they could see no glimmer of it. The forest was now so thick and lush with waterlogged greenery, they lost sight of the ruts. They were disoriented and some vocally regretful, convinced the ruts had long ago veered another direction, and they were never meant to travel through this jungle of mottled light.

But Agnes scampered along, certain of the feel of ruts below her feet. She saw them like an owl might see a mouse under a covering of leaves or a sheet of snow. But even if they weren't ruts, she knew this was a good way to go because, for all its imposing darkness, she had seen the glint from animal eyes. She felt their ease. This corridor was safe for them. Their bright eyes didn't dart. They watched not from fear but from languorousness. The ears swiveled mechanically, following sound the way a clock works, a clock without an alarm. Agnes felt safe. And she tried through the ease of her shoulders and her chipper whistle to make the others feel that way too.

Then, one day, as suddenly as the darkness had surrounded them, they broke out of it, at a cliff's edge, so suddenly Agnes might have tumbled over it if Carl hadn't grabbed the back of her tunic.

The forest had given way to nothing. The soft land crumbled down to water that stretched far, far, far across to another cliff face, which glistened green with colonies of wet ferns clinging to it. They'd never seen so much water in their lives. The Invisible River was a monster.

Above the fern-decked cliff rose endless fir tips sloping up and up and up into new white mountaintops. And a tall, steel, seemingly electrified fence in front of it all. A border. They looked at their map. What was the land? The Woodlots? Where were the factories and the smoke then? The river seemed a mile wide. But it was not on their map. Had they gone the wrong way?

There was no crossing this river. The fence looked as though it might be electrifying the water. Agnes thought she could hear the buzz of motors, but she was no longer sure what that sounded like, and how it differed from the roar of water. Or a horde of insects. It was all noise. She touched her fingers to her ears and found they were vibrating.

Agnes scuffed her feet at the soft ground, feeling for the ruts. She felt nothing but root and rock. She looked over her toes to the river below. The cliff face angled down, and jagged-trunked trees stuck up from the mud-and-rock mound. She scrunched her toes through her moccasins into the loose soil. The cliff hadn't always begun here.

To the left, Agnes saw that the trees retreated and a headland rose up. There, Agnes saw the ruts pock the ground and curve their way skyward. She tugged on Carl's hand and pointed.

"This way," Carl said to the others.

Agnes smiled. He'd done what she'd wanted and she hadn't even needed to speak. She felt like an animal of few words but imperative work. She felt like the alpha. With a nod or a snort, the herd followed. How long before they followed simply because she moved?

They wove through a last thicket of dark trees and broke out onto green high grasses that bent in the wind, which jostled them now that they weren't buffeted by the trees. Their skin tightened and pinched as the moisture they'd collected in the forest was stolen by the sun-dried air. They felt thirsty and tired immediately. At the highest point of the headland they could see the ruts head down, down, down to where the river released itself into what looked to be a tidal plain miles ahead. The cliffs softened themselves into rolling bluffs and spits that got swallowed up or exposed with the invisible tide. And far, far, far out they could see whitecaps at the river mouth and wondered if it could possibly be the sea. Consulting the map, they saw only a border marked by Xs. No other symbol. They'd always assumed it would be more of the same. Desert. Grassland. Mountain. They inhaled. Brine. Their mouths watered. It had to be the sea. There must be some mistake.

The newly visible river widened as they walked along, and the imposing fence across it veered away from them until it seemed quite small. Was the river theirs?

The ruts dropped them to the shore, and they continued next to the enormous river. It was more water than they'd seen in their lives. Moving so swiftly it looked to be hardly moving at all.

Now closer, they could see the riverbanks crowded with submerged debris. Old wood, planed but warped. Engines from large machines. Tires bigger around than six people circled finger to finger. Old rusted blades from big trunk saws. And furniture. Couches that at one time were plaid, or plastic. Old recliners with waterlogged woodland-scene upholstery. A whole intact side of a small log cabin.

Carl went up to a pile of fabric, wood, and muck and wrenched out from it a rusted crab pot. Farther down the beach he found a rod and reel. He twirled the spinner and it whirled. There was no line. He propped it across his shoulder and kept walking.

They were caught off guard by the sun's descent. So much of its arc happened behind the shrouded forest. They set up a rough camp near the riverbank. A quick meal of jerky, and then Carl and Dr. Harold tossed the crab pot in. The thick, salty air made them drowsy and they were asleep before the sky properly darkened.

In the morning they were roused by the high tide stinging their legs. A large moon was falling below the frothy horizon at the river's mouth. A differently mooned night and they might have stayed dry. At first they assumed the sting was from the coldness of the water. But then they discovered they were covered in a rash wherever the water had licked them.

Four were sent with the Cast Iron to find fresh water to wash with. They came back with cool moss water and sheets of sphagnum, and they all wiped down with them. The sting eased.

Carl pulled the crab pot up, careful not to touch the wet line with a bare hand. There was only mud, a couple red-shelled clams, and a yellowed crab with one eye and far too many appendages.

The Invisible River was a poisoned river. A clean version of the river would have provided all the food they could ever want. In another era they might have stayed along a river like this as long as they could. They would have fished for their food. Found mushrooms, or what else there must be to forage. They would have set up buildings and smokehouses for salmon and trout and deer and elk and bear. They would have started a new civilization on a river like this if it were clean and thriving. The Rangers would have had to force them to leave.

But the Poisoned River was a ghost river now, barren of most species, only mutated muck eaters at the bottom. They had barely noticed that above the sound of the raging water no birds called, no peepers croaked in the mud. The animals stuck to the dark protective woods, and they couldn't be blamed for steering clear of this poisoned shore. The Community did find feral grapes and hard beach plums that colored their shits with their stout purple skins. But otherwise, it was a dead landscape.

"Can we turn around yet?" Debra said.

"No, we haven't reached Post," Glen said.

"Do you really think there is a Post around here? Nothing else has been right on the map," Dr. Harold said, always supporting Debra.

"I think they are trying to kill us," said Val. "If it weren't for that fence, we definitely would have tried to cross. We'd be burning alive in this poison water."

"Which is why they put a fence there to stop us," said Glen. "Fences aren't meant to entice."

"I'm always enticed by a fence," Val said. "It's a challenge." When Carl nodded approval, she smiled.

"Well, Val, generally fences are a sign to stay away," Glen said. "It's not a challenge. A fence is a rule."

Carl snorted. "If you saw a *No Trespassing* sign, what would you do?" he asked.

"I would not trespass," said Glen.

"That's crazy."

"Would you?"

"Of course! Land isn't made to be owned."

"But all land is owned."

"Not this."

"Yes, it is, it's owned by the Administration. You waited until you had permission before you entered this land. You didn't just sneak onto it."

Val said, "I hate this conversation. It's making our life seem so boring."

"It *is* boring," Glen said. "Isn't that kind of the point?"

Carl's jaw dropped.

Agnes did not care about this conversation. Who cared about *why* or *how*? Who cared about *would* or *wouldn't*? She never understood why the adults were always discussing these words. *Should* and *shouldn't*. *Can* and *can't*. "*Is* and *do*," she muttered to herself. That's all that mattered. *Is* and *do*. Being and doing. Right now, and a little time from now.

Agnes walked along the tree line, away from the tidal zone and the Poisoned River. The ruts were gone again. She tried to picture a time when this river had been clean, inviting to shorebirds and osprey. She might look out and see fish so plentiful the water churned, their tails splashing her from the shore. It was from a book one of them had brought. About pioneers of a different sort who, upon landing on a shore, were first greeted by hordes of curious animals. That water roiled with life. And the land crawled with four-footed walkers, and yet there was enough for everyone. It was one of the tales they told around the fire at night. One that she found hardest to imagine and believe. She tried to believe in them all. That is something her mother told her to do.

Her mother had been the best storyteller in the Community, though she told stories least often. But she knew the magic of the unexpected, whether in story form or in real life. Agnes remembered her last birthday in the City, waking in the twilight, the banished sun peeking around edges of the drawn curtains. With groggy eyes she thought she saw something glowing by her bedside. A small plain white box. Inside it, a small pendant set snug in cotton. It was an orange-and-brown butterfly edged in yellow gold. Butterflies were gone, but she knew what it was from the old books her mother had shown her. It was the most elegant thing she'd ever seen, but what bewitched her was how it had appeared as if by magic. She knew, somewhere in her heart, that her mother must have snuck in during the deepest night so it would be there when Agnes woke up. But when she came out of her room, she didn't thank her mother and her mother didn't mention it. Didn't make note of it glinting around her neck. Her mother joined her silently in this game she'd started, where a piece of jewelry was so special, so important, it couldn't even be seen. Just felt there at her throat. For as long as she had it, Agnes pretended it was a gift from some other realm. From a place where everything was lovely and charmed and delicate. And her mother let her.

When she lost the butterfly necklace in the Wilderness, it was the Community's first fine.

*   *   *

WALKING ALONG THE shore, in and out of the headlands, they came upon several old recliners positioned in a circle around something that must have been a firepit. There was an indentation, some stones thrown about, but no fire had burned here for a long time. Tin cans were strewn around the circle and the children picked them up, turning them over in their hands, unaware of the rust or dangerous edges. The adults had forgotten about these things too until Brother cut his finger and the children were forced to drop their new toys. How long had these been here, and who had left them? Derelict Rangers? Had this corner been forgotten in the re-wilding? Escaped workers from the Woodlots? There couldn't possibly be escapees from across the Poisoned River. They wouldn't make it, would they?

"Sometimes it feels as though civilization is half a day's walk away," Debra said, eyeing the fence. The adults nodded solemnly. It was the kind of feeling Agnes knew her mother had. *Why are we even here? What is the point?* She never heard the children ask these questions. The answers were everywhere.

Beyond the circle of chairs, they found an old baby seat, one that a parent might have swung in the crook of the elbow or hooked into a car when cars had been useful. "A car seat," remembered Debra. Tied to its handle was a note, marker on plastic-covered note card, weathered but readable: *Her name is Rachel. Please take care of her.* There was no Rachel anymore. Their shoulders hunched again, weighed down by the greater world.

Agnes's hackles rose, and she lifted her eyes, nose, and circled, scouting what she could. The others dumbly circled around this empty omen as though wondering just where they were heading and what was waiting for them.

"Well, ahoy there!" a voice called.

Above them, at the zenith of the next headland, straddling the ruts, stood a man in a navy-blue tracksuit, a safari vest weighted with items like binoculars, knives, a bird book, and a poncho hanging out of its pockets, and a rifle held up, cocked and ready. He lifted a hand in a wave, his eye still trained through the scope.

"The gang's all here," he said. "We're just over this hump."

The Community's hands were on their knives, ready. They hadn't even had a moment to gasp.

The man lowered his rifle from his eye, his eyebrows raised. "They told us you'd be meeting us here?"

The Community slowly unclenched their hands and turned their heads to Carl, whose mouth was disappearing into a thin razor-sharp line.

"We're the new recruits you're picking up?" the man said.

They blinked.

Juan muttered, "Pickup location." He shook his head. "Pickup location?" He fumed. *Pick up* meant pick up *people*?"

"I thought they were giving us some fucking rice," said Debra.

"They definitely could have been more specific," said Glen.

"Fuck," said Val.

Agnes looked at Carl, who was surprisingly quiet. He stared up at the man and stroked his chin.

The man in the tracksuit put a hand over his eyes, trying to see them better. Then he clapped his hands gleefully. "Well, what do you know!" he cried. "You got the cast iron pot I sent!"

AND THEN THERE were twenty. Again.

The Newcomers were off the waitlist. A waitlist the Community had never heard of before. A waitlist that over the years had grown from a few names into hundreds, then thousands, then tens of thousands, then hundreds of thousands. Maybe more. That's what the Newcomers said.

They also said they had originally been bused to a different entrance, a place called Lower something or other, on a route that took them through a sliver of the Mines, but that there had been some unrest there and they had to turn around abruptly and change locations.

They said that after another long bus journey, they had been left at a desolate dock, blindfolded, and taken by a small motorboat, escorted onto the shore, and only when they could no longer hear the boat burbling away were they allowed to look.

They said they had been here on this beach for some time. Possibly months or more. They used to have a calendar.

"But you burned it," said Carl.

"Yeah," said the man in the tracksuit. This man who had sent them the Cast Iron many years ago. His name, he said, was Frank.

They said when they were dropped on the beach, they'd had watches too.

"But they broke," Carl said.

Frank nodded, looking reassured that someone understood the strange facts of their new lives.

Frank looked around at his group, and with regret said, "There were two more with us in the beginning."

"But they died." Carl waved his hand. "Don't worry, it happens."

"Don't blame yourselves," added Glen gently with an empathetic smile.

Carl rolled his eyes.

"Should we say what happened to them?" one of the women asked. She wore a torn animal-print skirt and glittery sandals.

Carl frowned. "Nope."

The Newcomers looked both relieved and even more stricken, glad to know they wouldn't be blamed, but alone and unsure what to do with their grief. The Community eyed them warily. They had not been looking for new people with new hang-ups. New grief. They had only gone where they were told to go. Now everything was different.

Agnes studied these new people carefully as the rest of the introductions were made. The way they looked was both strange and familiar to her. She inched closer and closer to a girl's shoe just so she could smell it. It was white and soft, like cotton. The eyelets and tongue made the shoe look like a lizard. There were no laces. She thought all shoes had laces. She had a strong memory of opening a closet and a smell wafting out. She knew that smell would belong to the shoe. But she got too close, and the girl with the shoe kicked at Agnes. The girl, older than Agnes, had been watching her approach. She bared her teeth, but the woman next to the girl slapped her arm and the girl howled dramatically.

"Pay attention, Patty," the woman snarled. The woman was definitely the girl's mother, Agnes thought, or otherwise related, as they had the same skeptical brow.

The girl rubbed her arm and frowned at Agnes, blaming her for everything. She tried to pull her foot closer to her body somehow, to keep it away from Agnes. But Agnes had already retreated.

The mother's name was Patricia, she told them all, and that was her daughter, Patty.

"You're both named Patricia?" Debra asked.

"I'm Patty," the girl whined. "Just Patty."

"And I'm just Patricia," said Patty's mother, rolling her eyes.

There was another girl who looked to be Patty's age named Celeste. She had a streak of blue in her hair and wore combat boots, which Agnes thought was one of the more sensible footwear choices of the group. The girl's mother, Helen, wore the ripped skirt and strappy sandals, her toenails covered in sparkly gold polish. The mother seemed embarrassed of her daughter, the way she stood next to her but apart, hugging her arms as though cold. The daughter seemed to feel likewise, slouching away, leaning toward Patty. Agnes watched the two girls briefly brush their hands together in solidarity.

Patty's dad was Frank. He did most of the talking for his group.

There were two other children, a little boy and a girl, young, with their mother. The mother was Linda, and the boy and girl were Joven and Dolores. The kids looked overwhelmed by the distance of the horizon and kept their eyes down. Sometimes the girl, Dolores, covered her nose, as though still unaccustomed to the smell of this place, even though they'd been there weeks, possibly months. It was so wet and rotting. So salted. When the girl looked up briefly, Agnes caught her eye and wrinkled her nose sympathetically. Dolores smiled shyly, looking just beyond Agnes, as though it was the closest her eyes could get. Joven wore glasses and had a buzz cut that made his hair look like a velvet cap. Dolores had braids, one on each side of her head, and formerly white socks with a folded cuff adorned with lace. The socks were smudged dark brown now, but the fold was still impossibly crisp, as though sewn into place. Dolores reminded Agnes of herself, when she was a young girl first here. Though Agnes would have been more excited than the girl seemed. But maybe she was misremembering. She might have been just as scared back then, with the new sights and sounds and smells, not able to look at much full on. But she couldn't remember. She could only remember being how she was now. She made a note to ask Glen.

"That's Jake," Frank said. "He's with us." He pointed to a boy whose bangs covered his eyes just like a curtain Agnes remembered from her apartment, one that swept to the side and was gathered in a hook. His ear was supposed to act as the hook, sweeping the bangs to the side. But it did a poor job, and he kept jerking his head to whip the hair out of his eyes. It seemed intentional that his eyes were covered, and yet it also seemed to Agnes that he wanted to see. It didn't make any sense to her. She stared at him, thinking of all the ways he could be killed here with hair like that. Then, he snapped his hair out of his eyes and smiled at her. She realized that he had been watching her. Watching her face work through all her thoughts on his hair. She hadn't noticed because he had hidden his eyes from her, tricking her into letting her guard down. It had been a trap, as effective as the dead drops they set for small animals. And now she could see that his smile was more of a smirk. A knowing look. He had good instincts. She felt a wave of respect and blushed.

The Newcomers had set up a makeshift camp from tents, and around their tents, they'd built a small collection of useless shacks. They said they'd found old boards and either had scavenged nails from this unexpected wasteland of civilized detritus or brought them in themselves. Either way, they seemed to have grown attached to their illegal structures. The Community only saw them as broken rules they would probably be penalized for. Around the perimeter of their camp were clumps of purple shit, pocked with skins. They'd been living off the hard beach plums and feral grapes and hadn't bothered to dig a pit toilet. Someone would have to search for each smeary shit in order to bury them.

Carl asked if they knew anything about the baby car seat and the missing baby, Rachel. The Newcomers said they did not and it was easy to believe them. They had no idea what was about to happen to them. With their cargo shorts and loafers, skirts and button-down shirts. The unbroken rubber soles of their shoes. They looked like they would not last long. With their fat stomachs and thighs. Their skin so soft and uncooked by the sun. They had all their toenails. All their toes. Their hair was smooth and unbroken and glinting in the sun. Agnes could barely remember when they themselves had been that fat and delicious-looking. But she knew they had been. A line of drool fell out of her mouth and into the sand.

"Okay, we've got a big Community now," Carl said. "We'll have to stay here for a few days, get more provisions. Introduce these New-comers here to how we do things. Tomorrow, first thing, we'll tear down these shacks."

"Why?" the Newcomers cried.

"Because you can't build structures here."

"Why not?"

"Are you serious?" Carl asked. He grabbed the Manual and threw it at them. It landed at their colorful covered feet.

"You should be familiar with this already," he said. "What did you do on all the buses? Watch movies?"

They exchanged sheepish looks.

"Name one rule."

"Hmm." Frank paused. *"Leave no trace?"*

"And what does that mean?"

They all looked at their feet.

"Are you telling me you're not familiar with *any* of our rules here?" Carl was getting worked up, which made Agnes snicker. Carl hated rules. But no one would know that from the way he was staring in-credulously at the Newcomers. He shook his head, his body slumped with dramatic disappointment. As though he thought the rules were the only thing that mattered.

"We didn't have a lot of time," cried Frank. "One day we get a call and now we're here." The others nodded.

Helen said, "We had a week to throw all this stuff together. It was crazy. We got the Manual on the bus, but . . ."

Carl sighed. "Well, I don't even know what to say. Honestly." He shook his head again, drenched in disappointment. "There's not a lot of time for catch up. And our success depends on us all following these rules." He paused, nodded his head emphatically. "These very important rules. You're going to have to follow me very closely to survive."

The Newcomers looked at Carl like he might save them. But a moment ago they hadn't looked like people who thought they needed saving. Carl had convinced them of that quickly. He'd scared them into believing whatever he said. It was just like what Carl did when he and Agnes played Hunted! When he was the hunter, he liked to give long speeches about mercy and compassion and would catch her and let her go several times before he killed her. When she was the hunter, she just killed him immediately. From the ground, pretending to be dead, Carl would whisper, "You're supposed to play with your prey a little—it's the best part." He liked the drama. But she didn't see the point.

The sun began to set and the bats arrived, clicking around their heads to see if they were edible, then flitting off to more palatable prey. The Community laid their skin beds in a wider circle around the Newcomers' ring of tents. To protect them, they said, but Agnes knew it was to contain them.

The Community built a fire and Carl made the Newcomers circle around it and read aloud sections from the Manual. Agnes hovered nearby and listened.

They skipped around, read Sections 2 through 2.18, Sections 4d, 4e, 4f, and 4g. The parts about micro trash, and hunting yield caps, and the part about Post check-ins and garbage weighing, and what they were allowed to write home about in letters. They read rules the Community didn't even follow anymore, the part about staying in one camp no longer than seven days being a key one.

They passed it around like a book of bedtime stories. Joven and Dolores leaned on their mother. They were asleep. The Manual was a boring story.

Agnes remembered the early days when they would read stories from the books around the fire. But she didn't remember ever reading the Manual. It was something only the adults had to read. It wasn't funny and had no characters or animals and nothing really happened. Just a lot of lines and dots and numbers and symbols. Not like in the *Book of Fables*. That was her favorite book, and it had been lost in a flash flood. She had almost been lost in the flood too. She had been reading at the riverbank, tapping toes on the cold wet sand, engrossed in the description of a deep dark wood where a girl walked alone, when she was yanked from behind, dropping the book in surprise, just as a large brown slide of water rushed by, thick and muddy and sudden, like a frog's tongue unfurling but never curling back. Glen had grabbed her. With her feet safe on the dry bank, she had a dreamlike memory of her name being called urgently again and again somewhere in the background of the fable about the stupid, careless girl and that misunderstood wolf.

When she looked down at her hands and realized the book was gone, she'd started to cry. "Because," she had said to Glen and her mother, who had sprinted up, her eyes wet and terrifying, "I didn't get to see what happened to the wolf." And then, she remembered, her mother began to cry and then Glen began to cry, and they were clutching her hard and they were all crying over this book that had been swept away. They would find it a week later when they crisscrossed downriver. It was torn by rocks or scavenged for nest materials. What remained was thick, bloated, the colors and black words smeared across the pages. Agnes picked it up, and the binding split in two. The heavy halves plunged from her hands. But she didn't cry this time. She felt no sadness at all, which made her wonder why they'd all been so upset when it was first lost. Was grief that short-lived?

After the *Book of Fables* disappeared, they'd begun to tell stories of their own around the fire. It made every day interesting, even if it had been a day marked only by the white sun or a sky filled with only one flat cloud. A day when no animal had stirred and barely anyone had spoken, except to signal when to stop and when to go. A story at the end of a day like that saved it.

Agnes watched Glen approach the fire. He stood and listened for a moment, until the Newcomers stopped reading and stared at him.

"You don't have to stop for me," Glen said. "I was just listening."

"Why?" Patricia asked.

"Don't you know all this stuff?" Frank said. They did not seem to appreciate being watched.

Glen stuttered. "Well, yeah, I just . . ." He hesitated, then sat down. "I just had a question."

"Okay?" Frank raised his eyebrows.

"I know we're all here now and we want to concentrate on surviving and all that, but I was just curious. Can you elaborate on how bad it is in the City?"

"What do you mean?" said Helen.

"I mean, you all have referenced how bad it is. So bad there's an extraordinarily long waitlist, and I get the sense that you're not all scientists, or adventurers, or people with very sick children. And that's kind of the roster we came in with. So I'm just curious if you could give me some context for just how bad it is. Because we could barely find the original twenty people to come here in the first place. So I'm just astonished people want to come here now."

Agnes had never seen Glen talk so much at once. He seemed nervous about his question. She looked at the Newcomers and their squinting eyes. Was he being rude somehow?

"When you say, 'We couldn't find people,' who's 'we'?" Frank asked.

"Me and my wife. We kind of got this experiment up and running."

The Newcomers looked at one another.

"I thought Carl started it," said Linda.

Glen looked struck. But he smiled. "Well, no. Carl was one of my students a long time ago. And he certainly helped. But no, it was me and Bea and Agnes. We were the first subjects." He touched Agnes's head and she blushed.

"Who is Bea?" said Patricia.

Glen looked stunned to realize they wouldn't know her. Of course they wouldn't know her. She wasn't here. He stuttered, "She's my wife. Agnes's mother."

"Did she die?"

"No, no, no." He shook his head violently. "She had to go back to the City."

A few of the Newcomers gasped.

"Why?" cried Helen.

"Her mother died. She had to go deal with it."

"Deal with what?" Helen asked, confused.

"Her mother's death."

"But her mother was dead," Frank said.

"Right."

"So why did she need to go back if she was dead? I can see if she was dying, but she was already dead, is that right?"

Glen swallowed. He nodded.

"There's no way she went back for that," said Frank.

"Excuse me?"

"No one would ever try to go to the City on purpose. Everyone's trying to leave."

"Don't be hyperbolic, Frank," Patricia said. "Not everyone is trying to leave. There's a lot of people you don't know."

"Well, there's a lot of people I *do* know, Patricia," Frank spat. "I know a lot more than you do." Agnes was surprised at his tone. He'd seemed benign.

Agnes saw Glen purse his lips as he often did when he was aggravated. He did it when he got mail from his department. He did it when Carl was giving a speech. Agnes put her hand on his arm and he took a breath.

"Sorry, Patricia," said Helen, "but I have to agree with Frank." She turned to Glen. "The City is not a place you return to. I'll bet she went somewhere else."

"No," Glen said calmly. "She's in the City."

"She probably went to the Private Lands," said Linda.

The Newcomers made sounds with their mouths, *tsk*s and clicks and *hmm*s, judgmental sounds, understanding sounds, sounds full of pity.

"I'm sure that's where she is," Frank said.

"Lucky woman," said Patricia.

"But she just left you behind, sweetie?" Helen cried, touching Agnes's cheek, and Agnes recoiled.

"Enough," Glen cried, and the entire camp fell silent. "I just want to know about the City. My wife is there. And I'm worried about her."

Agnes heard his voice tremble and she swallowed, stunned. How could he worry about her when clearly she hadn't worried about them? And all these people knew it too. Didn't he hear Helen? *She left us.*

Helen signed, exasperated. "What more do you need to know? It's bad. We left and there are many more trying."

Again the Newcomers made mouth noises to express their pity, and Glen's shoulders sank and he walked away.

The Newcomers fell into quieter sounds, clicking to themselves now, as though telegraphing private thoughts and ideas and feelings to one another that no one else could interpret, like a colony of bats. They were a tight group, and Agnes thought for the first time that maybe they were not as hapless as they seemed.

She turned to leave.

"Hey." A whisper came from the shadows.

Sitting just outside the circle of firelight, not paying attention, were the two girls Patty and Celeste and the boy Jake. They all stared into the fire with a look on each of their faces she couldn't decipher, though it wasn't altogether unfamiliar. Their faces were curiously blank.

Then Celeste peered at her. "What . . . is with your hair?"

Agnes touched its soft stubble. "It's short," she said.

The two girls looked at each other and rolled their eyes. "No kidding," Celeste said.

Patty said, "How old are you?"

"I don't know," said Agnes. "Probably twenty?"

The girls guffawed.

"No way," Patty said. "We're fourteen." She motioned to the three of them. The boy had yet to speak, but he watched Agnes from under those cascading bangs. She imagined a cougar leaping from above. He wouldn't know until the whoosh of its body parted those bangs and he would finally see. Oh, then he would see. But it would be too late. What a sad end. What an unnecessary impairment.

Celeste watched Agnes studying them. "I know what you're thinking," she said.

"You do?" Agnes asked.

"You're thinking how much we look alike." Celeste motioned to her and Patty. Agnes hadn't even been looking at them.

"We're twins," Patty said.

They looked nothing alike. One was the color of dry sand, the other of wet soil. One even seemed older by a couple of years. And they had different mothers. But Agnes nodded.

"Jake is my cousin," Patty said, hooking her thumb at him.

Agnes narrowed her eyes at him. "Is that true?"

"Yeah," he said. His voice was deeper than she would have expected. He had no facial hair, but he sounded like a man. His voice was not meek the way his shoulders were. He kept her gaze.

"I have a dead sister," Agnes said.

"Gross," Celeste said.

"So," Patty said, "did your mom really go back to the City?"

"Yeah," Agnes said. "And it killed her."

"So, she's dead too?"

"Yeah."

"Huh," said Celeste. "Then why did your dad say he was worried about her?"

"Glen? He won't accept that she's gone."

"That is so sad," the Twins murmured.

Agnes nodded. "I tell him she's not coming back and that we're fine without her." It wasn't something she'd ever told him out loud. They didn't often speak of her mother. But if he ever asked, it's what she would say. She thought it would make things easier on him to know. It was easier on her since she decided that was the story of her mother.

The Twins nodded. Agnes glanced at Jake and saw a skeptical look on his face.

"How did she die?" Jake mumbled.

Agnes blinked. "I told you. The City killed her."

"I know, but how?"

"I don't know."

"How do you know she's dead then?"

"I just do," Agnes snapped.

The Twins exchanged looks so meaningful that Agnes imagined they'd just shared everything they'd ever thought.

"Well, if it did kill her, I'm not surprised," said Celeste and shook her head like Agnes had seen Helen, her mother, do earlier. "I honestly don't think you could live here and go back to the City and survive. Like, the air would instantly kill you."

"Totally," said Patty.

"I guess," said Jake.

"Are there still a lot of sick kids in the City?"

"Oh, definitely," blurted Celeste.

"Were you sick?" Agnes asked.

Celeste shook her head. "When I was younger. But not anymore."

"But we have every right to be here," Patty cried.

"Whoa," said Jake, softly, soothingly. "Calm down, Patty."

Patty huffed like a deer in danger, and she glanced at Agnes with a sneer.

They fell into silence and listened to the words of the Manual. It was the part about the Wilderness State's system for fines. Fines for garbage, fines for entering restricted areas. The most absurd one to Agnes was the hefty fine for dying. She doubted as they read they even understood that's what it meant, it was so odd. Carl had explained it to her one day, skipping stones into the river. How even though your body would hopefully be scavenged, your clothing and personal items would need to be retrieved in order to lessen the impact, and that usually amounted to a rescue mission, the tab for which the dead person's family or next of kin would have to pay. "Yet another reason to stay alive," Carl had said to her.

Jake's attention had turned back to his shoes, and he flicked his hair repeatedly to try to see what he was cleaning.

"You're going to die out here, you know," Agnes said quietly. "And then they're going to have to find your body and airlift out what's left of it."

The Twins guffawed. "Wow," they said in unison.

Agnes flitted her hands in front of her eyes, pretending to be blinded. "Because of your hair."

Jake nodded seriously. "We're all going to die." He flipped his hair. "Someday."

Celeste flopped back dramatically into the evening sand. Patty followed closely behind.

Agnes cocked her head and peered at them. "Are they hurt?" she asked Jake.

"You are too much," Celeste said from the ground. She rose up again on an elbow and smiled before her face took on what seemed to be its natural scowl. "You'll have to let us know what the deal is here," she said. She cast withering looks around at the trees, the river, the birds flitting by, Agnes's soiled moccasins. "I mean, what the fuck is this place?"

"It's the Wilderness," Agnes said.

"And? I mean, what *is* that?"

Agnes looked at Jake. "It's the Wilderness," she said.

Celeste's eyes tumbled in their sockets, and she flopped to the ground again.

The Twins settled their gazes on the sky, and Agnes walked away. The Twins made her tired.

"The stars aren't that much better here," she heard Celeste complain.

"I was just thinking that," said Patty.

"I mean, what's the point?"

"Exactly."

Agnes looked back once more at Jake, who was still watching her. She felt how hunched her back had become under his gaze, so she straightened it. She had the urge to punch him, and so she ran as fast as she could to where the adults, of which she was one, were prepping meat.

*   *   *

THE NEXT MORNING they set about breaking down the shacks the Newcomers had erected. The boards of wood were hazards of rusted spikes and nails, slim ragged splinters and mold.

Agnes worked alone on one little shack. The outside was made of slats from old apple crates. The walls were dusty, broken-up paintings of idyllic apple farms. Sand crabs leapt around the sand floor. Each time Agnes pulled a board, dust and particulate burst into a cloud that enveloped her. She tried to cover her mouth, but it didn't help. After a few boards, Agnes stumbled outside as her whole body shook in a fit of coughing. Doubled over like that, staring through her watery eyes, she conjured an old memory and her stomach curled with dread. She remembered herself in her small bedroom, curled in her pink bed coughing into her pink sheets until a spray of red appeared, illuminated by the glare from the City's night lights. She saw her mother appear, scoop her to her chest, and run with her into the hall, down so many flights of stairs to another apartment. It was spare and smelled of bleach. It belonged to a private doctor her mother paid for emergencies. Almost no doctor worked on emergencies anymore because there were no emergencies anymore. Because of overpopulation, emergencies were thought of more or less as fate.

When her mother laid her on the doctor's cot, she saw her blood on her mother's shirt. It was not a blob, or smear. No, it looked as though her face had imprinted itself there in blood—a small eye hole, a smooth cheek, and a gaping mouth. Sometimes, now, walking in the woods, she would see a blot of color somewhere—lichen on a tree trunk, or a boulder sneering out from green grass—and think of this half face, her face. It was a death mask of a death she had cheated. She saw this mask many places, on many things. In other colors. The green blood of trees. Blue blood of water. Blowing white flower petals. Whatever made those things alive, whatever was the core that made them unknowable.

When she saw her mother again, it was the next day and the mark was gone. A new shirt. Clean, peach. Agnes remembered being angry that her mother would discard the mark of such a moment.

But it had happened before, those dashes to the doctor. They would happen again.

"She's building a tolerance," Agnes remembered the doctor saying of the medicine.

"What can you do about that?" her mother asked.

"Nothing. This is where we are. Unless you've got different air to breathe," she said, trailing off. Then she snorted bitterly because it was an absurd idea. Different air to breathe.

Agnes straightened back up, took a deep, careful breath of different air, and saw Dolores watching her. The girl hid partway behind one of the wayward shacks, a corner of wood-crate scrap, part of which read, *Regal*.

Dolores performed a few feeble coughs into her hand, mirroring Agnes's fit. Agnes imagined Dolores was trying to sympathize. Maybe it was her secret handshake. Yes, she'd most likely been sick too. She looked like she had, recently. She was skinny, her hair dull, her skin sallow. The dark under her eyes. The way she was so bound and careful in her body, as though a thoughtless move could bring on a painful coughing spasm. Agnes remembered it all somewhere in her body.

"Hey," Agnes said. Dolores's eyes got wide and bright, as though stunned to be seen. "How are you?"

Dolores's gulp was audible, but she stepped out from behind her shed and carefully over to Agnes.

"Why aren't there more kids like you and your brother in the group?" Agnes asked.

Again Dolores's eyes bugged at being asked a real question. She shrugged with her whole body as if to beg Agnes to believe her. She did not know.

She sat down and held out a small rubber ball and rolled it to Agnes's feet in the sand. She motioned for Agnes to roll it back, and so Agnes knelt.

"There was one," Dolores said.

"Oh," said Agnes.

"How many years are you?"

"I don't know," said Agnes.

"Really?"

"Really. I might be thirty years old. But probably I'm a lot younger than that. How old are you?"

"I'm three plus."

"That's nice."

"Are there flowers here?"

"There are many flowers here, but only during certain times of the year."

"What time of the year is it?"

"It's the fall."

"Are there flowers now?"

"Not really."

Dolores's eyes were big, and her small mouth pursed in thought.

She was lucky to be here. To be here and getting better. Agnes imagined that somewhere deep down she might know that. Briefly Agnes's mind was flooded with the image of a little ill Dolores sputtering blood uncontrollably, as Agnes herself had done. It was a vile and violent image, and she pushed it quickly from her mind. It was okay to remember herself like that, but it seemed cruel to put someone else through it, even if it was only in her imagination.

When they had first arrived in the Wilderness State, Agnes had been one of five children. Sister and Brother were still here, but Ali died quickly. Perhaps too sick already to handle such a physical life. There were other dangers here. The adults must have understood that.

She remembered Flor leaving when her mother, Maria, decided it had been a mistake to come. Her mother had gotten scared after the first death, and after a bear raided their camp. No one was hurt, but the bear refused to leave, luxuriating and shitting on their beds and trying to eat all their provisions. They went without food for two days while they stalked it, waiting for an opportunity to kill it. There were some hungry days while they figured it all out. At the next Post, Maria went to the Ranger at the front desk and said, "I surrender."

"Surrender? Surrender what?"

"I don't know. I renounce my Wilderness citizenship."

"Lady, what the fuck are you talking about?"

"I want to go home."

"Well, okay, then. Go home."

She stared at him blankly. "How?"

He pulled out a piece of paper. "Bus schedule. When you know the time you want to go, we can call you a taxi." Maybe they'd been there a month.

During the next spring Debra got a letter at Post from Maria. Little Flor had died.

"Well, she might have died here too." Debra forced a shrug. There were no guarantees.

Agnes smiled, and Dolores looked at her face seriously for a moment, then offered a small uncertain smile. Agnes had been a bit
older than Dolores when she had arrived. She couldn't think of how
it might feel to be three years old here. She wanted to say something
that would make the uncertainty in Dolores's face go away.

"Dolores," Linda barked, and Dolores sprinted off to her mother.
Linda peered at Agnes with curiosity and distrust as her daughter
slipped under her arm, the safest place, like a chick under wing. Dolores's face became serene. Agnes felt an aching absence. She remembered being that young, that easily safe. Agnes was happy to be an
adult now. But she missed feeling safe like that. It was gone from her
life for good.

With so many new faces to look at, she realized, she had not imagined her mother's face since before they'd entered the dark forest.
Every day before that she'd woken in the middle of a dream of her
mother's face. Not of her. Just of her face hovering over everything
the dream presented or told. In a dream where a coyote pack attacked
their camp, her mother's face was the moon, glowing over the car-
nage. In a dream of finding a hidden bunch of wild onions under
her pillow, once the dirt was brushed from the small white bulb, her
mother's face appeared in its pearly skin. Her mother was the face of
an owl Agnes had startled while on a frog-catching walk with Val.
No, that had to have been real, not a dream. They had caught frogs
and snails for dinner. And her mother had peered down at them with
irritation. Agnes swore she'd seen her mother's terrible face. Her angry mother, still angry at her.

Celeste shuffled up to Agnes with what seemed like pure dread in
her body.

"Ugh," she said, looking at Agnes expectantly.

"Ugh?" Agnes asked.

"UGH," Celeste said with more emphasis, her eyes surveying the
shanty demolition. "This is so dumb," she clarified.

"Why?"

Celeste pouted. "I miss my little house."

"In the City?" Agnes asked.

Celeste rolled her eyes. "No, here. It had a little window with flowery drapes. It had a smooth floor that I danced across and it smelled like roses."

"You're lying," Agnes said. "Nothing smells like roses here." She didn't remember the last time she'd smelled a rose. All she smelled was brine and rot and salt and fir.

Celeste shook her head. "I'm pretending, stupid."

Agnes nodded, but she wasn't sure what the difference was between pretending and lying.

Celeste said, "Besides, where would I get drapes? And there's nothing smooth for a million miles. But it makes me feel better."

"Why do you need to feel better?"

"Because I'm sad."

"Why?"

"Because I don't want to be here."

"Oh." Agnes looked down at the ground overcome, her mind racing. Chasing after something. A feeling. What was it? It was right at the tips of her reaching fingers—

"I was sad too," she sputtered, almost breathless.

"When?" Celeste said, her eyes slits, ready to take vengeance if she were made a fool.

"When I got here."

Celeste looked at the ants marching over Agnes's dirty moccasins, the stains on her smock from where she wiped her hands. Her hard dirt-smeared arms. The mud under her nails. "*You* were." She said it with skepticism.

"Yes," Agnes said slowly, the memory piecing itself together after being broken for so many years. She hadn't wanted to come here. She hadn't wanted to leave her friends. No matter how much blood she coughed up. She hadn't wanted to leave her pink bed. The bed her mother remade every morning so it looked as it might in a magazine. She hadn't really understood where they were going or what it would be like. But she could tell in the way her mother tensed her shoulders, tried to straighten her back to seem stronger, that it was a hard place. That there was danger. That her mother was afraid. And she looked around at their small but pleasant home and wondered, *Why?* Why would they leave a place they knew for a place they didn't know? She must have been four at that time, going on five. She'd worn socks with lace at the cuff just like Dolores had on, and she'd had braids too, just like Dolores. Her mother braided her hair when it was still wet from the bath the night before. Her hair would fray in a halo around her head from dreamy bouts with her pillow. She would go to the preschool in the basement of her building. She took naps and listened to stories there. She shared juice pouches with her friends. What were their names? She couldn't remember. She might remember them if her mother had spoken their names since they left. Told her stories of Agnes's life. But her mother only told stories of her own mother, Nana, or of Grandma, her own mother's mother, or of herself and Agnes. Agnes felt angry at her mother's self-centeredness. But then she remembered her mother wouldn't know any stories of Agnes and her friends. These were Agnes's private memories. How they squirted their juice pouches to make rainbows on the concrete, how they played with one another's hair during story time. She had forgotten the names of the girls she had shared those moments with. Those times were also times Agnes had been without her mother. The first and last times she had been on her own, until now.

She had a thought just then.

"No one really wanted to be here," she said to Celeste. "But we had to be."

"No one?" Celeste asked.

"Well, Carl probably did."

"Which one is Carl?"

Agnes pointed to Carl, who was picking grubs out from between the rotted boards of their torn-down shacks and popping them into his mouth.

"Oh, yeah," Celeste said. "That makes sense."

"He's not weird or anything," Agnes said, feeling protective of Carl, seeing him through this girl's eyes, seeing for the first time his dirt, realizing his odor, his matted hair, the zealousness in his eyes. "He just belongs here."

"Like you?"

Agnes flushed with pride and some shame. "Like me. Like me *now*." She spoke with slow surprise, unsure the words were really coming from her. "At first I wanted my mother to brush my hair every day because I didn't like it to get tangled." She pointed to her hatcheted hair. "I wore a white outfit off the bus," she said, wincing at the image, the brightness of the clothing under the dazzling sun. She squinted. It felt as if she were watching another little girl, a pleasant stranger. "My fingernails were painted," she said. "They were painted pink. Pink was my favorite color." Agnes started laughing, then laughing harder, and then Celeste joined in and they got stares from around the beach, especially from Patty. They stopped.

Celeste leaned in, whispered, "I brought nail polish."

Something in Agnes's stomach turned. She both wanted to see the color, color that wasn't of the earth, and also wanted nothing to do with something so unreal, so of her mother's world. A dead world.

"It would be hilarious to see it on you," Celeste said. She eyed Agnes's dirty fingernails.

"I think it would get in the way," Agnes said. Could she hunt with painted fingernails? Could she eat with her hands? Could she braid sinew into strong threads? Would it ever come off, or would she have to eat it off? Would she try to eat it off and grow dependent on its sustenance and die once it was gone? Her heart raced.

"It's pink," Celeste said.

Agnes opened her mouth to say no just as Celeste said, "Come on," and Agnes followed her.

Celeste trudged past the Community and the Newcomers, and Patty materialized to walk with them, a camaraderie beyond words. They silently crossed over into the forest, a line that was stark and sunny on one side and dank and dark on the other side.

Celeste counted, "One two three four . . ." to ten, and then she pivoted left. "One two three four . . ." to ten. She pivoted right. "One two three four . . ." to ten. She stopped. A boulder covered in moss. Celeste peeled back the moss in one wet green sheet and revealed a notch in the rock. From the notch, a neon-pink glow spread like a sunburst.

Celeste picked the bottle up like it was a baby bird, caressed it in her hands, modeled it to the other girls. "It's called Neon Dreamlife," she whispered, and Patty moaned.

"It has sparkles in it. But you can't see them until they're on your nails."

"Do me," Patty said. Celeste unscrewed the cap, and they all put their noses close to the opening and breathed in.

Patty coughed. "I love it."

Agnes's mouth watered. She wanted to drink the mercurial pink. Feel it coat her throat.

Celeste put her palm out and Patty slid her hand upon it.

Celeste swept the brush slowly across each fingernail, one two three times, clean, careful. Patty shivered. Her eyes were squeezed shut, anticipating a surprise.

"Don't touch anything," Celeste finally said. Patty opened her eyes.

The girls all drew closer to her hand. Patty wiggled her fingers. Agnes couldn't remember ever seeing such a vibrant color. Flowers, yes. But real flowers were coated with dust, or washed out in the sun's glare. Perhaps, she thought, once after a spring rain when the sun broke through the clouds she'd seen some violets gleaming purple, and that had been a shock to her eyes in the way Patty's nails were a shock. Sometimes the sunset was violently colorful. The color of just-spilled blood was shocking. Or when they butchered, pulled the stomach out whole, the red and blue veins like an anatomy diagram from one of her nana's old schoolbooks. That blue was bright and pure. But this pink, it hurt her eyes. It made her not want to share. She remembered her mother's magazine, and the bold colors she'd used in decorating. But even though the paper was glossy, it was still removed, distant. Pictures of a place she would never see in real life. Untouchable. Agnes reached out.

"No touch! Not dry!" Celeste screeched.

Agnes's hand darted back. Blood rose to her cheeks. She covered them with her hands. She knew the pink of her cheeks wasn't as pretty as the pink on Patty's fingers.

Patty was blowing on them like they were birthday candles.

"Do me," Agnes said.

"I'm not sure it'll stay on your nails." Celeste eyed them. "They're so dirty."

Agnes spit into her hand and wiped her nails.

Celeste pretended to puke. "You are disgusting," she said, and held out her palm.

Agnes slid her hand upon it.

"I'm only doing one nail. A test nail. I don't want to waste good polish if it's not going to stay."

"Please," Agnes whimpered.

"Do you want any polish or not?"

"Yes."

"Well, which one?"

Agnes looked at her scarred hands, her jagged nails, the dirt under them. She wiggled her left pinkie. "This one." It must be the finger she did the least with. It would stay cleaner longer, she thought. The polish would remain unchipped. Maybe forever. She stuck it in her mouth, tried to clean the nail with her tongue. Then wiped it on her smock.

She closed her eyes.

The brush was soft. Tickling. The liquid was cold going on. Like dipping her pinkie into a winter river's icy slurry. A thrill shot through her neck. Then, everything on her fingernail closed up, tightened, stopped breathing. She felt it being suffocated. She almost yelped, leapt up to run away. She hated it.

"Okay," Celeste said. "Go like this."

Agnes opened her eyes, saw Celeste blowing on her own hands, and looked down.

The pink was catching light she hadn't even known was present in the dark forest. It looked as though it moved on her nail, breathed more and more color into itself. She saw the speckles of glitter. Not too much. Just enough. It was alive and perfect.

Celeste screwed the lid back on.

"Aren't you going to do yours?"

"I'll wait for a special occasion."

"What special occasion would happen here?" Patty said.

"I'm sure there is something," Celeste said. "Don't people get married? Or throw parties? My mom loves to throw parties."

"Why are you here?" Agnes asked.

"Why are *you* here," Celeste responded, her eyes narrowing, suspicious again.

"I was sick."

"I've heard that before."

Agnes saw her bloodstained pillowcases again, the blood sprays never quite washing out. "No, I remember. I was. I was sick."

"So your mom brought you here to save you?"

Agnes caught her breath. She had not thought of it that way before. Her face burned, but she wasn't sure why. "I guess," she said. She didn't like this story, though. "And Glen," she said.

"Who is Glen?"

"My dad."

"Why do you call him Glen?"

"He's not my real dad."

"Yeah, you look nothing alike," said Patty.

"You act nothing alike," said Celeste.

"He's a great leader," Agnes said, her chest puffing at the thought that someone like him could be her dad.

The Twins burst out laughing.

"You are hilarious," said Celeste.

"He brought us here," Agnes said, confused.

"I thought you said your mom did."

"They both did."

"I'm sure it wasn't so simple." Celeste scowled. "My mom never does something unless it suits her."

"I don't know. My mom was pretty unhappy here I think. That's why she left."

"I thought she left because her mom died."

Agnes blinked. "Yeah, she did."

Celeste stared at her. "You must be, like, ten years old or something, right?"

"I'm much older than that," Agnes said.

"You could be eleven."

"I don't know how old I am," Agnes said.

"That's okay," Celeste said, throwing her arm around Agnes. "You're eleven. It's decided." Agnes didn't know if she liked Celeste. But she liked the weight of Celeste's soft meaty arm on her shoulder.

Celeste handed the nail polish to Patty, who laid it back in its notch like a baby being put down for a nap, drawing the moss back over it gently, patting it into place, then patting her glittering wet hands onto her face. "Dew is great for the skin," she said.

They trudged out of the woods and squinted into the harsh sun that bounced off the water. Agnes smelled the smoke of the fire being lit. Her stomach growled. She hid her beautifully painted fingernail in her fist.

*   *   *

THE NEXT DAY, Carl organized a chore day. He set up stations for all the major duties of the Community, and the Newcomers visited each and learned what would be expected of them day to day. There was some anticipation but mostly dread on their faces as almost all the jobs were dirty and smelly and maybe they worried they wouldn't be any good at them. They watched Debra stitching the stiff sinew thread through the tough hides to make new moccasins. She put out her hands so they could feel her calluses. The group that prepared the sinew thread had hands that would smell of animal insides until it wore away, which never happened before they needed to make more. The hide preparers sweated and coughed under the smoke. The smokers coughed and sweated in the smoker tent. And if carrying things seemed like a better deal than this hand labor, the Newcomers saw that the people who most often carried the Cast Iron and the Book Bag were bent-backed and stiff when they got up out of their beds in the morning.

"Why do you carry all these books? Haven't you read them all by now?" asked Patricia.

"Yes," said Dr. Harold, who was demonstrating different ways of carrying the Book Bag.

"Why keep them?"

"So we can read them again," Debra said with a curtness she mostly saved for Dr. Harold. He noticed and flashed her a smile. He often carried the bag because Debra liked books.

"It's good to have the history with us," said Glen with a nod.

"Why?" Patricia scrunched her nose.

Glen smiled. He opened his mouth, closed it. He smiled again. Agnes realized he didn't have an answer. No one had asked before.

Finally Carl jumped in and said, "History is good, is it not?" They treated it like a rhetorical question. No one answered.

"Well, what about this big pot?" Linda said. "I can't see how carrying something this heavy is worth it." She tried to lift it off the ground, grunting with exertion, but couldn't budge it. Linda was small. Almost as small as Agnes.

"It's worth it," the Community said in almost perfect unison, and Frank blushed.

The Newcomers murmured, understanding that the job of the pot carrier was important. But nobody would look at Dr. Harold, his arms around the cumbersome Book Bag.

Carl clapped. "Okay, now, hunting."

The Newcomers shuffled into line. Carl had set up a target down the beach. A pile of logs and a piece of hide stretched across it.

The Community had two working bows, so the Newcomers took turns. Each archer's arrow went in many different directions, and none came close to the target. It was an easy target too. Agnes could hit it without drawing her bow back very far. Not even the women with their small nimble hands were any good. Not even Jake, Agnes noted with disappointment. Maybe she could teach him.

"We're better with guns," Frank said, grimacing. His arrow flew toward the water.

"Guns don't last out here."

"Oh?"

"You run out of bullets quick," snapped Val.

"Can't we just order more?"

"We don't order things here," said Val.

"Delivery is unpredictable," said Glen, chuckling.

Agnes knew he'd meant it as a light comment, but several of the Newcomer adults rolled their eyes. Maybe they thought Glen was laughing at them. Or maybe they thought he was foolish. The Twins and Jake stared slack-jawed at Glen.

"Look, we all need to be good at things in order to survive," Carl said. "Some of us will be better than others at things. That's okay. As long as everyone pulls weight of some kind. But it helps if we all know how to do all the jobs."

The Newcomers nodded. It was clear they liked Carl more than anyone else. They already looked to him for answers.

Carl continued, "Even though only some of us will become regular hunters for the Community, we all have to get comfortable with the bow and arrow. What kind of training did you do before you came here?"

"Training?" whispered Helen.

"Yes, training. I assume you all knew that bow hunting was the norm. Even if it's just that you read some books on archery . . . anything."

Carl looked around at the Newcomers. No one said anything.

Carl clapped. "Well, okay. It doesn't matter. When I'm through with you, you won't need guns."

Carl bowed to Patty's mom. "You are, again?"

"Patricia."

Carl looked at Patty. "And you're Patricia too?"

Patty's mom opened her mouth to speak, but Patty screamed, "I'm just Patty! And she's just my mom!"

Patricia snapped, "Calm down." She took a deep breath and let it out in a long *phew*. She turned to Carl. "Why don't you all just call me Patty's mom then," she said, letting out a peal of laughter that didn't sound like laughter at all.

"Okay, Patty's mom, I bet you did something to prepare, didn't you?" Carl winked.

"I read a few books." Patty's mom raised her chin, triumphant.

Patty guffawed. "No, you didn't."

Carl turned to the sullen, skinny girl. "And young lady, what did you do?"

"Nothing. I'm a kid."

Celeste snorted. "You're a young lady."

Patty and Celeste laughed and laughed.

"Quiet!" Carl's eyes flared. The Twins immediately fell silent and traded looks of disdain. But Agnes could see them blushing too.

"Show me your hands," he demanded.

They thrust out their hands.

Carl grabbed one in each of his hands, squeezed each, prodded, turned them over, clasped their forearms, and then slapped their palms.

"Ow," they said in unison.

He squeezed their arms. *Hmm-hmm*ing to himself. He pulled on their fingers and pressed his thumbs into their palms.

"I think we've got some naturals here," he said. Patty's parents and Celeste's mom applauded. The Newcomers straightened, as though excited that their own had impressed Carl.

"Do you think you young ladies can hit that target?"

They scowled.

"I think you can," said Carl. He waited for them to fill the silence. He was in teacher mode, but Agnes imagined he was not used to teenage girls.

"What do you think?"

Celeste rolled her eyes angrily.

"Just tell us what to do," Patty muttered.

Carl handed them each a bow and arrow.

The first arrows they shot dropped at their feet.

"This is stupid," Patty said.

Carl handed them new arrows, and Celeste stomped her feet in protest. "Mom!"

Her mother had a growling voice, hoarse, as though screaming was a large part of her life. "Celeste," she said, "just do it, for fuck's sake."

Celeste's arrow went wild to the right, as did Patty's.

"Again," Carl said.

"No," Celeste screamed with the fury of an animal caught in a trap. Her shrillness made Agnes's ears pop. But despite her protests, she drew back her arrow alongside Patty. Agnes was fascinated how they could look so furious and so bored at the same time.

The Twins let their arrows fly, barely looking at anything. But the arrows sailed right through the heart of the target. Their arrows almost split each other. Seeing this, Celeste's fury disappeared and she was pure boredom once again.

Agnes thought they might be the most beautiful people she'd ever seen. The Twins' fury was sudden and unbounded. It was messy and illogical, and she didn't know enough words to describe how it made her feel. But she knew it was powerful. And she knew that somewhere she had this power in her as well. She tried to think when she'd ever observed animals with such unexpected ferocity and she wasn't sure she had. Because while animals became ferocious for obvious reasons, she couldn't quite figure out what the Twins' emotion was born from.

"Again," Carl said.

Celeste didn't scream this time. She just rolled her eyes and drew back, as did Patty. Figuring out how to do it had anesthetized them. They both released sighs that Agnes had only seen dying animals emit. They nailed their target.

"How did you two get such good aim?" Carl asked.

"Slingshotting rats," said Celeste.

"You saw rats?" Agnes asked, amazed. "In the City?" She'd never seen any animal in the City.

"You probably lived in a nicer zone than we did," sniped Patty.

"But I didn't even know there *were* any rats left in the City."

"Oh, then you *definitely* lived in a nicer zone than we did," Celeste said, and the Twins roared.

Carl shook his head. "Doesn't explain anything. Slingshots—it's a whole different set of muscles."

Patty said, "Well, they were pretty big slingshots." She raised her chin proudly, just as her mother had.

He looked at Celeste.

"They were pretty big rats," said Celeste, dead straight.

Carl chuckled. Delighted, he clapped his hands and said, "Can't say it matters! Time to hunt!"

He put his arms around the Twins chummily, and they immediately slunk out from under him and back together like magnets.

For a time after they disappeared into the woods, Agnes heard peals of laughter, sometimes screams. She felt haunted by the sounds, even though she knew it was the Twins.

Toward evening, the two girls and Carl came back with a doe and a fawn. The one deer had most certainly refused to leave the other, and so both perished. The small fawn was draped around Carl's shoulders, its pink tongue swinging slightly side to side. The doe's neck was torn open, probably by a ragged arrow tip. And one of its hind legs was turned around. It looked as though after merely stunning it with the arrow, the girls had wrestled it to death.

Carl dropped the fawn off in the spot where they would butcher, and then approached those around the fire shaking his head, his eyes wide. A spray of blood colored his shirt; blood congealed in his beard. "They basically pummeled that poor animal to death," he said.

"And you let them?" Debra scolded.

"They have to learn." He broke into a grin. He had enjoyed it.

The Twins dragged the doe to where the knives were kept with short pulls and grunts. The spilled blood left a trail from the kill site in the forest to the beach. For the rest of their days on the beach, they never saw another animal skulking in the woods or emerging onto the beach. Blood is a warning sign, which the Twins didn't know yet.

*   *   *

SINCE THEY COULDN'T stay along the Poisoned River, they decided to head back the way they came. Really, Carl had decided. Really, Carl, with support from the Newcomers, had decided. By the end of their days on the Poisoned River, it was clear the Newcomers officially saw Carl as the leader, even though the original Community had never had an official leader. Now, they did.

Agnes had attended the meeting around the fire, though none of the other young people had. She was surprised, and thought Celeste, Patty, and Jake ought to be there. But the Newcomers looked at her skeptically when she took a seat within the circle. When Carl sat next to her, she saw their expressions change. Their eyebrows raised and they nodded to themselves. Carl had validated her being there. Did he know that? Is that why he had done it? Her leg twitched.

"So," Glen began, because he always began meetings. He'd had the most experience with all his meetings at the University. "We need to make a plan for next steps. But before we do, we need to explain how we make decisions here." He nodded to Debra, who explained consensus.

The Newcomers nodded slowly when she was done. Then their faces contorted as though they'd eaten something subtly disgusting.

"That sounds hard," said Linda.

"It is hard," said Carl.

"Like, maybe too hard," said Frank.

Carl nodded, looking around the circle. Glen opened his mouth to speak, but Carl cut him off. "Yeah, I think you're right, Frank. It's just too hard with such a big group."

It hadn't been what Frank said, but Frank nodded anyway.

"Besides, we don't always make decisions by consensus," said Carl, reassuringly.

"Yes, we do," said Debra.

"No," Carl said, "remember when I suggested we walk a day off route for water?"

"Yeah, and we did it, because we all agreed to," said Debra.

Val jumped in. "I don't think you're remembering that right, Debra."

"Oh, I'm remembering just fine, dear." Debra looked at Glen for help.

"Look, Carl," Glen said, "a bigger group doesn't mean we have to stop deciding as a group."

"We had this many before and we did just fine," muttered Debra. Debra loved consensus.

"Hey," Carl said, his hands up, "I'm just looking out for the best interests of our Community. Our *new* Community." He nodded to the Newcomers. "I think now that we are a new and larger group, we should decide *as a group* how to make decisions. As *this* group. Not our old group. Perhaps the Newcomers don't see the logic in consensus. I know I never did."

"Neither did I," said Val.

"You don't like consensus because you want to be in charge," snapped Debra.

"Well, I don't think I like consensus either," said Frank. "It doesn't feel very representative."

The Newcomers nodded.

"It's completely representative," cried Debra.

"But what if," Helen asked, "we are voting and everyone votes one way and I don't want to vote that way. But I'm looking around the circle and everyone is really mad at me and so I go along with the vote?"

"That doesn't happen," said Debra.

"Hold on, Debra," Val said. She turned to Helen. "It's happened to me."

Helen touched her throat and nodded at Val with wet, sympathetic eyes.

"That's making me realize," Frank said, "that I'd rather have my own vote, be counted, and accept the outcome, regardless of what it is."

Carl nodded. "It seems that the Newcomers would like a new way to make decisions."

Val clapped her hands. "Let's vote." The rest of the Community protested briefly. But there was not much to do about it. With Carl and Val and the Newcomers, the rest of them were, Agnes saw, outnumbered.

"That's a majority," said Carl.

"But we need consensus to vote out consensus," said Debra.

"Listen to yourself," Carl said.

"But—"

"Consensus is no more. That's a wrap."

"Can I bring up something I've noticed?" Frank said. He looked right at Carl when he asked.

"Go ahead," Carl said benevolently.

"It's a lot of effort to keep changing work responsibilities. We've only been with you a little while, but I'm already confused about who does what. It seems like your system could use some updating."

"I'm listening," said Carl eagerly.

"I think from now on, we"—he motioned to the Newcomers—"should deal with cooking and rationing the food. It's the easiest thing for us newbies to do. That way we don't always have to decide every day. It's a lot of work to shift responsibilities."

Carl nodded. "It is a lot of work."

"We don't shift every day," Debra said. "We have a system we use to organize work. It's very easy." Her face was contorted by her disbelief.

"But the system necessitates a vote. Decisions," Frank said. "It's a lot compared to just knowing I make breakfast every morning."

"It is a lot," Carl said.

"Yes, I've always thought it was just too much," said Val.

"But we've always done it this way and it works," said Debra.

"Well," said Carl, "maybe it's time to try something different. We have to be flexible out here, Debra."

"Let's vote," Val said.

The old members of the Community were outnumbered.

"Looks like we'll have the Newcomers cook and divvy out food from now on," said Carl. "This will really help a lot." He turned to Frank. "I'm so glad you brought that up."

Frank beamed. "Can I bring up one more thing then?"

"Shoot."

"Can we stop being called the Newcomers? I mean, aren't we part of the Community?"

Carl laughed. "Well, one thing at a time."

"What does that mean?" Frank's face stormed.

"I think it's important to remember that we are, in a way, elders. Teachers. And you are still learning. I think there needs to be a distinction until we are all on more equal footing. So you will continue to be the Newcomers. And we'll be the Originals. No, we'll be the Origina*lists*! And together we will be one Community." Carl pressed his hands together and bowed.

"But someday we'll stop being called the Newcomers?" Frank asked.

"We'll see."

"With all due respect, Carl," Juan said. "The Originalists? Shouldn't we talk before we decide on something like a name?"

"Nope." Carl leaned back, smiling, his head resting in his laced fingers. Juan blinked in surprise. "Well, I think this was a very productive meeting, don't you?"

Frank, his brow furrowed, opened his mouth to say more, but Patty's mom squeezed his arm and shook her head.

Val snickered.

Agnes looked around the circle. The Originalists stared at Carl and the Newcomers with dropped jaws. Frank looked a bit sour about the name, but overall the Newcomers seemed pleased. At first glance, Glen looked almost amused. But she'd seen this face before, after her mother disappeared. It wasn't surprise, or even entirely resignation, though that was present too. Agnes hadn't been able to interpret it then, but now, in context, it was very obvious, even as he tried to paste a smile on his face when he turned to look at her. Glen was scared.

*   *   *

THE ORIGINALISTS HAD never traveled swiftly, being a large group with heavy gear and children, but still their pace was greatly hindered by the Newcomers. This new larger Community left a trampled forest in their wake, and the Originalists wondered, would they get penalized as a whole group now? Or would the Rangers penalize the Newcomers for obvious Newcomer issues? When the Originalists were new, they'd been punished harshly. Fined, threatened with expulsion. Would the Newcomers be treated the same?

At their lunch break, the Newcomers flung their bodies upon the moss, groaning as they went down. The Twins and Jake leaned against trees while the Originalists and all the young children squatted, their arms crossed over their knees, ready to bounce up if they needed to.

Agnes appraised them all like they were a new herd of deer. She wanted to know which was the loner buck. Which was the dominant doe? Which would vie for more territory and authority? Which would die first?

Frank was a tall, thick man with soft hands and easily blistered feet. He had either appointed himself the leader of the Newcomers or simply become it accidentally. But Agnes noticed he paused before making decisions. He looked around. He was uncertain and beyond his depth. And he angered easily.

A better leader would have been Linda, who ruled her children, Joven and Dolores, firmly. But her hands were full. She sighed and sat heavily whenever the group stopped. Joven's buzz cut was going to grow out like a mop on his head, and Agnes could tell that Dolores's increasingly matted and tangled hair had once been precious. Her mother probably had brushed it every night at home. But no longer. Joven and Dolores would flourish here, but Linda was too tired to be much of a leader. Too bad, Agnes thought.

Agnes watched Joven and Dolores watching Sister and Brother, who watched them back. Sister and Brother were a little older than Joven, but not by much. Maybe they would become friends. She hoped they would like Pinecone because she was tired of him following her around.

Celeste's mom, Helen, was interested in all the men in camp. She tied her long hair back in a kerchief. She tied off her long skirt to show her brown legs. They were meaty the way legs had been in the City, but here they looked out of place. Helen's legs made Agnes hungry, and perhaps they made Carl hungry too, because she saw him gaze at them often.

Agnes's cheeks warmed. She became alert. Across the fire Jake's eyebrows were raised and wriggling, and he jerked his head slightly to the left. Agnes followed the directive and saw Debra gazing at Helen's legs too and tracing her collarbone with one searching finger. Agnes looked back at Jake and he shrugged. She subtly tipped her head to her right where Dr. Harold sat, and even though she could not see his face, she knew he would be staring at Debra. Jake followed and his eyes widened, and he broke into an awe-filled grin. Agnes hadn't seen him really smile yet. Just seen his thin-lipped smirk, frown, or pensive expression. He had a broad gap between his two front teeth, his teeth the color of a buttercup, his tongue pink like a field mouse's nose. His grin turned down into a small smile that softened his eyes, and he looked at her across the circle and shook his head a bit, and kept smiling like he was really happy about something and couldn't shake it. It was something Agnes hadn't seen very often in her life. For all they had here, she realized, they didn't often have joy. Not this kind. She wanted to burn it into her memory in case she never encountered it again.

She turned her attention back to Helen and her legs. Helen wasn't helpless. But she was impatient. And that could be dangerous here. What about Patty's mom? She seemed nervous and short-tempered. Agnes thought she was probably capable of making a stupid mistake. Maybe she would be the first to die. Perhaps it would be one of the children. But this thought struck her as sad, and she vowed to protect Dolores and Joven. If not the children, then who? Agnes wondered if Jake would think her game dreadful. Was this a weird thing to think about? She was sure nothing would happen to Celeste, Patty, or Jake. They were too strong and sharp behind their sneers. In Agnes's opinion, Linda was untouchable. Perhaps Frank. He had the ability to be cunning. She'd seen it in the meeting, though she imagined that was more Carl's influence than Frank's initiative. No, he was an unprepared person, not just here in a new environment but possibly in every situation. But his weakness, Agnes decided, was his ignorance of this fact. Agnes watched him. He reached his hand out to something in front of him. A frog jumped. And Frank jumped too, even though he'd been watching and poking at the frog. Frank threw his head back and laughed, elbowed Patty's mom, who closed her eyes, waiting for the moment to pass. Forget even that the frog was a poisonous varietal. Frank was startled by things he himself put into motion. Yes, Agnes thought, Frank would be the first to die.

*   *   *

AFTER SEVERAL DAYS of sunless walking in the wet forest, they burst out into a thin, open forest dotted with orange-skinned pines. They raised their arms and hands to ward off the pressure of the unveiled sun on their eyes. They peeked out from behind fingers and balled fists trying to acclimate to the newly identifiable day.

Though the forest thickened and thinned, the tree skins turning from orange to white back to orange, it remained cool, airy, and dry, and was, for some reason, empty of useful life. They would need provisions soon. So for several days they walked and camped quickly, lying mostly under open skies, eating jerky, cooking minimally.

Eventually this forest delivered them to the edge of a tall ridge that crumbled at their feet to the valley floor. It was possibly a hundred trees tall or more. The valley was foggy and muted as though the morning sky had fallen to earth. Just below them on an outcrop, Agnes saw a swatch of red. A glint, something shiny, or at least it had been shiny once. Something that caught the light like nothing else in nature. Something plastic. The Newcomers didn't notice it. They were too recently acquainted with plastic. So it didn't register to them as anything notable. But all of the Originalists snapped their heads toward it immediately upon stepping to the edge of the ridge.

It took a moment for the Originalists to see the gleam of blond fur. The matte brown of old blood and the dark hollowness of the crevice of a big joint like the hip. A body. A human body with a red plastic poncho and straw-like blond hair, tufted like the worried fur on the hindquarters of a deer. A body almost intact except for the gouges in its pelvis, where something had tried to find nourishment. Had it been an attack, or had something scavenged on this mysterious body? The body lay on a small outcrop just before the ridge gave way to thin air. Carl and Juan carefully picked their way among ridge rocks to retrieve it.

The man had been naturally pale, but patches of his skin had turned maroon and scabby after what must have been a violent and blistering sunburn. Still on his head was a green cap with a wide tail that covered his neck. Under the tail his skin was soft and cool. Agnes pressed her fingers against its rubberiness. He wore cargo shorts and a fanny pack. The shorts were sun-bleached, and the fanny pack had been torn open by something small but vicious. A badger maybe. Whatever had been in it—food, jerky perhaps—was gone now.

They stared at the body, taking in all the details they could make sense of. His hiking shoes, the one white sock and the bloody one. His bushy mustache with a short growth of patchy beard. A handkerchief remained neatly tied around his neck. A spotting scope hung there too. He looked like a man out for some birding, and the Originalists wondered if it might be a Ranger they'd not met before enjoying some off-hours. But that pale neck. No pale Ranger could remain that fair. And the burn. No pale Ranger would let a burn go so wrong. The shorts might be regulation, but the shoes weren't. No Ranger would wear shoes. They wore boots. And that fanny pack. That fanny pack.

Carl turned to the Newcomers. "I thought you said there weren't more of you."

"There aren't," Frank said. "He's not with us."

"Then who would he be with?" Val said, taking on the accusatory stance that Carl had introduced.

The Newcomers shrugged. They were too new to have a guess.

The Originalists looked at one another, then back at the man. A rube. A know-nothing. Out of his depth but out here nonetheless. Deep out here. How could someone like this get through the entrance? Get this far? Where was his gear? Was there a camp? Were there more like him?

Debra said, "He was probably visiting one of the Rangers and got lost. He's probably a relative."

"Or . . ." Linda said. She looked around, cleared her throat. "I mean, I don't know. I just got here. But are there other groups here?"

"What do you mean?"

"I mean other groups like you. Like us. Who are out here, living like this."

"Of course not," Carl said. But he looked puzzled. He cocked his head at the corpse and bit his lip, which Agnes had never seen him do.

Val snapped her support. "What a stupid question," she said, an angry speck of spit landing on the dead man's cheek.

Linda huffed and Agnes saw her look around, perhaps trying to catch a sympathetic eye, but everyone else was mesmerized, nodding at the corpse, a new thought dawning on them.

*   *   *

THEY LEFT THE body and walked the ridge until they found land that eased down to the lowlands, and camped at the bottom under its looming face. It wasn't until they were under it that they realized it was Winter Ridge, a ridge they'd named because it always looked snow-dusted, no matter the season. But it didn't seem possible it could be Winter Ridge. They'd been so far from it. Had they accidentally followed new ruts, some shortcut, and been delivered here? Or was the Wilderness more compact than they had imagined? The Originalists tilted their heads back to see its white stone face evergreened in lush, pleasant patches. It was the closest thing some of them could get to nostalgia, a feeling of home. To see Winter Ridge meant that not too far away was their lovely hidden Valley nearest to Middle Post. Where they'd camped for almost a whole season, a few years ago, before the idea of constant moving had settled in. Being run out of that place by Rangers had felt like being cast out of a homeland, that Valley where they had become a family of sorts. With the cool, lazy river, the perfect protective bluffs, the cave that Agnes liked to play in, where her mother had kept her secret prized possessions, the secret grasses where her sister was born.

With heads still craning toward the ridge face, they circled up.

Carl said, "We're low on provisions. We're going to have to do a big hunt. We'll have to stay here for days to process it all, not to mention we'll need to make more bags to carry it. So take care to set the camp up well."

Agnes squatted by the fire, moving dead pine needles into shapes, wondering if such a move offended the pine needles, which might prefer their own shape. Carl approached her.

"Don't you think there will be deer toward the end of the meadow?" he asked.

"Yeah," said Agnes.

"Good. Go scout the dominant."

"Okay."

Agnes walked into the meadow. She knew the deer were that way because the wind was blowing that direction and they liked to be downwind from predators, which today was the Community.

"Hey."

She stopped.

Jake jogged up. "Can I come?"

"Why?"

"So I can see how you do stuff. I need to learn stuff. Like, what are you doing?"

"Scouting the does."

"Why?"

"To find the dominant one."

"Why?"

Agnes scoffed. "*Why?* What do you mean, why?"

"I mean why." Jake flipped his hair. "I don't know any of this stuff."

Agnes sighed. "Come on."

They walked until Agnes could see a herd. Then they walked a hundred more feet, and Agnes pointed to the ground and got down. Jake got down next to her. They crawled slowly another hundred feet and stopped.

She pulled out the spotting scope and sat very still and watched the herd in the grass. She noted the markings on the biggest females. There were two that she thought could be the dominant. Their width. The shape of the snout. She brushed her hand back and forth across the grass, making an unnatural noise and movement, but not an alarming one. The deer heads popped up. The ears swiveled. All of them had reacted. So Agnes waited awhile, then clapped. The female with the highest white stockings snapped her muzzle toward the sound, paused, then snorted, and all the deer took off across the meadow.

"Okay," Agnes said, standing up.

"Okay what?"

"We can go back."

"Did you find out which one was dominant?"

"Yeah," Agnes said.

"Which one?"

"You don't know?"

"I don't."

Agnes whistled. This was a lot of work. "The one who snorted. She was the dominant."

"And what do you do with that information?"

"If we kill her first, the others are easier to hunt. She's their leader. Without her, they don't know how to protect themselves."

"That's sad."

"No, it's not."

"But what about the babies?"

"Without the dominant, they're even easier to kill."

Jake winced. "No."

"They are very useful. Their skins come right off."

"Please stop."

"They're good to practice on for the kids. You should practice on one."

"Never."

"You will *have to* practice on one."

"Is this legal?"

"Why wouldn't it be?" Agnes stopped. She knew there were things that were forbidden here, but this, she couldn't imagine taking advantage of evolution being one of them. "It's evolution."

"But you're not allowed to grow things or build houses."

"And?"

"Well, isn't that kind of evolutionary?"

"It's not the same."

"Isn't it?"

"No, it isn't." She said it firmly, but she wasn't sure. She would have to ask Glen. She hated needing to ask things. She'd rather just know. But Jake's questions were catching her off guard. Not too long ago everyone in the group had basically known the same things, and agreed on most. Not anymore. It was tiring. They acted so different from her, the Twins and Jake. They asked such different questions, noticed such different things. They did not take for granted what she took for granted. It made her curious, but she also hated it. Hated that they were different. It made her feel different. She knew that in the place where they came from she would be considered strange. But she had come from there too.

She changed the subject. "Are the Twins really twins?"

"No. They just met on the bus as far as I know."

"Is *Patty* short for *Patricia*?"

"No, it's just *Patty*."

"Is that a normal name?" Agnes only really knew the names of the Originalists, the Rangers, and names that came up in books they carried, names from earlier times, names from fables. They were grand-sounding. But Patty was so *Patty*. And *Patty* wasn't a name like *Val*, short for something more enjoyable to say. *Valeria* was a song she could sing. Her own mother's name was short for *Beatrice*. *Beatrice* was a name that stopped her cold. But her mother's name wasn't a name she ever had reason to say. And probably never would now that she was gone, dead, done. She wished she could remember the names of her friends from the City.

"It's not *not* a normal name," said Jake.

"Hmm."

"Actually they were both named Celeste at first, and for a few days they went as Celeste 1 and Celeste 2. Then Blue-Hair Celeste and Plain Celeste. Then Plain Celeste announced her name was Patty. And so now they are Celeste and Patty."

"Why *Patty*?"

"My guess is she always wanted to be named Patty."

"But she gets so mad when people call her Patricia."

"Well, that's because her name is Patty." Jake shrugged. "Wouldn't you be mad if people called you something else, like Agnestia, or something?"

"But that's not my name."

"Exactly."

Jake flicked his head back, removing his bangs from his face. Agnes watched them slide back. She felt in her pocket for something to cut them with, but her knife was at camp.

On their way back, they came across a rattlesnake in the grass, and before she could warn him, the snake struck out at Jake. But he'd already altered his path, arcing away from where the snake was. He hadn't acknowledged it or jumped, or even asked, *What's that sound?* which she would have expected since he was so new. He never broke his pace, and he kept going on about the Myth of the Private Lands, as he called it, which Agnes had tuned out once she heard the first tell-tale shakes of the rattle. Somehow, he'd noticed the snake and given it room enough that he didn't have to be concerned, even though it wasn't enough room for the snake to not feel anxious. Agnes guessed that if she put her fingers to his wrist she'd discover that his pulse was steady, his skin cool. She spent the rest of the walk and the day pondering this realization, and later fell asleep to images of defensive goshawks, a rutting moose, cougars hovering in the trees. Their terrorizing faces confronting Jake's tranquility. It took a lot for someone new to the Wilderness not to be startled by all it had to display. But a lot of what?

*   *   *

THEY CAMPED UNDER Winter Ridge for several nights, hunting, restocking, gathering pine nuts from the trees that hung heavy with cones, skinning game and smoking it. The smoking tent was up and running, and everyone had a job, shadowed by a Newcomer who scurried behind trying to learn it all. The hum of a village in the shadow of the Ridge. It was so familiar.

Two trucks of Rangers rode up to their camp one morning. Ranger Bob drove one truck. The other truck carried two Rangers the Community didn't recognize. They got out of their truck tentatively, conferring quietly with each other. Ranger Bob stayed in his truck.

Agnes waved and started to walk up to his truck. Her mother had always liked Ranger Bob, and so had she. She'd never seen him outside Post before. But before she could get close, he shook his head and shooed her away. He pulled out a clipboard and a pen and stared intently at the other two Rangers. She stayed put, but she scowled and hoped he would see. She wanted a treat.

The Rangers took attendance with a new roster, one that included the Newcomers. When Bea's name was called, there was silence. The Rangers looked at them with irritation. Then one said, "Oh, she's the deserter."

They conferred.

"Then why is she on this list?"

"Dunno, this is the list Bob gave us."

"Should we cross her off?"

"No, we're not supposed to do that. Bob made the list, so . . ."

"So just leave her name and mark her absent?"

"You're asking the wrong guy."

"Well, you're the guy who said not to cross it off, so far as I'm concerned you are the absolute right guy."

"Why don't we ask Bob?"

"Do you want to get fired?"

"Hey, Meg, can you calm down?"

They stared at each other, breathing fast for a moment. Then the anger slowly melted from their faces. Finally, they laughed.

"Okay, folks," the Ranger named Meg said, addressing the group again. "You know why we're here, dontcha?"

"You'll need to move on," the other Ranger said.

They walked around, pointing to the bent and blistered grass under the smoking tent, the pit toilet that was too full. "You know you need to dig a new hole once it reaches halfway," said Ranger Meg, jabbing into the pit with a stick. They claimed the pinyons had been overharvested.

"This all needs to go," the other Ranger said, drawing a circle in the air that was supposed to encompass all their belongings and them.

"And make sure you do a micro trash sweep because I can see a lot of it," Ranger Meg said, gesturing at a patch of clean dirt.

"Should we go to Middle Post?" Glen asked.

The Rangers shook their heads. "No. This time you'll go to Upper Middle."

The Rangers turned to go.

"Wait," Glen said. "What do you know about the chairs down by the river where we picked up these new recruits?"

"What chairs?"

"Well, a circle of chairs, old recliners, sofas. All organized as though there's been a meeting sometime in the past."

"The recent past," Val cut in.

Ranger Meg and the other Ranger looked at each other. Again

they stared intently. The other Ranger muttered through stiff ventriloquist lips, "Should we get Bob?"

Ranger Meg shook her head. She turned to the Community. "Don't know what you're talking about," she said. "And so we don't need to worry about it."

"Okay, well, what about the body up on Winter Ridge, do you know about that?" Val was riled up.

Carl elbowed her.

The Rangers exchanged looks while trying to seem like they weren't.

"Don't know what you're talking about," Ranger Meg said again, but her tone was high and excited.

"A body, you say? Where'd you say again?" the other Ranger asked. His voice had taken on a dramatic curiosity.

Carl elbowed Val again to keep her mouth shut.

"On Winter Ridge," Carl said casually. He poked a finger into the air above him. "Up there. We figured he was a visitor of one of the Rangers. He wasn't dressed for the place."

Ranger Meg and the other Ranger exchanged more looks. "Oh, right," Ranger Meg said. "That must be Brad's uncle."

"What?" the other Ranger said.

"You know, Brad's uncle," Ranger Meg hissed.

"Brad—"

"We got it," Ranger Meg said. "We'll get on that. Poor Brad. Anything else?"

The Originalists and the Newcomers shook their heads cautiously.

The two Rangers went back to their truck and filled out their own paperwork. Agnes turned toward Ranger Bob.

Now he was smiling, beckoning her. But his smile turned into a frown as she got closer.

He rolled down his window.

"You doing okay?"

"Yeah," she said.

"You sure?"

"Yeah. Why?"

He shrugged. "You're skinny."

She looked down at herself. She always looked like this. She looked back at the Community. The Newcomers were still fat and the Originalists were still skinny, just like it had always been. But she saw Glen slumped on a log. He looked the skinniest. He'd developed an awful, wracking cough recently, and looking at him now, she realized how sick he looked. Agnes said, "Now, Glen—he's really skinny. I think he's sick. He coughs a lot. Can you help him?"

Ranger Bob looked around. Lowered his voice. "You know I can't, sweetie."

She stepped onto the runner of the truck and tried to peer inside. She wanted him to give her a treat. He once gave her a banana. Another time an apple.

"You look real hungry."

Her eyes widened. She stuck out her tongue, pawed her hands, and begged like a kit. "Don't you have something for me?"

"I'm serious. You sure you're okay?" he asked again. His quietness made her feel like he was stalling.

She slapped her hands on the door. "I want a treat," she said sternly.

He chuckled. "Well, you seem okay, that's for sure." He dug into his pocket and brought out two green lollipops. "I brought your favorite. Now don't tell anyone," he said. "Put them in your bag. I wish I had more."

She slid them into her bag. The plastic crinkled. It was so loud. "Shhh," she said. She looked at them in the bottom of her bag, catching light, the green so unnatural. It was a lollipop, she knew, but she couldn't remember when she'd ever had one. Why did he think they were her favorite? "What're you doing here?"

"On patrol."

"I didn't think you ever left Middle Post."

He laughed. "Well, I have a new job. I train new Rangers." He nodded over to where the Rangers were anxiously leafing through papers. He shook his head. "I'm out and about a lot now."

"Do you miss Middle Post?"

"Well, Middle Post is closed now."

"Forever?"

"I'm not sure. I hope not. I kind of prefer just hanging out at Post if you want to know the truth, but this is a good job too. I get to see more. And it pays the bills." He shrugged.

"What kind of bills does a Ranger have?"

"Regular old bills. Everyone has bills."

"I don't."

"You're a kid."

Agnes puffed her chest. "I'm a leader."

Ranger Bob's eyes widened in surprise; then he became very solemn and saluted her.

"You don't have to do that," she said bashfully.

"I think I'll try to talk to your mom soon," he said. "Do you want me to tell her anything for you?"

She blinked. "How are you going to talk to my mom?" she said.

"I'm going to call her. On the phone. I want to tell her I saw you and Glen."

"But she's dead."

His face fell, but then he smiled. "Sweetheart, she's okay. She's just in the City. You know that."

Agnes gripped the door. She thought she might fall. It's not that she didn't know, deep down, that her mother wasn't dead. But she felt dead. What Agnes couldn't believe was that she might be so easily accessible. A telephone. If Agnes was by a telephone, the distance might not have seemed so vast. But she lived in the Wilderness. Her mother was running around the City taking calls from Ranger Bob.

"Do you talk to her often?"

"No, but I've talked to her."

"Why?"

"She asked me to look out for you. Have *you* talked to her?"

Agnes frowned. "Of course not."

"Not even at Post? They were supposed to let you call her."

Agnes's eyes swam. She studied Ranger Bob's knuckle hair on the hand that was slung over the steering wheel. She couldn't remember the last time they'd been to Post. Or if she had ever used a telephone in her life. She shook her head.

"Oh. Well." He searched for something to say.

"How is she?" Agnes asked. She kept her tone even like an adult would.

"She's okay. She misses you like crazy."

Agnes laughed like an adult would, like Val often did, theatrically, cynically. "Ha-ha," she said. "Now that's funny."

"She does."

Agnes laughed for real. Something newly bitter released from her. "Maybe," she said. She squatted down to play with the dirt, but her body felt achy as though she had aged and become someone like Dr. Harold, who always cursed his stiff knees in the mornings.

"Well, I'm going to tell her I saw you. You and Glen."

"If you want." Agnes didn't look up.

He started his car.

"Who is Brad?" she asked.

"Brad?"

"Ranger Brad? Wasn't his uncle visiting?"

He scrunched his face, still worried. "There's no Ranger Brad. Is this one of your make-believe games?"

"Yeah," she said. "I heard the coyotes talking about him." She smiled and he laughed. She had offered a lightened mood and so his shoulders relaxed.

"Well," he said, "Brad's uncle must be a friend of theirs then. You tell that Carl to give you some extra food tonight. Tell him Bob said to."

She nodded. She would never do that. She got the same amount as everyone else. She was certain of it.

Late that night, as most of the Originalists and Newcomers slept, searchlights played high above on Winter Ridge, the hum of a helicopter circled around them. A truck's lights washed over where the ridge dropped and swept against low-lying clouds. From where the Community slept it looked like a silent invasion.

Most were asleep, but Agnes and Jake saw the lights. They saw because they stayed up later than everyone else and had been doing so since the new moon. Sitting together, most often silently. Staring into the fire and wondering about what the other was wondering about.

They watched the lights curiously for a few moments.

"What is that? Is that aliens?" Jake asked.

"It's Rangers."

They lit the ends of sticks in the fire and took them away from the sleeping Community, picking their way in the dim dark through the grasses. They spelled out words in the air with the lit ends of the sticks, drawing with the embers secret messages for the invaders above.

Agnes wrote, *Liars* and *Cowards*. And, *Hi Brad's uncle.*

Jake wrote, *Dicks.*

The words burned into their sight so that they read them again and again against their eyelids whenever they blinked.

"They're so dumb," Jake said, walking back to the fire.

"Why?"

"If they'd searched for the body in the day, we probably wouldn't have seen them. Certainly not their lights. Maybe we might have heard them."

Agnes *hmm*ed. It had been a sunny day. She would have seen the glint of the sun off the metal of the trucks. She would have heard the helicopter when it was many miles away. Tonight, with low-lying clouds, was a good night to try. If the clouds had hugged the Ridge as the Rangers must have assumed they would, their lights would have been mostly invisible. The clouds would have dampened the sound of the helicopter and made it sound possibly like some wild horses running close by but out of sight. Or some strange bug ticking nearby. The Rangers' luck ran out when the clouds for a time left a gap that just happened to encompass the search party and the group below with clear cool air and a window to the starry sky. A middle-of-the-night search meant they had planned well, but nature worked against them, as it often did. And she and Jake had worked against them too, by being awake. She *hmm*ed again and let Jake continue with his theory. She liked that he was trying to understand this new world of his, even if he got it so wrong. Someday soon, she'd explain the Rangers to him. That they were much smarter than they sometimes appeared, and much more powerful too. And that, even though the Rangers had attempted to conduct the search for the corpse in secret, they really didn't need to hide anything from the Community. Ultimately the Community didn't matter. The Community, as she understood it, had no power. Her mother had tried to have good relationships with all the Rangers, but as far as Agnes could tell, the only trustworthy Ranger was Ranger Bob. Jake didn't need to know all of that now. These were things she'd just begun to understand, and she had liked her world better before she understood them. His wrongness made him seem innocent, and that made her feel protective of him.

They walked slowly toward the fire, and she slipped her calloused hand into his soft hand and heard his faint gasp of private delight in the darkness, believed she could hear the shifting muscles from the beginning of a smile because her hearing was that good. They walked like that to the edge of camp, then slid their hands from each other and walked alone to their own beds, Agnes's next to Glen's snoring lump and Jake next to Frank, though not in that family's bed. Agnes saw that Jake's own bed was slightly to the side, which saddened Agnes, that he had to be a little bit alone. She had never asked him about his family, she realized. Was she supposed to? She watched Jake crouch, pull his sleep skin back, and disappear into the blackness of the ground just as the fire smoked out.

*   *   *

THEY PACKED ALL morning. The smoking tent came down. The curing tent came down. The components were rolled into their buckskin bags and fastened on the packs strapped to the designated carriers, which were Patty's mom and Linda that day. "Trial by fire," Linda said as she hoisted her laden pack. Patty's mom stumbled under the weight, surprised that Agnes had handed it to her as though it weighed much less. Smoked meat was passed around. The precious skin-scraping bones. Packs of smoked bones. Extra bones were buried. Tanned hides were draped on backs because they still needed time before they would be ready. Each of the hide carriers smelled only the rich and rotten musk of the brains used to tan as they moved through the blooming sage country under the steady sun.

After a few days, Agnes thought she could see the remnants of a trail as they neared their familiar Valley. Barely perceptible, but she could see it. It could be an animal trail, but something told her it was the softened ground made from their own deerskin slippers, or from their old rubber soles so long ago.

She knew this place well, even though she'd never led through it. The way the land sloped up on the left, toward the caves where her mother, Glen, and she had spent their time. The secret grasses on the right, where her sister had been almost born. Agnes peered into that place as they walked, remembering how her mother squatted and swayed, her head down, and that strange moment when she lifted a glistening lump and kissed it. From where Agnes was perched, she had seen her mother kneeling for a long time. She knelt in complete stillness for what felt like hours. Then her mother stood, kicked a coyote, and walked away, and Agnes ran back to the cave where Glen napped.

Madeline's place was soft with new grasses, and it made Agnes think they might be near some anniversary time, but she couldn't think of how long it had been. Time was lost on everyone here. She didn't care much for it, but now, it seemed sad to her that her little sister had no one marking time for her. She'd never thought of the dead that way. But as she led the group into the Valley, she saw it as something desolate, a place where nothing had been until this moment, even though she knew it was really full of everything.

Her mother hadn't told her the girl's name, but Agnes had heard her and Glen use it in private, secretly talking in the night under the skins. She remembered watching her mother return to the cave that day, how she squatted to wash herself, how she stared at the game Agnes and Glen were playing but didn't join in, how she nuzzled her pillow, though her face wore no expression. Her mother was, it had seemed to Agnes, gone, though her body remained. And then how, sometime later, she was leading them back to camp as though it were any day, and if Agnes hadn't known better, she would not have thought anything bad had just happened. There would be a shield around her mother for days that made it impossible for Agnes to touch her until they slept, when she would cuff herself to her mother's ankle. She had needed to be close to her mother because she missed her sister, even though the girl had never been real. Agnes had wanted to ask for comfort but didn't know how. She'd wondered if she ought to have given comfort to her mother. But her mother was a wall and Agnes assumed her mother didn't need anything from her. She never did. Agnes decided it was Madeline who might need some comfort. And so she had sneaked to her burial spot the next night to keep her company.

There had been nothing left. She saw some thin bones tossed under a bush. She picked one up and bent it between her thumb and index finger. It was soft. It glittered with wetness under the moonlight. Agnes felt a desire tugging at her. She wanted something. Something to remember. To connect to Madeline somehow. But she didn't want the bones. They could still be scavenged and helpful to something. She picked up one of the broad green leaves her mother had laid over the body. Agnes put it to her nose to smell it, but it clung, sticky to the tip. She pulled it away, and in the night's black light she could see it was covered in thickened, sticky blood. Agnes's nose and cheek were wet with it. She didn't wipe it off. She felt the slow tickle as the blood's last moisture evaporated and her sister remained. She smeared more on. As it dried, it tightened her skin so that it was hard to frown, or smile, or talk. Like when she and her mother used to smear mud on their faces during rainy days. "We're at a spa," her mother would exclaim as she wiped mud across Agnes's cheek. Agnes didn't know what a spa was, but she loved anytime her mother laughed.

Agnes wore the blood mask back to camp but wiped it off with her spit-covered palm so her mother or Glen wouldn't see. What a strange thing to have done. She couldn't say why she'd done it.

She hadn't thought of the girl in a long time. She hadn't known what to think about her. But now, again, she felt a deep lonesomeness for Madeline, who probably had no idea how long it had been since she didn't survive. What a sad thing, to have never been alive in this place.

Agnes stopped walking and looked around for Glen, suddenly wanting to hold his hand. But he was far back, behind the group, slowly making his way, his cough breaking the day's silence to its own beat. He never wanted her to walk with him anymore. She knew he worried that he would hold her back. He knew she liked leading. She saw that it pained him to tell her no, so she had stopped asking. She watched him scanning the landscape. He knew where they were too. She began to walk again. They walked down and up and down and up to their first home, the place the lazy river slithered through, their lovely hidden Valley.

Their old camp was lush and overgrown like it had been when they first arrived. Before they'd trampled certain grasses, or harvested too many dry sage branches for tanning. It really did look better without them there, Agnes thought. She felt a wave of regret that they had returned. But then her stomach danced and warmed because being back felt so nice.

She had carried the tools so she brought them over to the natural ring of stones and set up their work area. She saw Glen setting up their bed where they'd always put their sleep circle. It would need to be bigger this time, with the Newcomers. A few Newcomers joined him. Frank, Patty's mom, and Linda. Then Carl and Val walked up, and they were all talking with Glen. *Poor Glen,* Agnes thought. He was so small and skinny compared to the rest of them. So bent while they stood so straight. From their circle she heard his hacking cough. It was as though his lungs never cleared out the excess moisture from the dank forest. In his sleep, Agnes would nudge him over onto his side. Something her mother would do for her when she was ill. Or put her bag under his head to elevate him so the phlegm couldn't gather and pool. When they walked, he was mostly fine. Moving helped. The worst time was when he lay down at night. Then, he sputtered like he was drowning in his own wet breaths.

What are they talking about? Agnes wondered. She set up the smoker. Without consensus it was hard to figure out when decisions were being made. She used to see all the adults congregate together, and she knew they were debating in order to decide something. Now any small group of adults could be discussing anything. When Carl was involved, perhaps a decision was being made. She peered back and saw that Glen was walking away, with a skin over his shoulder. Carl and Val hovered by the sleeping circle, leaning into each other, talking quietly. Watching Glen go.

Agnes bounded over. "Why is Glen walking away with his bedding? Where is he going?"

"He's going to sleep somewhere else, away from camp, until he gets better," said Carl breezily.

"What? Why?"

"He's worried that he's bothering people who are trying to sleep. With his coughing. I mean, it's continuous. Quite irritating. He volunteered to sleep elsewhere. Until he's better."

"But he can't sleep out there. He should sleep closer to the fire if anything. He needs to keep warm."

"People will still hear him." Carl traded his pleasant tone for something more straightforward.

"Then why doesn't everyone else move?"

Carl and Val snorted. "Come on, Agnes," said Val.

"That's an absurd thing to suggest. All of us move just so Glen can be comfortable?" Carl laughed.

"Stop laughing." Agnes stomped her foot.

Val looked stern. "Hey now, you know we're already doing him a favor. You should be grateful."

"What do you mean?"

Val said, "Sweetheart, he's very sick. If he were anyone else, we would have left him behind by now. He's holding us back."

"No, he isn't. The Newcomers are."

"No, it's Glen," Carl snapped.

"Hey," Val said softly to Carl. She put a hand out, as though to try to hush him. But she put her hand on Agnes's shoulder instead.

Agnes felt her lip tremble. *No, no, no*, she thought. She clenched her fists to keep her feelings in control. She took a breath. "But—"

"But we're not going to do that to him," Val said. "We're not going to do that to you."

"You sent him away," Agnes said, barely audible.

"It was his idea," spat Carl. "He volunteered. Go ask him. Or better, go join him if you'd like." He started to walk away.

She blinked. She had not thought to do that. The fire was so warm and the camp was where everyone was. Why would anyone sleep out there? *He'll never let me*, she told herself. *Who lets you do anything?* a voice said. *Do what you want.*

"Okay, I will." She gathered up her skins.

Carl turned and laughed. "Oh, that's great. See you in the middle of the night when you come running back."

"You don't think I'm brave?"

"You're a child. You can only be so brave."

Val raised her eyebrows at Carl.

"What?" Carl cried. "She's always had the group around her. Who knows how she'll do alone."

Agnes started to walk off. "I won't be alone. I'll be with Glen."

"Right. He's a great shield."

She stomped her feet again and yelled, "He is!" And then her voice wavered and her eyes got wet. She trudged after Glen. Behind her she heard Val scolding Carl: "And you're just going to let her go?"

"She has to learn," he scolded back.

Glen had walked off, toward Madeline's place, but he'd not made it far before he stopped to sit. He was hunched over his legs in the middle of the sage, his blankets in a heap next to him. He looked so tired. She gathered his skins and he groaned.

"What are you doing?" he said.

"I'm going to carry your stuff." She slung it over her other shoulder. She had several skins now draped around her. They almost touched the ground.

"No, I mean, what are you doing here? With your bedding."

"Our bedding."

"I left it for you."

"Well, I'm coming with you. Where do you want to go?"

"No, no, honey, you keep your bed with the others. Go back."

"No, I'm staying with you."

"No, Agnes, I mean it. You have to go back. This isn't good for you."

"No."

"Agnes, you have to."

Agnes threw the skins down. "Don't tell me what to do," she screamed. Her small fists clenched, strained at her sides, and she thought she might punch Glen, except that she loved Glen so much. Even though she had led the whole Community here, from the Poisoned River, all over the Wilderness really, even though she knew she had made herself essential to the group, she felt helpless right now. She felt helpless and embarrassed thinking of how she'd asked Ranger Bob for help and he'd said no. How all she had done since then was try to help Glen sleep. That's all. He wasn't any better and she didn't know how to make him better. How could she not know how to help Glen when she could do so much else?

She felt Glen's arm around her shoulder. She realized she was crying fiercely into her fists. White stars burst behind her eyes.

"Shhh," he said, and stroked her hair. "Come on," he said. His voice was steady and clear, not raspy like it had been a moment ago, and for so long before that. With her sight blurry from tears he resembled the strong man who had brought them here. His back straight, his arm heavy on her shoulder, weighted with muscles. "We're going to find a really good spot," he said. He kissed the top of her head and gathered up the bedding effortlessly as though it were as light as a leaf. But she saw him wobble as he straightened. Knew this was taking all he had. He was mustering everything he could to take care of her, even though really he needed her to take care of him. She was ashamed at how good this made her feel. She whimpered and let him lead her away. "I know just the place," he said. He took her up a scramble of rocks to their cave.

* * *

THEY BUILT A little fire when the sun began to set. They lay on their backs, in the skins, their arms behind their heads looking for shooting stars. When something came to mind, they said it. But mostly they lay quiet.

Jake had brought them a bowl of food to share from dinner. He'd sat with them for a little while.

When he left, Agnes reached into her bag. "I have a treat," she said. She pulled out the two green lollipops.

Glen's eyes flared like embers in wind. "Ooh."

They each tore the cellophane carefully, folded and tucked it into Agnes's bag. "It would be bad for these to catch in the wind," she said very seriously.

"On three," said Glen.

"One."

"Two."

They put the green sticks to their mouths.

Agnes puckered. She couldn't remember ever tasting such a flavor. Like taking a bite of honeycomb and a rose hip at the same time. Crab apples. They had encountered some a few years ago. Her mouth watered and the sides of her tongue shriveled. She wanted to spit. But there was also a sweetness in the back of her throat. She looked at Glen. His eyes were closed, the corners of his mouth smiling as he drew the lollipop in and out of his mouth, making *mmmmm* sounds.

"Do you like it?" she asked.

He drew the lollipop out slowly, his eyes still closed. "I love it."

"I don't know."

His eyes flashed open. "Really? You used to love lollipops. Though I guess you were a fan of orange."

"Really?"

"Oh, yes. Your mother would buy bags of lollipops and collect all the orange ones and keep them in a drawer. You got one a week. You would go crazy."

"I don't remember."

"You were young."

"I remember a lot of things, though."

"Well, this was a small thing." He shrugged.

"What did she do with the others?"

"She handed them out to the kids in the building." He chuckled. "We ate a lot of them."

"What was her favorite?"

"Oh, green. She liked it because it's not a flavor of something. It's just a flavor."

"It's not something?"

"I guess it's supposed to be apple, but it isn't."

"I thought it was like crab apples."

"That's what you tasted?"

"Yes, I tasted it."

"That makes sense. Do you want your lollipop?"

"No."

"Can I have it?"

But Agnes was already handing it to him.

Agnes asked, "She would give other kids lollipops?"

"Yeah, she used to give the kids lots of things. Stuff that you out-grew. Or toys you didn't want. There weren't a lot of kids in the build-ing. Only a few younger than you. Do you remember them?"

"No." Agnes couldn't imagine a building that size with only a few kids. Even still she couldn't picture them. "Did I know them?"

"Oh, yeah. The ones who lived around us. You were all friends. You would run up and down the hallways together. Especially af-ter curfew. It annoyed everyone. But the parents thought it was fun. We would meet in someone's apartment and drink. Of course, that was before you got sick. You and the others." He drummed his fin-gers against his chin. "I think their names were Wei and Miguel and Sarah." He laughed. "Wow. I can't believe I remember."

"I don't remember them," Agnes said again. But truthfully she was forming a picture in her mind of the fluorescent lights and the con-crete floor of the hallway. Of one end getting closer, the sound of panting and screams. Then a new view, or the other end of the hall, and launching toward it. She heard adult laughter behind a door. Ice touching the sides of a glass. Her cheeks hurt. Her eyes were wet. She was smiling. A door clicked. A body came out into the hallway, and Agnes collided with it. No. Jumped onto it. Into the arms. Arms lift-ing her up. The eyes shining. Smiling face of her mother. Something astringent on her breath. The door ajar and the sounds coming from inside now seemed raucous.

"Okay, okay, bedtime for everyone," she said. Agnes and the children *booed*. The adults inside *booed*. Her mother stumbling back, theatrically, barely holding on to Agnes, who was wrapped around her, arms around neck, legs gripped around her waist.

"How am I the bad guy?" her mother cried. Agnes buried her face in her mother's neck. She could smell the heat of her—it was always hot in the building; none of the windows opened. She could smell whatever they had been drinking. Then Agnes smelled Glen because he had appeared and pretended to eat her nose. Then she could only remember the feeling of sleep. Of warmth, of cool sheets, her mother's dry lips. "Good night, sweetheart."

A shooting star drew a blue line above them.

How awful it must have been, Agnes thought, to leave such a nice life.

*   *   *

AFTER A MORNING hunt, Agnes and other Originalists scraped and washed and stretched skins by the fire while the Newcomers explored the area.

Val appeared next to Agnes and sat down.

"How are you, kiddo?"

"Fine."

"Friends?" Val held out her hand.

Agnes shook it. "Friends."

Val caressed Agnes's head. "Your hair looks ridiculous, by the way," she said, a *tsk* in her voice. But she was speaking softly too. She was trying to be kind in the ways Val could be kind.

Agnes touched it. To the touch, her shorn head growing out all at once made her imagine a scene from an old wildlife special that lived in her memory like an image through fog. Of an immature lion with an immature mane. One skulking on the outskirts of the pride, not ready to take on the alpha. Yet.

"You're going to have to decide if you want to have some self-respect and cut it again, or if you're going to look stupid while it grows to your butt." Val's eyebrows, so shaped and black they looked painted on, wiggled. "It's really so stupid-looking," she said, smiling.

"Cut it please," Agnes said.

"Okay." Val clapped her hands. "You'll look fierce."

"I want to look like a young lion who is ready to be a leader."

"Well, sure, that sounds like it could be fierce."

Val got on her knees, and Agnes sat against her and took off her shirt.

Agnes closed her eyes as Val pinched sections of her hair to cut.

The strands lifted in the wind like dandelion seeds.

"Make a wish," Val said.

"I did."

"What was it?"

"If I tell you, it won't come true."

"Oh, sweetie, it won't come true regardless. What was it?"

"I wished that my mom didn't suffer," Agnes said. She hadn't really wished that, but thought it would make her seem noble.

"Well, that's very selfless of you. Next time, though, make a wish for yourself."

"But you said they don't come true."

"If you make wishes for other people, like the one you made, you'll never know. If you make wishes for yourself, at least you'll find out. See my logic?"

"Yes, I see it. What did you wish for?"

"A baby."

"Babies aren't so great."

"You're right about that."

"Then why?" Agnes heard the whispering snip of the scissors behind her ear.

"Because I want one. And I hate when I don't get what I want."

Agnes thought of Val's life, or what she knew of it. She liked Val. A lot more than many did. She had never thought of Val as someone who hadn't gotten what she wanted. But she guessed she didn't really have a sense for everything Val wanted. And if it was a baby, then she certainly didn't have that, and she had certainly tried. A lot. Everyone knew about that.

"Okay, you are done, m'dear. Looking good if I do say so myself."

Val put her hand in front of Agnes as though it were a mirror. "See, take a look."

Agnes stared into the calluses of Val's hand and touched her hair. She cooed, something she somehow knew to do from watching the women greet one another with air kisses outside their office buildings. "I love it," Agnes cried. She pretended she had on layers of lipstick and smiled like she imagined one would with layers of lipstick on. Her lips full, sticky, hard to move, covered in mud. It was funny to her that she could remember such strange images that had nothing to do with her daily life and never would again. Made-up women in an unbelievable world. She giggled like she'd seen them giggle, her fingers to her collarbone, her chin up at attention.

"You are a hilarious weirdo," Val said, planting a quick kiss on the top of Agnes's shorn head and bounding off to help with lunch. Agnes decided a swim would be a good way to rinse off, and a swim would be good for Glen.

He sat on a log whittling a piece of wood into a hook, his hands covered in small bloody nicks. Agnes stood over him for a moment before he looked up, and when he looked up, it was a slow, stiff, painful movement. He smiled.

"*Que bonita*," he said, touching his own hair to show what he meant.

"Thank you, Glen."

He picked a stray hair off her smock. "Make a wish," he said.

"I did already."

"Then I will." He closed his eyes, held the hair to his lips to kiss it before blowing it into the wind.

He smiled up at her, squinting into the sun behind her.

"Do you want to swim with me?" she asked.

He shook his head, mouthed *no*, still smiling and squinting at her. He grasped one of her hands and wagged it back and forth. "So proud of you, my girl," he said. His voice was reedy again, and fell into a whisper at the end.

"Thanks, Glen."

He let go and went back to whittling, and she stood there for a moment more, wanting to somehow change his mind but not knowing how.

Everyone, even the smallest of the Newcomers, was busy around camp, but still Agnes went to the river. She knew she was neglecting important work. That worm of irresponsibility squiggled against her ribs, made her feel like a kid again, without a worry or duty, and she secretly cherished the feeling.

Her toes in the cold water, she thought about washing parties with her mother, when they'd wash the special rags they used to have in the river. They were just old strips of cotton T-shirts, repurposed by Debra. But they had been one of the last remnants of the City that they relied on daily. She'd been much smaller, her mother sometimes seemed nervous to have her go too deep into the water. But now Agnes was a swimmer. She flopped toward a deeper pool in the lazy river, dunking her whole self under and scrubbing the loose hairs from her scalp, shoulders, chest.

She rolled over, flippered her hands to stay submerged, and opened her eyes to see the blue of the sky through the water, see the sun's effects, diluted by her depth. In other parts of this river, it picked up speed and became dangerous. If she tried to stay still, she could feel that pull beginning even here. Small and gentle, but an unmistakable tug. She wouldn't notice it if she were standing or washing, or even treading upright. But once she relaxed, she could move quite swiftly downriver. But where she was, the river slithered back and forth, like a cold snake. And there was no danger, as far as she could tell.

She thought back to Ranger Bob. The way he had looked at her after he gave her the lollipops. The skin between his eyes sagging down in a deep *V* of worry. She remembered that look from their very first day. Their trip had been exhausting. Her mother was exhausted. Her face blotchy and laced with red veins like cobwebs from crying. Agnes remembered that on their last day at home, her mother and Nana had fought.

"You can't go," Nana had said.

Her mother was flustered and upset. But more, confused. "I have to go. Why are you making this harder?"

"Because it's so stupid." Nana had scrunched her fists and face, like in the cartoons that Agnes watched when smoke would come out of someone's ears if they were mad. Nana was very mad.

"This is not stupid, Mom. It's important. Don't you care about Agnes?"

Nana's eyes got big, and she blinked them at Agnes as though seeing her for the first time. Her anger softened and she smiled. She reached out to hug Agnes, and Agnes stepped toward her, but her mother's heavy arm pushed her back behind her. Then her nana howled.

Seeing her nana with tears falling made Agnes's chest constrict. She felt her throat tighten and the water rise to her eyes and she heard her mother become angry. All was cut short, though, when her mother threw a glass against the wall.

"Don't tell me what to do," her mother screamed. Nana screamed, "But I'm so scared." Agnes slunk away from her mother's arm and moved herself toward her room slowly so as not to be detected.

She needn't have worried. Neither woman noticed her leave. Even though they claimed to be fighting about her, they had forgotten she was there. They were wailing at each other now, accented by hysterical words. She'd never seen anything like it before. Now, of course, she knew the Twins, and they acted in a very similar fashion. Now she could marvel at it. But at the time, she remembered being scared.

Agnes had shut the door to her room that night, slowly releasing the knob so the click was hushed. The pain in their voices dulled by the barrier of the door. Agnes walked around the room and touched the things that belonged to her, trying to hear if they had something to tell her. She tapped her fingers on the window and waited for a response. She put her head into her pillowcase and stretched it across her face and breathed through the cotton weave. She lay down like that on her bed, her head on her pillow inside the case. That's how she fell asleep. She woke up to her mother pulling things from her drawers.

"What are you doing?" she muffled from inside the pillowcase.

"Oh, good, you're alive," her mother said, distracted by filling a backpack with Agnes's warm clothes. Her voice was ground down, powdery. Her eyes were bloodshot. She had not slept. She wore a giant T-shirt Agnes had never seen before, and puffy socks pulled up to her knees. Her hair was in a fallen side ponytail. She looked like an unhappy adult dressed as a once-happy child. "Sweetheart, can you pick two things that are the most special things to you? That you wouldn't mind carrying around with you for a long time?"

"Why?"

"Because we're going away. And you might not see your other things for a while."

Agnes nodded solemnly. "Is Nana gone?"

"Nana is gone. Bring two things to me in my room, okay?" Her mother hurriedly kissed the top of her head.

Agnes chose her stuffed unicorn and her butterfly necklace. She lost the necklace within the first couple of months in the Wilderness.

"Oh, we were looking for it everywhere. How did you find it?" her mother had cried when a Ranger reported the discovery.

"We find everything," the Ranger said. His stony face ground down her mother's smile. He wouldn't give her the necklace back. He said it would be kept in the evidence room.

"Evidence of what?" her mother had asked.

"Of your failure to follow rules."

That was the earliest interaction Agnes remembered with a Ranger other than Ranger Bob, who had led them on their intake day.

She thought about her mother living in the City, there for Nana even though Nana was dead. She didn't understand it. Agnes loved Nana too. *But I'm alive.*

From under the current Agnes felt a disturbance from the bank and popped her head up, alarmed.

Patty and Celeste, naked and knock-kneed, were wading into the river.

"You are a cheater," Celeste sang. "Skipping work like that."

Agnes's heart burned with shame. "I've never skipped work before," she said, sinking underwater up to her nose and looking woefully back toward camp.

"Oh." Celeste frowned. "I figured you were a badass. You should do it more," she said.

"Ugh, I had to whittle," Patty said. "And now I have splinters." She waggled her swollen red fingers. She had bad splinters and would probably need to see Dr. Harold.

"At least you didn't have to touch the dead things like I did." Celeste scrunched her face in disgust.

"But you love dead things," Agnes said, and Celeste rolled her eyes.

The girls floated on their backs and watched a few bullet-shaped clouds speed across the sky. That wind was high, though, and around them nothing moved.

"This is a pretty okay place," Celeste said, her voice slightly wistful.

"It's the first place I remember," Agnes said.

"Was it the first place you went?"

"One of them. Yes. It's near the Post where we entered."

"We haven't been to Post yet," Patty whined.

"It's not special."

"But there are snacks!"

"Only in some. Most of the snacks are gone from the machines. There's water. That's about the best thing."

"And handsome Rangers?" Patty asked.

"The Rangers are *old*," Agnes said. She and Celeste laughed at Patty.

"They don't seem so old," Patty said quietly.

"Rangers aren't worth your time," Celeste said.

"Why do you say that?" Agnes asked.

"Oh, you can just tell, right, Agnes?"

Agnes was surprised Celeste had come to that conclusion so quickly. "Yeah, I guess."

"*I guess*," Patty mocked for no reason.

They continued to float. Agnes listened for sounds of bird wings and the occasional splash of their hands in the water.

Agnes felt like she was dozing, but she didn't know if it was possible to fall asleep in the water. When she heard the Twins scream, she was slow to move, as though she were floating in sap. She flailed to stand and looked around. She saw no threat. The Twins were cowering up to their necks in the water. Then she noticed they screamed with smiling mouths. She rubbed her eyes again and looked.

Jake stood on the bank, his arms hanging confused, his mouth agape, trying to say something but not being able to over their screams of, Agnes now realized, pleasure.

"Jake! We're naked!" Celeste squealed.

The girls turned their attention to Agnes.

"Get down, Agnes," Patty screamed, her eyes squeezed shut.

"Why?" Agnes asked.

Patty screamed, "Because you're naked!"

"So?"

The Twins laughed hysterically, water rushing into their mouths. They looked like they were drowning.

Turning to Jake, her hands on her bony hips, Agnes said, "Does it bother you?"

"No," Jake said, his eyes trained on the ground.

"See?" Agnes said to the Twins, submerged to their shoulders. Patty and Celeste cackled maniacally like Debra did. Like Val still did sometimes. Their faces guffawing all over the place.

"You are so weird," the Twins screamed in unison. And Agnes

felt a sting of jealousy. She'd never said the same thing as another person at the same time. It seemed impossible. *How did you do that?* she wanted to ask, but now they were staring at her body and she felt unwelcome.

"I'm leaving," she said. She walked toward where Jake stood, and he stepped back from the shore as though afraid, turned around and started to walk in small circles, his head down.

Agnes put her smock back on. "Come on," she said to Jake.

He followed her downriver from the Twins. "I see you cut your hair," Jake said to the ground.

"Yes," Agnes said.

"How come?"

"Because it looked immature, like a baby lion."

"What do baby lions look like?"

"Like furry babies."

"Oh."

"What?"

"Well, I liked your hair. I thought it was cool. Shaggy." He smiled. "I mean, it's cool now too."

Agnes felt a blush come on, which she quickly turned into anger. "Well, I think your hair is stupid and I always have."

"Why?" he said, his voice high-pitched and sad.

"Your bangs. You're going to get yourself killed."

"Because of my bangs?"

"They cover your eyes. You're going to trip over a rock. A cougar is going to attack from above. You'll flip your hair too hard and break your own neck." She stopped, a little breathless.

"It sounds like you've thought a lot about my hair."

"About how it's going to kill you, yes. I have."

"I'm going to take that as a compliment. Because it means you're thinking of me."

Again, Agnes felt heat rush to her neck, her cheeks. "Just because you're new. Your hair is dumb and it's going to kill you one of these days and someone needs to tell you."

"Do others think this?"

"Well, it's not like I talk about your hair all the time," Agnes snapped. "But I'm sure everyone knows except you."

Jake nodded. "Will you cut it for me?"

She thought of her fingers in those stupid soft bangs, trying to cut a straight line that would allow Jake to still look like Jake. Agnes realized she was holding her breath. She exhaled slowly.

Jake watched her thoughts race across her face. But his smile faded as she remained silent. "Or, you don't have to," he stammered.

"No, I want to."

"Okay." He seemed unsure.

"I really want to. I really, really want to."

"Okay." He seemed happier.

Agnes started running, yelling "Stay there" at Jake. He stayed.

She ran and smiled the whole way to get the scissors from Val. She returned to Jake with a pounding heart.

She breathed deeply a few times. "How do you want your hair?"

"Like yours?"

"But I thought we were just doing your bangs?"

"Do whatever you want. I trust you."

Agnes looked at him nervously. She thought of touching his whole head so close to his scalp. Of having to fold his ears forward the way Val had folded hers, so they wouldn't get nicked. Of peering close at the back of his neck to get a clean cut, of breathing on his neck and having him feel that and know something new about her.

"Just your bangs for now," she said.

She cupped water from the river in her hands and wet his hair down. She straightened the bangs down his face and the ends curled under his chin. With him sitting and her standing, she was hunched down to reach his face. She tilted his chin up, but then the bangs parted and slipped to either side of his ear. She could hear the Twins splashing upriver. Jake watched everything she did.

She settled in front of him, cross-legged, and tried to get leverage that way. But she was too far. So she knelt, her knees touching his knees, and leaned toward him and realized her face would have to be so close to his face for her to do this. She tried to pull back and wobbled, as though she might fall to the side, and he put a hand on her hip to steady her, and then kept it there long after she was steadied. His hand sat light and tentative, but still it was there warming her through her smock.

Agnes held her breath, and when she absolutely had to, she exhaled slowly out of the corner of her mouth, careful not to hit him in the face with the old air from her lungs.

She didn't really know how to cut hair like his. What were bangs, anyway?

She pulled his bangs taut, made small snips. Jake cast his eyes to the side, his mouth small and shaped somewhere between a smile and a frown, as though concentrating on something. As chunks of hair fell away, she wanted to tuck them into her pocket. She wanted to feather them across her face when they were dry.

Agnes didn't want the haircut to end. And when it did she said, "Oh no," because now he would have to take his hand away and this moment would never happen again.

"What?"

Agnes tried to cover up her disappointment. "I did a bad job. You look weird."

"How weird?"

"I didn't realize your hair would stand up like that if I cut it so short." It looked like a tuft of moss atop his head.

He touched the stand of upright hairs, and Agnes felt cold air rush to the spot where he'd had his hand. She shivered.

"I think it'll be okay," he said. He smiled. "Thank you." He stood up and helped her to her feet. Some strands of hair lifted from his chest and floated away.

"Make a wish," Agnes said.

"That's kids' stuff," he said. "You can have it."

Jake began to walk away.

Agnes blurted, "Don't you need to swim to get the hair off?"

"Nah, I'm good," he said.

"Okay."

"Thanks again," he said and turned to leave. He flipped his hair, the hair that wasn't there anymore, and broke into a run.

"Stop doing that," Agnes whispered to his retreating body.

Agnes took the long route to the cave rather than swing by camp. She didn't want to be seen and pulled into work. She didn't want to work today. She tried to think if she'd ever felt that way before. What was it about today that made her want to be apart from everyone? She'd felt an unfamiliar heaviness in her chest and when she reached the cave she dropped to the ground.

She wondered why Jake had run away after a moment that, to her, had felt big, heavy, as though dozens of elk pelts were being piled on top of her. Her arms had been hard to move under the weight of whatever it was she had been feeling. Hadn't he felt it too? Was it possible he hadn't? More than possible, she thought. What if it was very likely he hadn't? She tried to remember his delighted gasp when she'd grabbed his hand by the fire, or the warm tingling where his hand had lain on her hip, but now she saw them differently and wondered if she had it all wrong. Perhaps it was friendly, brotherly. The heat she had felt was her own embarrassment and not something between them. His gasp had been alarm. Discomfort. Far from feeling brotherly, perhaps he hated her. Perhaps she filled him with disgust.

She startled to feel something brush her leg and looked down to see a cheeky squirrel picking at some crust on her smock. She hadn't even noticed it approach. She'd been too preoccupied wondering what Jake had been thinking.

"No more," she said to herself. Thinking of him had become dangerous. Her feelings could get her maimed or killed.

"What if you had been a cougar?" she said to the squirrel. "I'd be dead."

The squirrel squeaked at her, agreeing she had made a mistake. *Yes*, it chittered, *it's best to not think about the boy.*

"Thank you," Agnes said. "I'll stop thinking about him." She brushed her hands off in front of her. "Done," she said, and sighed.

Agnes stood up from where she'd squatted, brushed off her legs, and went into the cave, to the back where her mother had hidden the pillow and magazine, but they were gone.

The heaviness in her chest inched up to her throat. She guessed it had to do with being somewhere so familiar when such familiarity wasn't supposed to exist anymore. Not for them. Not in this life. Wasn't that part of the point? To kill off their sense of home? To have them feel at home anywhere? Or nowhere? Were they the same thing?

When she returned to where she'd been sitting, she noticed a rusty red spot on the ground. She looked around, squatted to touch it, and felt something loosen inside her. She stepped away and saw a new drop on the ground. She touched the inside of her leg; her hand came away with a small smear of the same rust red. She touched the smear to her tongue. Iron, metal, winter. Blood. She squatted and pulled her smock up so she could see the ground between her feet. She watched small drops of red fall slowly. *Drip. Drip.* Like time passing. She watched the drop's edge become ragged in the dirt. She felt the drops release from her with a light, wet tickle. One drop. Two drops. Three drops. To ten. And then it stopped.

She knew what it was. She was excited to tell Val. A little embarrassed to tell Glen. She wondered if there was some special ritual they'd dreamed up for this kind of thing. Obviously, women in the Community got their periods, but she was the first to get her *first* period here. She felt wild. Useful. Right. She grinned and felt a bubble in her chest that she thought was excitement. But when it rose and burst in her throat, loneliness was what was left.

Looking down at her smock, she noticed a few hairs. Long dark ones. They had to be snippets of Jake's bangs. She carefully picked them off, collected them together like the tip of a very fine paintbrush, and stroked them across her cheek. She lightly dragged them to her neck, a touch so soft she had to concentrate hard to even feel it, but in that concentration her pulse quickened. She gazed down at the camp, watched the blurry shape of Jake stoking the fire. She moved the hairs over her lips and smiled. She smelled them. They smelled like nothing. She curled her tongue around them. They tasted like nothing. She put them in her mouth. Ground them down with her teeth. Then she filled her mouth with spit and swallowed them.

* * *

NEW COLD WINDS had arrived and were charging the air around them, turning it buzzy and sharp. The Community built the campfire a little larger that morning and pulled their skins from their bed. Soon the animals would retreat to the mountain foothills and they would follow, congregating in the hollows until the snowmelt raised the rivers.

They had been in this camp too long. It was too easy to stay in the Valley. The game was good. The river was close. To some of them, it still felt like home. They were avoiding making their next walking plan when they saw a figure approaching. Assuming it was a Ranger coming to tell them to leave, a few groaned, and they all went back to staring at the fire, eating their porridge.

But as the figure got closer, they could see it wasn't a Ranger. Too small. Not in uniform. No truck.

The Originalists and Newcomers all touched the place on their bodies where they kept a knife or a rock, whatever weapon they held onto for safety.

As the person drew closer, they could see it was a middle-aged woman, soft around the middle, with a sensible haircut under a deep brimmed hat and good hiking boots, the kind a Ranger would wear. The kind someone would wear who knew the kind of walking necessary in the Wilderness State. The exact opposite of the footwear the Newcomers had arrived in.

The stranger's face was in shadow, but she moved quickly around sage and rocks like she knew the terrain.

"Is she one of yours?" Carl whispered to Frank.

"No."

"Must be a new one then. Why didn't they tell us someone was coming?"

Frank shrugged. "Don't ask me."

Carl rose to greet the stranger, his hand on his knife.

Agnes slunk to a rock, ahead of Carl. She felt a need to get closer. She watched the stranger approach. Her pulse quickened. Her neck prickled.

The woman finally overtook the edge of camp, her face obscured by the hat. She walked toward Carl, who had been briskly approaching, but slowed, suddenly full of uncertainty.

The woman tipped her hat back off her face and then they could see her. The camp hushed. Even the birds hushed. The deer huffed, stamped, and bounded away.

"Well, don't all say hello at once," said Bea, her hands on her hips. She laughed from behind a scowling smile, a kind of laugh they'd never heard from her. Her breath turned to smoke in the cold morning air.

Part V

FRIEND OR FOE

AGNES WATCHED HER mother that first day from the depths of a dream. At times seeing her felt as jarring as a nightmare.

Bea had walked up to camp like a dangerous stranger. Like a Ranger. Laughing and gruff. Her back and neck tight. Ready to start citing violations, threats. Her breath fogged out of her mouth as though she were a furious winter animal. But Agnes had known before anyone else who it was. When they still had their hands on the knives or stones, Agnes was cowering, trying to disappear.

Carl had greeted her mother first.

"Well, look who it is," he cooed, embracing her longer than necessary, laughing in her ear, then strangely listing with her as though they were slow-dancing.

Her mother frowned. "Am I in the right place?" she said over his shoulder.

"Yes," he said. "Everything's different now."

"No shit," she'd murmured as she pulled away and looked around. People had begun to gather. Curious faces peered at her.

Her mother ducked her head and lowered her voice as though to tell a secret, and it was in a way. Agnes could not hear it.

"In off the waitlist," Carl said, sweeping his arm toward the rest of camp. "We've doubled in size!"

"That's a lot of people to feed."

"Nothing we can't handle," he said, taking Bea's hand.

Agnes saw her mother frown again. She looked around the camp for something, casually at first, then frantic, as though fearful she wouldn't find it. Then her eyes locked on Agnes. Flashes of emotions crossed her face. They quickly resolved into a frown. Then a tearful smile. But Agnes could only see the frown, her mother's hand kneading Carl's absently as she gazed at Agnes.

Her mother floated to her, drawn like a magnet.

"Hey, you look great," Carl called after her, licking his lips. He looked famished.

Agnes froze on the stone where she perched and willed herself to become the stone, or become stone-like, a wall of stone. Stony in the face of this person. Even as her heart thumped and her eyes watered as though she'd eaten something bitter and sour, unripe. *Play dead*, she instructed herself.

Agnes felt a hand on her shoulder and realized Val was there next to her. Perhaps had been next to her the whole time, watching Carl and her mother, perhaps feeling as bewildered as Agnes did right now. Agnes looked up at Val. Her face was twisted, disappointed, no doubt, to be looking at Bea again. Val had a much clearer sense of her feelings. Agnes tried to conjure a similar clear disappointment, but she couldn't.

Her mother stopped a foot away from Agnes, her face a mask of emotions, none of which Agnes understood. Her mother didn't reach for her. Agnes's stoniness had kept her at bay. She shivered there perched on her lonely rock, her knees up and hugged to her, her toes gripping.

Finally her mother cleared her throat, and Agnes instantly opened herself to whatever her mother would say after so long.

"Why is my daughter so skinny?" she barked, eyeing Val.

Agnes blinked. *She is not even talking to me.*

Val squeezed Agnes's shoulder hard. "She's always been skinny."

Bea looked around at all the new faces gawking at her. Her face was accusatory, but her eyes were welling. "She's skinnier than every single person here," Bea choked.

"I hadn't noticed," said Val.

Bea nudged Agnes's chin up with her knuckle. "Why are you so skinny? Are you not getting enough food?"

Her voice lashed Agnes's ears. Her nudge felt like a blow.

Agnes pulled her face back down. She was embarrassed. Scared. Angry. She clamped her mouth shut.

"What the fuck is going on here, Carl?" Bea was saying, walking away from Agnes.

"Calm down, for fuck's sake," Carl muttered, all the warmth of his first greeting gone. "You sound like a damn lunatic. Agnes is fine."

Her mother's voice had dropped, hushed to make her words private, though they weren't. "So help me if you've been keeping food from her. Where is Glen? He better not be wasting away too. You motherfucker, Carl."

Agnes looked down at herself. She thought she looked normal. Like she always did. Her stomach growled as it always did. Didn't everyone's? She pulled at her smock and let it drape back.

Carl grabbed her mother by the arm and leaned in close, hissing something into her ear, his finger at her neck, as though it were the point of something more cutting. Her mother's face flickered through emotions, and then she gasped and recoiled from Carl, her face filled with disgust but also sadness. She watched Carl walk away, a slight tremble in her hand. She looked around at all the people watching her, all the new eyes. Agnes noticed the Originalists were pretending to be busy, their ears perked, their heads down, much like Agnes herself had been. But the Newcomers were at attention, their jaws slack, staring unabashedly at Carl and her mother's exchange.

Bea straightened and turned back to Agnes. Her face was bloodless. She moved slowly toward her. Breathed cautiously as though catching her breath. "But look at you," she finally said, her voice pitched high. "You're grown up now. I go away for a little tiny bit and you're all grown up, I guess."

Even with feigned pleasantness, Agnes could hear accusation in her voice.

"I guess—" said Agnes, faltering. She tried to steady her voice, but it was coming out haltingly, as though she might cry. Her throat was heating up, and soon, she felt, she might be sputtering and she did not want that. "I guess you've been gone awhile, Bea," she muttered, and the tremble calmed slightly when she saw her mother wince. Even Val breathed in sharply. Or was she stifling a laugh?

Her mother recovered. "I think I still prefer *Mom*," she said, smiling again. "Besides it hasn't been that long, has it?" She looked from Agnes to Val, then around to see if anyone was watching.

Everyone was watching.

Val said, "It's been a very long time."

"No," Bea said, her voice insistent and irritated. "Not that long."

But Agnes knew they'd seen snows right after her mother had left, then lived among blooms, then summer-dried grasses, turning leaves, and now the scent of snow was in the air again. It's what they used to call a year, and that's how long her mother had been gone. Her mother would never admit that, though. She might claim the weather could not be trusted. Agnes opened her mouth to speak, but her mother's eyes prompted her to shut it. There was no argument to be had. The emotion of the reunion had already flared when their eyes had locked. If her mother felt bad or was sorry, then Agnes had missed the signal. And now it was a memory.

"And your hair," her mother said. "What happened to your beautiful hair?" She reached out and smoothed a hand over Agnes's head.

Agnes ducked out from under her hand.

"Okay, that's enough." Her mother snapped her fingers. And Agnes begrudgingly brought her head back for inspection.

"Who cut it?"

Agnes shrugged.

"Well," her mother said, cupping Agnes's head, "at least your skull is perfectly round. I did a good job turning you in your crib. You don't see a skull that lovely and round every day. I guess I was a good mother after all, huh?" She laughed and looked to Val, who flashed a false, sour smile back at her. "Well," her mother said, "I love your hair short. It's very you."

"I'm growing it out," Agnes mumbled, picking the grime from between her toes and balling it with her fingers.

Agnes's mother stepped toward her. "Come here," she commanded, wrapping her arms around her daughter, pulling her from her stone perch slowly so Agnes's legs unfolded and planted beneath her. Agnes wiped the toe jam onto her mother's hip as she lightly pressed her hands against her. She was offering an approximation of affection, a studied version of it. It felt like what her mother often offered. Then Agnes slid from her embrace, back onto the stone as though she had always been a part of it. Her arms lay across her knees, her head propped, bored, atop her arms. She watched the fire. She felt dizzy. She willed her mother to move on.

"What are you doing back?" Val said, more accusation than question.

"I was just wondering that myself," her mother said. "Where is Glen?" But it wasn't a question for anyone in particular. She knew where Glen was.

Her mother grabbed Agnes's arm and she tumbled off the stone. Agnes's legs wobbled underneath her. She'd never felt as unsteady, knocked over.

Her mother headed straight to the caves. It was as natural as if her mother and Glen had planned this meeting long ago. Her mother had a sense for Glen, as though she had sniffed him out. Would her mother still have had a sense for Agnes if she had been the one off in the cave? Agnes thought of her stormy face as she'd looked out among the new and old faces at camp and found Agnes's. How her mother had spoken not to her but to Val. How stupid her heart had felt. How silly it was to want or feel anything. But she stopped her mind's progression and rewound, tried to think again of the moment when their eyes had met. And hadn't there been a momentary calm when the tumult, for both of them, had halted? *If I could just stay in that*, she thought. It was a thought, a yearning, that helped her gather her balance, get her feet right and under her. A thought that relaxed her arm and shoulder and allowed her to slip her hand into her mother's as they walked.

*   *   *

GLEN WAS FACEDOWN on a skin at the mouth of the cave, his arm flung over his head. He looked like a pile of discarded branches. Agnes felt a pang once again. She'd only slept there with him a couple of nights before he insisted she return to the camp. He didn't want her to become an outcast. She hadn't gone to see him yesterday. There had been too much to do. But without her, he had no company. Agnes peered at her mother's face as they approached, trying to register the emotion there. Would she keep Glen company now? Would he want her to? She didn't remember ever seeing him angry after her mother left. Agnes braced for what that might look like.

Her mother toed Glen's armpit, and he moved his arm and peered up at her.

"You're back," he croaked.

"I'm back," she said.

"I heard the cheers."

They both laughed.

Agnes frowned. There had been no cheering. She looked from face to face, her eyes like crickets pinging back and forth. This was not what she had expected.

"Sorry I didn't get up," Glen said, rolling over.

"It's okay," her mother said.

"I'm weak."

"I know."

"You were gone a long time."

"I know."

He was quiet. "It's okay," he said, and Agnes knew he meant it.

Agnes blinked in surprise. How could he not be angry? Her mother hadn't even apologized.

Glen sat up a bit against a rock. "I did not think you'd come back, though."

"I almost didn't." She cast her eyes toward Agnes but would not meet her gaze.

"I wish you hadn't," Glen said. And Agnes startled at his declaration. And at his tone. He sounded sad.

Glen scooted to the side of the skin, and her mother lay next to him.

"Oh, you poor man," her mother said. "There's nothing left."

Her mother pulled a skin over the two of them and he tried to push it away, but she held tight and he relented. They lay there like that, quietly. They seemed to have forgotten that Agnes was there. She crouched at their feet.

Agnes could see her mother's eyes, open and alert. They gleamed, catching light as she roamed them over Glen's skinny and forlorn body. Then she closed them and they lay, as though asleep. They were so peaceful. Agnes had not imagined they could look like this ever again. Her parents together in the hum of near sleep. Agnes's foot began to bounce. She longed to join them, but felt strangely unwelcome.

She waited a few minutes, then slipped under the pelt, at the feet of her parents. She curled up and found her mother's ankle and encircled her hand around it. But her mother pulled it away. Agnes took this as proof that she was indeed intruding and prepared to retreat. But then, her mother's foot returned and slid under Agnes's side. And Agnes clamped onto her ankle so she could not take it away again.

Glen sighed. "Things have changed."

"I can see that."

"No, but it's more."

Agnes held her breath for the more. Glen lifted his head slightly, as though to peer down at her. She shut her eyes.

Her mother cleared her throat and shifted subjects. "Aren't you going to ask me why I left?"

"I know why you left. Your mother died," he said, his voice quieter.

She did not say anything for a few minutes.

"But when your mother died, you didn't leave," she said finally.

"I didn't like my mother," he said.

"I didn't like your mother either," she said.

They laughed.

"Do you feel better?" Glen asked.

"No." She sighed. "What are things like here now?"

"Not good. What are things like in the City?"

"Not good."

They laughed again.

Agnes didn't think any of this was funny.

"Is Carl in charge?"

"Basically."

"And everyone is okay with that?" Her mother's voice was accusatory as it rushed out.

"Well, no. But enough people are. The Newcomers really flocked to him."

"I see." She paused. "You should still be in charge," she said.

"I was never in charge, Bea. We all were." He sighed, tired now of talking.

"It was never true consensus."

"Yes, it was." Glen raised his voice as much as Glen ever raised his voice.

"We discussed. You offered a thought and we agreed with you."

"That's not true."

"It's true enough. And it worked."

Glen sighed. "Now Carl and his people make the decisions."

"Like not feeding you and Agnes. Or the others, as far as I could tell. How did that happen?"

"A couple of Newcomers took over dishing meals."

"And they give you less food?"

"There's no evidence of anything like that."

"But—"

"They're just taking care of their own first. It's probably subconscious. They don't even know they're doing it. I mean, they're all very nice. It's a nice group," he said, and Bea cackled.

"You and your bright side. There's no way they don't know what they're doing."

"Well, I guess you'd know." His voice was sharp. He was exhausted and bewildered, and somewhere underneath all that maybe he was angry. Agnes felt foolish for not seeing it before.

Agnes heard her mother breathe quickly like she was about to spit back some explanation, her whole body tensing to make her point. But she released it all with a long slow exhale.

They were silent again.

Agnes felt her mother shift and lean into Glen. She said quietly, "So, you want me to get rid of them?"

Glen chuckled.

"And by that I mean murder them?"

Glen erupted into laughter that led to choking coughs. Agnes looked at her mother, and she was grinning quietly to herself as she enjoyed Glen's moment of happiness. Agnes hadn't heard him laugh this much since before her mother had left. Since before that. Since, she realized, before Madeline.

He regained his breath and squeezed her mother. "I missed you."

"I missed you too." Her mother tucked into him more, her foot shifting away from Agnes slightly. Agnes held tight.

"What can I do?" Her mother's voice sounded small. Like Agnes's used to. When she lived in the City. When there was so much that was bigger than her. So much beyond her control. When she didn't realize she had any control.

"Make nice," he said. "Just make nice."

Agnes heard them kiss.

"I feel like such an idiot for bringing you here," Glen said. "Both of you."

"You know what would have happened if you hadn't."

"I just feel so stupid that I didn't see this coming. I thought a group of people who wanted to be here would figure out how to be here together."

"Should we break off from the rest of the Community?"

"I think it's safer to be a part of it than to be a potential enemy."

Her mother nodded.

"Besides, it's against the Manual to splinter."

"And we wouldn't want to make the Manual angry."

"Bea."

"Sorry."

Agnes felt them melt closer to each other. And then felt Glen soften as he drifted to sleep. But she knew her mother was awake. She knew they were both monitoring Glen's breathing.

Birds somberly called to their friends in the sagebrush somewhere near her feet. A dark cloud lay across the sky like a dirt path.

"Why are you back?" Agnes whispered, not sure if it was more of a complaint or a question.

Her mother's muffled reply floated down over the skin, over Glen's small body. "Because you and Glen needed me."

Agnes bristled. For a moment she felt like the time away had rendered her mother readable. Agnes no longer felt so mystified by her. "Wrong," Agnes snapped.

Her mother's sigh floated down to her ear. "Then why am I back, Agnes?"

"Because *you* needed *us*," Agnes said, mustering as much confidence as she would need to sound convincing.

"That is true too," her mother said. Her voice was as flat as the shadows that crept away from them now that the sun had reached its zenith and had begun to fall. She did not say more.

Agnes was surprised into silence. Even if she was right about her mother, it hadn't offered any relief. Knowing her mother's reasoning didn't mean she understood it. If her mother did indeed need her,

Agnes still didn't know what that need felt like. She tucked her hands between her knees and curled into herself to make her own warmth.

*   *   *

AGNES FOUND HER mother shadowing the morning chores, as though attempting to relearn them. The morning crew that day were mostly Newcomers who somehow still weren't very good at their jobs. They seemed not to know what to do with her mother, so she simply stood to the side observing as they chaotically dished out porridge, or later haphazardly did the camp kitchen clean, her arms crossed and her brow frowning. Agnes imagined her mother was not so much relearning as critiquing.

When the food was put away, bowls cleaned, wood added and the fire stoked, Frank stood up, wiped his hands on his jeans, because he still had jeans, though they had been thoroughly patched with elk hide scraps by now, and walked over to her mother.

"Hi," he said, extending his hand.

"Hi," her mother said.

"I'm Frank," he said.

"Hi, Frank," she said, not offering her name in return.

He smiled at her expectantly. When he got no response, he nodded his head at Agnes. She reluctantly returned the gesture and sidestepped slowly up to them.

Frank smiled. "Hi, Agnes."

"Hi."

To Bea he said, "So you must be Agnes's mom?"

"I am," her mother said.

"And so you're back from the Private Lands?"

"Excuse me?"

"You decided to come back?"

"Yes. From the City."

"Oh." Frank frowned. "I thought you were in the Private Lands."

"I don't know why you thought that, but I was in the City."

"That's what someone said. You ran off with a Ranger to the Private Lands and you were raising a family out there."

"That's absurd. My family is right here." She pinched Agnes's shoulder and drew her to her side.

Frank pointed at Agnes. "I thought you told me that."

"Did you now?" her mother said.

"No," said Agnes. "I said you were dead."

Her mother flinched. She saw it.

Frank eyed them nervously. "Well, I don't remember who said what. It doesn't really matter, does it?" He laughed. "But," he continued, "I imagine you're proud of this girl here. I would have thought she was the leader of this Community when we first met."

"How interesting. Just how proud do you imagine I am?"

"Well," Frank said, eyes darting between the two, "pretty darn proud, I'd say."

They all nodded and fell into silence, as though waiting for her mother to say she was proud. But Agnes knew she wouldn't say that. Not when some stranger told her to. Her mother did not like being told how to feel. And Agnes could tell her mother did not like the Newcomers. Her mother then, without a word, left the camp. Headed back in the direction of Glen. Agnes stood there limp-armed, injured at not having been invited. And hesitant to visit Glen herself, something she'd never been hesitant to do before.

When her mother returned, she spent the rest of the day greeting and meeting everyone. Agnes had never seen her so social. She approached the old Originalists with hugs and whispers. First Juan. They laughed and spoke conspiratorially. "Tell me everything," she heard him hiss. Then Debra, who embraced her mother and wouldn't let her mother pull away until she was done. She even hugged Dr. Harold. No one seemed to have anything against her for leaving. Except Val, Agnes noted. *But that's because Val wants to protect me,* she thought. Her mother didn't approach Val, and Val pretended not to notice her mother making the rounds. Her mother approached Carl several times during the day, as though she kept remembering things to tell him. She would put her hand on his shoulder, speak, and then they would laugh, or they would turn serious. It felt like they had very important business, though they'd never had important business before. Agnes watched Val watch this. Val frowned all day.

When her mother went up to a Newcomer, she flashed smiles galore. She was ingratiating and humble. She leaned in and touched the Newcomer's arm. She approached Frank again and had him laughing within seconds.

Once everyone was met, re-met, cajoled, placated, charmed, her mother retreated to the sidelines and observed. When she helped with chores, she did not lead, did not offer opinions, did not say much. Just watched. She was studying how the Community had come to work in her absence.

Agnes watched her mother watch everyone else. She wanted to know what her mother was seeing so she could know what her mother was thinking. She watched for what her mother would notice about everyone after time away, or on first observing them.

Agnes saw that Frank was broad and tall, but weak. His stomach skin hung wrinkled and sagging as though he'd just given birth. A formerly well-fed man. A beer-bellied man. Agnes saw his fingertips were stained and shredded and scabbed over like all of their fingertips had been when they first arrived. Unused to the coarseness of bark and stones, of the tannins of skins and nut husks, wild foods. But whereas the Newcomers' hands were all now properly calloused, his were still scabbed over. He was not working as hard as everyone else, though he always seemed to be in the middle of some chore. He had Carl's ear, though, and that meant something.

She noticed that Patty's mom was unhappy with how much time Patty spent with Celeste. Agnes noticed that she was also unhappy with how much time Frank spent with Carl. Patty's mom busied herself with chores around camp. She acted busy to hide that she was lonely, bored, and possibly feeling scorned. Agnes saw that Joven and Dolores were spending more time with Jake than with their mother, Linda, who was spending most of her time with Carl, when Carl wasn't spending his time with Val or Frank. Or Helen, Agnes noticed. Her mother spent a lot of time watching Carl. Carl and his grayed temples, something Agnes had not noticed before. She saw that Debra was hiding a subtle limp. Agnes felt foolish for missing some of these things.

She saw that Val wore Carl's oversized buckskin jacket as though she were hiding—or protecting—her belly. She did this whenever she hoped she was pregnant, which was often. She wanted a child so badly. But she had just had her period. It was one of those things that could not remain private in a Community like this. Agnes felt bad for Val, who she feared would scowl till her dying breath if she could not have this one thing.

Val looked small in Carl's coat, but actually she looked healthy, plump almost. What Agnes then noticed was how skinny all the Originalists were. The Newcomers looked as though they still held onto some of their City fat. And Carl and Val looked solid and healthy. But the other Originalists were lanky, shadows of themselves. Skinniest was Glen.

She watched her mother watch Glen, and Agnes felt broken-hearted. She saw then that the Newcomers mostly avoided Glen, who had wandered back to camp for a meal, a serene look on his face as he waited in line with a bowl. His legs bowed unnaturally. His ribs showed through his hunched back. None of this was so different from the other bodies around, and it was all what Agnes had seen before. But what Agnes saw for the first time, and what she was certain her mother had noticed, was that he stumbled. His sure-footedness was gone. He walked worse than the Newcomers, who weren't used to stones and roots, the way the ground had natural variations unlike the smooth concrete floors and level streets of the City. It was a big difference. Glen's feet seemed to have forgotten the texture of the earth. It was the kind of thing that would be hard to come back from.

*   *   *

THAT NIGHT BEA joined the Community around the fire after dinner. This was the time when everyone was able to relax. The time
when stories were told or reminiscences shared. Bea knew this tradi-
tion. She knew people had questions for her. Agnes imagined that's
why she had avoided it as long as she had. She had been back for three
days. When Bea sat down, the group murmured. Carl announced,
"Our storyteller has arrived." There was even a smattering of ap-
plause. Bea blushed, visible even in firelight, as she took a seat. She
spoke quietly, and the Community leaned in.

She had taken four trucks and a cargo plane to get back to the City.
The first thing she did was shower until the water allotment ran out.
Then, twenty-four hours later, she showered again until the water
allotment ran out. Then she binged on spaghetti and potato chips.
Then she was sick for several days. And then for several more days
she felt afraid to leave the building. The City was loud and bright, the
sun gleaming off every surface. She closed all the curtains and curled
into bed for days. People around the fire closed their eyes, imagining doing that too. When she gathered the courage, she went out
and took care of some business, she said, flinching at the memory, and
Agnes knew she meant tending to Nana's affairs. And then, she said,
she explored.

"What did you see?" they asked.

"I saw some beautiful sunsets because of the smog. There's even
more smog than before. The buildings seem taller, which I didn't think
possible, and their steel and glass reflected those sunsets in a really
pretty way."

"What else?"

"There were so many different vegetables in the market, such
bright colors. I could have stood and looked at the produce forever."

"What did you eat?"

"Well . . ." She paused, embarrassed. "The lines were incredibly long, and often, by the time I got into the store, most of the freshest food was gone. You had to go early in the morning. So I mostly ate potatoes and green peppers." She saw their disappointment. "But a few times I did manage to purchase some beautiful fruit and greens." She brightened.

"And?"

"They were good." Their eyes egged her on. "Perfect-looking." She shook her head. "But not what I remember. Pretty colors but not a lot of flavor. The wild onions here are astounding in comparison."

People began to shift uncomfortably.

"Well, what else did you see?" said Debra, a bit of an edge in her voice.

"I went into a store that sold kitchenware, and all the pots and pans are so pretty and clean."

They waited.

"And?"

She thought and they held onto her silence. "Honestly," she said, drooping, "I saw mostly terrible stuff."

The Newcomers nodded. The Originalists said, "Different terrible stuff? Or the same terrible stuff as before?"

"The same, but worse."

She told them there was more debris in the streets. The smog hung low like a fog you walked through. Lines snaked out of every shop. Fights breaking out over something like broccoli.

She said more people were squeezing into the existing buildings because there was no room to build more. "Plus, there's no more sand for concrete."

"What?"

Bea shrugged. "Look, I don't know. That's just what I heard."

On her floor of the building, it seemed like each apartment now held several families instead of just one. But even as that was happening, she said, several of the children from the building had died. She looked at Agnes, wet-eyed. Agnes felt a lurch inside as she tried to re-member the names of her friends. Glen had remembered them—why couldn't she? They were dead now. She wasn't.

Bea said there were many more people who lived on the street, but she didn't know where they went after curfew.

"Underground," said Frank, matter-of-factly. Patty's mom swatted him. "Let her talk," she snapped. Patty's mom was drunk on Bea's information. As though secretly she loved the City and all its flaws.

"Just outside the City limits, there are camps. I think they go there. I don't know how they get through the checkpoints, though."

Frank whispered "Underground" out of the side of his mouth, away from his wife.

"The trees, that handful of surviving trees scattered and gated around the City? All dead. Someone bombed them all. Some counter-cultural group." The Newcomers nodded again. *"Gangs,"* mouthed Frank.

"There was violence everywhere instead of in smaller pockets. I was afraid when I was outside. People ring your bell and you can't answer the door. It's not safe." The Newcomers nodded at this too. They seemed to know about it all. Bea had seen the City they left be-hind. There was not much new she could tell them, but still it seemed they'd hoped for something different.

Bea fell into silence, and everyone, especially the Originalists, looked disappointed. This isn't what they hoped new stories from the City would be like.

Not that long ago, Agnes remembered, they were telling stories *about* her mother. They referred to her as the Deserter in the sto-ries. They imagined the many lives she might be leading then. They called them Ballads, and they took some wild turns, as stories do. Some ended with her heading up a new Administration and tearing down the buildings of the City, though they never decided where people would live after that. That wasn't the job of fire-time stories.

Recently, after spending the season in the mountains, Juan had told a Ballad that ended with Bea opening the borders of the Wilderness State so others could come in.

"But," Patty's mom had said, "we don't want that. Do we?"

They looked around the fire and shook their heads. No one wanted more people to come. The Newcomers disliked the idea most of all.

"If you let more people in, soon it's gonna look like the City," said Frank.

Linda had picked up the tale then, and Bea was back safely in the City, where she'd found a hovel of rats on the outskirts and was ruler of their gang. She was married and pregnant again, this time with a litter of rats with human hands. She and her rat gang were resisters looking to overthrow the Administration.

"What's an Administration?" Pinecone had asked. No one answered him.

Agnes hated the stories at first, when her mother's absence was fresh and hurtful. She blocked out those early stories. As time passed, and she started listening, she would think about adding to the story and realize she had nothing to say. She found it impossible to imagine what her mother was doing in the City. It had to have changed. Her mother certainly had changed. And so it seemed impossible that her mother was actually there.

That's when Agnes started a new strain of Ballads.

"You know she never made it to the City, don't you?" Agnes had said one night around the fire.

They were silent for a moment.

Then Debra started to nod her head. "I heard she perished in the Fallow Lands."

"I heard she was imprisoned and now works the Mines," said Linda.

The scenarios tumbled out of their mouths.

"She missed greens too much, so she's gone to work the Greenhouses."

"She was barred from the City and is hiding in the Refineries."

"She's sandbagging along the New Coast."

"She's a Meat™ maker."

"She's on the Flotilla."

"She's in the Private Lands," Val offered.

Some of the Newcomers *ooh*ed at the thought. They thought the Private Lands were real, and Agnes knew that if they'd had a choice, they'd rather be there than the Wilderness.

But Carl said, "Oh, come on, Val. There's no such thing."

But if there were such a thing, everyone would feel so betrayed. And Val knew that.

"She's in the Farmland drinking milk," said Juan.

They groaned amorously for milk.

"She's sitting on the hill over there," Agnes said. "Watching us."

Deep down, they all thought this was the most believable story.

They crawled into their beds thinking of the Deserter watching over them. Some of them thought her dead, because it was less eerie to imagine her watching over them as a spirit than as a stalker. That was what Agnes wanted. For others to think her mother was dead. She was tired of being the only one who believed it.

Across the fire now, her mother seemed tired, drained. Her shoulders slumped as though conjuring the City had taxed her beyond her powers. "Is there anything else you want to know," she mumbled, trying to seem engaged. She was trying to impress—Agnes could see that. She was the Newcomer now, or that's how she might have felt. Agnes imagined she did not like that feeling.

Juan cleared his throat. "Well, so we know the City is terrible." He looked around and everyone nodded. Some rolled their eyes. Her mother bowed her head, as though embarrassed. She had always been the best storyteller. But this story was proving hard to tell. Juan continued, encouragingly, "But what I want to know is . . ." He paused for effect. "Did you drink any milk?"

The group tittered, bashful. They wanted good memories, not

warnings. Her mother laughed, almost delightedly, as though she had found a purpose. And with her face newly animated, said, "Did I drink milk? *Did I drink milk!*"

Agnes stood and left the fire.

She could hear her mother finally captivating the group. She'd found her stride. The Community *ooh*ed and *aah*ed and giggled, and her mother laughed that strange laugh. Her mother must be making everything up now. Or these things were true and it was the bad parts she'd made up. How could such a terrible place make so many people happy like this?

Agnes curled at the bottom of the bed and shivered. Glen was in the cave, sleeping there still. Agnes couldn't warm the skins herself. It was why a family was nice to have out here.

She stared into the sky, wide-awake for a long while, tracking night fliers above her and the roaming stars. Eventually she heard people retiring to the beds, the talk around the fire subdued to a murmur.

Her mother arrived soundlessly. She pulled a skin from the top and lay under it, hugging her knees up, keeping her feet away from her daughter.

Agnes huffed.

Her mother murmured, "But why don't you come up here and sleep where it's really warm."

"Because I sleep down here." She added, "And maybe Glen will come."

"He won't," her mother said, and then her hands were gripping Agnes's arm and leg, dragging her up to hold her against her stomach. Her mother's chin dug sharply on the top of her head.

"Did you have fun stalking me all day?" her mother cooed. Agnes squirmed. "You don't have to watch me all the time," she said. "I'm not going to leave."

Agnes went limp like prey. It hadn't occurred to her that she was keeping tabs on her mother for fear she'd leave. She just didn't trust her.

"I know you are angry with me. But someday you won't be." Her mother spoke calmly, as though hypnotizing her. She stroked Agnes's new short hair abrasively. And Agnes felt a pang, the memory of a comforting pain, of her mother brushing out the snarls of her child-ish long hair under the electric lights of their apartment.

"I'm sorry I left," she said, "but now I'm back. I had my reasons. Okay?" Her mother's body quickly warmed the bed; then the heat melted Agnes and she curled herself into her mother. She had missed this feeling. She felt as though she'd just put down something heavy that she'd carried for many miles. Her muscles burned as they relaxed.

Agnes felt youngest again. Somewhere in her deepest memory, she recalled that when she felt really sick, but also other times, the only way to feel better was to crawl into her mother's bed. To learn anything about the world, about life, or about her, Agnes had to nes-tle alongside her.

Agnes let out a relieved sigh so long it sounded mournful. "Did you really drink a lot of milk?" she asked.

"Sometimes you have to give the people what they want."

Agnes frowned, and her mother must have felt the frown on her arm because she said, "I drank a little, honey. It's really too expensive to drink it all the time."

"Describe it."

"Cold, creamy. Like cold spring water and animal fat. It coats your whole mouth. And when you're thirsty, it's better than water. If it's cold."

"I remember."

"Do you? But do you remember that it tastes bad after you've swal-lowed it? Like a minute later, it's already old in your mouth. Gross."

"Was it always like that?"

"I think our tastes have changed. But I can't tell them that. I don't want to ruin milk for everyone."

"But you made them miss it still."

"It's better to miss something you can't have than think there's nothing worth missing."

"Then why did you tell me?" Agnes had loved milk.

"Because you can handle it."

Agnes blushed. She knew this was a compliment. She wormed closer. "What else didn't you tell them?"

"Are you sure you want to know?"

Agnes nodded eagerly.

Her mother told her that there were animals in the City. Not just the rats that had been in some parts but now different types of animals. No one ever saw them because they came out at night, after curfew. But she went outside after curfew and was alone in the empty streets under the towers of steel and glass and stone, and she saw their eyes in alleys, saw them scurry by. Rats, of course, but also raccoons, opossums, snakes, coyotes. Just before curfew lifted, they went back into hiding. She told Agnes that the stars were even better than they were here. Something she'd never known because she'd not been outside after curfew when the lights of the City were cut. But in the middle of the night the smog cleared for her and she saw the dust of galaxies.

"Does that mean we're going back?" Agnes asked. Perhaps her mother had spent so much time there trying to prepare for their inevitable return. She had never really wanted to be here in the Wilderness. Agnes knew that.

But her mother became stern, scary. "No," she snapped. "We can never go back."

"Why?"

"There's nothing for us there. There's nothing there for anyone. And more people are seeing that now."

"Like the Newcomers?"

Her mother made a small grunt acknowledging them. "I'll bet we're going to get a lot more Newcomers the longer we are here. But I promise you, whatever happens, we will not return to the City."

"But what if we have to leave?" Agnes swallowed hard. It was not a possibility she had considered before. But her mother had brought the outside world back with her when she returned. And it was affecting how Agnes saw her future.

"We won't."

"But if we have to. Where else would we go?"

Her mother paused, lowered her voice, and said, "I would take us to the Private Lands."

Agnes waited for her mother to laugh. Her mother hated conspiracy theories, and the story of the Private Lands was the biggest one she knew. Her mother used to say that the Private Lands were what people believed in when they'd lost all hope. She meant it disparagingly. Agnes had heard a lot more about the Private Lands from Jake and the Twins. Their parents, the adult Newcomers, all believed in it. But Jake and the Twins didn't. They'd been born into this world as it was. They didn't imagine there could be some secret alternative. Why would there be?

"But," Agnes ventured, "the Private Lands aren't real."

Her mother leaned in and whispered. "That's what I used to think too. But here's another thing I didn't tell them." She nodded her head to the fire. "They *are* real. And I know where they are."

"Where?" Agnes felt like she was talking to a child laying out her make-believe world.

"Near here. You have to cross the Mines panhandle, but then you are there, in one of the corners. Apparently it's an enormous place."

"Did you try to go there?" Agnes asked, knowing that she must have. If she'd been gone so long in a place as terrible as the City, it had to be because she was trying to get somewhere that promised to be better.

"No, of course not. I was trying to get back to you."

"You must have. It's why you were gone so long."

"I wasn't gone that long," her mother insisted, as though she couldn't accept the real length of her absence.

"You were gone so long," cried Agnes.

"Agnes." Her mother's tone was a warning.

"Didn't you miss me?" Agnes blurted from behind her own private wall.

"Of course I missed you."

Agnes sat bolt upright. "Then how could you?" A thought, one she'd never had before, pressed itself between her eyes like a cold finger. *I would have come.* Agnes had spent all her time wondering why her mother had left, but she hadn't thought to wonder why her mother hadn't grabbed her by the hand as she'd run. Said, *Come on, come on,* and fled, not *from* Agnes but *with* her. Agnes hadn't thought to include herself in the possibilities of that life because her mother hadn't thought to. Had she been thinking at all?

Her mother shushed her and pulled her back into her lap. "Come back," she hissed, and squeezed Agnes hard, possessively. "I love you more than you can understand," she said. "I would do anything for you." She growled, "You're mine," reclaiming Agnes as a creature that could not exist without her.

Agnes stiffened, withdrew her limbs, her self, and crawled back under the corner of the pelt, curled up. She did not want her mother's aggressive overtures of love. She wanted her back rubbed, her cheek caressed. She wanted murmurs against her neck. Her hand held lightly. She wanted to not have to ask questions. To be confused. She wanted confessions she didn't have to demand. She hated her mother's fierce love. Because fierce love never lasted. Fierce love now meant that later, there would be no love, or at least that's what it would feel like. Agnes wanted a mild mother, one who seemed to love her exactly the same every day. She thought, *Mild mothers don't run away.*

Her mother did not try to wrestle her back again. Rather, she watched Agnes for a moment before she closed her bright animal eyes.

Agnes hated that her mind would not let her curl back into her mother. Would not let her run to her without a care or worry or resentment. Would not let her forget that cloud of dust her mother had disappeared into. Yet Agnes shivered in her absence still. Would her mother's whims ever not matter? She fell asleep to the exhalation of her mother's spent breath, and to the urgency of her own thrumming heart.

*   *   *

IN THE MORNING, Agnes woke up under shadow. The Twins stood between her and the sun, disapproving looks on their faces. Her mother was nowhere.

"Let's go," the Twins said in unison.

Agnes stretched out of bed and silently fell in line with them.

"We have decided something," said Celeste as they reached the edge of camp.

"Yes," said Patty. "We have decided there's something really messed up about your mother."

"You said she was dead," Celeste said. "How is she not dead?"

"I thought she was dead," said Agnes.

"Are you a liar?"

"No," cried Agnes. "I thought she *was* dead," she mumbled again.

"Well, are you happy that she's not?" Patty asked.

Agnes thought about the conversation last night, the way she'd relaxed in her mother's arms, how one touch could offer comfort and the lack of it could trigger pain. She thought of how cold she had been upon waking up alone. She did not remember such an empty feeling when her mother had been gone for all that time. Agnes had kept herself warm. It was as though she felt her absence most when she was close enough to touch.

Agnes shrugged. "I guess. I don't know." She stopped. The Twins stopped. "Would your moms ever leave you?" she asked.

Patty shook her head, and Agnes believed her.

"No way," said Celeste. "But I don't think it's because she loves me. She's just too scared to leave me. She hates to do anything by herself. She can't even go to the shit pit by herself."

"Really?"

"Yes. During the day I have to go with her."

"What if you're not there?"

"Maybe she finds someone else, but honestly, I think she holds it. And in the night—" She stopped. "I shouldn't tell you."

"What?"

"She just pees right behind her bed."

"In the sleeping circle?"

"Yeah. She wakes me up to be a lookout, and then she wraps one of the skins around her and squats. It's ridiculous."

"That is so gross," Patty whined.

"Has she gotten caught?"

"Once. She crawled back into bed, and we heard someone say, '*Tsk-tsk*, naughty Helen.'"

"Who was it?"

Celeste rolled her eyes. "Carl, duh."

"Ew," breathed Patty, stepping closer to Celeste.

"Did he say anything in the morning?"

"Oh, probably. I'm sure my mom fucked him and then he was cool with it."

"What?" Agnes and Patty shrieked.

"Oh, yeah," said Celeste. "They are totally fucking."

"Carl?" Agnes said.

"Carl is fucking everyone, basically."

"Not my mom," said Patty.

Celeste raised her eyebrows at Agnes.

They walked again, in silence.

Agnes felt a hand on her shoulder, and Celeste was there, in step and leaning in. "She must have had her reasons," she said. She shrugged. "Right?"

Agnes shrugged back. "She must have."

The Twins led Agnes to a place they called the Patch, a spot they had found with a nice view and a blanket of soft baby grasses. It was

Madeline's place, but the Twins didn't know that and Agnes didn't tell them. It would have grossed them out and they never would have returned. And Agnes thought Madeline might like some company.

Jake was already there, reclining against a rock, the jackrabbit pillow she'd made him propping up his head. She smiled at this. Pillows were absurd out here, but so was he, in a way. His black jeans were shredded into rags at the bottom. But she remembered they'd been like that when she'd first seen him. It wasn't hardship. It was style. His canvas high-tops were still perfectly folded over, and the white rubber toe was still white, even though he'd been walking in them for many, many, many seasons. His bangs were growing out quickly. Agnes would have to offer him another haircut again soon. She blushed.

They weren't supposed to use fur for superfluous things. It was supposed to be used only for warmth. For things like hats and mitten liners. Or to wrap around your neck or your middle on the coldest days. She'd caught the rabbit because it was lame, quaking under a sage. Alone. She'd lunged and caught it by the ears when it fled and tangled itself in the scrubby branches. It was too young to know how to get away. Agnes hated catching animals that way. It was unfair. She was a better hunter than that, and she believed they deserved the chance to be better animals. Also, it was against the rules to hunt young prey. But it appeared to have been abandoned by its mother and the rest of the litter. In that moment, catching it and breaking its neck swiftly felt much kinder than what it otherwise might go through.

She should have donated the fur to the Community, and the meat too. But she'd kept both. She had told Jake that he should hide the pillow. It was nice to share a secret with him. It was nice, also, to break the rules with him. So he took it out only when away from camp. Only around her and the Twins. The pillow was soft, and she enjoyed watching him touch it to his cheek, or absentmindedly stroke it while he told her about something interesting he'd seen that day, or when he wanted to reminisce about the City, because, of all the Newcomers, he seemed to miss it the most.

They sat in a circle and Jake dug into his bag. He pulled out a skin pouch, uncinched it, and handed it to Patty. "One piece each," he reminded them.

Patty pulled out a piece of rabbit jerky and passed it to Celeste.

Celeste peered inside. "You took the biggest one," she muttered. She chose one, scowling, and passed the bag to Agnes. When it returned to Jake, he counted what was left.

"Four more pieces," he said after taking his piece. "I think we should make more."

That lame rabbit had been the first. They'd caught two more and dried the meat, tanned the hides. The Twins now had secret pillows too. But they kept their secret pillows in a secret place.

"Who wants to check the trap?" Jake asked as they chewed their jerky thoughtfully.

Celeste said, "I'll go." She rose and disappeared into the thick bushes where they had set out the dead-drop trap Agnes had made from some branches and a flat rock.

A few minutes later they heard a rustling and footsteps.

"Did it catch?" Agnes called out.

"Did what catch?"

They all spun their heads toward the new voice.

Bea emerged. "Did what catch?" she asked again, frowning, eyes piercing Agnes, as though she already knew the answer.

Agnes mumbled, "Nothing."

"What are you doing here?" her mother asked, her voice a frightening mixture of calm and outrage.

Agnes's mouth dried up. Her mother looked around, her mouth screwing between anger and sorrow. Agnes followed her gaze and saw what her mother saw. Jake's ridiculous shoes. The way Patty picked at the patches of her pants so that they would need to be sewn much sooner than if she'd just left them alone. Agnes saw how close she was sitting to Jake. How their butterflied knees touched. Agnes drew hers in, hugged them, and rocked. She tucked her lips into her mouth. Agnes saw her mother see how they lounged comfortably right where Madeline had been. Agnes might as well be lying on a pile of cleaned and bleached bones. She felt monstrous.

"Answer me," her mother said.

"Nothing."

She saw her mother's hand tremble as it lifted to wipe her brow and knead her eyes. She looked around again and focused on Jake. "What is that?"

"A pillow," he said.

"Where did you get it?"

He tipped his head at Agnes.

"I made it for him," said Agnes.

"We don't use fur for pillows, Agnes. You know that."

"But it was just one fur," Agnes lied.

"He can use skins like everyone else. If you want to do something nice, you can show him how you fold a skin to be *like* a pillow."

"You have a pillow," Agnes said.

"I *had* a pillow," her mother corrected her. "I don't anymore. And it wasn't made at the expense of the Community."

"It caught!" Celeste came bounding out of the bushes with a jack-rabbit by its ears. It kicked its legs as she skipped, swinging it like it was an extension of her arm. Its pelvis looked crushed, but it was still alive. When Celeste saw Bea, she stopped. She looked at the hare. It gave a plaintive cry to whatever hare friend might hear it.

Her mother appraised Celeste, the hare, Agnes, her proximity to Jake, and Patty's attempt to secretly chew jerky.

"The pillow is one thing," she said, "but really, Agnes. Rogue hunting? Keeping food from the Community? That is unacceptable."

"What do you care about the Community?" Agnes snapped, jumping to her feet. "Drinking your milk, breaking curfew. We were better off when we thought you were dead."

Somewhere Agnes heard a gasp. She was not sure where it came from, and wouldn't have been surprised if it had come from her own dry throat.

Her mother's face arched in surprise. She slapped Agnes.

The birds in the bushes were still and silent. Jake had leapt to his feet, but he stayed back.

Her mother's face was on fire. "You think because you lead our walks that makes you an adult. Adults follow the rules or face the consequences. You're still shielded from it all. I won't always be able to protect you, Agnes."

Celeste snorted. "When did you ever protect her?" she said. "I've certainly never seen it."

"And just who the fuck are you?" spat Bea.

Celeste clamped her mouth shut. She looked years younger than she was, like a child on the verge of blubbering. She broke the rabbit's neck urgently, as though trying to reclaim some standing.

"There are ways you can get in real trouble out here, Agnes," her mother said. "This isn't a game."

"I know that."

"Do you?" A worried look overcame her but was quickly replaced again with anger. What was she so angry about? She saw her mother eye the limp rabbit a split second before she swiped the rabbit from Celeste, leaving the girl's hands empty, coated in clumps of fur.

"This animal isn't yours," her mother said, shaking droplets of blood from the slack rabbit's mouth at the Twins and Jake. "It belongs to everyone. And you—" She turned to Agnes, her eyes bloodshot. "This place," she snarled, pointing to the ground, "isn't yours either."

A ghostly feeling formed in Agnes's gut. Something familiar but covered in cobwebs. She stomped her feet. Clenched her fists. "I hate you," she said, forming each word into a hard stone that rolled off her tongue and dropped dead at her mother's feet.

Fleetingly, between postures, her mother gave herself away, slumping more desperately than anything Agnes had seen. Their eyes briefly met. Her mother's held a question, one as desperate as her stance, as needful and longing-filled. Then, like in an eclipse, that vulnerable look was blacked out by one that was hard, intimidating, unloving.

She turned away, throwing that new strange laugh of hers over her shoulder at Agnes. "Of course you hate me," she barked. "I'm your mother." With the rabbit flapping against her thigh, leaving blood splats behind, she disappeared back into the brush. She became untouchable again.

*   *   *

AS AGNES APPROACHED bed that night, she found Glen lying stiffly in the skins. Her mother lay next to him. Their hands touched, index fingers hooked to each other, but no other part of them made contact along their length. They stared up into the sky as though paralyzed, comatose, dead. But when Agnes stood over them, Glen smiled with great effort, his eyes red-rimmed. Her mother's smile was taut and unwelcoming. Still, Glen and her mother scooted apart and made room for her in between them. She didn't understand.

"Come lie down here for the night," Glen said.

Her mother had scooted almost all the way off the bed. *Probably so she would be as far from me as possible*, Agnes thought.

Agnes lay between them. Her mother and Glen held hands over her. Her mother was fidgety, picking at Glen's fingers with hers, as though preoccupied, or nervous. Agnes wondered if it had to do with what she had said to her. She had never said it before. She didn't really hate her mother. Yet her mother had laughed it off. She seemed to expect it.

Agnes turned to her mother slightly. She remembered then how she had often crept into her mother's room in the early dawn. Agnes woke up too early, before the sun was even lightening the sky, but her body, her mind, wouldn't let her fall back to sleep. Her mother would be asleep in her bed on her side. Always open to her, even in sleep. Agnes would curl into her, and her mother's arm would automatically envelop her. And like that, Agnes could doze again until her mother's alarm buzzed.

Agnes scooted toward her mother, but her mother turned away. Her body tense, a barrier, a wall. Glen tried to pull Agnes back, but she reached out, clasped her mother's shoulder, and tried to roll her back.

"I'm sorry, Mama," she whispered, trying to get closer, rooting into her neck, her soft cheek.

But her mother was now rolling away and was up, up to her feet. Quiet like an animal.

Agnes sat up. Glen tried to pull her back down.

"Back to sleep," he sang anxiously.

But she jerked her arm away.

Her mother was slinking across the circle of beds. She stopped at Carl and Val's bed, then crawled under the hide with them. The firelight flickered over them. Around the circle of beds, eyes peered, curious. A moment later, a confused moan, and then a still sleeping Val rolled out from the skins onto the cold dirt. From her sleep, Val clawed at the air, then awoke fully, became alert and reached toward them, for Carl, under the skins. But Bea emerged again, drew her fist back, and struck Val's face. Agnes heard the crunch of bones. Heard Val's cry of pain. Heard the Community's quiet gasps around the sleep circle. Val clasped her nose, but her mother pried Val's hand away and punched her again. And again. Val screamed and howled, then gurgling, turned away. She curled, hand to her face, wheezing through a mangled nose.

Agnes saw her mother use her leg to shove Val's balled-up body away from the bed and farther out into the uncertain glow of the half-moon.

Under where her mother now lay with Carl, there was some commotion, some wrestling; then Agnes heard unmistakable sounds. Animal sounds. Something she'd seen countless times in the wild but couldn't reconcile with the vision before her. Her mother on top of

Carl, bucking as though on horseback. This normal act of life she thought she had figured out becoming strange again. She felt indignant. Around the circle, people brazenly watched the spectacle. Val howled with rage as she crawled away, grabbing Dr. Harold's pelt from his bed, dragging it with her. He let her have it.

Agnes finally wrung the shock from her eyes and sprang up. To stop her mother. To demand an explanation. To punish her. To console Val. To harm Carl. She didn't know what feeling was strongest. But as she rose, a hand clasped her arm and roughly pulled her back down. It was Glen.

"Stay here," he said.

"But Glen—"

"Stay here," he hissed. His grip felt like a shackle.

"But—"

Before she could say another word, he covered her mouth. She felt him quivering, overcome with some emotion. Anger. Sadness. She couldn't tell. She'd never seen him overcome with either.

"It's okay," he said. His voice came from deep in the reeds of his throat.

She thought of her fight with her mother earlier. Of her mother's defeated posture before her knowing laugh. Agnes hadn't spoken to her for the rest of the day. At dinner, her mother had kept her distance. Made small talk with everyone, all the people she used to not spare a thought for. She'd seen her mother throw her head back and laugh at something Dr. Harold had said. Dr. Harold of all people. Then her mother had settled to eat her ration next to Carl. They had huddled strangely close, whispered intensely under the usually light dinner-time chatter. Their conversation serious, sometimes heated. So, so, so close.

Agnes shook her head, trying to dislodge the image, let it fall to the dirt. She felt ill.

"Glen, this is my fault," she said.

"No, it isn't."

"We had a fight."

"This isn't your fault," Glen said. "You can't understand it now, but I promise you it isn't your fault."

She was so tired of not understanding. To not know how it worked made her feel estranged from the world.

Glen didn't say more. He squeezed his eyes shut and started to hum. He leaned closer and hummed in Agnes's ear, and it filled her up with a song that was familiar to her even though it wasn't something that Debra or Juan sang around the fire. It wasn't a song Patty, Celeste, and Jake had tried to tell her about when they talked about all the music they missed. It was something she remembered from when she was younger. When she was sick. A song that floated in under her closed door. A song Glen and her mother listened to on nights when they finished a bottle of wine together. When the sound of silverware clinking against the dinner plates sounded to her like a faint bell signaling the start of something. He hummed it into her ear and covered her other ear with his warm hand. And she was back in her bed, on the mattress that held a small imprint of her because she'd lain on it so much of her short life, back in a place where she had been worse than unwell, but where, she thought, she had been happy.

She squeezed her eyes shut too and her lashes collected hot tears.

Earlier that day, after the slap, after the rabbit, Jake had asked Agnes what her mother's name was.

"Why are you asking me that?" A mote of dread had deepened within Agnes. She didn't want to think about her mother.

"Because I've noticed no one—none of us new people, that is—calls her by her name. We all just call her your mom. *Agnes's mom*."

"Then call her that," Agnes had said angrily, not thinking it could mean anything.

Now, even with eyes clenched and ears covered, Agnes could feel the tension around the fire. The stillness from ears perked and listening to the gripping rhythm of bodies, of Carl calling out "Bea," and a sound that must have been from her mother—a grunt that sounded like it came from behind clenched teeth. Everyone wanting to be alert when something big took place, when the world as they knew it changed. Even the deer that munched dewy grass on the outskirts of the camp were listening. They bleated to their young, to their mates, to make sure they were there and safe. Then they snorted out into the night beyond their sight, *Friend or foe? Friend or foe?* to warn off the unwelcome. In the distance Agnes was certain she heard the wolves howl back. *Foe.*

The Newcomers had called this stranger who'd walked in from the desert *Agnes's mom* because that's how she had let herself be introduced.

They knew her name now.

Part VI

TO THE CALDERA

THEY WERE WAITING for the Gatherers to come back from the mountains with the pine nut harvest when a lone Ranger appeared on horseback.

They hadn't seen a Ranger in three winters. Maybe four. Somehow Agnes could still remember that counting winters was the same as counting years, but she was no longer sure how many had passed. Things had changed since Bea and Carl began leading. Winters were milder. Fire season was longer. Water was becoming harder to find. They spent less time in the mountains. After their last Big Walk, Bea and Carl had refused to do a cross-map migration as in seasons before. Instead, they kept the Community confined to one expansive basin surrounded by small ranges. The Basin was nice enough. It had what they needed. It wasn't beautiful exactly, but they found great comfort there. They landed in the same place twice. Three times. Five times. They hovered. Once they'd found the Basin, they just kept moving around it without ever really leaving.

But it sometimes meant needing longer excursions to harvest or hunt in the places they might, in previous seasons, simply have migrated to. When Gatherers went out to harvest the pine nuts from the foothills and mountains, it meant that the rest of the Community waited in place for longer periods of time, until the Gatherers returned. Same with the Hunters, who, depending on the season, had to track game into those same foothills and mountains. Their camps stood for much longer. At one Community meeting, there was even talk of erecting a smokehouse that was sturdier. More stable. They stopped short of calling it permanent, though that's what they meant. No one said, *We can't*. Or, *We shouldn't*. Or, *This is totally against the rules*. They just talked about it like it was normal for nomadic people to build a permanent structure in this strictly leave-no-trace Wilderness State.

They blamed Big Walk V for that.

Big Walk V had been a hard and grueling walk. Harder and more grueling than Big Walks III or IV, which had been worlds harder and more grueling than the first Big Walk, or Big Walk II. Big Walk V had felt like a forced march. The Rangers were like coals under their feet, their heat unbearable. Whenever they appeared, the Community had to scramble and push ahead. And it felt like the Rangers appeared whenever they had stopped to take a breath. Their resources dwindled, and they were only afforded a few stops along rivers long enough to hunt and process their kills to bulk up their food stores. So they hunted to eat each day and chewed jerky and ate pemmican and hoped their bedding, skins, and clothes lasted, and when they didn't, they wore them in tatters.

They lost a Newcomer newborn on that walk. The first baby born in some time. The first death in some time too. It was a surprisingly difficult loss for a group of people used to losses. Linda, who had not even wanted another baby, wept for days.

But what more is there to say about walking at this point? It takes as long as it takes. Is as difficult as the terrain and not more. The weather varies. Though they saw new things, they were just variations on the things they'd seen on past walks. Hills that looked as though they were moving were only different from past hills because, for whatever reason, these hills looked as though they were moving faster. And in reality, none of the hills had ever moved. Their tips seemed sharper, more like horns than the tongues of past hills from past walks. They were all still hills. And the Community was still a little breathless going up them, even after all this time.

It wasn't that they were fatigued or bored with their surroundings. It was a privilege to experience this sameness. To be able to settle into routine. To luxuriate in one place for far too long and not be too surprised by anything. A dank, heavy-limbed forest would always be pleasurable, even if they were no longer shocked by the salamanders they found under every rotting thing. They still were going to scoop out the slippery sacs of beady eggs from every water-filled depression they encountered. Not because it was thrilling, but because they could. And because they were hungry. Had they ever really been adventurers?

If there was a bright side to the cruelty of Big Walk V, it was that they had ended up somewhere quiet, peaceful. Somewhere, it seemed, the Rangers weren't interested in visiting. Or maybe, they hoped, the Rangers had other things to worry about. Glen sometimes worried out loud about the study. During their third winter in and around the Basin, undisturbed by Rangers or directives to visit Post, he wondered what it meant that they weren't checking in for questionnaires and blood work and physicals. But no one else worried. No one else missed the study.

"I didn't say I missed it," Glen would insist, but he wouldn't say more.

Val had finally become pregnant after the last snows fell. And she was round and red-cheeked and wobbling like an acorn by the time this Ranger showed up alone on horseback. He seemed more apparition than man. It had been so long, he couldn't possibly be real. He didn't introduce himself.

"You have to move along," he muttered down from his silver speckled mare. "You've been here too long."

"And you've been *gone* too long," said Bea.

"We have a lot going on," he said flatly. He closed his eyes as though remembering a nightmare. He sighed. "We work, you know. It's not an easy job. So please let me do it quickly." He pinched the bridge of his nose with fatigue. "You've been here too long. Time to move along."

"What's with the horse?" Bea asked.

"Please don't change the subject."

Bea made doe eyes. "What? I want to know. I love horses." She scratched under the mare's chin, and the horse snorted appreciatively.

"Research shows that trucks are too damaging to the ecosystem."

"You needed research for that?"

The Ranger scowled. "Of course not. But we didn't know the degree to which they damage it. They leave a supertrace." His face was pained thinking about all the supertrace he'd left on the land. "So we are all on horseback now." He slid out of his saddle awkwardly.

"That's a big change," she said.

"Lots of big changes with the new Administration."

"What Administration is that?" Carl asked.

The adults all laughed at that, especially the Newcomers. While they laughed, the Ranger knit his eyebrows and took notes.

When he finished writing he said, "Get going."

"We have to wait for our Gatherers to return," Bea said.

"Where are they?"

"In the mountains."

"Why aren't you all in the mountains with them?"

"Because we're here."

With an annoyed flourish, the Ranger opened his notebook again. "You should be gathering together," he said through clenched teeth, furiously scribbling their trespasses. "You shouldn't be waiting for anyone. You're nomadic. There is nowhere you are allowed to just wait. You are supposed to one, stay together; two, keep moving; and three, do things as you move." His counting fingers formed a two-barreled gun.

"We have to stop to hunt and gather and process," said Bea.

"Besides, even nomadic people eventually settled," said Carl. It was a very uncharacteristic thing for him to say, but he had turned an ankle that year and it had made walking a little less enjoyable for him.

That's when the Ranger saw their smoker. He shook his head disgustedly. "You people." He walked around it, threw open the hooding, took pictures of it, scribbled more notes. Then, he pulled out a flask from his back pocket and a box of matches from his backpack, shook the liquid from the flask all over the smoker, and threw a match in. It lit up.

Building the smoker had taken an entire summer of harvesting wood from the foothills and dragging the wood back to camp. They'd never done so much exhausting work. Even during the years when they had walked for what seemed like years. Creating permanence was much harder work than walking, it turned out. They watched the smoker burn. There was nothing they could do. It had definitely been against the rules.

"Aren't you worried about that fire spreading?" Bea's voice quaked with anger, and maybe a little sadness.

"Not really. My horse is fast." He winked at Bea.

She spit at his feet.

"Watch yourself," he sneered. After a little trouble and cursing, he got back on his horse. Nodding to the fiery smoker, he cried, "Not a trace!" as he galloped away.

They hadn't restocked their water yet that day, so the Community smothered the fire with a few skins from their beds. They gagged as the deer hair and skin smoldered and smoked.

The next day they sent the Hunters out to the foothills for more meat.

They worried that to move again would give up their claim on the land, though they had no claim on the land. So they did not pack up camp. They stayed put against all logic. Their instinct told them to.

*   *   *

WITH THE HUNTERS off hunting and the Gatherers still gathering, Agnes and Glen were helping Debra and Jake sew. Sister and Brother and Pinecone were there too, but they were only making knots in the sinew and then being scolded by Debra.

Staying put had led to increased food, increased growth and girth, and the need for new clothes. For Agnes most of all. Perhaps she really had been too skinny like her mother said, but now she touched her cheeks to feel them spring back, jiggle under her fingertips. She was no longer an up-and-down arrangement of bones. Now she possessed a shape, albeit slight. She wasn't sure anyone else would notice it, but she noticed it. When she lay down, everything felt different. Her body met the ground differently. She had grown taller too. She was now almost as tall as Val. She looked right at Val's nose when they stood together. But she was still one of the shortest people in the Community. Much shorter than her mother, who was as tall as the men.

Agnes watched Glen slowly peel sinew strands from a dry deer tendon. He had jowls again, and they quivered as his fingers trailed up and down the tendon. Her mother's first order of business after she joined Carl as leader had been to reinstate Glen into the Community. Cooks weren't allowed to cut his rations, or any of the Originalists' rations, any longer. They claimed they never had, but the Originalists became undeniably plumper in the season that followed this new mandate. Bea even had Glen's rations increased for a time, until he became stocky again, regained his strength, and became solid on his feet. It was required that Glen be engaged in at least one conversation per day with a member of the Community other than Agnes. Each person took a turn. It wasn't hard for the Originalists since they'd known him so long, though it could be awkward with Carl glowering at them. And if they didn't spend time with him, Bea glowered. It was hard to be an Originalist sometimes.

For the Newcomers it was even harder. They really had to make an effort to think of him as part of the Community. He was always on the outskirts or walking far behind. That Agnes spent a lot of time with him and brought him food and washed the wounds he collected from tripping and stumbling had taught them he belonged in some way, but they had not really believed he was the pioneer of this group, that he'd started this Community in the Wilderness State, even though that's what they'd been told. They always believed it was Carl, and Carl never corrected them. And even after they knew, they still preferred to think it was Carl. Carl was strong, decisive, unkind when he needed to be. They just liked Carl better. Carl's story, as told to them by Carl, was a better story.

But Carl, it turned out, hadn't any grand plan for leadership. No agenda or way forward. He just wanted to be leader and have everything go through him. Once that was secured, he delighted in being the enforcer.

Bea was the one in charge. But far from being a disruptive leader, she kept the Community abiding by rules even more stringently than they had before. "We will give the Rangers no reason to think of us," she would say. "Our ideal is that they forget we are here." Every rule in the Manual was followed to a T. Until the Basin.

The sun arced over their bent heads. Agnes felt her legs getting hot. They splayed out in front of her. She paused and took a moment to drape a cloth over Glen's head so he would not get sun-tired.

Agnes softened sinew in her mouth as she watched Jake stitching pieces of hide together. He was making a patchwork buckskin blanket. His fingers were white from the force needed to pull the bone needle and sinew through. His hands were fully calloused. When he touched Agnes, his fingertips were as rough as dried seed pods. He said he could barely feel her skin against them. So he would sometimes trace his cheek, the tip of his nose, the inside of his wrist along her skin. Something more sensitive. He was her life mate. They had decided. They would make a family and rear their young, and then, at an age when it seemed their young could take care of themselves, they would send them away to find their own land to explore. And then they'd have more young.

"What age were you thinking," Jake had asked.

"I think probably by six," said Agnes.

Jake paled. "What?"

"You don't agree?" She absorbed his silence, studied the incredulous look on his face. "I guess I could be convinced to wait till seven
or eight?"

"Agnes, that is way too young."

Now she felt incredulous. "Bears do it at two. Why can't our
babies?"

"Because we're not bears."

"Our babies will be better than bears!" Though she wondered if
anything could truly be better than bears.

"Weren't you about six when you came here?"

"Five. I think? I don't remember."

"Think about when you were that young. Would you have wanted
to be on your own? Finding your own food, defending against predators. You, at five or six? Alone?"

When she first got here, of course she had been useless in the Wilderness. But that was because she was from the City. She knew beds
and clean plates. She knew toilets. She knew about the predators in
the City, but they were a different kind of predator, and it was a different kind of danger. She had needed time to adjust and learn about
this new place. But she believed that by the following spring, she had
developed the abilities and skills needed to lead the Community, if
anyone would have let her then. She knew then almost everything
she knew now about living here. The things she didn't understand
well were people and that hadn't changed much. But surviving—she
understood that. It had been one of the first things she understood
here. Really, what else was there? Hunting, processing, tracking, water source, basic clothing and shelter, weather, the different gifts and
threats from flora and fauna. Being alone on a stormy night. Being
alone when you knew a big cat was nearby. Being alone when you
heard footsteps and didn't know what they belonged to. These things
were hard at any age. But a six-year-old possesses logic. They can
think themselves out of fear if they have to. If they are left alone to.
Her mother had left her when she was maybe ten? Eleven? Twelve?

That had been very hard, but not because of survival preparedness. And if the whole Community had left her, she would have been sad, but she still could have survived. What did age matter?

"I don't know," she said. Jake still stared at her with doubt. "Why, what age were you thinking?"

"Sixteen? Seventeen? Or whatever is legal."

"Legal? What's that?"

Jake hung his head in exasperation. Agnes felt her blood heating up. She did not want her children coddled. She didn't know how old she was now. Maybe she was fourteen or fifteen or fifty-nine. Sometimes she felt older than them all. She'd been leading their walks for a long time now. And she'd been capable of surviving on her own just fine, thank you. She was brave. She was skilled. She was a watcher. She could take care of herself. And she would take care of Jake. And a baby. And anyone else who came along. Until they didn't need her anymore.

"Let's drop it," Jake said, possibly sensing Agnes was building an argument.

Agnes had agreed. They didn't need a *parenting philosophy*, as Jake called it, because every month Agnes bled.

The Twins said she would have to have real sex to get pregnant and what they were doing wasn't sex. Agnes knew it wasn't real sex but didn't know how to make it real sex. Jake thought they were too young. He thought the walking was too hard to have kids right now. The weather was too unpredictable. He was embarrassed that they would have to tell Glen. He was scared of her mother. Wasn't a newborn a burden on the Community? There was no rush, really, he always said.

"But you want to have young, right?" she would say.

Jake rolled his eyes. "I call them children, and yes, I'd like to have some."

"Because it sounds like you aren't sure."

"No, I'm sure."

"Okay, then." She would reach for his pants, and he'd shackle her wrists with his hand.

"Please, Agnes. You're too aggressive."

This always stumped Agnes because she didn't know how else to be. She tried to move more slowly for his pants, hoping that would seem less alarming to him. But he still dodged her.

She had asked politely. She had made intellectual arguments. She'd offered what she knew of statistics, of the need to grow the population in the Wilderness State. To stake some kind of claim here. She couldn't imagine an elk going to so much trouble to mate. She had even tried to trick him one day by insisting the anthill they'd been sitting next to belonged to a rare poisonous kind of ant and that they needed to undress quickly to make sure no ants were on their bodies. But she'd felt ashamed of her cunning as he stood there blushing at their nudity, trusting fully that she had only meant to protect him from ants. She had walked away, mumbling for him to get dressed. The last time they had been alone together, she had decided to be blunt. She turned around, pulled her tunic up, and pushed her backside into him, and they both tumbled over.

He rolled away. "No, I told you."

She clenched her fists in frustration.

He smiled. "Are you going to hit me?"

"No," she said. She hid her hands behind her back so she could relax them and pretend they had never been clenched.

"We can do other stuff."

"Okay," she had said and led him to a spot between some sage bushes, and there they rubbed together with their clothes on. It's not that she didn't enjoy it. She liked panting and wrestling with Jake. They giggled and squeaked like weasels at play, and they were always relaxed and gentle afterward, like they were floating on a lazy river. She just didn't see the point of it. She had needs. And this did not satisfy them.

Agnes slowly pulled the softened sinew from her mouth, and Jake blushed even though he had not seemed to be looking at her. She heard the return whistle of the Gatherers. The mellow toot on carved bone, in long and short bursts.

Then, on their heels, the horn of the Hunters, which Carl had fashioned out of a rock sheep's ridged, pearly horn.

Agnes bounded up, pushed the wet sinew into Jake's hand. "I did a really good job with this one."

"You better have." He smiled shyly at his palm, where the sinew glistened with her spit.

The Hunters and Gatherers arrived, and Agnes could see four jackrabbit heads, their limp ears flopping with each step. A deer lay across Juan's shoulders. Ahead of them Joven walked with his deer, probably so they wouldn't get spooked from the scent of the dead one.

Joven's deer were a mother and juvenile that had recently crept closer to the border of the Community's camp in the Basin. They were probably looking for protection from predators and were hoping the Community wasn't one. One morning, Joven went out and fed them pine nuts. He had been told not to, but he didn't listen, or perhaps he did not want to follow the rule. He was young. He was a Newcomer. He had other ideas.

The adults had a long meeting about Joven and the wild deer he was feeding, arguing for or against breaking the rules. Some insisted that when they needed the deer for food, it would be a good resource. The deer made Joven happy, and usually he was a somber little boy. But others simply said, "We can't domesticate wild animals. Even if it's an accident. We'll get in so much trouble." "But they're already hovering around us," the pro-deer camp argued. "At what point do they just become ours?" "When we feed them," said the anti-deer camp. "Well, they're already fed, so they're already ours." The pro-deer camp cheered and the anti-deer camp booed, and they got so loud and angry Carl and Bea had to make a call. They decided to let the deer stay.

"Our first foray into animal husbandry," they said, putting on cheerful faces.

"Which is not why we're here," said Debra, the anti-deer camp leader. "This is really bad precedent, people." She shook her head.

"Well," Carl said, "we're also supposed to be leaving this Basin once in a while, so if you want to follow the rules, why don't you run along."

"Oh, shut up, Carl," Debra said, and she stepped toward him angrily. But Frank stepped toward her as she did. He was imposing. He somehow got bulkier the longer he was here, rather than waste away as most everyone else had. Debra stepped back. She'd been right, though. Domestication was very against the rules. Even Agnes had read this rule. It was rule number two on the second page of the Manual.

Now the deer shadowed Joven everywhere while keeping a wary distance from everyone else.

Joven took the deer round to the sleeping circle, where they munched on sage and then lay next to his bed and curiously nosed the deerskin bedding. They lay their gentle necks over his torso when he slept.

The Community got to processing what they had brought back. Linda lit the smoker. They'd patched it after the fire. It worked almost as well. Skinners skinned the rabbits, then scraped hides. Carl and the Twins worked on the deer. Carl had the strength to wrestle its bulk, but the Twins had the finesse to work clean in the skinning and gutting and butchering. Everyone could process a deer, but their hides were immaculate and their cuts were beautiful.

By the middle of the night they'd gotten meat into the smoker. Hides had been scraped, soaked, and stretched before they lost the sun. They made cuts by firelight. They formed a chain of hands to move strips from the fire to the smoker to be hung.

Then they tumbled into bed, where the smaller children were already asleep.

At first light, after only a few hours of sleep, five Rangers rode into camp on horseback. They were different Rangers than the one

Ranger who had visited before. They wore new uniforms. Gone was the Ranger green. These new uniforms were a watery blue. Crisp white handkerchiefs circled their necks. Their badges were the only thing that announced they were still Rangers, though the Community recognized some of them.

The Rangers carried rifles, slung over their shoulders. And when they hopped off their horses, they held the rifles up, ready.

"What's going on here?" Carl stretched and rubbed his eyes. His words were garbled by a yawn.

"We're here to move you off this land," one of the Rangers said. He was likely the head Ranger. His horse was the tallest one, and he wore a different hat from the others.

"No, I mean, what's with the outfits? They're new."

"They're not outfits. They're uniforms."

"Well, they're new."

"So they are." The head Ranger stood up a bit taller. It seemed he liked the new look, liked the starchiness of the clothes. His boots were new too.

"You look like an army."

"We have a new mandate."

"What's the mandate?"

The Rangers gave one another long, meaningful looks. The head Ranger spoke. "That's classified."

"How come?"

"Because it's classified."

"No, how come you have a new mandate?"

"There's a new Administration."

"That was fast," Carl said.

The Community laughed.

"Don't get smart," the head Ranger said. "You need to move along. As you've been told. Repeatedly."

"Just once, actually," said Bea.

"Once is more than enough. Oh, for fuck's sake." The head Ranger's shoulders fell as he spotted Joven's deer lying with him in his bed. "What are those?"

"What are what?" Bea asked. The deer stood up on their twiggy legs and hovered over Joven, who sat up in his bed and rubbed his eyes. They all blinked at the Rangers.

The head Ranger pointed at the deer. "Those."

"Oh, just some deer," said Bea.

"They look awfully comfortable around you."

"We were just about to get them to shoo."

"You're not supposed to do that."

"Do what? Get them to shoo?"

"Stop it. You're not supposed to have deer following you around like dogs."

The deer stood plucky, their ears taut, as though they knew they were being talked about.

A bearded Ranger ran at the deer, but they merely bowed their heads.

The Rangers looked to Carl.

"It just sort of happened." Carl shrugged.

The mother deer bent toward Joven and nuzzled her nose into his clenched fist until he opened it. The deer licked his palm.

"They do that for the salt," Joven explained in his small, high voice, his velveteen hair shining in the sun.

The head Ranger shook his head. He withdrew a pistol from his holster. "You know I have to destroy these." He turned to Carl. "Unless you want to do it yourself. Are you the head guy around here?"

Carl scowled.

Bea stepped up. "I am," she said.

"They're not wild anymore. It'll give the others the wrong idea," he said and cocked the pistol. The deer stared steadily at the gun in his hand, hoping it was food. Their big eyes quivered in their sockets, their ears twitched, taking in all the nature around them, all the signs and signals. It looked to Agnes like they were smiling.

"*Jovencito, ven acá rápido, rápido*," Linda hissed, urgently wagging her hand at her side.

But the head Ranger swiftly strode the few paces to the deer and shot a bullet in the juvenile's head, then the mother's head, and they dropped and shook on the ground, kicked up dust, grunted and mewled, then stopped.

Joven held very still, trying to blink away his shock. Quiet tears fell. The deer had fallen next to him. One of their tender necks lay across his ankle. He had blood on his chest and above his eye. Pooling in his bed. Linda ran to him.

The head Ranger cast a victorious look at the boy. "The kid must really like deer," he said.

Carl lunged at him, but Bea put her body between them.

The head Ranger looked back at his men. "This is contraband, so I guess we'll need to take it with." He twirled his finger, and the four other Rangers picked up the animals and flung them across their horses' backs. The deer hung limp, their tongues red and lolling, blood burbling from the bullet holes as though from a ground spring. The horses whinnied nervously. They did not like the weight of death on their backs. But the Rangers did not mount. They turned back to the Community, holding their rifles across their chests.

The head Ranger said, "Well?"

"Well, what?" Bea said.

"What are you waiting for?"

"An apology?"

The Rangers laughed, and Bea laughed haughtily with them.

"Not happening," the lead Ranger said.

"Some instructions then, I guess."

"Start packing."

"Now?"

"Yes."

"Are you just going to stand there and watch?"

"Oh, we'll help a little," he said and smiled. The Rangers went to the smoker, the repaired and functioning and in-use smoker, and set it on fire again. Then the Rangers mounted their horses and rode off.

The Community used several more skins to extinguish the fire. They inspected what was left to salvage. They tidied up the camp and made breakfast and stared dumbly at the campfire as the children, minus Joven, yelled and wrestled around them. No one made a move to pack. Instead, they had the Hunters return to the foothills the next day for an overnight or two, to replace the skins they'd just sacrificed in the fire and the meat they'd lost in the smoker.

Two mornings later they heard an incessant mechanical whir as the wind in the Basin picked up. In the distance, zipping low toward them, they saw a helicopter. Soon they were spitting dust from their mouths and covering their ears and eyes. The helicopter hovered above them. A raspy megaphone blared down.

"You have been ordered to clear this camp immediately."

"We can't sleep first?" Carl yelled up.

"You have been ordered to clear this camp immediately."

"Oh, it's not a real helicopter," Frank said. "It's too small. It might be a drone."

"It's too big to be a drone," said Carl.

"But it's too small to be a helicopter."

"Maybe drones are bigger now."

"Maybe helicopters are smaller."

"It's just a fucking Ranger toy," said Val.

A loud noise—a thumping, clanking, grinding, shrieking noise—followed, and they all covered their ears.

All the birds bolted away from the bushes. The children cried.

"You have been ordered to clear this camp immediately," they heard over the industrial din.

They looked around at one another.

Bea sighed loudly and yelled, "Well, it seems the time has come to say goodbye to our pleasant Basin."

They all nodded. They covered their ears and dragged themselves around camp packing things away. They had been there a long while. They no longer remembered how best to pack it all. They had accumulated too many things. How had they accumulated so much? How had they accumulated anything other than food? It took them two days to pack. By then the Hunters had returned. There was nothing to do with their kills but leave them for scavengers. They had no time to skin, butcher, strip, soak, stretch, smoke, and dry. A total waste. They walked around camp looking for micro trash, and the whole time what they now called the metal bird hovered above them, screeching for them to get out, leaving a few times for, they assumed, fuel or power, though they couldn't imagine from where.

When they finished, they stood under the metal bird and looked up, shielding their eyes.

"Now what?" Bea yelled.

A yellow light blinked on its belly as though relaying the message. "Await instructions," it intoned, and then it zagged away, leaving them with a phantom echo of the screeching soundtrack in their ears. They sat on their buckskin packs and waited. Later that day, a small but fast-moving cloud of dust emerged from the horizon. They heard the whinny of horses and the clomp of hooves. It was the five Rangers, their uniforms as crisp and clean as before. The head Ranger wordlessly handed Bea an envelope.

Inside was a new directive: *We are opening a new Post! Travel to the Caldera summit for the grand opening event!* There were hand-drawn balloons in the corners of the paper.

"You're throwing a party?" Bea said.

The head Ranger shrugged. "Sure, why not? How often do we open up a new Post?"

"Why are you inviting us?"

The head Ranger smiled hard, with all his teeth. "Well, because the Post is for you."

"Is the party on a specific day?"

"No, we'll just have it when you get there."

"So you'll just be ready to party?"

"Yes, do you have a problem with that?" He had tired of the conversation.

"Do you have any idea how long it will take to get here?"

"For me, it'd take about six weeks of good daily mileage. For you?" He chuckled. "Six *months*. Minimum." The other Rangers laughed hard behind him.

The adults nodded, but this idea was lost on Agnes. "How many moons is that?" she asked.

The head Ranger snorted. "Many. I've never seen anything move slower than your caravan."

Bea rolled her eyes. "Yeah, yeah, so we've heard. You know, we're carrying a lot of stuff."

"Well, maybe you should pare down. I'm sure real nomads didn't have so many possessions."

"We are real nomads."

The Rangers laughed hard again.

Bea crossed her arms. "We're also walking with children and they slow us down."

Agnes's face burned. She stomped her foot. "We do not! I'm the one who has to wait for you." She felt tears rising. She was a good leader.

"I'm not talking about you," her mother snapped. "I'm talking about the children."

This stunned Agnes. She had not known that her mother thought of her as something other than just a kid. She thought her mother only saw her as that strange girl imitating her in a cave. Her mother dismissed her, and then other times exalted her abilities. She rarely seemed happy that Agnes was leading, but never interfered. It had originally been Carl's idea, and it had begun when her mother was gone. But her mother could be dismissive with everyone. So perhaps being treated like that simply meant her mother thought of her as a peer.

Bea eyed the head Ranger skeptically. "Our map doesn't really show the Caldera, not in any useful way." She looked in the envelope. "Is there a new map?"

"You'll get a map when you need a map," he said, and without any warning he pointed his rifle into the distance and fired. The sound flew away from them, across the Basin, stopping at nothing, shaking dry sage branches and alarming the bugs, voles, birds who were still around.

The five Rangers on their horses corralled them like cattle. "Let's go, let's go, let's go," they hollered.

Startled into action, Bea led the Community stumbling across the Basin. She wouldn't let Agnes do it alone, keeping a step ahead of her no matter how fast Agnes tried to go.

Over the course of what must have been half of the fall, the Rangers shepherded them away from their pleasant Basin. At sundown, the Rangers would disappear and reappear at morning to keep the Community moving. They marched them back into those high desert places where they'd spent so many years. They walked them deep into the sage sea, favoring bad camp spots over good ones. They bypassed good water sources, only offering them slow, slight streams, or larval standing water. Where they walked them, the game was scarce. And so was shade. It was hard to imagine the route choice wasn't intentionally cruel. The head Ranger had a habit of whistling all day atop his horse as the Community dragged themselves forward.

They were far from the Basin now. Delivered back to the emptiest high desert where they didn't have the impulse to idle. One night the Rangers left and did not show up the next morning. Or the morning after. They left behind a new map and they never returned. They'd done their job.

*   *   *

THE ORIGINALISTS HAD seen the Caldera when they had first arrived. Day one. Not because it was so close to Middle Post—though it was certainly not distant—but because it was so tall and lonely in its height. It sat heavy on the horizon, an upside-down triangle, white in winter and green in spring, the tip-top point broken off, creating a catchall for anything that might stumble in. Well beyond it was the first mountain range they'd ever explored. The range was a shadowy hump on the horizon. The Caldera stood alone.

Agnes remembered it as a white hat atop the bald, sunburnt head of the high desert. The endless desert, its ruddy dirt and camphor scent after a rain. Its errant arms of sage and brush and grasses. Then there it was. A triangle hat belonging to a dunce.

"It's like a pyramid of snowballs," they explained to the Newcomers, who had never seen it.

"Like a colorless kite stuck in the sand."

"A geometric marble end table."

"A slice of white pizza, with the tip bit off."

"White pizza," murmured Patty.

But the only thing the Originalists had ever really known about the Caldera was that it was off-limits.

In their previous map there'd been a black circle where the Caldera would have stood. And black circles meant *do not enter.*

On this new map, the Caldera was at the top center, a white triangle with a red flag sticking out of its concave top. All around it were messy green triangles for trees.

"Didn't the maps used to have actual information on them?" huffed Val, her arms wrapped around her bulging stomach.

"Don't start with the maps again," Bea said.

"It's just that they're always wrong. Who's their mapmaker? One of their fucking kids?"

"It has all the info we need. Water is marked, it has topography, and all the landscape types are color-coded. What else do you need?"

"Well, what's all this?" Val said, waving her hand around a swath of space between where they stood and the Caldera. It was the color of the parchment the map was printed on.

"It's"—Bea looked at the key—"nothing important."

Val snorted. "I'll bet you ten pine nuts it's gonna feel pretty important when we're in the middle of it."

"What's your problem?"

"What's yours? You're so into the map. Did you make it or something?"

"Oh, come on, Val," Carl said. "Now you're just being stupid."

"No, you're stupid," Val shouted, her stance defensive, threatening even. Then she clamped her mouth shut and drummed her fingernails on her belly, as though to distract herself. Carl rolled his eyes at her. So Agnes patted her on the back, and Val, sniffling, grabbed her hand and gave it a squeeze. Val was not herself. Or on second thought, Agnes thought, she was a very extreme version of herself.

"We need to find water," said Bea. "Good water." She poked her finger at all the spots on the map that looked blue between their position and the Caldera. "I think this is where we should head." She jabbed at a large blue blob that looked like it would be a few days' walk. "This blue line here must be a stream. It's about halfway. Hopefully it won't be dry."

"Well, we'll definitely have water at the Caldera, so there's that," said Dr. Harold.

"We need water before that, Harold," said Debra.

"Well, I know that, Debra." He smiled aggressively.

"Are we sure there's even a lake at the Caldera? The map doesn't show the very top," said Frank.

"There's two lakes," murmured Bea, measuring distances with her spread fingers.

"How do you know?" Carl said.

Bea looked up. "Oh, Bob told me. He said there was one good lake and one bad lake. And the good lake was good for drinking and swimming."

Debra squealed, "Swimming!"

"When did he tell you this?" asked Carl.

"Oh, gosh," said Bea, standing up and stretching out her knees. "At intake? Our first day," she translated for the Newcomers. "We could see it on the horizon. I asked him about it."

"And you still remember?"

"Are you kidding? I think about it all the time."

"I can't believe you didn't tell me about the lakes," Debra said in a scolding voice.

"Debra, you would have run off that very day."

"Oh, I would have, you're right." They laughed. Debra loved lakes and was unhappy that they somehow never encountered anything more than shallow rivers and murky springs.

Agnes looked over her mother's shoulder at the map. It was clear to her, looking at it now, that these lakes her mother sought were no longer lakes. The evidence was in their outline. The outline of the lake was bolder and bluer than the interior, as though it were meant to be a barrier between different times, between then and now. She could see the same thing in the alkali lakes, though they were colored pale blue. Around that pale blue there was also a blue outline. A dark blue. A thirsty blue. That line between then and now. Or between what they were hoping to find and what they would find.

Agnes began to see the map as a story rather than a piece of truth. Something that changed based on what their needs were. It wasn't something to orient their lives to. It was a suggestion rather than a directive. They didn't have to follow it. Did they realize that? She noted the location of the sun in the sky and turned in a circle, peering at each slice of land in front of her. She could name the places they'd been that lay in each direction. Corroborating it with the map, she was right each time. They had senses. So why did they still use a map that lost them as often as it oriented them?

Because they'd been told to. Because it was in the Manual that they should always refer to the map. That's why. Because the Posts were on the map and the Posts were important. But she could name where the Posts were in each specific slice of landscape. Couldn't everyone?

Even the new Caldera Post. If it was on the Caldera, she knew how to get to it. No, the map was useless, and more important, it was endangering them. It was the last hand of civilization they wouldn't let go of.

"We should just follow the animals," interrupted Agnes.

"What?" her mother said.

"If we follow the animals, they'll show us where the water is."

Her mother smiled. "That's a good idea, sweetheart," she said, patting Agnes on the head. "But we've got a solid plan here we're going to follow. I feel really good about it."

*   *   *

THEY EXPECTED TO reach the lake in a few days, but by the time the moon had waxed from crescent to full, they still hadn't arrived. They found and followed the stream for a day, but it was mostly dry. They rationed water. Agnes again suggested they follow the animals and her mother shushed her.

They had to be close, she said.

They were close. In fact, they soon realized, they were next to the lake. Had been walking along it for miles. It was an enormous lake, or had been at one time. Now it was just a lakebed. No, a former lakebed. A lake that likely hadn't been a lake for generations or more. Filled now with nothing but tall, rippling yellowed grass. A grass lake. On the map it was a quenching bright blue.

"I told you—the maps are always wrong," Val cried.

"Oh, shut up, Val," Bea sputtered. "The stream was right!" She chewed on her fingers anxiously.

"I guess we keep walking to the next lake on the map then," said Carl. "Bea?"

"I don't understand how there's no lake here," she mumbled through her fingers, as if speaking to herself.

"The map is old," said Dr. Harold.

"But this isn't how it's supposed to be."

"Well, how was it supposed to be?" said Glen, gently.

She blinked up at him, a worried look. "It said there would be water here."

"And it was wrong," said Val valiantly.

"Let me think," Bea snapped. Then she breathed long and slow. "There needs to be water on this route. We need it." She sounded defeated. "Let's camp here tonight." The Community got to work setting a quick camp. They couldn't make a fire. Not here in this parched sea of grass. So they pulled out jerky for dinner. They unrolled beds. Most were too busy to notice when Bea murmured, "I'm going for a walk," and then headed out into the high grasses. But Agnes noticed. She waited and then snuck away, catching her mother's track, the subtly disturbed, parted grass she'd left behind.

Her mother was circling the grass lake, taking a long arced path, but then, after a good while of walking blind in the high grass, Agnes saw a treetop peek above it all in the distance, and just past where she stood, she saw that the grasses ended. She moved stealthily to the edge and peered between the coarse shoots.

Her mother stood before the tree with something in her hand, squinting at it. Then she dug into her bag and pulled out a little pad of paper and small pencil she'd brought back with her from the City. She jotted something, tore the paper from the pad, crumpled it up, and pressed it into a hole in the tree. She stepped back from the tree, looked up into its branches as if contemplating climbing it. Then she turned around and walked back toward the grasses where Agnes hid.

"You can come out now, Agnes," she called into the grass lake.

Agnes flushed and slowly stepped into the open.

"You know you can just ask me."

"But you won't tell me."

"Well, you can still ask." Her mother smirked.

"What were you doing?"

"Saying hello to a squirrel friend of mine."

"Mom."

"Agnes."

"What's going on?"

"Nothing, and that is the truth. Sometimes I like to leave something behind. You never know who or what will find it. It's one of the things that keeps me sane out here."

Agnes knew she would not get any further with this questioning and was angry at her mother for wanting to play games.

Bea saw her anger. "When there is something to know," she said, "I'll tell you." She pinched Agnes's cheek and said, "Don't grow up too fast," and laughed when Agnes swatted her hand away. She had known it would anger Agnes even more, and that was why she'd done it.

She put a hand on Agnes's shoulder and squeezed, and they walked back through the grass together like that. Her mother tried to make the gesture feel maternal, but Agnes knew she was being escorted.

Her mother shared a bed with her that night, and whenever Agnes stirred and peeked to see if her mother was sleeping, her mother's eyes would be peering at her, bright amber and in control. "Go to sleep, Agnes," she would say, a singsong command. Eventually Agnes drifted into a frustrated sleep, and she would not have been surprised if her mother had stayed awake the whole night just to keep Agnes from slinking off to find what she had hidden.

When Agnes woke, it was late. She felt groggy. Her body stiff. Water rationing was taking its toll. She lay trying to block the rising sun, which seemed intent to beam right into her eyes and her eyes only.

The camp was droning. People were lethargic, dried out. When they were packed up, they gathered in a droopy circle. The places where they'd slept were flattened, and it felt like they were corralled by a grass fence on all sides.

Bea said flatly, "I was doing some scouting of that cluster of lakes yesterday."

"And?" said Carl.

"I think it's a dead end. So I think we should do what Agnes said."

She turned to Agnes. "Follow the animals." Bea smiled at her, her eyes gleaming with instinct. Agnes felt her heart flutter, tugging itself between pride and disgust, love and anger. Her mother was lying to the Community. But she was also putting Agnes in charge. Agnes smiled back, from deep inside. She couldn't help it, even as her stomach began to ache. She hated how easy it was for her to love her mother. How hard it was to remain indignant when her mother hurt her. She would always love her mother. Even when her mother didn't deserve it. It filled her with shame, and with yearning too. Agnes bit her smile to make it retreat back inside. She watched her mother's smile retreat then too.

*   *   *

AGNES HAD KNOWN they were following animal trails for days before anyone else realized it. She'd seen them clearly branded into the sameness of the sage sea for a few sunsets. She saw the broken branches and, looking ahead, could see a phantom path made among their snapped-off ends. Trails like this beamed away from her in all directions. One trail crossed with another, and as she walked, they each funneled into some kind of wide avenue where hundreds of creatures had trampled through.

When they came upon their first congregation of creatures, she stopped, put her hands on her hips, and said, "See?"

A day before, a storm had come through, briefly dumping rain on them as they walked across the plain. They'd been able to collect a gulp of water by turning over cups and hats, cupping their palms or turning their open mouths to the sky. The earth sopped it up fast, though, and as quickly as it had rained, the ground felt dry again.

But here, a depression had collected much of that storm. It seemed to be a dependable water source, well visited, thoroughly trampled. Barely any sage remained.

The animals had been rendered languid by the water. Elk sat on the ground made cool by their wet bodies. Buffalo stood in the water flicking their tails. Birds dipped up and down in the air above, buoyed by the rising moisture. Rabbits cleaned behind their ears. All was quiet except for the regular chirps and squeaks of the sentinel animals keeping watch for predators.

The Community set up camp a ways off from the water source to avoid potential trampling. They set about cooking and putting their beds together in silence to match the serenity of the watering hole at dusk. They heard the clicking of bats and the humming of insect legs. The bigger animals murmured quietly to one another as the night fell. And just as everything seemed to have bedded down, there was a momentary cacophony. Elk bugled; buffalo snorted. The ducks quacked. The small vermin squeaked, and far-off wolves howled. It was as though they all were saying good night. It felt strange to no longer be alone.

When the watering hole became mud and the animals moved on, the Community packed up and moved on too. They stayed in water this way, migrating with the animals from watering hole to watering hole.

Since the grass lake, Val had ballooned and become breathless. She kept her arms wrapped around her middle as though trying to keep everything in. She lost her words in the middle of a conversation as her body clenched, beginning to begin labor. Val scowling and smiling in equal measure that it was finally happening.

She birthed Baby Egret amid the lows of the animals at their third watering hole. She called him Baby Egret as though to ensure no one confused him with one of the milk-white birds tiptoeing through the mud. The birth was easy and quick, and Val appeared very satisfied by that. Baby Egret was cleaned and wrapped in a new buckskin sling Debra had made for him. The camp bustled to make them comfortable, but soon everything calmed down and it was a day like any other. Only with a new voice in the mix. A loud, reedy one.

Agnes noticed that the animals at that watering hole were very interested in the new sound from their camp. Females, mothers, approached the camp, sniffing the air, excited and alert. They swiv-eled their ears. Baby Egret sounded like their babies. Plaintive and needful and demanding. Agnes knew they wanted to help. To show Val how to soothe the infant. How to feed him. How to protect him. They assumed Baby Egret was one of them, and Agnes had felt a small pang of jealousy over that.

But walking ahead of the Community, Agnes felt proud to be lead-ing, just another kind of creature on a mass migration. Just creatures finding water the way all creatures must. It wasn't that she didn't always feel this way each day they'd been out here. That she was just another animal. But there was something about the scope of what she could see now. How massive it was. They often saw animals: a herd of deer, mating hawks, a wolf pack. The elk herd was the largest group of animals they ever came across all at once, other than flocks of birds. But flocks of birds didn't have the same battered hooves as the elk, the same sweaty fur.

Looking across the vast plain and seeing all the animals moving as one, in one direction, with the same needs, she felt a part of the place in a way she hadn't before. She'd never realized she felt apart from it. But she guessed she had in some unknowable way. It was their reliance on the water spigots. On the maps. On the fact that they checked in with Rangers. They were never fully living on their own. Not like these animals were every day. Not until now. And she was leading. She thought about a conversation she'd had with Jake when he'd first arrived, when he'd asked how long she thought she would be staying. He had no concept that the Wilderness State would be for-ever, having just arrived, bewildered. But she'd never considered they would ever leave. When they left the City, her mother hadn't called it a trip, or an adventure, or something temporary. She had said, "This is our new home." At the thought of leaving here, her breath caught in her throat. She felt like that small girl again, listless and coughing, turning a handkerchief red. Unable to assert force on the world. But that was no longer her. She was no longer that small girl, curiously watching from a distance, from behind her mother or behind Glen. Tentatively reaching out to touch a wet deer nose, breaking through a spider's new morning web, wiping dew and silk from her face with surprise. Now she was the head elk. The point of the *V*. The dominant doe. She was a part of it all. It all depended on her.

Agnes sprinted ahead. She heard Val call for her to wait. Glen croaked for her to slow down. Her mother ordered her to stop. But she whooped in response and ran faster. She spooked the deer, which veered away. The geese above got smaller as they rose to retreat from such ecstasy. This was the last breath of that little girl. Agnes grinned. She did a cartwheel, whooped again. If she'd had something in her hands to dig deep into the dirt with, she would have buried her younger self. Instead, she made squishing sounds as she pretended to dig around in her guts. Then she dramatically pantomimed pulling something out of her, the heart of that little girl, and with one last whoop she threw it up into the geese and they honked and veered off again, raining shit down around her.

Then Agnes waited for the others to catch up.

*   *   *

THE CLOSER THEY got to the foothills, the greener and softer the world became. The weight of the air changed. There was water again in every breath, and soon they hoped they would find it running clean and easy from small springs and brooks. They passed solitary pinyons and collected the nuts when they could to process later. Pinecone asked to carry the bag. "Because of my name," he said. He carried it with a seriousness that made Agnes laugh, a little unkindly, she realized when she noticed that others smiled at Pinecone's focus. Finally, the tippy tops of the mountains came into view and the Community veered toward them. They left the migratory masses behind. The watering holes. The camaraderie. The safety of the group.

Glen had become ragged, hoarse, weak again. He'd developed a limp from simple movement rather than from some traumatic injury.

He hid it as well as he could. In the night, he was coughing again, and in the morning he gingerly stepped and winced, stepped and winced, as though pained by even small moves. The Community had water now, but the water rationing they'd gone through had taken a toll on Glen.

One of the nights after they left the last watering hole, Agnes had seen him walking off at dusk, dragging a single blanket. Agnes tried to join him, but he forbade it. Agnes had begun to read Glen's physical wavering like people read the weather signs in the sky. A halo around the moon meant rain. When Glen disappeared, something bad would happen.

It took a few nights for Bea to realize Glen was sleeping on the outskirts of the camp again. That it took her mother so long to notice confirmed Agnes's belief that not only was she a bad mother, she was a bad wife as well. *As if I needed confirmation*, Agnes thought.

"Why didn't you tell me he was doing that?" her mother muttered, throwing debris into the campfire.

"I didn't think you cared."

"Of course I care," she said in a tense hushed whisper. "Do you know why he's doing it?"

"Maybe he's dying," Agnes said.

Her mother's face burned. "What did you just say?"

Agnes swallowed. "Maybe he's dying," she said, quieter, afraid. She said it because she believed maybe he was. It's what many animals did when they were dying. She prepared to continue with these explanations. But Bea turned to her, her face wild, not with anger but with fear, and every part of her advanced as if to slap Agnes. Agnes cringed, certain she could feel her mother's hand just at her cheek. But the slap never came. Agnes opened one eye and saw her mother walking away from the light of the fire, directly toward where Glen was, as though he were true north. She did not return to camp before Agnes went to sleep. And she was not there when Agnes woke in the earliest silver dawn.

Agnes found them huddled just far enough that the light from the campfire would be visible as a glow on the horizon, not flickering flames. She squatted just an old pine's length from them, but if they saw her, they did not acknowledge her. They behaved as though they were alone, somewhere private, not under the open sky.

Glen reclined on his belongings. Patches of his beard were gray, and it covered what Agnes knew were sunken cheeks. He looked like a scrap of hide too small and ragged to do much with.

Bea sat beside him, leaning over him, lounging almost. She had a brutish wooden bowl next to her and a rag in her hand. She dipped it into the bowl, and it came up dripping. She ran the wet rag down the center of Glen's chest.

Glen sighed, and his shoulders released apart, as though she'd unlocked them from his breastbone. He laid his head back.

Agnes watched, perplexed. How could he feel relaxed in her hands after she'd disappeared and now abandoned him for Carl? How could he accept her love? Tenderness needed to be accompanied by something else to matter, something like loyalty.

After Bea joined Carl, she made sure Glen was cared for. But as far as Agnes had seen, she did none of the caring herself. Until now, Bea had kept her distance. If she observed Glen at all, it was from afar. Perhaps her mother's privacy had made it feel as though her love for Glen was over. But now, here, that was clearly wrong. Sometimes Agnes doubted her mother's motives for things, assuming she held onto quieter additional desires. But there was nothing ambiguous here as Agnes watched her mother kiss Glen tenderly on the cheeks, the temples, his closed eyelids, his forehead, as he smiled blissfully and sadly; then, when she kissed his mouth, his body reached for hers. He was in love. And so, it seemed, was her mother. Agnes thought back to all that time without her mother after her mother had abandoned them. She couldn't remember Glen showing a moment of anger. As though he was certain she had only acted out of necessity, and therefore he could cast no blame.

She watched from the shadows as Bea lay in Glen's arms, her head on his bony chest, lifting slightly with each breath. Their eyes were closed, but they were not asleep. Agnes felt warmth in her chest, and she remembered that this was how they'd slept for years. Her mother and Glen in each other's arms and Agnes at their feet. Watching them together, Agnes felt heartsick. She wanted to be a part of that family bed again, to be the one they wanted to share tender time with. Did they miss her right now? Did they miss the feel of her hands around their ankles?

*   *   *

THE COMMUNITY STAYED put for a few nights and processed the pheasants the Hunters had rustled up.

Bea joined Agnes at bedtime now that Glen was off in the outskirts. But her mother curled much too tight in a ball, on purpose, Agnes thought, and it left Agnes restless and cold throughout the night. She didn't want to sleep like that again. One night, Agnes left the warmth of the fire in search of Glen.

It looked like he had a fire going too. But she realized that what she thought she saw, a glow on the horizon, a little black snake of smoke slithering up the dark blue dusk sky, was much, much, much farther away and must not be a fire at all. Maybe it was some remnant of sunset. The smoke nothing but an illusion.

"Hi, sweetie," she heard Glen say.

"How did you know it was me?"

"I could tell from the sound of your footsteps."

Agnes was proud of Glen for discerning her approach, but she was also embarrassed that she'd been detected so easily.

"Don't worry," Glen said, sensing her disappointment. As she got closer, she could see him smiling. "I only know your footsteps. And that's only because I spend a lot of time listening for them. No one else would be able to hear you."

"Good," she said and squatted down next to him. "Can you come back to camp?"

"I'd prefer to stay out here."

"But I'm cold when I sleep."

"Isn't your mother sleeping with you? She said she would."

"Yes, but she doesn't keep me warm. She doesn't like me to touch her."

"Of course she does."

"No, she pulls away when I reach for her foot."

"Maybe she's just asleep."

"No, she's awake. She's doing it on purpose."

"Agnes, I find that hard to believe."

"It's true. She doesn't want to be with me. She doesn't like me." Agnes felt a surge of pressure in her chest, as though she might sputter into coughs. Her eyes watered.

"Your mother loves you very much. Everything she does, she does for you."

"That's not true."

"It's mostly true."

"She does a lot for herself."

"Don't you?"

Agnes thought that counterpoint was unfair. She wasn't someone's mom. But she didn't say that. "You don't," she said.

"Sure I do."

"No, you don't, and you certainly wouldn't if you had your own kids."

"Oh," Glen said and frowned.

"What's wrong?"

"I thought I had my own kid. She's this funny little girl who says dumb things sometimes. Like how her dad doesn't have any kids."

"You know what I mean. You're not my actual dad."

"I feel like I am," he said.

"I know. I just was thinking about Madeline."

Glen looked slapped. "Oh."

"Sorry."

"No, it's okay. It's nice to hear her name. I didn't know you knew it."

"I do."

"Did your mother tell you?"

"No."

"But you heard it."

"Yes."

Glen smiled. "You hear everything, don't you?"

Agnes smiled and bowed her head proudly. "It's my job."

"No," he said, frowning again. "Your job is to be young."

"I'm sorry I said her name."

He chuckled. "You can say her name. It's nice to hear it—I wasn't lying." He smiled. "I don't talk about her because she's not here. And you are. And you're my girl. But if she were here, I would treat Madeline like I treat you. Like your mother treats you."

"Hmm," said Agnes. She was unconvinced.

In front of them a pair of amber eyes blinked near to the ground.

"Mouse or mole or vole or troll?" Glen said.

"Troll," Agnes said.

"That's what I thought too. Scoot, troll," he said, and the creature scampered away. Glen coughed. Then said, "Sometimes I feel bad for keeping you here. I think maybe we should have left when you got better."

"Don't." Agnes said this forcefully.

"Oh?"

Agnes wanted to say more, but she found that when she opened her mouth to speak, she only choked on a rising feeling. She looked around at the black sky, the near-invisible line of the horizon. She listened to the bats clicking their whereabouts and finding her. The breeze cooled her skin after such a hot day. Sitting alone next to Glen, her dad, in the open air among the animals and the Community. Who would she even be now if they hadn't come here?

"I never want to leave," she said.

Glen pulled her close and kissed her forehead. "I know you don't," he said, still frowning.

"Will you please come back to camp?" Agnes said. "I'm lonely at night."

"But your mother."

"She'll go sleep with Carl. It's where she wants to be anyway." Agnes flinched a bit at having said such a thing to Glen. It was cruel.

But Glen laughed, a reedy empty laugh. "Oh, Agnes. What you don't know about your mother could fill a canyon."

"I know more than you think."

"Oh?"

"I know that she thinks she is protecting us."

"But . . . ?" Glen asked.

"I don't need her to protect me. And neither do you. Even if we needed help, there are other ways."

"Your mother knows what she's doing. And I know what she's doing. We're a team."

"How can you say that when she's with Carl?"

Glen's voice became slow and emphatic. "I know what she's doing," he said again, trying to make it true. "She knows what she's doing. We're a team."

Agnes looked at Glen. "You're a fool," she said quietly. Though she knew it was unkind, she could think of no other way to say it.

Glen blinked. Agnes thought his eyes got wet for a moment, but nothing escaped them. "Maybe," he said.

They were quiet. A ground owl filled in the blanks. A cloud rushed to hide the moon. Agnes shivered.

Glen stretched dramatically, then slapped his thighs. "But," he said loudly, with forced cheer, "to answer your question, yes, I will come back to the sleep circle. My feet were getting awfully cold out here."

Agnes smiled. She helped him up, noticing the way his knees trembled. But he steadied himself without her help. She gathered his bedding, and they walked. She felt like she was the youngest member of a herd and he was the eldest, the most important. She knew no one else thought of him that way, but she felt proud beside him. She didn't think he needed to be the leader to still be important, though she understood that wasn't the way of the herd. She threw his pelts over her shoulder to free her hand, which she slipped into his.

Agnes smiled as they walked and kept her smile even when she noticed her mother watching them approach, her face pinched and disapproving. As they got to the edge of camp, Bea rose from her seat and went to the bed she'd been sharing with Agnes. She picked up her own pelt just as they arrived at the family's spot in the circle. She gave Agnes a tight smile. Agnes tried to mirror it, to mock her mother. But instead of feeling mocked, Agnes thought she saw a laugh behind her mother's eyes. Her mother did not acknowledge Glen. She walked over to where Carl was lounging and put her skins down with his.

Agnes looked up at Glen and was surprised to see he was not watching her mother walk away. He was smiling down at Agnes. He pinched her cheek.

"It's bedtime. Ready, Freddy?" he asked.

"My name's not Freddy," she said.

"It isn't?" He scratched his head. "I could have sworn . . ." It was a thing he used to say to her whenever they were preparing to leave the apartment. Back so long ago when she was a little girl and he was her mother's boyfriend and they were about to step into the harsh, crowded world outside their cozy home.

*   *   *

AS THE COMMUNITY ate their supper and the horizon devoured the sun, Agnes's hackles rose. She looked around the fire and saw that most of the others were still, alert, listening. Each of their heads whipped toward the sound of a single crunch.

They peered into the growing dusk. Agnes saw the shadow of a man, shoulders hunched. It looked as though his hands were thrust into pockets. But his details were lost in the murky light and sage surrounding him.

"Who the hell are you?" Carl yelled at the shadow.

The shadow flinched, lowered himself into a cowering pose. His hair caught the sun's thrown blazes of red.

"Fuck off," Carl yelled.

The shadow loped away, looking back every few paces, the sad whites of his eyes shining, his tongue drooping from his mouth.

"He needs water," Debra said.

"We need water," Carl said.

"We have water." Debra looked at Bea.

Bea said, "No water."

The Community pretended to turn attention again to the fire, where the flames rioted. They kept their hands on their primitive weapons.

"Juan and I will keep watch till morning," said Carl. The shadow retreated and was not sensed again that night.

The next day the Community was on edge, everyone disrupting their work to scan the horizon for a return of the slinking shadow.

The next night it came. This time closer and more reminiscent of a man. A man with the kind of mangy beard found on corpses. Like the dead man on the ridge and his dead beard. *Brad's uncle.* Agnes sneered at the memory. This man in front of them wore madras shorts and thin-soled City shoes. A water tube slung around his torso, deflated, empty. He knelt. He thrust his hands out, palms upraised. His eyes were low and averted.

"He needs water," Debra said.

"We need water," Carl said.

"We have water," Debra said. She looked to Bea again.

Bea sighed. She flicked her hand. "Give him a cup of water."

Carl punched his hand against his thigh, his lips tight and bloodless. But he stood up and found a wooden cup that had been tossed into the dirt. Without brushing it off, he filled it with water and walked it away from the fire, not toward the man but far to his right, to make the man have to crawl to get it.

The Community turned their attention back to the fire. They heard rustling, the grunt of exertion. They heard a slurp, a gasp, a cough. Then they heard nothing. When they bedded down, they assumed he bedded down as well, right where he'd drunk the water. Frank and Linda patrolled that night.

In the earliest part of morning, they woke to a shriek. Debra's. She was standing, a pelt clutched around her. The man in the madras shorts was in her bed, curled up like a pill bug. His eyes bulged and his muscles tensed in preparation for an escape, though he didn't move.

"Okay, that's it," Carl said. "Get up."

"I'm sorry," the man said into his hands.

"Get up."

"I was cold," the man said from the ground.

"Get up."

"Can I have some soup?"

"Get. Up."

"I'm a good worker."

Carl pulled the man up by his armpits, and for a moment the man remained curled, his legs pulled to his chest, his whole body hovering over the dirt. Then he slowly let his legs down and they saw that he was very tall, stringy. Carl appraised him. He might be either very strong or very weak.

"Let's go," Carl said. He marched the man back out into the bushes.

When Carl pivoted to return to camp, the man in the madras shorts reached for him. It was a plaintive reach, one of desperation, sorrow even. They could all see that. But Carl took it as aggression, and he grabbed the man's arm and lunged at his throat. Carl and the man slapped at each other's faces. Their hands and fingers clawed, but their wrists broke form and rendered every move ineffective. They had never seen Carl fight before. It turned out he wasn't very good at it.

The men spun in a circle, their feet shuffling, as though dancing, slapping at each other to avoid getting slapped. Finally Carl landed a punch in the center of the man's face and he went down to one knee holding his nose. Carl kicked the man's foot out from under him, and the man fell to the side, his hands at his face, his knees tucked again. He stayed down.

Carl returned to camp and the Community went about their day.

They cleaned up from breakfast. They did small tasks, tidied as though guests were expected. They turned the meat in the smoker, stretched skins. The Gatherers went out in small groups to gather. They did what they could to distract themselves from the presence of the man. But, nervous, they did their tasks poorly. They scraped a hole into one of the skins. Meat fell into the smoking fire. A batch of pine nuts was ruined.

During supper, the man crawled closer, his tongue hanging out, dirt crusted. Carl walked to him, grabbed him by the collar of his fleece pullover, and dragged his limp, long frame back past the edge of camp.

He sat between sage bushes, exactly where he'd fallen that morning. He broke off the leaves and slowly ate them. It was not sustenance and would eventually make him ill. As they fell asleep, they heard him crawl away. They heard the wet slap of diarrhea against the dirt and the man whimpering.

In the morning, Debra woke again to find the man tangled in her skins, and Carl pushed him to the boundary and fought him again. They did the same dance they had done, but for a much shorter amount of time. Carl landed a punch after only a few turns on their dusty dance floor, and the man crumbled.

This cycle repeated itself over the next two nights and mornings. Debra began to sleep in Juan's bed. In the morning, the man would be found in Debra's bed, luxuriating in the comfort and space. And Carl would drag him away from camp.

On the third night, around the fire, Debra said, "I brought him scraps yesterday."

"That's not allowed," said Dr. Harold bitterly.

"I don't care," said Debra. "And I'm going to do it again tonight."

"Debra, why?" Bea asked.

"Because I want my bed back," she said. Juan scowled at her and she scowled back. "He kicks in his sleep."

"She steals the covers," he said. They each pawed at their own bleary eyes.

"He's not going away," Glen croaked. "Maybe we should discuss what to do?"

"Let me handle it," said Carl. The conversation ended there.

As people retired to their beds, Carl walked to where the man crouched and kicked him. They saw the man trying to flatten against the ground as Carl lifted him with kicks to his abdomen.

"Stay down," Carl demanded, though it was clear the man had no intention of fighting back. Carl kicked him over onto his back and straddled him. He pulled his head up by his hair, and he landed four punches to his face. When he let go of his hair, the man's head fell back to the ground, as if returning to where it belonged. Carl leaned toward him, secret-telling distance, and stayed like that as everyone else held their breath. Then Carl walked back to camp and crawled into his bed, where Bea lay waiting.

In the morning, the man was building a fire poorly. His lips were full and purple. His cheeks distended like a harvesting chipmunk's.

The breakfast crew took over and the man watched carefully, taking notes with no paper. When they all sat around the fire to eat, he sat too. And when they were given a bowl of blackened rice, he was given one too.

"This is Adam," Carl said.

"Hi, Adam," they all said.

Adam tried to smile, but no emotion escaped his swollen face.

"Tell us a little about yourself, Adam," said Debra.

And that's when they heard that there were other people in the Wilderness State. That they'd been here for some time. And that more were coming.

His chin quivering with anger, Carl declared them, whoever they were, to be Trespassers. But Adam said they already had a name. They called themselves the Mavericks.

SISTER AND BROTHER and Pinecone woke from nightmares in which they were blindfolded and dragged away in the purple night to the Mavericks' dirty hovels. They said they pictured a kind of wild man the adults knew did not exist. A wild man covered in dirt, animal blood dripping from his mouth. The kind of wild man City dwellers had perhaps always imagined the Community to be. But probably these other people looked like Adam. Their City clothes were dirty and hanging on them, but were still City clothes. Their hair was too long but still evoked the last professional cut they'd received. The soles of their shoes were splitting, but they were rubber soles. They still had jeans. They still had unbroken eyeglasses. They would look ruined by the Wilderness, not at one with it. What they wondered was, while Adam seemed harmless enough, would the others be?

According to Adam, the City the Community had known was nothing compared to how it was now, and that is why people were fleeing, making such a risky trek to hide in the last place they could. The last wilderness. Whenever the Newcomers would try to nod their heads knowingly, being the previous most recent City dwellers, Adam would point at them and bark, "No, you don't know. You don't know."

His storytelling went on for days. But then, one night, he went quiet. They thought it might be fun to have a new audience who hadn't heard their own stories, the ones about the beginning, the Ballads they'd created from their history. So Juan told them, creeping around the circle, his eyes beaming emotion, making faces, hands fluttering in pantomime. He'd done some amateur theatre in the City, he told them, which was new information.

Adam sat there politely the first night, then distractedly the second. On the third, he stuck his thumb out and thrust it down. "Boo," he said as Juan recounted a treacherous hunt. Juan froze.

"Excuse me?" said Bea.

"I said, 'Boo.'" Adam stuck his tongue out. "Your stories are a snooze. And while I'm at it, boo-hoo, poor you." He rubbed his fists into his eyes and said, "*Waah*. Hardship? You had it so easy! You guys just walked right in. I bet they flew you over in a cargo plane."

The Community said nothing since it was true.

"You walked up to the door of the Wilderness State and it was wide-open. Practically given a red carpet. Now you want to hear about hardship, I'll tell you about hardship. We had to escape the City. We didn't have a cargo plane take us. We had to walk to get here. We bribed truck drivers if we were lucky enough to see one. It took months and months. We evaded the authorities the whole way. The ones that made it anyway. And there are plenty who didn't, okay. Okay?" He shouted and they startled, and some of them obediently nodded their heads. "But we've been here for years and you didn't even suspect it. We all know who you are. We've seen your bare asses when you shit. And you've never even suspected we existed."

The Community was dumbstruck.

Carl latched onto what he could. "Years?" he said. "Then why are your clothes still so new?"

"I didn't say I had been here for years. We. Us. The Mavericks."

"How did you manage to hook up with them if we've never seen them?"

"I guess I'm a better explorer than you."

This angered Carl. "I think you're an ex-Ranger who got fired and went nuts and didn't want to leave."

"No, I'm a Maverick. I'm on the team. We don't follow their rules.

We make our own rules." Adam popped his arm and made a muscle. It quivered effortlully. He still looked dangerously undernourished. It was hard to know if he was telling them a story or the truth.

"We get in trouble when you don't follow the rules," Carl complained. "We get blamed."

Again, Adam wrenched at his eyes. "Boo-fucking-hoo. Try being on the run 24/7."

"We don't have to run," said Carl. "Because we're allowed to be here."

Adam snarled, jealousy rising to the surface.

Bea perked up. "And that is a good distinction. We are allowed to be here. You're not. Why, we could just call the Rangers right now and let them know we have ourselves a Maverick. Maybe that's what we ought to do."

For the first time Adam looked distraught, not superior. "You have a phone?"

"Of course we have a phone," Bea guffawed. They did not have a phone.

Adam blanched. "Please don't." He crawled on his knees over to Bea. "Please, I can't go back. I won't talk about the Mavericks anymore. I'll be good. I promise."

With Adam cowering it was hard to continue with the threat. Bea nodded.

Debra glared at her as Adam rose, shaking, and went to sleep under a tree.

"That was so mean, Bea," she scolded.

Debra followed Adam, Agnes assumed to console him. She must have also told him there were no phones because after that it was *Mavericks this* and *Mavericks that* for days. It sounded at times like Adam was a superfan of the Mavericks and not necessarily one himself.

After that Debra and Adam were inseparable, which upset Dr. Harold a great deal.

"I don't see why we are harboring this . . . this fugitive," Dr. Harold muttered whenever anyone was in earshot.

"Oh, enough," Debra huffed. "He has as much right to be here as we do."

"That is patently false," Dr. Harold sniped back. "He has zero right to be here. And we have one hundred percent right to be here. We have official paperwork."

"It's a free country," she said.

Juan snorted, "No, it's not, Debra." He was still bitter from having shared a bed with her.

"But it's against the rules," Dr. Harold said quietly.

"Since when are you such a stickler for the rules?" Debra snapped.

Dr. Harold's jaw dropped. "Debra, I've always been a stickler for the rules," he said, clearly hurt. "Did you not know that?"

Debra shrugged, irritated, distracted. "Adam," she barked, and his hand shot up from the sleeping circle where he was lounging and she went and lay down with him.

Dr. Harold looked down at the ground, dejected. Patty's mom patted his arm.

It was hard to know what to do with Adam. They trained him in camp chores. He was okay at working but not great. They didn't want to show him how to do too much because all the things they had learned over the years now felt valuable. It was knowledge they felt they should protect and keep secret. So they butchered, tanned, darned, mended and sewed, shot arrows, hulled rice, shelled pine nuts, filtered water all with their backs to him. Debra showed him how to sew with sinew even though they'd told her not to, but otherwise they thought they kept their skills and secrets hidden. They didn't know if he was a foe. But they knew he wasn't their friend.

Still, Adam found out about things they would have preferred he not know.

"Why are you headed to the Caldera?" he asked while skulking in the shadows one evening. Carl and Bea were laying out their planned route for the next days.

"It's where we were told to go," said Bea.

"Hmm," he said.

They started discussing again, but in whispers.

"Why were you told to go there?" he interrupted again. He squinted at them. "I mean, do you even know?"

"Of course we know. There's a party."

"A party?" Adam howled.

"Yeah, there's a new Post on the Caldera and they're having a party to celebrate."

"The only thing on the Caldera is their Lodge and that's their special meeting place. Believe me, you wouldn't be invited to any party the Rangers were throwing at the Lodge. They hate you."

"No, they don't." Bea sat a little straighter. "They're having the party *for* us."

"Hmm," he said again, stroking his chin and peering at Bea. "I thought you were, like, the smart one."

"Don't start," Carl snapped.

Adam raised his hands. "Hey, I'm just saying, I wouldn't trust what the Rangers told me. Especially if they invited me to a party. What are they going to do when you get there, roast you over an open fire?"

Bea rolled her eyes. "Don't be an idiot. We've known the Rangers for a long time. Yes, some of them are assholes. Many, even. But not all. We have a relationship."

Adam howled again, but he kept whatever made him laugh to himself.

"Well," said Helen. "I can't wait to get there. I need a good party."

"I've always wanted to see the Caldera," said Dr. Harold. "We weren't allowed to go before."

Adam's eyes danced over their faces. "Amazing that you just go where you're told to go and avoid what you're told to avoid. *Yes, sir, no, sir.* I mean, getting here took some creativity, I'll give you that.

But honestly, haven't you evolved yet? What happened to free will? Didn't you talk about that, Carl, in one of those stupid interviews you did forever ago?"

"Do you ever want to eat again?" threatened Carl.

Adam put his hands up. "I didn't mean to offend," he said. Though it was obvious he had. Debra cackled alone.

Adam was lounging by the fire, his feet up on the Cast Iron, chewing on a twig. "I just know I wouldn't go if I were you." He shrugged.

Bea glared. "Well, nobody asked you to go," she said matter-of-factly. "You can go wherever you want. But we're going to the Caldera. And we're going in the morning."

Adam smirked. "A unanimous decision I see."

"This conversation is over," said Carl. "You can sleep out there." He waved his hand into the dark. "With Glen."

"You can sleep with me, Adam," said Debra, sneering at Carl.

Agnes looked at Carl. His face was raging. She looked to her mother and saw that she was angry too, but in a very different way.

As Agnes fell asleep, she could hear their curt, cross whispers.

*   *   *

THE COMMUNITY WOKE to a scream. Debra's. She was standing by her bed, a skin wrapped around her. Her eyes were fixed on the bedding at her feet. Adam usually slept there, but now the bed was empty except for a pool of blood on the skins.

Carl knelt over the blood and dipped his finger in it. He sniffed it. Licked it. His face screwed. "This is rabbit blood," he said.

"How do you know?" said Debra.

"You can taste the rabbit." He waved his hand at it. "See for yourself."

Some tried it. They nodded.

It was rabbit blood.

"What an amateur," Carl scoffed. "Did he think we wouldn't taste the blood?"

The camp had been overturned. A pouch of meat was gone, some sewing and patching materials, two skins they had just finished tanning, and the Cast Iron.

"That son of a bitch," said Frank.

"Well, he certainly had help," said Carl. "He couldn't carry the Cast Iron by himself."

Debra sniffed. "He's stronger than you think."

"Why are you defending him?" Carl said.

Debra's face crumpled. "I don't know," she cried, flinging herself to her bed, into the blood and everything.

The group tightened their circle. Some thought he'd acted alone and staged a violent kidnapping. Some thought he must have reconnected with Mavericks, who helped him. Maybe it had been a setup from the beginning. He'd been a plant. A mole. Whatever he was, he was also a scoundrel.

Agnes thought he was probably just strong enough to carry all of that alone. It's why he took only one pouch of meat. A group would have taken more.

They searched for clues to the direction the Cast Iron might have been taken. They reported evidence like broken twigs and a footprint, some scratched bark, and a chunk of fallen jerky all at the edge of the forest, heading toward the Caldera.

"Well, we know the direction he went," said Helen.

"Or *they* went," whispered Patty's mom.

"I think we should try to overtake him," said Carl. "He can't get far carrying that pot." Carl's fist twitched, opened and closed, as though he could see Adam right in front of him.

Debra welled up again. "Don't hurt him."

Agnes couldn't remember seeing Debra ever cry before today, even when her wife had left early on. Or when Caroline died. She hadn't thought Debra was capable of it. Agnes crouched to where Debra was curled and put her hand on her back. "I'm sorry, Debra."

"Don't give her any pity," said Bea. "This is all her fault."

"Me?" Debra shrieked through a sob. "You told him he couldn't come to the Caldera."

"Well you're the one who wanted to give him water in the first place."

"But you're the one who said we could," said Debra. "You're the leader. It's your job to say no. So this is your fault," she screamed.

Agnes couldn't remember ever hearing Debra scream before today either. It was turning out to be an interesting day for Debra.

Bea's fists clenched at her sides. She looked as though she had an army of words heaving against her gritted teeth. But she held them all back and finally said, "We have to try to track him. That pot is too valuable to us. That bag had a lot of meat in it. And that pemmican is irreplaceable when winter comes. Oh, for fuck's sake, stop crying, Debra."

*   *   *

THEY PACKED QUICKLY and headed into the cinder cone forest.

The forest rolled out before them. Thick with tall trees but not shrouded like it had seemed from its edges. Under the canopy, birds zipped tree to tree and all sounds had an echo, though there was no clear reason why. After a couple of days, Agnes could see, through breaks in the vegetation, what looked like dunes. Scattered cinder cones around the base of the Caldera. Their tops were sandy and bare, their slopes speckled with skinny firs. They had been bubbling baby cauldrons, but now they were long dead.

They'd been racing, quick camping, sleeping for only a few hours a night, eating jerky as they went. Carl was leading. He was like a wolf with meat on the nose. The children were having to run sometimes to keep up. The line of them was stretched long into the forest. But it was Glen who really struggled. After a couple of nights, he'd barely made it to camp before they were up and walking again. He didn't get up with them. He sat hunched over his knees, shaking his head, heaving. Agnes stood with him. Carl was already blazing some kind of trail out of view.

"Mom," Agnes yelled. Her mother reappeared quickly from up the path and saw Glen. She looked like she might collapse, but then she barked angrily, "Everyone drop your things—we're camping tonight." She dropped her bag and sprinted ahead to where Carl was hustling along.

People dropped their bags and milled around. Some of the Newcomers cast irritated glances at Glen, some of the Originalists too. They had left people behind in the past. But this was Glen. And this was different, Agnes thought. Wasn't it?

Her mother was gone a long time. The camp was set up, a mix between a quick camp and something longer, since the Community didn't know the amount of time they'd be there. A fire had been set up, but the beds were basic, a circle of one pelt per family.

Agnes heard them before she saw them. A rising cacophony made from two angry voices. When Bea came back down the mountain, her eyes were dancing and her jaw was set. She plunked down by Glen, who was curled by the fire. They were close enough to touch, but she didn't touch him. She chewed on her knuckles instead. Carl followed after, furious in every movement. A walking argument. But he kept his mouth shut.

Debra was the first to speak. "How long will we be here?"

"Until we are all rested and able to continue," Bea said flatly.

Carl paced by some wimpy trees. At times he would stop, spread an arm like he was about to speak. But he would say nothing. Just tuck his arm back and begin pacing again. No one spoke and no one wanted to look at anyone else. Finally, Carl took his pelt into the woods. Agnes expected Val to follow with Baby Egret, but she didn't. It seemed she hardly registered he'd gone.

The camp tension lightened slightly. Bea sighed a long, tortured sigh. Debra got a bag of jerky and passed it around.

Agnes went to sit next to her mother. "What did you tell Carl?"

"I told him we were only as strong as our weakest member."

"What did he say?"

She shook her head. "Glen just needs some sleep. He'll be fine tomorrow. And I'll lead so we can keep a healthy pace."

"I could lead," said Agnes.

But her mother looked at her. She looked weary, troubled. "No, I don't want you up there. In case we run into anything."

Just then Baby Egret's caterwaul ricocheted off the tree trunks and Agnes flinched.

Her mother laughed. "You think that's bad. That is nothing compared to you. The neighbors, they moved to another floor because of it."

"No, they didn't," Agnes said, a smile creeping to her face.

"Yeah, they did," her mother insisted. "You were so loud. Such a ruckus. But you didn't have colic like Baby Egret. You just liked to scream. You were mostly happy. So I didn't mind."

Agnes listened to Egret and tried to imagine herself that young, and she couldn't. She was so much older now, so far away from her childhood she had trouble conjuring it. She flushed and wrapped her arms around her waist. It had been too long since she bled last and she wondered if she wasn't bleeding because she was pregnant. She smiled a little at the thought. She didn't want to tell anyone her suspicions just yet. It felt like a secret she ought to keep to herself. At least for a little while. She had finally convinced Jake to have real sex. His face was rose red and his voice so quiet she had to keep asking "What" to his murmurings. "I love you," he would whisper into her neck. She didn't know about that. But she did know when he tensed and became very still, his eyes rolling skyward, that she had someone else's life inside her for the first time.

"Why did you do it?"

"Why did I do what?"

"Have me? Have a baby?" Agnes wasn't sure if she'd ever asked this. When her mother looked at her as though struck by a thought that caused her great emotion, one she didn't want to share, Agnes was certain she hadn't.

Her mother opened and closed her mouth several times. "I don't know how to answer that."

Agnes tried to help. "Well, probably because you wanted to be a mom?" That seemed easy enough, she thought.

Bea smiled. Her eyes got wet, and she touched Agnes's cheek as though she were brushing away dirt.

"Something like that." Then she laughed seeing the irritation of a bad answer flit across Agnes's face. Agnes's frown turned to a smile. She always smiled when she made her mother laugh.

"Big answer please," Agnes sang and reached one of her small hands out to play with the fringe of her mother's tunic. Her mother played with the fringe adjacent, and their fingers entangled.

"The small answer is I wanted to be a mom."

"Okay."

"The big answer, I guess, is I wanted to be *my* mom. To live her life. The life I knew would work out. With the kid and with everything working out okay. It wasn't even necessarily the life I wanted. It's just what I assumed would happen. I wasn't very adventurous, I guess."

"And was it just like that?"

"Oh no, it wasn't like that at all."

"Why?"

"Well, my mom raising me had already happened. And I knew that everything had turned out okay. But when I had you, I realized that nothing was certain. We were at the very beginning together and anything could happen. It's obvious now, but for some reason it came as a shock to me. When you got sick, I had a hard time believing it. I remember thinking, *This isn't supposed to happen.* So I got scared. It wasn't all scary, of course, but I remember being scared a lot when you were little."

Agnes didn't need her mother to tell her that it was both nice and not nice to have a child. It was always there on her face.

Nervously, Agnes said, "I wonder if I'll have babies." She hoped she'd said it in a casual tone, one that wouldn't give away why she was saying it.

Bea smiled. "If you want to, you'll have them."

"Do you think I'd be good at it?"

"I think you'd be great at it."

"Will it hurt?" Agnes said, not sure what to imagine but imagining that it would occur in the thick woods in the dark or on a smelly playa, her anguish making birds caw and fly away. She'd heard some of the women give birth and it seemed awful. But she remembered secretly watching as her mother birthed Madeline's little body. Her mother hadn't looked to be in very much pain, and had been mostly silent, until after it was all over and she clenched her fists and screamed.

"It will definitely hurt," Bea said. "But the pain of labor doesn't last forever. That's just the very first part. There's so much more to being a mom."

"Like what?"

Bea cackled. "Like what," she said. "Like what," she said again, pulling Agnes up into a tight hug. Agnes squirmed but couldn't free herself. She coughed and sputtered, made her unhappiness known in grunts. But it just made Bea laugh and squeeze harder, rocking her back and forth like she was a baby again. Agnes always felt so much younger in her mother's arms. Her legs splayed across her mother's lap, her arms like doll arms pinned uselessly at her sides. And so she relented to the swaying and her mother's hard love and almost, almost, almost fell asleep.

Agnes awoke warm and happy because they had all slept, Glen and Bea and Agnes, in a huddle by the fire. It was the first time since her mother had returned that they'd been together as a family asleep. Or as a family doing much else. The sun sliced between tree trunks on its way out of the ground. The rest of camp seemed to be asleep. She watched a robin hurry up to her as though it had something urgent to tell her. Then stop. Then hurry up. Then stop. Then the robin took off and a shadow overcame the sun and chilled her. She squinted up. Carl's face was blocking the light, staring down at them. He didn't speak. He didn't wake her mother or Glen. They still lay in a pile, her mother's head atop her pressed hands on Glen's side, her shoulder fitted into his stomach, his skinny body curled, protective, around her. Carl paused only briefly and then prowled by, his bright eyes taking it all in.

*   *   *

AFTER THREE DAYS, Glen was walking around again spritely, eager. He got in line for breakfast and ate a full bowl of porridge. He helped clean up even though it wasn't his job. And then he scouted for micro trash even though they weren't packing up. He wore the oddest smile, Agnes thought. He looked serene. The rest, it seemed, had done wonders for him. Agnes noticed her mother watching him over the previous days, happy. As though admiring her accomplishment.

After breakfast, Carl called a meeting around the fire.

"We've had our rest and it seems time to get moving. The lucky thing is Adam couldn't have gotten far with the Cast Iron. But he could have changed course. I want to send a couple groups out in different directions to track. We'll meet back here just after the sun crests. Then we can still get in some walking for the day. Linda, Juan, and Helen, follow the arc of the sunset. Patty's mom, Dr. Harold, and Jake, head toward the sunrise. And Frank, me, and Glen will head up the mountain. Everyone else will stay back with Val and Bea."

"Wait," Bea said, confused. "Glen should stay back. I can go instead."

"Bea, I want to go," Glen said with that odd smile. "I'm the reason we lost Adam's trail. I want to help get us back on track."

Bea narrowed her eyes at him. "No. It's not a good idea. You should stay here."

Everyone stared.

"No, Bea, I've got to pull my weight. Carl's right."

Her mother's eyes flared at Carl. "What do you mean, Carl is right? What has Carl said?" Her face was a full-on panicked sneer, while Carl looked calm and bored.

"I can't just succumb. That's not why I'm here."

"You're here because our daughter's life depended on it, remember? And because you like pretending to be a caveman."

Glen winced. "That's not nice, Bea."

"I don't care. You're not going tracking. I'll go."

Carl said, "I don't want you to go, Bea. We need leadership here. We can't just leave the kids alone with Val, no offense, and Glen, who you're saying is too weak to walk. We don't know who is out there. Plus, he's going to be walking for days, so he might as well start now."

"Bea," Glen said, "I need to do this."

"Maybe you should try listening to Glen for a change," said Carl. "He understands that we have to keep agile. We have to be flexible. Or else we'll never survive."

Bea stared hard at Carl, then at Glen. She looked like she might cry. But she laughed her haughty laugh instead. "Well, then, if Glen wants to go, who am I to stop him?"

Glen put his cheek to Agnes's cheek. "Bye, honey." He squeezed her mother's hand and seemed reluctant to let go, his odd morning smile giving way to a glumness at the corners of his mouth.

Agnes watched her mother process all the information coming her way, trying to sort out what was real and what wasn't. Carl and Glen both peered at Bea holding Glen's hand, fighting to remain neutral. Agnes saw a deep distrust in her eyes. A blatant worry. It made Agnes's heart skip a beat. She realized this was the first time she'd seen them interact publicly since her mother had returned. Even when they'd all slept by the fire together, they hadn't spoken. Upon waking, her mother had silently walked away, and Agnes took her place keeping Glen warm, keeping him company.

Glen was the first to let go, but he had to pry his hand from her mother's, her grip was so desperate.

*   *   *

EVERYONE ELSE HAD returned by the time Carl and Frank came back alone. Carl carried a fox around his neck, its tongue limp and pink. He stopped in front of Bea. "It was an accident, I promise," he said, his face flat, his eyes averted. "I tried to bring him back, but he insisted I leave him." He jerked his head in the direction he'd come. "About two miles up."

Carl knelt, drew his skinning knife, and went to work on the fox, its eyes so dead they looked like Xs.

Without a word Bea moved briskly in the direction Carl had come. Agnes followed several paces behind, quietly, unsure if her mother even knew she was there. She had trouble keeping up. She didn't remember the last time she'd seen her mother move so quickly. Agnes stopped. No, she remembered.

She watched her mother running up the mountain, with her beeline, her singular purpose, and saw her running for that truck, crawling over that driver and disappearing. But there was no one for her mother to run away with this time. There was nowhere for her to go. Agnes repeated this to herself, a bird call in her head. She sprinted to catch up, to follow her mother from a safe distance, as she so often did.

In the forest Bea called for Glen, and after a while Agnes heard him reply, "Oh, hi," with an ambivalent shrug in his voice. He repeated "Hi" so Bea could find him. And when she reached him and was standing over him, her hands to her face, he smiled and his voice turned affectionate and forlorn. "Oh, hi," he said, smiling sadly up at her.

Bea burst into tears.

Agnes froze.

"Oh no, oh no, oh no." Bea fell to her knees. "What have you done?" she said, cupping his face.

"I fell down," he said.

His leg was twisted at the hip. The knee almost pointing behind. There was a gash on the side of his head that was the pink of inside flesh. Agnes crept closer until she was next to them. She saw blood pooling in his ear.

"You must be in so much pain," said Bea.

"An excruciating amount."

"But you're so calm," said Agnes.

"I'm happy to see you two." He smiled and then Agnes noticed the tear trails through his dirty face. Dry now. His eyes vibrated at her. He was in shock.

"Carl said it was an accident," Bea said. "Was it an accident?"

Glen shrugged. "Yeah." He smiled at Bea and then up at Agnes, his eyes pooling. "It was an accident."

None of them mentioned trying to get him back to camp. There was nothing to be done. They all knew it.

Glen sighed. "I guess we should have gone to the Private Lands after all," he said, looking up at Bea.

Bea laid her head on his chest. "Oh, Glen," she said, her voice breaking.

Glen licked his finger and rubbed Bea's cheek.

"You look ridiculous," he said.

Bea laughed through tears.

But Glen said, "No, I'm serious. You look silly. This is silly. This whole thing. Go home," he said. It was as though he'd just woken up from a dream clear-eyed and certain.

Bea sat up. "What do you mean, go home?"

"I mean go home. This is all stupid. The goal has been achieved. Agnes is healthy. You don't really need to be living like this anymore, do you? So go home."

Bea stood up. She crossed her arms in front of her deerskin clothes as though embarrassed of them. For a moment she seemed not to know what to do. Then she kicked dirt at him.

He chuckled and reached for her ankle. He gripped it, massaging behind her anklebone with his thumb. "There you go, getting mad at something perfectly reasonable. My mad Bea."

"No," she said.

"Always so mad," he continued, moving his hand up to her calf. "That's the first thing I liked about you. You got things done. You did. I mean look at her." He pointed to Agnes. "Now go home."

"There is no home," she said, her voice cracking again.

"See, there you go again. Of course there's a home."

She kicked him for real, and he winced. "I had plans for us and they were working."

Agnes stepped toward them, on instinct, to protect, but Glen didn't seem affected.

"I'm sorry I ruined them," he said, running his hand up her calf, over its ropy muscle, dusted and grimy. "I love you, Mad Bea. Please take Agnes home."

"Don't tell me what to do," Bea said.

"It's over."

"You don't know what it's like in the City."

"I know it's bad. It was always bad and we did all right. Go home. Think about what's next. You were right, this was always a stupid thing to have done."

"I never said that."

"Of course you did. You said it all the time. And you were right."

"Don't say that."

"Do it for Agnes. She's strong now. She doesn't need you to protect her in this way anymore."

"Don't tell me about my daughter."

His smile drooped at the corners. He released her leg, dusted it with his hand. The muscle quivered. He rolled moaning onto his side and into as much of a ball as he could. His dead leg dragged behind.

Agnes watched her mother stand over Glen, peering hard at his back, at the worn deerskin that covered it, the pelt worn through in places because no one had ever given him a new skin to wear nor a raw skin to fashion into something. He wasn't a good hunter, and whenever he did catch something, he never kept anything good like the hide for himself. Agnes thought of the many pants he'd made her from the skins of deer he hunted. Everyone gave her little garments or scraps to make clothes from. They all did that for the children. So she had barely noticed that Glen did so with his meager amounts, even as it meant he went without.

"You should have done more," Bea accused, choking on the words, part anger, part despair. She put her foot against that worn skin and shoved his limp body.

"Please don't kick me anymore." He curled tighter, his head hiding in his hands as though he expected a beating. "You may have noticed I'm not doing well."

Bea pushed him with her foot again.

Agnes hauled her little leg back and kicked her mother's leg.

"Hey," both Glen and Bea cried.

Glen snapped, surprisingly harsh, "Don't kick your mother."

Agnes's tears sprouted. "But she's kicking you."

"She's allowed to kick me. But you're not allowed to kick her. Do you hear me?"

Agnes did not remember Glen ever raising his voice at her. Her mind spun. She felt hot and short of breath. She squeezed her eyes shut. *Count to ten*, she thought. *Then it will all make sense.* She counted to ten, opened her eyes.

Glen's hand was on Agnes's foot, his somber smile, his welling eyes looking at her. "Hey, I love you." Agnes knew her eyes were wet now, but she didn't feel the tears.

Bea whimpered and shrugged off her coat, made just before these last snows had ended, warm, fluffy, still smelling of smoke and the animal, and laid it over him.

"Thank you," he said, pulling the arm of the coat closer and feeding the edge into his mouth. He bit down and groaned. It was a dark, violent noise.

After, he looked at Agnes. "I've been thinking," he said, his voice a bit muffled by the coat. "Maybe you should be in school?"

Bea felt his forehead. "Are you delirious?"

"I'm serious."

"You rhymed," said Agnes, and smiled her best crooked smile at him. Glen coughed, shivered. Hugged the coat again.

Agnes's throat tightened, and she felt ashamed for saying something so lighthearted. Her heart sank like a boulder.

But then Glen said, "Ha-ha-ha," in this new shrugging voice, almost droll, and they all, incredibly, laughed. Her mother and Glen laughed uproariously, till more tears came out of their eyes.

The laughter trailed off, and Agnes watched Glen's smile slowly remove itself from his face. She watched every twitch as it disappeared because it would be the last one she saw. She felt him leaving. She looked at her mother. Did she feel it too?

"Shhh," Bea said, even though no one was making any noise. As if to discourage any more talking, or maybe she was trying to soothe them. Still cupping Glen's cheek, she said, "Agnes, I think it's time for you to go back now."

"Why?" Her voice was shrill, out of control.

"Because."

"Are you going back?"

"No, I'm going to stay here a bit longer."

"I don't want to leave." Agnes dropped to her knees next to Glen. He was still smiling at her, sad, in agony, but steady. She balled her hands in her lap.

"Agnes," her mother said, "I want you to go back and let everyone know we're here. I want you to stay there until I return. Tell them not to leave. Tell Carl not to leave."

"No. Please."

"Agnes, go back to the camp."

Glen touched her foot. "It's okay," he said. "We can say goodbye now."

Agnes couldn't move. She knew she would never see Glen again, and that was bad enough. But she didn't trust she would see her mother again either.

"Agnes," her mother said again, firmly.

Agnes put her fingers to her mouth and chewed their tips.

Glen gently took her fingers out of her mouth and squeezed her hand. "She'll come back, I promise."

Her mother's face went bloodless while Agnes blushed, exposed and raw. Known.

What would they do without Glen to translate?

Agnes leaned to kiss Glen on the forehead.

"My darling daughter," he said. His lips were dry and his smile disappeared into his skin, but his eyes were wet and beaming up at her. "I couldn't be prouder of you," he said.

Her mother put her hand on Agnes's shoulder and drew her back to her feet, turned her around, and with an outstretched arm firmly directed her toward camp.

Agnes walked away slowly. Then she stopped.

"Agnes," her mother warned.

She started walking again, stopping every few steps to wait until her mother ordered her forward again. When she stopped receiving orders, perhaps because she was obscured from view, or simply because they were done with her, she stopped and just listened.

Their voices were soft, unintelligible except for a few words here and there. *Please. Never. Soon.* It was just like when she was a small girl in her small bedroom in her small pink bed, listening to them be the adults in the kitchen, making a meal they didn't share with her, a much more special meal than she had been given. The clink of glasses and the thunk of a wine bottle. Some music playing lightly, their laughter happy, or their voices concerned if they were talking about something important. Piecing it all together without seeing it, just staring into the darkness of her room, the City outside dark after curfew. She always felt safe.

Now it wasn't so much what they were saying. In fact, like then, she couldn't decipher the content. It was more the feeling, what lay in the bottom tones of their voices. A kind of comfort, ease. It was the same tone as back then. It was familiar. How people felt about one another was always in the voice. In the way they talked to one another when they thought they were alone.

Agnes returned to camp and, without waiting for dark, slid into the bed of skins she had shared with her parents at one time in the past. Jake arrived and slipped under the covers. He tried to hold her, but she pushed him away. This was her family's bed. He tried to crawl back in, as though he knew what Agnes needed better than she did, and so she kicked him. He yelped in surprise and scooted away. Agnes shivered half awake until the sun set and rose again. In the morning, Jake brought her food she didn't eat. She watched the ants overtake the bowl and thought of all the food Glen had passed along to her. Food he hadn't eaten himself, that had led him to get weak and die. And how she had happily accepted that food, thoughtlessly, because she was the child and that is just what people did for children. She thought she could carry more weight during their treks and that was all she had needed to do to help him, to protect him. There were so many more things he had needed.

The next day, just as they were lining up for dinner, her mother walked out of the darkness and back into camp. She was wearing her coat again. A streak of Glen's blood was painted across its left arm.

She did not walk up to Agnes first. Instead she went to Carl. He put his hand on her shoulder and she shrugged it off. They exchanged some words, serious at first, angry even, in low voices. Then less so. Then just quiet. And then they laughed. Bea tossed her head back as she laughed, as though she was carefree. Agnes saw furious stars.

After dinner, Bea finally approached Agnes by the fire. She put her arms around her and kissed her forehead.

"Glen loved you so much," she said.

Agnes stood rigid and still as though her mother were a predator and she were prey. She wanted to run away. She wanted to fling her arms around her mother's neck and sob. She didn't move a muscle.

Bea squeezed her harder. "Agnes, it's okay if you want to cry."

Agnes mumbled, "Okay."

Her mother took her by the shoulders and peered at her face, but Agnes averted her eyes. Looked at the brown bugs crawling from the wood, trying to escape the fire that was probably ravaging their home. Seeing her mother laughing with Carl. Seeing her mother running for that truck. Remembering holding Glen's hand on all the walks they had to do without her mother.

Her mother said, "I'll move my bedding and we'll share again. I think that would be nice. Would you like that?"

"No," said Agnes. "I'm fine by myself."

"Are you sure?" her mother said.

She sounded disappointed, so Agnes's heart leapt, then plummeted. "Yes," Agnes said.

"Okay," her mother said, and tried to hug her again.

"Is he dead?" Agnes asked, her eyes still peering hard at the ground. Of course he was. But she wanted her mother to say it.

"Yes, he is."

"Did you have to kill him, or did he die on his own?" Agnes's mouth was taut, bitter; her stomach churned. Her voice was steady.

Her mother's knees wobbled at Agnes's question. She looked like she might stumble into the fire. "Agnes," she gasped. But then she choked out, "He died."

"Did you do the ritual? Did you stay for the buzzards? And the coyotes?" She wanted to barrage her like a gale would. She wanted to be relentless.

Agnes looked up at her mother for the first time. She wanted to see her damage. To see her hurt as much as Agnes had been hurt. As much as Glen had been hurt.

Her mother's face was a dark cloud. Her eyes were bloodshot, and the skin around her eyes welted red as though she'd been pummeled.

Her face was streaked almost clean from dried tears. She looked like she'd been crying, and crying hard, for days. Then how had she been laughing with Carl? Agnes choked on her breaths. Panicking. She had invited a new kind of hardness between them when, she now realized, before there had only been simple grief. Something they could have shared. Agnes felt a wave of shame, an impulse to drop to her knees, erase what she'd just said. But there was no going back from it. It was too late. Why did her mother insist on being so many people at once when Agnes only needed her to be the one? Her mother's face stormed, seeming at odds with even itself. She looked like a deer might look when Agnes was about to cut its throat. There was a current of despair there, but also a bolt that went through it. She knew to hold tight then, to lean on the legs. Because that bolt was its last defense.

Her mother turned to the fire, now standing shoulder to shoulder with her daughter. Not looking at her, she said, "There are some things you don't understand. You think you do. But you don't. I hope you never have to."

For the first time Agnes believed her mother was right about this. Agnes looked at her mother's profile in the firelight. It was dreadful.

"I love you," her mother seethed. "I know you love me."

Agnes's eyes filled with hot remorseful tears. She reached out, but her mother flinched angrily, and Agnes froze.

Her mother continued in the slowest, hardest voice Agnes had heard come from her. "But if you don't like what you're seeing, Agnes Day—" Her mother spit into the fire. It hissed in the coal's red core. "Then you'd better cover your fucking eyes."

All the light of the night was snuffed out.

Her mother turned away from her and joined Carl in bed.

IT WAS OBVIOUS when they had arrived at the top of the Caldera because the winds shifted from blowing at their backs to blowing in their faces. The land across seemed flat, but only because they'd been on the side of a mountain for so long. They hadn't had a vantage in a long time. But at the top here, the highest thing around, they could see where they'd come from. They saw the extent of their up-and-down trekking over the past seasons. The Caldera had wide, swelling foothills. They saw how many cinder cones popped up from the tree-covered landscape. Some were bare-topped. But others were pint-sized volcanoes, thick black cauldron bubbles covered almost to the top now with trees.

In the further distance they saw plumes of smoke, and hazy skies at the horizon in each direction. Fires in the sage sea. Fires in the mountains. The air was singed. It made the top look like an aged photograph of a place that no longer existed.

As they approached the middle, they walked downhill again. They were walking into the Caldera proper, the volcano's pock. Its wound. It was eerily quiet, as though nothing lived there. It was unlike any landscape they'd been to, barren and full all at once.

Around a bend the lakes emerged. One black and one blue. The closer they got, the more the black one evolved into a deep murky green and the blue one became white like the clouded sky above it.

The lakes were bordered by tall pines, with the greenest needles Agnes had seen in a long time and tall rusty-orange trunks. Healthy trees. Not thirsty like what they'd seen lately. They were watered well by the lakes and snowmelt. So much vibrancy in a landscape marred by lava. The obsidian flows were glassy fingers reaching for the lakes. Elsewhere, those fingers were rough, the rock sharp, reddened, and treacherous. Pumice cliffs and peaks surrounded the lakes and the Caldera rim. Between the lakes lay a flow that had hardened as it had swirled, molten, like a hurricane around its own eye.

"We are swimming in those lakes," said Debra in a reverent whisper. "I don't care how cold they are."

They quickened their pace.

Their feet crunched, and that sound ricocheted back from what they were descending into. They walked over hardened lava rather than pick their way among the trees, even though the understory was clean. Dead, even. The path clear. But they wanted to have clear views. They didn't know who else was here. It was likely they were alone. It certainly felt like they were alone. They'd never found Adam's track again. But it was also possible he was lurking close by. And maybe other Trespassers were with him.

Overhead, birds of prey soared, but Agnes didn't hear songbirds or insects, the cautious chattering of the squirrels. But there had to be something alive here. If for no other reason than to feed the circling raptors. Then she watched a large eagle swoop down, dip its talons into the lake, and bound up with a sizable fish. The lakes had been stocked at some point.

"Finally, some decent fishing," Carl said.

They descended and found a structure, what was supposed to be the Caldera Post. It was boarded up, and looked to have been that way for a while. It was ramshackle and boards covered some windows. It reminded Agnes of something she might have seen in a book or magazine from long ago. A log lodge. On a mountain lake. A great room with great windows soaring three stories. Two wings spreading from it, full of what must be guest rooms. Something built for enjoyment. It was clearly the Ranger's Lodge.

They halfheartedly tried doors, but none of them really wanted inside. Outside, a breeze blew; the sun twinkled over the lake surface. In front of the Lodge was a stretch of sandy beach. Dramatic cliffs rose on either side. It was beautiful. Their unease from earlier dissipated as they set up camp on the shore. Carl sent the children to find sticks, and he set about making poles for fishing. He pulled out a fly and line he'd kept in his bag since they'd first arrived. It was possibly the only thing that had survived since the very beginning. Besides the Manual. And some of the books and knives.

That night they camped in a semicircle around the fire on the shore of the lake. The stars felt closer than ever before. They twinkled big and dangled from the sky like hanging lights. The wind blew the smell of fires away. The smog lifted. For the first time they noticed the heavy scent of water and hot rock cooling under the evening sky. Their bellies were full of flame-cooked fish. Their fingers were sticky with the fish's oils. They picked scales from their teeth and burned the fine bones in the fire.

They woke in the morning and stood around. There was enough fish for breakfast, lunch, and dinner. Camp was set up; firewood was gathered and plentiful.

"Isn't there something we should be doing?" asked Dr. Harold.

"What do we usually do with our time?" asked Linda.

"Hunt, skin, tan, smoke, sew, gather—" Carl said.

"But there's nothing started right now, and we have plenty," said Linda. "So we have—"

"The morning off?" Debra asked.

Before anyone could reply, Debra was running toward the lake, pulling her smock over her head.

Linda and Dr. Harold followed. Then Val with Baby Egret and Carl. Then Frank and Patty's mom. Soon everyone was stripped down and in the water.

Only the adults had ever really learned to swim. The rest of them had figured it out in the deeper parts of the bigger streams. Once or twice in very slow parts of a rare wide river.

The children splashed around near the beach. The teenagers paddled sloppily out to where their feet could just touch. The adults took smooth strokes and popped underwater, flicked their feet like fishtails.

Her mother had taught Agnes how to swim at the first river they'd camped at. And before that, back in the City, she'd made Agnes practice holding her breath in the bathtub. When Agnes would snort in water, flail up gasping, her mother would be there with a towel to wipe off her face.

"See," she would say. "You panicked, but you're fine. Water won't hurt you if you know how to behave around it."

In the rivers during those earliest days, her mother would hold her around the waist and have Agnes put her face in the slow-moving current. Agnes would flail until she calmed down and began to paddle, her mother's arms never unwrapping from around her.

Agnes had seen how Debra taught Pinecone to swim. And how Sister and Brother had learned from Juan. All by nearly drowning. They learned fast. But they didn't like the water now. They all stayed close to the beach, only going in up to their navels.

Agnes paddled up to Jake and the Twins. They hopped on their tiptoes in a circle, looking up into the sky, then down into the clear water.

Agnes could see all their toes scraping the sand. The water felt oily, but when she lifted her hand out, it slipped off cleanly and left nothing behind but her cold taut skin. No silt. No slime. Pure. She swam a few strokes to where the bottom dropped away and dunked her head and looked down. Far, far, far below, the lake-bottom dunes looked as though they shifted with every kick of her feet. Above her head a sheer rock wall sloped as vertically as a slope could and still be considered a slope.

Agnes scanned the water's surface and spied her mother doing somersaults farther out. Just her head, then the curve of her upper back, her bottom, then crossed ankles and feet. It was graceless. It looked fun. Her mother looked like the little girl she probably was the last time she did a somersault underwater. She came up, spouting water from her mouth and grinning.

Once, back in the City, after one of the breathing lessons her mother had given her in the tub, her mother had gotten into the tub with her.

"Okay, sit like this," her mother had said, crossing her legs, sitting up very straight. "We used to do this when I was a kid. It's stupid. But funny. I don't know if it will be as funny in the tub. But let's try."

"Okay," Agnes had said in her reedy, high voice. Her mother seemed hulking across from her in the tub. There was so much more of her. So much more skin, so much more face and leg. So much more hair. Agnes remembered feeling like ten Agneses could fit inside her mother. And then she was reminded that she had come from there. That she'd lived there, breathing water in her mother's guts.

"Just imagine we're underwater," her mother said. "Our hair is floating all around, like it does when you lie on the bottom of the tub." Her mother tussled her own hair so it was wild and looked like it could be lilting in water. She tussled Agnes's hair.

"Imagine that we're holding our breath," her mother said, bulging her cheeks out and widening her eyes. "And then," she said, "hold your hand like this," and she put her left hand out flat, palm up. "And your other hand like this." She pinched all her fingers together except for her pinkie, which jabbed out. "It's like you're holding a teacup," she said. "And now you drink your tea like this." She lifted her pinched fingers to her puckered mouth. "It's an underwater tea party," her mother said, sipping imaginary tea from the imaginary teacup, the bathwater barely to her hips.

It was a ridiculous game because neither one of them was underwater. The absurdity made them giggle, and whatever Agnes was doing with her face—she was only trying to imitate her mother—made her mother laugh until she had tears in her eyes.

Agnes smiled at the memory of such an easy time between them and tentatively paddled her way over to where Bea was tumbling.

When she reached her mother, Bea stopped flipping and treaded water cautiously. Her eyes countered Agnes warily. Agnes had avoided her since Glen. She thought her mother had avoided her too. She didn't know what to say to make anything better. To be sorry. To be forgiven. So she had said nothing at all. But for the first time in a long time, the thought of her mother had made her happy. She had to do something with that.

"Do you want to have a tea party?" she asked shyly.

Her mother spit water out of her mouth like a fountain. She smiled, looking relieved. "Do I ever!" she said. "Do you remember how?"

"I think so," Agnes said, and placed her hand out flat and pinched her fingers and rounded her lips to sip, treading frantically.

Her mother laughed. "You have to sit cross-legged too."

Agnes pulled her legs up into a knot. She toppled, sank, laughed. She splashed her hands to right herself.

"Okay, now try it underwater."

Agnes dropped below the surface.

Her mother dropped too and looked at Agnes trying hard to stay upright with the teacup in her hand. She smiled and pointed down, down, down and launched herself deeper. Agnes surfaced to get more air and then followed her mother.

The weight from the water above and around her kept Agnes upright and allowed her occasional moments to sit and sip without needing her arms to stay under.

Her mother's sit-and-sip was effortless. Her hands slid up and down to her lips. Her cheeks were not puffed out with air, but rather she kept all the air deep inside. Her mother's eyes were glassy like the water around her. She looked like she was sitting at their table at home. Except for her hair. Her hair curled like sage branches. Her mother was more beautiful than the mermaids in the fable from her favorite lost book.

Agnes looked to the bottom. The sandy ripples were still. She became aware of how everything was still and quiet. She could only hear a thumping in her ears. Her own heartbeat. She looked across at her mother and saw the artery at her throat pulsing. With each thrum in her mother's neck, she heard a thrum in her ears. The only sound beneath the water was the beating of their own hearts together, the coursing of their blood. And then, when her mother laughed, the bubbles spilled from her like it was her very life escaping. Agnes wanted to grab all those bubbles and gobble them up so she could have it forever.

She felt a mournful longing for her mother, as though she were far away, untouchable. The water made Bea look like she was behind a plate of glass. Agnes reached for her, but she was just far enough away that she couldn't grab hold. She tried again, and her mother dodged her hand and smiled. She thought it was a game. So Agnes shook her head *no* and thrust both hands out anxiously to show her how much she needed her, and finally she caught a handful of her mother's wisping hair and pulled, trying to catch her.

Her mother's face grimaced, and a moan full of bubbles escaped her as she pried Agnes's hand away. She scowled back at Agnes. But then her face turned panicked and she yanked Agnes to her, grabbed her by the waist, kicked her up to the surface.

At the surface, Agnes sputtered and coughed and realized she'd been trying to breathe underwater. She hadn't been aware, so fixated she'd been on reaching her mother. She felt like she'd been asleep. The only proof it hadn't been a dream was everything around her. The water. The cliffs. Her mother's arms were around her, pulling her back to shore. She looked around her in a daze at the sun glinting off the basalt rocks, the white and black obsidian. The waxy clusters of pine needles. It was as though the whole Caldera glittered.

Celeste and Patty and Jake watching her be pulled to shore.

"Good job, Agnes," said Celeste. "Real nice form." The Twins snickered.

Agnes didn't care. She just let herself be dragged, weightless in the water, her head safely above, her body cool, her mother's arm around her, like in the rivers of those early days, when she was just her mother's little girl, who had just grown out of being her mother's little baby. She felt like a baby again. She dangled her arms and legs and burbled her lips across the surface as she was dragged along.

Bea got Agnes to the fire and put her coat around her. Everyone was still swimming. Agnes could hear all their voices echoing off the Caldera walls, sounding as far away as ghosts.

"No more swimming for you," her mother said.

"Okay," Agnes said.

Her mother's eyebrows went up. "Okay? Well, then, okay."

Her mother had expected an argument, but Agnes didn't want to argue anymore. She let her mother tend to her as she slumped and stared into the fire. It reminded her of being sick. Feeling this warmth flitting around her, draping blankets across her shoulders, brushing the hair out of her eyes. Wiping away drool or snot, blood if she'd been coughing. Feeling that her hand was being held when she was somewhere between awake and asleep. Being sick had been awful, but being cared for felt nice. She missed it. She knew her mother was still caring for her all the time. But it was behind the scenes. It was secret. It was strategic. It wasn't the same.

Many in the Community were floating now. Their arms out, heads bobbing. They looked asleep. The sun glided across the sky on its daily path. How did it feel about going the same way every day?

Agnes laid her head against her mother's shoulder, still cool from the water.

"Are we going to have to leave here?" Agnes asked. Saying the words made her chest hard.

"Why do you ask that?"

"I wondered if the study would end with Glen gone." She felt her mother's body stiffen under her head.

Her mother sighed. "The study can go on without Glen."

Agnes felt a wave of shame for saying his name. He had been gone a short time, but it felt like years. And yet she also felt that he wasn't really gone at all. He was just off somewhere in seclusion, trying not to disturb people's sleep with his cough. She was toggling between grief about his absence and anticipation of his return. It was a hopeful place she did not want to be removed from. Agnes and her mother fell silent again. Glen was something they shared. Agnes thought that perhaps they resented that in some way, and would prefer to each keep him for themselves.

She watched a dragonfly patrol where the water met the shore, tracking small bugs. Agnes was sure she could hear the swift quiver of its tissue wings because she was sure she could hear everything. She had thought she could hear a heartbeat in her stomach and had made Jake listen. "That's just your guts," he'd said. "No," she said. "There's something else." But not long after that, she bled, heavily. She was disappointed, but more, she was embarrassed to have her body fail her. She reported the apparent miscarriage to Jake curtly and answered his questions evasively until he stopped asking them. He wanted to understand how she felt. But she didn't know how she felt. She didn't understand why she wept for a sac of blood that had not yet, in the end, had a heart. She had slipped her fingers through the slick mass looking for it. It was not there. She had wanted to tell her mother, but she felt ashamed. Her mother had lost Madeline, whose heartbeat Agnes had heard. Her mother had put Agnes's ear to her stomach and said, "Now, shhhh." And there it had been. Just like a frightened jackrabbit. Madeline had been a whole, real baby, just not all the way grown. Agnes had birthed heartless blood. So like she did with the pregnancy itself, she kept its loss from her mother.

The strange thing she found herself wanting to ask her mother, though, was not about having and losing an unfinished baby, but about the feelings of worry she had begun to have, before she bled, and even after. That her baby would suffer, or had suffered, some-how. It was a vague but overwhelming feeling that draped itself upon her at different moments. When she lay down to sleep. When she felt an electric surge and knew it was her body and the baby communicating. Even when she was no longer pregnant, that feeling of ants in her stomach would tickle her with busy worry. Things felt different now. Because Glen was gone. But it was more than that. She felt it, but she had no words for it. What if there was an end written for them already? But she couldn't ask her mother about all this. It felt overly human. Rationalizing and worrying and preparing. It felt unlike herself. As though she'd already been changed by the child, even though they would never meet.

In the shallows, the children and teens played an ancient game of Marco Polo. The adults were swimming over to join. Their shrieks and calls echoed off the rocks, and it sounded as though new explorers were calling from beyond the trees, all around the summit.

"Is it true what Adam said?" Agnes asked. "That people are flooding into the Wilderness State?"

"I'm guessing it's greatly exaggerated but perhaps not untrue."

"Does that mean we'll have to leave?"

"Agnes, why are you so fixated on leaving?"

"Because I don't want to go back to the City."

"But why do you worry we will?"

Agnes shrugged. "Everything is different now."

Her mother didn't ask her to explain. "Try not to worry. Besides, leaving here doesn't have to be the end of the world." Her mother paused and smoothed her matted hair, as though deciding to say what she said next. "We've got the Private Lands."

"This again!" Agnes sat up. A rage was bubbling. "I suppose this is the big plan you've been working on. And I suppose you've got it all figured out."

Her mother sniffed. "As a matter of fact, I have."

"Okay, and how are you going to get us there?"

"I know a guy," her mother said.

"And the money?"

Bea looked surprised. "What do you know about it?"

"I know you need money. The Newcomers told me."

"Well." She squinted. "We have the money."

"For everyone?"

Bea shrugged. "We'd have to see. But we definitely have enough for us."

Agnes knew that meant no. And that at some point in the future her mother had a plan to leave the others behind. That wasn't shocking to Agnes. It was life in the Wilderness. And it was not shocking that her mother seemed to think nothing of making that decision. More shocking to Agnes was that her mother would embark on something like this on faith alone.

"Who is this guy?"

"He's a guy I know."

"How long have you known him?"

"Awhile."

"When did you meet him?"

Her mother thought. "Around the time we left the City."

"Is the guy you know trustworthy?"

"Agnes," her mother said sharply. "Of course he is. Do you think I would work with someone I couldn't trust?"

But all Agnes could think of was that there was a guy willing to take her mother somewhere that didn't exist if she gave him all her money. And that didn't seem trustworthy.

"What's his name?"

"Sweetheart, don't worry," her mother said.

"Mom."

"I'm not going to tell you that."

"Did Glen know?"

Her mother winced. "He knew enough."

Agnes felt betrayed. Her mother was planning to take her away from here without even asking what she wanted. "But I like it here."

"But we can't stay here forever."

"Why not?"

"Oh, Agnes, we just can't." Her mother said it as if it was the most obvious of thoughts.

"Well, no one told me that," she snapped, to hide the unevenness of her voice. She choked back what she was feeling, rubbed her face roughly to push back tears and her own fear.

Her mother relented and tried to soften the conversation. "Look, we probably won't have to leave. I just don't want you to be haunted by worry. Whatever happens, I have a plan for us. Try to trust me on this one. The Private Lands are a real option for us. I promise I can get us there. It would be a good life."

"I like this life."

"Well, so do I," her mother said. "This is only a backup plan." But Agnes didn't believe her.

*   *   *

TWO DAYS AFTER they summited the Caldera, set up camp, spent hours swimming, and ate their fill of fish, they heard the faraway crunch of footsteps echoing off the Caldera walls during breakfast cleanup. It sounded like an army of people, a large and heavy-footed horde, but they had learned that sound grew larger in the Caldera. So they were alarmed, but not terrified. As the footsteps became louder and closer, the Community grabbed sticks and knives, the bows and arrows, big stones, anything they could. Together they moved toward the sound, holding their weapons ready.

Several Rangers moved single file out of the forest. And from behind the Community came the *beep beep* of a horn. They all startled and turned to see a van driving in from behind the Lodge. Ranger Bob hopped out and saluted cheerily.

Her mother laughed. "How did you get that up here?" she called to him as he and other Rangers from the van approached.

"We drove," Ranger Bob said. "There's a service road on the other side," he said. And Agnes saw a few of the Rangers smirk at this revelation, and was reminded that to some of them, this was a game. She watched Ranger Bob, curious how he fit into that. He just smiled his Ranger Bob smile.

They converged on the beach, and it had the feeling of a reunion between estranged family members. Ranger Bob shook hands with members of the Community, who seemed confused by the gesture. He patted Agnes on the head and said, "And last but not least," looking around for one more. And not finding him, he frowned and put his arm around Agnes's shoulder. He was Glen's height. A little stockier, but older like Glen. He squeezed. It felt nice.

"I thought you said this place was getting renovated," said Bea.

"It is. You should have seen it before."

"But it's all boarded up," said Juan.

"We just do that so people don't mess with it."

"Who would mess with it?"

The Rangers exchanged looks. "Why don't we go in and sit down and have a talk. Just the leaders." Carl and Bea stepped forward.

"Why just the leaders?" said Debra.

"Because some decisions need to get made."

Agnes stepped forward too. "I'm a leader."

"Just because you lead us places doesn't make you an actual leader," said Carl.

"To me it does," said Debra. And Val said, "To me too."

"If decisions are getting made, I want Agnes there," said Celeste. "I want one of us there."

"What do you mean, one of us?"

Celeste said, "A kid."

Carl said, "I thought you weren't kids."

"We have different values than you, so this is a time I don't want to be lumped in with adults."

Bea huffed and began to walk. Carl followed, and so did Agnes. As Agnes walked into the Lodge, she noticed a box of notepads, with pencils, just like her mother carried. She swiped one. There were new Rangers at the table. No one welcomed her into the room. Agnes took a seat and waited out the Rangers' confused silence.

"It's fine," said Bea, waving her hand at Agnes. "She can be here." But her mother shook her head all the same.

There were two Rangers at either side of the door, their hands folded in front of their belts, their legs apart. *They are guarding the door,* Agnes thought. Another was planted at a door in the back of the hall and another on the other side of the big soaring windows overlooking the lake. Agnes could see her Community out there. Debra and Pine-cone swimming, others cooking and prepping dinner. Jake and the Twins were milling around in some bushes near the window, curious, maybe protective, until two Rangers escorted them back to camp.

Ranger Bob sat at the head of the table and made some announcements about the fire they'd smelled and about the movement of a wolf pack into the area. "In case you get lucky enough to see them," he said. He was all smiles as usual and kindly-voiced. But he had someone next to him who gritted his teeth and rolled his eyes often. He was introduced as Ranger Bob's boss, and he had one more stripe on his uniform than Ranger Bob. Just one, but it seemed like one made a big difference. Ranger Bob looked at him a lot. He clearly wanted to make the man happy, and it was unclear if he was succeeding.

Ranger Bob paused, then cleared his throat. "So, and this bit is important. The study has concluded."

Carl and Bea blinked stupidly like deer.

"What does that mean for us?" said Carl.

"Well"—Ranger Bob smiled—"it means you have to go home."

"To—" said Carl.

"The City."

"What?" Her mother's voice came sharp and angry. Even though she had just told Agnes that she had contingency plans for such a moment, she seemed utterly blindsided.

"Hold on," said Ranger Bob. "We may have another option to offer you. But we'll need something from you in return." He shot a glance at his boss. "We've been battling a scourge for a few years. Something we wanted to keep from you. For the sake of the study. But it has come to my attention that you are no longer ignorant of the fact that we have some Trespassers in our midst." Carl smiled, seeming happy they had used his term, but then he quickly scowled as if to try to hide his giddiness.

Bea made a surprised face and opened her mouth to express shock at the idea. But Ranger Bob held up his hand. "Save it, Bea," he said. "We know about Adam." Bea then looked surprised anew, as if thinking, *How?*

They told the same story Adam had told them, but this time it sounded much more real and plausible. A group of people—no one knew how large—had been living in the Wilderness for several years. Having most likely crossed over from the Mines, but possibly at other points. People who had disappeared from the City, who had been run out of the City or could not survive there, were now surviving here. In the beginning, their presence was half believed. Some Rangers thought it possible. Others denied it. Ranger Bob bowed his head sheepishly. He had thought it inconceivable. They eventually gathered evidence. Motion cameras in the woods caught videos of blurry images moving from behind trees in places far from where the Community would have been. They had enough evidence that they were not only here, but had been here for quite a while. And there were many.

"And what does that have to do with us?" said Carl.

"We would like your help. We haven't been able to infiltrate this group. But we think that maybe you can."

"What do we have to do?"

"What you've always done," said Ranger Bob. "Walk, hunt, live. But in a predetermined place. We've pinpointed the quadrant where we think most are hiding. We will transport you there. And I will join the Community, pretending to be one of you. I'll carry a tracker and alert headquarters when they are found."

"And if we do this, we get to stay?"

Ranger Bob smiled. "No, not exactly. You get to stay while you make contact, of course. But once we have intercepted the Trespassers and rounded them up, then we will secure passage for you to the Private Lands."

Carl laughed. "Fuck you, Bob."

"I know it isn't the Wilderness State but—"

"It's bullshit is what it is. There's no Private Lands."

"I can assure you there is. And if you help us, you can live there for the rest of your lives and never have to return to the City ever again."

Carl started to stand, angry, but Bea grabbed his arm and pulled him down to her. She whispered furiously in his ear, and as she did, he slowly sank back into his seat.

"What if we can't connect with them?" Bea asked. "What if we try and fail? Do we still get to go to the Private Lands?"

Ranger Bob and his boss exchanged eyebrow raises. His boss scowled, and Ranger Bob turned to Bea and smiled. "We have no doubt you'll find them."

"But we've never found them before," said Bea. "Adam came to *us*. Why do you think we'll know how to find them now?"

"You found that dead guy," spat the Boss. His eyes shifted from face to face, deeply distrustful of what he saw.

"He was one?"

"Yes."

"But he was dead. He couldn't hide."

The Boss slammed back in his chair. Agnes didn't understand what made him so upset. The Boss waved his hand at Ranger Bob, as though to say, *Go ahead*.

"We know they want to rendezvous with you," said Ranger Bob.

"They want to steal our stuff," said Carl.

"Very likely."

"How do you know?"

"We have intel."

"What intel? How?"

"That's classified."

Bea snorted. "Oh, come on." But Bob put a hand up to quiet her, and she quieted, immediately.

"This is an important operation. We need to bring this trespassing to light. To send a message to anyone who thinks it's a good idea to follow in their footsteps."

"The message being, *Stay out*," said Bea, filling in the blanks.

"Yes."

Agnes looked out the window. She saw her Community and the vast Caldera ecosystem behind them. They were specks. And the Caldera was a speck on the map. It had taken them seasons to get here from the Basin, which they had spent seasons getting to.

"But there's plenty of room," said Agnes.

"What do you mean?" asked Ranger Bob.

"I mean, it's a big Wilderness. So what if some people stay?"

"The Wilderness State is changing. It has a new mandate. No one can be here."

Agnes scoffed. "How can you have a Wilderness without any people?"

The Boss answered. "The study has clearly shown that you can't have a Wilderness *with* people."

This struck Agnes as ridiculous. "You wouldn't even know we were here if we hid. There'd be no trace of us."

The Boss sneered. "Oh, if you hid, we'd find you and we'd round you up."

Before she could say more, her mother hissed, "Quiet, Agnes."

Carl said, "I have a question. Why don't *we* just carry the tracker and press the alert button when we find them?" He looked despondent. Life as they knew it was over, and on top of that they had to work with the Rangers?

Ranger Bob and the Boss looked at each other, deciding what to say. Then Ranger Bob smiled. "We don't trust that you'll do it." He shrugged. "Sorry."

Agnes braced for Carl to rage at this, to feel babysat. But he sat there contemplating it, and surprisingly, he said, "That's fair," accepting the provisions. Adding, "Just as long as we are still in charge."

Bob raised his palms, a sign of mild surrender. "Of course. I'm just there for the button." He smiled. "And a little adventure too. I don't mind getting away from the uniform." The Boss rolled his eyes, his mouth sharp and disapproving, but Bob smiled through it.

"And what if we don't help?"

"Well, we sincerely hope you do."

"But what if we don't?"

"Like we said, the study is over," said the Boss. "You'll fill out some paperwork. And then go home. To the City." He crossed his arms. "Tomorrow."

"It's a good deal," said Ranger Bob in a soothing, coaxing voice, the kind of voice Agnes used on skinny, needful, hungry hares when they'd noticed her but hadn't run yet. He stared at Bea and smiled until he couldn't smile anymore. His face blanked and briefly he frowned, and Agnes saw how tired they all looked. How dirty and wrinkled their uniforms were, the tongues of their boots askew, shirttails untucked. When usually they looked so official, proud and clean.

Bea turned to Carl and held his eye for a long time. Then she looked out the window at the Community, everyone enjoying their time here, relaxing, perhaps thinking how nice it would be to relax for good. Perhaps thinking of them on a bus back to the City, weeping. Agnes couldn't figure out what she was calculating. But she was nonetheless surprised when her mother said, "Okay. We'll do it. We'll help." She nodded at Carl and he nodded, sullenly, back. She didn't ask for Agnes's opinion. No one did. And Agnes didn't offer it. She had heard what she needed to hear.

They left the table and went to their own corners. The Boss peered at Ranger Bob, clearly unhappy. Perhaps he had simply wanted to kick them out and Ranger Bob had managed to buy them more time. Agnes watched the Boss checking doors, whispering to the Rangers standing guard, casting looks back at her mother, Carl, Ranger Bob, and then to Agnes herself. She caught his eye, the color of the sky when it was blazing. The color of nothing. She guessed Ranger Bob trusted him because he was his boss and she guessed people trusted their bosses. And she knew her mother did because her mother trusted Ranger Bob. But Agnes didn't trust this man. Not at all.

*   *   *

AROUND THE FIRE, Bea presented the news to the Community as though it were just another directive. As though they were lucky to get the chance to stay a little while longer. And then, what a gift to relax and live a life of peace in the Private Lands.

"So they're forcing us to turn on those poor people?" Debra scowled.

"Trespassers, Debra," snapped Carl.

"It's that or be sent home," Bea said. "Tomorrow." She'd said this a few times already, wanting this to be the main takeaway from the announcement. Bea made a rueful face Agnes knew was fake and she realized that this must be part of her mother's plan somehow. But she couldn't imagine how.

"So there was a choice?" Val's voice was shrill, and she laughed short and awfully. "And this is what you chose for everyone?" she said to Carl, the words dripping distastefully from her mouth.

"It's a good deal," he said to Val in the same coaxing voice Ranger Bob had used.

Val shook her head. She turned to Agnes, forlorn. "You too, Agnes?"

Agnes looked past everyone and at the Caldera wall, trying to find something to lock onto, something solid. She felt her mother's eyes on her. "No," she said.

"Agnes," warned her mother.

Agnes met her gaze. "I'm staying here. I'm going to stay and disappear. Just like the Trespassers."

Bea's mouth went slack, but it was Carl who venomously spit, "Like hell you are. This isn't a decision you get to make."

But Celeste spoke over him. "We can't carry everything we'd need ourselves," she calculated, knowing already their numbers would be diminished.

"We'd need to leave most of our stuff behind. We can't take our books. We can't take our kitchen. We won't need the Manual. The Cast Iron is gone. We can take only something for warmth. Some food, water. Knives. Weapons. Only what you can carry on your backs. Tight against your backs."

"But we need this stuff," said Juan. Agnes knew he was thinking mostly of his paints.

"We'll start over," said Agnes. "New bowls and beds and clothes. We'll need only what is absolutely essential. But we can find whatever we need after we find a better place to hide. We've done it before. When we were new. We'll do it again."

Her mother was looking at her like she'd just been slapped.

Again, Carl spat, "We aren't splitting. We are staying together on this or it doesn't work."

"Don't tell her what to do," yelled Debra, moving next to Agnes. "You're not telling me what to do either, Carl."

"Yes, I am. I'm the leader. And so let me tell you you're not being smart. If some of us run, all of us get fucked. They'll never trust us to make contact with Trespassers if half of us run and *become* Trespassers. They'll send us back to the City. All of us." Carl's voice cracked, and a chill went through Agnes. "If you run, you ruin this chance we have at something more."

"Not necessarily," said Val, though now her voice was softened. She bit her lip.

"Oh, come on, Val." Carl sneered. "Use that little brain of yours."

"Oh, you fucker," said Val, and then Baby Egret woke, squalling, hungry, papoosed against her. "Dammit," Val growled, thrusting her hands deep down her front and latching Baby Egret to her. When she straightened, she had tears streaming down her face. "Well, fuck," she screamed into her hand while Egret nursed.

Carl was right, Agnes realized, and she imagined Val had just realized it too. The Rangers would never reward those who remained. They would only notice who was gone. And they would punish everyone. She felt a hand on her arm and recoiled, thinking it was a hand meant to ensnare her. But it was Jake. He walked his fingers down to hers and held her hand tight.

"But you hate following the rules," Val wailed to Carl, accusingly.

"I'm not going to run away and hide like a fugitive. I have a right to be here." He lifted his chin. "Running away is cowardly," he said.

Val laughed. And then she laughed more, tears streaming, shaking wildly until Baby Egret shook loose from her nipple and squalled again.

"I honestly don't see what's so funny," sniffed Carl, and then he cast looks around. "This thing you want to do is going to get us all in trouble."

"You can't trust the Rangers, Carl," pleaded Val. "You know that. They are looking out for themselves. Why do you think they won't round you up when they round up the Trespassers?"

"I trust them more than I trust a bunch of people who came here uninvited and are ruining it for the rest of us." Spittle foamed in the corners of his mouth, and Agnes understood. Carl was bitter. He had been given something special that was being taken away, and he needed someone to blame. Val nodded and took a step toward Agnes. Agnes noticed the Community members shifting positions. People crept closer to her or to her mother. They were quietly making decisions about the rest of their lives.

She looked at her mother, who had been strangely silent. Her mother's face was blank. Somewhere in her head she was lost in a maze of calculations.

Frank said, "Well, I think it's easy to take their word on the Private Lands existing. We've all seen the footage."

"*We* haven't," said Agnes. "The original Community. We left the City certain the Private Lands were a story dreamed up by crazy people. Now we're expected to believe they are real, and more, that we get to live there? Who are *we* that we get to live there? What have we done except betray others who want the same thing we want? To be here. We can all run, together. We know how to hide."

Celeste was behind Agnes, muttering "Patty" and wagging her hand. Patty's parents were behind Bea, hissing for Patty to join them. Poor Patty in the middle. The Newcomer adults had always wanted to go to the Private Lands. This deal with the Rangers must have felt like a miracle, and they weren't going to waste it. But the younger Newcomers had a very different feeling about their future, as young people often do.

"I'm not going back there," Carl said. "Your mother has told me everything I need to know about the City. And now about the Private Lands." Agnes realized he was speaking only to her. His eyes were steady even as his voice wavered. "We have to be unified on this," said Carl.

"Oh, now you need a unanimous decision? You need consensus!" Debra laughed. "That is perfect."

"Oh, shut up, Debra," he said.

"Fuck you, Carl. You've reached the limit of your power."

"Don't bet on it," said Carl, putting his finger up to Debra's face.

What happened next took seconds, but to Agnes it felt as though sunsets and sunrises had passed, and by the end she was wrung out, starved, unquenched, bereft, but clearheaded.

Carl turned fast like a jackrabbit toward the Lodge and screamed, "Rangers!"

And just as quickly Jake brought him to the ground. Jake, wiry and desperate, stepped on his knee and grabbed his foot as everyone watched agape. Carl howled and flopped to get away, but he was pinned. Agnes could see the instinct take over in Jake and knew that he was about to drop his weight and twist in such a way that would irreparably break Carl's leg. A broken leg would leave him defenseless. He would not survive. The Rangers would leave him there to die. Or maybe, if he was lucky, they would pity him and ride him out so he could return to the City. Was that a death sentence too?

Carl panted, slobbered, "Please, please."

"Stop," Agnes yelled.

Jake froze, peered up.

"You'll kill him."

"So?" Jake scowled.

Agnes thought of Glen. Of his shrug and his twisted leg and of how he had been protecting them even then. She shook her head. "Don't," she said.

Jake, angry and ashamed, untangled himself quickly and threw Carl's leg down. He couldn't look up at the faces around him. He just ran toward the woods, yelling, "Agnes, come on!"

Now Agnes saw that some people had already run. Linda and Dolores and Joven were pulling whatever gear they could and running full-armed into the wooded slopes. Celeste was pulling Patty toward the woods, Patty blubbering, her arm reaching toward her mother and father, while her legs were fleeing with Celeste. Helen and Frank and Patty's mom screamed for their daughters, but they did not follow. Once the Twins' bags were slung over their shoulders, the girls never looked back. Debra had slipped out with Pinecone, but Sister and Brother were cowering behind Juan, who was standing shocked behind Bea. Val and Baby Egret were calmly walking away, not fearful or panicked. Egret was cradled sideways, nursing, and Val wouldn't want to jostle him.

Agnes knew she too was moving, but she couldn't feel it. She felt stuck, immobile. Her silent mother looked stuck too, her face morphing like storm skies while Carl rolled around on the ground behind her, perhaps already damaged beyond repair. Her mother stood offering empty palms, her shoulders at once tense and slumped, like the curve of a boulder. Agnes watched her mouth twitching, as though wishing to open and scream *Ranger* too so that Agnes would be captured. She watched her mother's hand twitch, and Agnes imagined it reaching out to keep her there, or, maybe, just say goodbye. Agnes took a tentative step backwards, watching all this emotion inside her mother that she would not release. Few members of the Community remained. The people who chose to run had run.

The ones who remained, Agnes saw herself in their eyes. She was too wild, something uncontrollable and wholly selfish, and while that had served them well in the past, now her survival instinct seemed to disgust them. She looked again at her mother, and felt a longing that almost knocked her down, to be curled up with her, not under skins around the fire, not with her hand clamped around her mother's cold ankle. She wished to be curled up in her mother's lap in her own small bed, or in her mother's bigger bed, on the sofa by the window, peering out any window at the white sky, living their life in that City apartment because they had never known life anywhere else. If she'd never come here, if she'd known nothing else, couldn't she be happy with what they'd had?

"Mom," Agnes said, taking another step back.

Her mother's mouth settled in a hard thin line, and she stepped urgently toward Agnes, reaching.

Agnes ran.

AGNES CAME TO a clear outcrop and looked down at the land below, angry, bewildered, and terrified that she had lost contact with everyone. Where had Jake gone? Dolores and her mother and brother? The Twins? Val and Baby Egret? How could everything have changed so suddenly? The tangled cinder cone forest hugged the Caldera like a parasite. And beyond she saw a set of lights traveling across the desert toward the Caldera. A vehicle. A large one. Then a hand slipped over her mouth.

"Don't let them hear you," her mother hissed in her ear. Agnes felt a flush of relief until her mother dragged her into the trees.

Agnes tried to dig in her heels. "Mom," she hissed.

"Don't speak."

"Mom," Agnes screamed, and her mother stopped in shock.

"Are you trying to get caught?"

"Where are we going?" Agnes hissed.

"We have to get to the eastern foot of the Caldera."

"Why?" Agnes's voice shook. She was disoriented and enraged by her mother's hand shackled around her arm.

"We are meeting Bob."

"No way. I'm not going to a Ranger."

"We have to. It's all planned."

"What do you mean, it's all planned?"

"Getting to the Private Lands. We were trying to get dropped close to the border before we made a run, but thanks to you, now we'll have to stow away in some truck. Make the long trek from here. It certainly won't be pleasant. But I don't think we'll get caught."

"What are you talking about?"

"My plan!" Her mother made fists and looked wild. "The plan I had with Bob. He was going to take us to the border and get us across and to the Private Lands." She scowled. "Don't look at me like that. It was a good plan, Agnes."

"And that's why we're at the Caldera? To meet with Bob?"

"Yes, so he could have a reason to bring us to the border quickly."

"But why?"

"Because they were going to send us back to the City!"

"So there are no Trespassers to find?"

Bea's eyes grew wide. "Oh, I didn't say that. There are Trespassers here. The ones Adam told us about. The Mavericks. We don't see them, but they see us."

"So Adam wasn't a part of this?"

"Oh no, Adam was a surprise. But a helpful one."

"Did you tell Bob about Adam?"

"I had to."

"But how? We haven't been to Post in years."

"We leave notes for each other."

"Where?"

"In trees," her mother muttered.

The grass lake. Agnes remembered her mother tucking something into a tree's trunk. It had been for Bob. "For how long?"

"Since I came back. We've been communicating since then." Her mother looked ashamed, unveiled. Her mother seemed unfathomably complicated and mysterious again. Briefly. Then she looked terrified.

"Why would he do something so risky for us?"

"Because we're friends."

"Mom."

"He wants to be there too. It's not just the study. The whole Wilderness State is ending. He needs somewhere to go."

"So he'd come with us?"

"There's nowhere else to go," her mother said impatiently.

"Isn't he married?"

"When did you become so old-fashioned?" her mother snapped.

"Is he married?"

"No," she snapped. "Not anymore. And not that it matters." Her mother blushed. "This plan is a good plan. A solid plan. You need to come with me."

"Now?"

"Now!"

Agnes saw that what people had taken for strength and leadership in her mother might just have been desperation, a manic instinct to survive. She didn't know if there was a difference. Shouldn't there be?

"I'm not going."

"Agnes. You'll get found. You'll get sent back. Or worse."

"I'm staying here."

"For what? With who? Everyone is scattered."

"We can find them like you found me." Agnes made the call to regroup. Her mother again clamped her hand over her mouth.

"I didn't find you, Agnes. I tracked you. Easily, I'll add. And so will the Rangers."

Panicked, Agnes flipped through some thoughts. "But the Private Lands aren't even real."

"Of course they're real."

"How do you know?"

"Bob told me."

"How does he know?"

"He's been there!"

"He said that?"

"Well, he knows people who have been. Shit, I don't know, Agnes. I just know we need to go." Her voice was hushed hysteria.

Agnes ground her teeth. Of all the absurd plans. How could Agnes know something so clearly while her mother believed the opposite wholeheartedly? She tried to keep her voice measured. "I know you're trying to protect me, but the City is right where we'll end up if we go to him. They need us as bait. There's no other reward for us other than this place right here. The Private Lands are not real. He's lying to you."

"He wouldn't," her mother said, and it was such a simple belief. It was the only thing to believe in. She'd probably believed in it for a long time. She'd probably been leaving notes in the trees for years, planning for the time when she would have to find another way to save Agnes, herself. She probably thought she had no other choice.

Agnes heard a call. She waited, listening. She heard it again. "See, there's one of our own. We need to regroup."

"No way," her mother said and grabbed her again. And again Agnes wrenched away.

"I'm not going," Agnes screamed. "This is my home."

"Stop!" Her mother shook her by the shoulders desperately. "This is no one's home." She looked exasperated, as though Agnes didn't understand something very simple about the world. "You can't hide forever."

Agnes shook her mother off. Tears sprang. Of course she could hide forever, she thought indignantly. She knew this land better than they did. She would not get caught. She was offended her mother thought otherwise.

"Why would I go anywhere with you? You left me."

"This again?" her mother roared in frustration. "Why can't you look at all the other times I was here? Why is our whole relationship that?"

"Because you left me alone."

"You weren't alone."

"You left me in the Wilderness."

"You LOVE the Wilderness."

"Because mothers don't do that."

"Well, this mother did." Her mother choked on her words they came out so fast. "How are you going to deal with that? This mother loves you. And this mother left. And this mother came back. And this mother will never be forgiven for it."

"That's right."

"Oh, I know. You don't need to tell me."

Her mother crumpled to the ground as though her legs were just dirt, crumbly anthills holding her up. Her knees splayed, and her hands came together ready to be shackled as though she'd just given up on any future. So did Agnes. In the exact same way. Like a shadow.

"I know I hurt you," her mother said. "I never wanted to. Ever. In my whole life I never wanted to. But I did anyway. I'm sorry."

"You shouldn't have done it."

"But I did it."

"I want you to say you shouldn't have done it."

"I can't."

"Why not?"

"Because it wouldn't be true. It was important for me. It may not have been good for us, but it was, I think, good for you. It led us to this point. And now we have a chance." She shook her head. "I never lied to you, Agnes, and I'm not going to start now."

"I wish you would."

Bea blinked. Surprised. "You don't mean that."

"Yes, I do," Agnes said, her voice peaking hysterically, her fists clenched.

"I shouldn't have done it," her mother said quickly, trying to give Agnes what she wanted. "I shouldn't have left you. It was a mistake. I ruined everything."

Of course her mother had lied to her before—they both knew that—but still, she'd been right about this lie. This lie dropped like a dead animal at Agnes's feet. It made her feel awful to think it had all been for nothing. Even though she could see in her mother's face that some part of her wished she'd never left too, it didn't matter. She had left. And everything, ultimately, had been fine. No one had died. This mother left. This mother came back. This mother loved her. And Agnes didn't know how to forgive her. Even though the lie felt awful, the truth felt worse. There was nothing that could be done but let time pass.

"I do love you, Mama," she whispered.

Her mother whimpered. Her face contorting as though all the feelings she'd ever felt were wrenching across it.

She leaned over and clung to Agnes, kissing her face and head, nuzzling her neck like she used to do when Agnes was a child. "Was I wrong? Should I not have brought you here?" Her mother wept now.

"No, Mama, I belong here."

"That's what I mean," she sobbed. "When we leave, how will you live?"

"But I'm not leaving here," Agnes said.

"You can't stay." A growl permeated her sobs.

"I'm not going."

"It's the only thing that makes sense." Her mother's anger was bubbling.

"I'm not going anywhere." Agnes's voice rose, her fists clenched vehemently.

"It's suicide."

"Mom, I'm not going with you."

Her mother's eyes quivered furiously. "Yes, you are."

Bea grabbed Agnes's arm, her hand a claw. Her voice was a haunted scream.

But Agnes seized her mother by the throat and pushed her down. Her mother choked but wouldn't release Agnes. Agnes drove her fist at her mother's eye, and her mother's whole face broke into anguished surprise. Her eye reddened and swelled instantly and she sputtered, but Agnes had to hit her again before her mother let go.

"Oh no," Bea said, gasping, unable to breathe. Then she opened her mouth wide and shook with mad, breathless laughter.

Agnes released her throat.

Her mother caught her breath, all the while staring at Agnes with shocked and shining eyes. "Oh no," she said again, and then unleashed a shrill bolt of laughter Agnes had only ever heard from her nana.

Agnes stood up.

"Oh no," her mother said again, and from underneath the laughter a wail rose. Something low that seemed to rise out of her guts. "Oh no, oh no, oh no."

Agnes turned away.

"My baby," her mother sputtered, snot and tears bursting from her. "Oh, my baby. My baby girl." She wrung her hands violently. "I hope you get to stay."

Agnes started to walk deeper into the forest, away from the outcrop. Away from her mother.

"What a wonder you are," she heard her mother say, not to her, but to the air, the lands below, the sky, the forest, to herself. "See? Look at her," she said as though confiding in a friend. "Look at that *wonder*. I *was* a good mother."

Was she making one last argument? No. There was something else in her voice. Maybe it was her way of saying goodbye. Or maybe, Agnes thought, it was just now dawning on her that it could be true.

Agnes looked back, furtively. Her mother was doubled over, crouched like an animal, her clawed hand digging at her own heart, watching her. Sobbing. And smiling. More than smiling. Beaming.

Agnes felt both relief and anger. She felt respected, free. And alone alone alone.

Through the trees behind her mother, Agnes could see the broken line of the horizon where the sun was setting. The light of the day was being blotted out as though somewhere shades were being drawn.

Part VII

THE ROUNDUP

AGNES SPENT THE night asleep in a tree. From there she watched her mother sit, stunned, then ease herself up and limp downhill to find Bob, until she became lost to the trees. Agnes heard a whir of something. A helicopter or drone throughout the night. A searching light swept over the Caldera slopes. There was no deal for the remaining Community members, she was certain. They either had run too or were bound for the bus. What if they were all there hiding? But the forest was quiet except for the surveillance. The animals who lived there were listening. Trying to figure out what to do next.

In the morning Agnes climbed down to find the others. She made some of their calls, like a chattering squirrel followed by an irritated jay, a coyote *yip* after a hawk's complaining *eeyEE*. Eventually she heard a call back. Over the course of days, weeks maybe, she found the Twins, Val and Baby Egret, Linda and Dolores and Joven, Debra and Pinecone, and Dr. Harold, who had run at the last minute. Then, thankfully, she found Jake.

As a group they drifted deeper into the cinder cone forest, trying to become lost. They knew how to listen. They knew how to hide. They spread out across the forest alone or in pairs rather than walking together, always within calling distance of another person or two. In this way, if they did come upon Rangers, they would not all be captured at once. They did not camp together in case Rangers ambushed them as they slept. But every few days when the tree shadows were their longest, they would congregate just to be together.

Sometimes, when they came back together, someone was missing. At first it was Dr. Harold. They hoped he had decided to venture out on his own, perhaps thinking he had a better chance. When Linda and Dolores disappeared and only Joven followed the calls to return, he was badly shaken and wouldn't talk for days. But eventually he would tell them it was the Rangers. He had been trees away trying to corner a squirrel. He fit himself into a hollow in a stump and waited there for days before he dared come out of hiding. Over several seasons, their numbers dwindled as they put more and more distance between themselves and the Caldera.

What happened then was people would appear out of nowhere, tentative and afraid. They would come out of hiding. Someone who had been listening, discerning, learning the Community's call and taking the risk of revealing themselves in exchange for some company, some security. *Friend? Friend? Friend?* They were Trespassers. They were looking for the Mavericks.

Some were alone, though they usually had not begun that way. Others were a part of a still-intact small group who had paid and bribed and walked their way from the City and sneaked in from the Mines. They had all found little markers in the woods, abandoned campsites, deer hooves and innards left behind after butchering, hatchets stuck in trees. Little clues to the presence of others. Some wore shoddy clothes of deerskin that had been poorly scraped and still held on to bits of flesh and smelled like rot. Others were in new boots, with the new trekking poles, new cookware, and new sleeping bags, the kind the Community had come with in the beginning. One couple they absorbed thought they had been in the Wilderness for over a year. Another group still had watches that worked. They were pretty sure they still knew the date. Men, women, and children. Grandparents, single mothers and fathers who had left behind an ill spouse. Or a spouse who had refused to leave. Or who had not been told about the plan to begin with. They'd all fled the City, they said, because they had no other choice. Now they were splintered and hungry. They said the Rangers pursued them relentlessly. They heard that the Mavericks could live undetected in the Wilderness for years, and had thrived and somehow evaded capture. They wanted the Mavericks to help them disappear too.

Upon finding the Community, these poor souls would ask in hopeful whispers, "Are you the Mavericks?"

Agnes would put a hand on their shoulder. "No," she would tell them. "But we can do all that. We can help you."

Each day they spread out in what seemed an endless line, splitting and coming back together when necessary, like a *V* of migrating geese. At times, walking through the forest or the plain, Agnes would swear that the Wilderness now teemed with people.

*   *   *

AGNES WAS HUNKERED in a stand of trees near the foothills at sundown, listening for the call of her group, when she heard the unmistakable sound of something curiously alive in a tree nearby. They had somehow made it back through the mountains, to the other side, through the sage sea to the Basin, which they hoped the Rangers still disliked traveling to.

She crept closer, tree by tree, stepping soundlessly, using everything she had learned in her life to go undetected. Invisible behind a skinny alder, she paused and watched a tree tremble in a way trees didn't tremble. Then a very young girl fell to the ground, landing like a big cat on her feet and hands, in a deerskin smock, mud on her face and grass in her gnarled hair. The girl opened her mouth big as though to yelp or holler, but made no sound. But a moment later she cocked her ear and then bolted in that direction, silently. She couldn't have been older than four.

Agnes made her call. She listened. She made the call again. The small forest was silent for a moment. Then she heard a hesitant call back. Agnes quietly moved toward the sound.

Slumped under a tree was a woman in skins cradling an emaciated girl in patched jeans stained with urine and feces. The woman's eyes were circled in bruise purple. Her lips were parched. They appeared to be dead. But the younger girl, the one Agnes had seen, was crouched in front of them, a guard. She was vibrant, and after a moment of watching Agnes, she leapt up and climbed the tree the dead lay under.

"Hello," said Agnes as the girl perched on a branch that reached toward Agnes.

"Hi," the girl mewed.

"I like your dress."

"Gracias."

"Is this your mother?"

"Yes."

Agnes smiled kindly.

"And my sister," the girl whispered.

Agnes nodded. "Do you know how long you've been here?"

The girl shrugged.

"Do you know how old you are?"

The girl shrugged again.

"That's okay. It doesn't matter. Are you alone now?"

The girl nodded, her eyes becoming big and wet briefly, as though letting herself see the situation as it was. Then quickly, as she straddled the tree branch, she began to beat her chest. She opened her mouth again and looked as though she were whooping loudly, as Agnes had seen her do earlier, but she made no noise. Even with no sound, the unbridled emotion in her was obvious, natural. She looked at Agnes and put her finger to her own lips. "Quietly," she said, no doubt repeating a mother trying desperately to keep a wild and boundless girl hidden.

Agnes's hackles rose then. She cocked her head. The girl did too. They had both heard something.

Agnes smiled. "I have a lot of friends here. A lot of kids your age. And we live here. Would you like to meet them?"

The girl slid down from the tree like a rivulet. Her feet were dirty and tough, and there were no shoes or socks to be seen. She stood next to the bodies without looking at them.

"Hurry now," Agnes said, reaching her hand out. The girl took it, but once she was next to Agnes, she climbed up into her arms and rested her head in Agnes's neck.

Agnes carried the girl the rest of the day. The girl fell asleep on her shoulder from time to time. She cried out in her sleep occasionally. She peed herself, and Agnes felt it run down her own leg. But Agnes kept walking, carrying the shivering girl, who was finally able to be scared and tired, calling out to her companions in the quiet night air. And when she could not walk any longer, she laid them both down to sleep.

In the morning, Agnes woke to the girl's face an inch away from hers, peering down at her nose.

"What's your name?" the girl asked hesitantly.

"Agnes. What's yours?"

The girl looked up at her with her spooked and knowing eyes. "It's Fern."

"How nice. I love ferns."

"No, not the plant." She scowled. "It's short for *Fernanda*." She stuck out her tongue as though the name were a bad taste in her mouth.

"Well, it's a lovely-sounding name."

"*Fernanda* means *adventurer*. My mamá told me."

"I like that."

"But everyone thinks Fern is just a plant."

"It's a great plant."

The girl squinted at Agnes. "I'm looking for something very secret and special. Can I trust you?"

"Of course."

Fern pulled out a map from under her shirt, where she had fabric wrapped around her torso. *"Aquí es donde guardo todo,"* she whispered. She smoothed the map out for Agnes. The girl had drawn it. Under her scrawls was what looked to be an old bus schedule. There were upside-down *W* mountains, lakes of blue *U*s and *V*s. Forests of green circles atop thick brown lines. It was of no place, but it could be any place.

She pointed to a big bold *X*. "This is the Place."

"And what's there?"

Fern looked up with silver moon eyes. "Everything good," she said with reverence.

"Well"—Agnes smiled—"let's try to find it." She stood up and took the girl's hand. As they walked the girl kept up a nervous chatter, and Agnes *hmm*ed and listened for danger in the bushes.

For a day, they wandered in the night calling to the others. Eventually, in an open valley, they heard a response. In an abandoned coyote den, she found some of her companions huddled. The whites of their eyes shining from the starlight that could reach that far down into the earth. Jake and a boy they'd found who said his name was Egg. Val and Baby Egret. Debra and Pinecone. The Twins now had Joven and a stranger's child they were caring for. There were others hidden not too far away. Everyone had a child now. The children had appeared to them over the course of their walk, wandering alone in the Wilderness, somehow surviving longer than those caretakers who had brought them here.

Agnes was relieved to see them all but couldn't help thinking they were living a terrible life. Compared to what their lives had been like not long ago, this seemed like an awful way to live. Then she thought of Fern's mother and sister in the woods. At least they were alive. They were together.

They wandered the Wilderness, pretending to look for the Place in Fern's map, a place they came to imagine was the very last place they could go. But in reality, they were only trying to evade Rangers. They encountered more people. People who shared news, news of others, news of Administration changes, news of Ranger sightings, people who offered lifesaving food and water, shared their hiding places. People who were likely eventually captured or worse. There were so many people in the Wilderness.

The Rangers were like bounding cougars who never seemed to tire. In the old days, before the Roundup, Agnes had thought the Rangers had seemed official, in charge, but also a little hapless. They split their time between the Wilderness State and behind a desk at Post. But now it was as though they rode their horses on the tailwinds of the runners. Spurred on like apex predators would be. Bounding after them, never seeming to tire. The Originalists, the Newcomers, these Trespassers, people who now formed this entirely new Community, Wilderness refugees, were just deer in a herd with no option but to push on. They would run out of a will to live before they ran out of land to live off of. The Rangers had governed them with rules. The tedium of paperwork and bureaucracy had hidden what relentless hunters they were.

Eventually the new Community could no longer stay together, even spreading out through the forest, calling to one another, only coming together in brief moments. They had to split up in a real way. They decided it had to be groups of two. An adult would travel with a child. Everyone needed a buddy, they told the children. They tried to make it seem fun.

"It's like hide-and-seek," Agnes explained to the children who were each standing next to their buddy, while their buddies were anxiously snapping their heads toward every errant sound. "We're all hiding now, and then we will find each other," said Agnes.

Pinecone looked skeptical. He'd aged into a stickler of a boy who cherished rules. "But only one person does the finding in hide-and-seek, and they try to find everyone," he said in a scolding voice.

"Well," Agnes said, "in this game we find each other."

"Or we could just stay together," said Fern.

"We can't."

"Why not?"

"That's not part of the game."

"But staying together sounds more fun."

Agnes felt her throat clench. "It's too dangerous," she said.

Fern leaned toward Agnes and whispered loudly, "I thought you said we were playing a game."

"I lied," Agnes said, touching Fern's cheek. "I promise I'll never do it again."

Each of the adults got some kind of provision, pelt, water, something to help them out on their own, but no one had everything they would need. They secured what they had to their bodies to make it easy to run.

Agnes looked at Jake, standing there with his hand on the shoulder of Egg. Agnes thought about how once she had believed children could live on their own in the Wilderness at this age with the right exposure. She thought about how Egg still cried every night. But then she looked at Fern, who had spent most of her life here. Could she? If she had to? *It doesn't matter*, Agnes thought, *because I would never leave her.* That is what Jake had understood in that conversation, but she hadn't. She smiled at Jake.

"I'll find you," said Agnes.

The other adults were sprinting away with the children.

Jake nodded, pulled her to him. They were life mates. They had chosen each other. Jake kissed the top of her head. They heard a snap from the direction they had come. Big. Maybe it was a bear. Maybe it was a cougar. *If only.* She felt them both startle as though they had been lost in a reverie there, holding each other. As though days might have passed. But once they heard the noise, they each grabbed their child's hand and ran apart without saying another word.

WHEN THE LEAVES had turned yellow in the small craggy mountains of what they'd discovered was a coastal range, Agnes and Fern crossed paths with two women claiming to be Mavericks who gave them food and water and entertained them through a fireless, starless evening. They were gossips and had news about many of the Rangers Agnes had known long ago, about this new strange place near the Wilderness State border where buildings were one or two stories tall and were surrounded by green grass and flowers. They gossiped about new people in the Administration, people Agnes had never heard about. People who may not even have existed. But it didn't matter what they said. Agnes hadn't seen anyone besides Fern since the snows last ended. It was fun to hear new stories again.

"How on earth do you know all this?" Agnes asked.

"We talk to everyone," the woman with green eyes said.

"But there's no one here!" Agnes said, chuckling carefully. Fern's head was in her lap, the sleeping girl's breathing sounding like wind in the trees.

The women gaped at each other. "No one here? My dear, everyone who is anyone is here. But they will never tell you who they are."

"We've run across two former presidents here!"

"And that famous actor. What's his name? The one in the action films. But he was a mess. I can't imagine he survived." They clicked their tongues.

"Oh, and just the other day we met a remarkable woman. She had lived here for many, many years. She had raised her family here. She had been a great leader of one of the original communities," she said. "She told us such stories about her exploits, and we realized we had heard her story before. The story was the Ballad of Beatrice. The woman was Beatrice herself."

Agnes managed to choke, "No, it wasn't."

"It was her," the woman cried. "She knew all the things Beatrice would know." The women rattled off facts about her mother that anyone could have known, but Agnes still felt her heart galloping.

"Where did you see her?" Agnes snapped, and the women startled at the tone. They looked at each other and had a silent but lengthy conversation.

"It's late, dear," the green-eyed woman said.

"We are going to sleep now," the other woman said, eyeing Agnes warily.

"No, please, where did you see her?" Agnes insisted.

"Well, it wasn't that long ago," she said through a fake yawn. "So perhaps she's still very near."

And even though Agnes knew it was impossible, she pictured her mother crouching in a tree above her, ready to pounce and carry her away. Agnes felt her cheeks become wet and knew she would go with her mother this time.

*   *   *

IN THE BOTTOM of her bag she found the small notebook like the one her mother had always carried with her, the small pencil stuck in the wires. She wrote a note, half in pictographs and half in alphabet letters, because although her mother had taught her how to write, she never had had a reason to learn it well. She rolled the note and left it in the knot of the tree they camped near. She wanted her mother to be able to find her. Just in case she was looking. Agnes left notes in trees all through the mellow mountains she and Fern wandered. She sharpened her miniature pencil on rocks. She wrote notes to her mother until the paper in the small notebook ran out. And then she left things she thought her mother would know were put there by her. Leaves, acorns, pine needles tied in a bow.

She wanted her mother to find her.

But she was found by Ranger Bob instead.

One bright morning in the headlands, after a foggy wind-filled night, Agnes awoke under a shadow where no shadow should be.

"Rise and shine, Agnes."

She squinted open an eye and saw Ranger Bob looming over her. His mustachioed frown was sympathetic.

She heard horse hooves prancing in the grass, announcing the presence of more Rangers. She felt next to her for Fern, but she was not there. Agnes sprang to her feet.

"Don't run," Ranger Bob warned. He wore a new uniform. This one was scarlet, with badges down the arms. A thick vest covering his chest shone under the sun in an unnatural way like plastic. He had two guns, one on each hip, and his hand was ready on one. It glinted in the sun, along with his wedding band. He had a different hat and different badges from the other Rangers, who held back, alert, waiting for his instructions. "I'm afraid playtime is over," he said.

"Are you in charge now?"

"I've been in charge for some time," he said. Ranger Bob straightened almost imperceptibly. But Agnes noticed his pride. "I'd like this to go smoothly," he said. "I was always fond of you."

Agnes heard a rustle in the bushes behind her.

Fern came bounding out from the bushes, yelling, "Agnes, Agnes, it's the Place! I think it's the Place!"

The Rangers drew their guns.

"No," Agnes yelled, throwing her hands up.

Fern halted, her eyes large and wet like ponds. She had a rabbit by the ears, and it kicked its scrappy legs at the air. Ranger Bob whistled through his teeth and waved his arm down. The Rangers lowered their guns.

"Who's this?" Ranger Bob asked, softening his voice so as not to startle her.

Agnes waved Fern toward her and put her arm around her.

"This is my daughter."

Ranger Bob smiled. "Well, that's nice."

Agnes hugged Fern tighter.

Ranger Bob took his hand off his gun and brought out plastic circles that had hung on his belt. He put them around Agnes's wrists and closed them. "I think you're the last of the Community."

"I doubt that," said Agnes.

"No, I'm pretty sure we got everyone. They were easy once you split up."

"Is that so?"

"Yeah. You probably should have stayed together."

"Why?"

"Because without you leading them, they were easy pickings." He took Agnes gently by the elbow. "I'm not going to cuff your daughter. I don't want to scare her. But I trust you'll make sure she behaves." He smiled at her just like Ranger Bob had always smiled at her. Then he yanked them forward.

Ranger Bob walked a pace ahead, pulling them along like wild horses by a new hard bridle. Agnes's grip on Fern's hand was desperate and white-hot. Had she failed? Was there more that she could have done? What if she had told everyone to go with her mother? To the Private Lands? Would they be safe? Would they be together?

She stopped. "Where is my mother?"

"I don't know where your mother is."

"The last time I saw her, she said she was meeting you. She said you promised to take her to the Private Lands. Did you?"

Ranger Bob's mustache twitched and his face darkened. "Sweetheart, there are no Private Lands."

"But the deal you made. And she said you two had a plan. She said you said you'd take us," Agnes said. "Didn't you say you'd take us?"

He slowed and his shoulders tensed. "People say a lot of things. It doesn't mean they will happen. Your mother and I . . ." He paused. "We said a lot of things to each other." He looked as though he might say more, but he didn't.

Agnes finally formed a clear idea of what they'd said to each other and why. Her mother had said what she had needed to say so that he would help her, help her daughter, help her family. And Ranger Bob had said anything he felt like saying because he could.

Her hackles rose.

EPILOGUE

OFFICIALLY, THE ROUNDUP lasted three months, but a small group of the Wilderness refugees evaded capture and lived on in hiding for three more years. The Rangers did not publicize this. They kept searching and were not kind when all were found. But that's another story.

During the Roundup nearly two thousand unauthorized people were found and extracted from the Wilderness State. There were only ever supposed to be twenty.

This history was called the Great Wilderness Roundup. During an unexpectedly progressive and brief moment in time, it was referred to as the Ranger Rampage. And someday, when those of us who lived there—who ran from the Roundup so we could remain there—are dead and gone, I'm sure it will cease to be known at all.

They told me I lasted thirteen years, the last three on the run. When they finally found me, I had Fern in my care. A little girl who had only ever known the starry sky I grew up with. Who only knew the warmth of elk hide and the joy of the rare wild plum, the jolt from walking through a field where wild chive secretly grew, the green and bitter scent in her nostrils. I'd tear a bit and put it in her mouth, and she'd smirk with distaste and also with knowing. All natural things are known and understood somewhere inside a natural being. Those were good years, being on the run with Fern. I thought of her as my daughter even though she called me Agnes.

When I had first arrived in the Wilderness, the uncommon bustle of twenty humans had brought prairie dogs out of their holes to watch. Deer snapped their heads up from the grasses. Hawks made tight circles above our heads. Nothing made a sound. Though I'd been young, it was something I never forgot.

When we left the Wilderness, it wasn't really a wilderness anymore. From the back of a Ranger truck, we watched the Valley we had spent our early years in come into view. The one with my family's cave. The one nearest to Middle Post. The one with the Caldera overlooking it. The one that had been the first place that felt like a home. Madeline's Valley. Yellow tape fluttered in the wind, marking off squares of land as far as I could see. Some squares were dug up. Many contained buildings in some state of construction.

"What are those?" asked Fern.

"Those are houses."

"What are houses?"

"They're buildings that people live in."

"Like in the City?" Fern had only heard of the City with its skyscrapers. Who knows what she pictured in her mind.

"No, you wouldn't find these in the City. Only a few people will live in these. Maybe even just one."

"Did you live in a house?"

"No, I lived in the City."

"Well, then, how do you know about them?"

"I've seen them in magazines."

"Who is going to live in them?"

"Important people."

Fern's eyes got big. "Are *we* going to live in them?"

"No, *cariño*, those houses are not for us."

We drove by a squat large stone building. A perfect rectangle with large windows flanking a grand doorway, *Hidden Valley Elementary School* carved above it. There was no one out. Perhaps no one lived here yet. Or maybe it was one of those holidays when families hopped into the car to drive the Boundary Road. We drove by a town center, a main street with a small grocer and other shops, past a park and a playground, and the Hidden Valley Library too, just before we turned onto a road that stretched away from town and out of the Wilderness. Everything was laid out according to some fabled map of how things used to be a long time ago. So this was the Wilderness State's new mandate. It turned out there were Private Lands after all.

The road out was clean and paved black. A fresh yellow line painted down the middle. At the end of that road was a gate and a barbed fence like we'd seen across the Poisoned River. When we looked back at the gate sliding shut, we could see the Caldera standing sharp and white over the rooftops of the town.

*　　*　　*

IN THE RESETTLEMENT complex on the outskirts of the City, where Fern and I are housed, I don't recognize anyone, though supposedly we have all been picked up in the Wilderness. There was one boy I thought might be Baby Egret, but the boy was a toddler now and the years in between had been full of changes. I thought he looked like Carl and Val, but he barely spoke and his hands shook as he picked up the wooden blocks he seemed determined to stack. He did not appear to remember me when I knelt in front of him. An older woman was caring for him. I asked her about Val, but she just shook her head. No. The woman answered no to all of my questions, even when they were contradictory. *Is she here? No. Was she captured? No. Is she dead? No.* I couldn't be sure if the woman even knew Val, or if the boy was even Baby Egret. So I left the woman and the boy alone after that.

"Is there another complex?" I asked a guard after I'd explored and asked around after Jake, Val, Celeste, and the others we had met on the run, in hiding. The guard glumly shook her head. Everyone that got picked up was here.

It's not that I believed the guard, but I didn't know what to make of their absence. I felt somewhere in me that my companions had to be somewhere, alive. At least a few. At least Jake. I felt it. Felt him. Though what good is that feeling if he isn't here with me?

Other Wilderness refugees in the complex swear they are missing people too. And they swear those people are alive. People swear they've heard of other Resettlement complexes elsewhere in the City, flung far from one another along the City's border. Which means we're all here; we just aren't together. Some find this enraging. Some find hope in it. But who can say if it's even true?

I looked for my mother but never found her. She would have heard of our capture because we were reported on for a while, but she never came to claim me. I don't know if she made it out. I like to imagine my mother, as much a friend as the Rangers ever had, might have been shown some mercy.

I lost almost everything in that Wilderness. I lost everyone. I lost Jake. Twice I bled heavy and late, and those were losses to me. I even missed Pinecone sometimes. This wild Fern, this girl I call my daughter, was someone else's daughter in the Wilderness. She lost her mother, a sister, and ended up with me. I've watched loss daily, but sometimes it's my mother I miss the most.

*   *   *

NOW IT IS just me and my Fern.

She is probably seven years old now, as scraggly as a coyote pup and as curious too. When she was young and in the Wilderness and we were on the run, sometimes she didn't bother to walk. She just sprinted on all fours as fast as any of us were walking. She loped alongside a coyote we encountered once by a stream, and the coyote, convinced of her feral canine-ness, yipped and bounced around her.

Here, in the City, she takes all of this concrete, bustle, decay in with interest. She's inquisitive as she wanders around, as though it is just another wilderness to explore. Another part of the map we had yet to unfold. A thing to become part of. She calls it her New Wilderness. "It's yours too," she says to me. But I know it isn't.

She has her bad nights, dreams of her mother, her sister. Dreams of all the messages she grew up hearing from the coyotes, the wolves, the elk, the magpies, the peepers, the crickets, and the snakes. Here, the message is untranslatable. It's an ever-present hiss, gurgle, hum, and then a scream. It comes from the Refineries. But Fern listens hard to it, as though someday she'll know what it's saying.

"It has to be saying *something*, Agnes," she says. "It's making noise."

Here's what I've discovered. If you follow the fence from our Re-settlement complex out to its farthest point, where it meets another fence at ninety degrees, there is a hole cut there. We squeeze through the fence hole and then we are in a marsh. The marsh borders the Re-fineries. It absorbs the heat from the machinery, and at night it steams against the cold air. At night, just like my mother said, there is life in the marsh. In the day you'd think it was dead. But that's because the creatures know they are rare, and rare things never last. We go through the fence and wait until the curfew alarms screech and the sun finally sets, and then, quietly, a frog will croak. A mallard will moan.

Someday, someone who doesn't want the hole to be there will find it. They'll close it up and there will be no way in. The fence is high, its top barbed and electrified. I'm squirreling money away for wire cutters so that when this happens I can make a new hole, and when that one is covered, I can make another.

The ground is worn under the fence hole. I know others come here. Sometimes in the night, when we are exchanging calls with a bullfrog, I even hear a rustle that I know is human. I put my hand over Fern's mouth because even through the Roundup she never fully learned to be afraid of what she couldn't see. But I've learned. I know better. It's not safe to make yourself known in a place you're not supposed to be. We must always hide. But even though we're hiding, I have a sense that the people who come here at night come for the same reasons we do. Escape from the world as we know it now. To know the world as it once was.

I bring my Fern here, cutting into her night's sleep, because I want her to remember what she knew in the beginning of her life. What I knew my whole young life. The other night when I tried to rouse her, she rubbed her eyes sleepily, whined and kicked. She didn't want to go. She threw the blanket up over her head. Eventually I cajoled her out of bed, but I'm afraid of the day when I can't. When she becomes obstinate. When she becomes different from me. What will we share if we can't share this? Will we be nothing but strangers? I want to grab her in these moments, squeeze her too hard, growl into her hair, never let her go. But she always wriggles free, unfazed, or maybe with a small eye roll. She knows she has everything I can give her. I think of my mother in these moments. She was someone who never did what I expected her to. When she looked at me, I didn't understand what her look meant. She looked at me sharp-eyed, her mouth twisting and pained. As though looking at me hurt her sometimes. I didn't understand it until I had the chance to care for this little Fern and I looked at her and saw all that came before and all that would come after and all its potential awfulness and certain beauty and it was too much for me to bear. I looked away, scared, disgusted, overcome with love, on the verge of crying and laughing, and finally, finally, finally I began to know my mother.

*　　*　　*

I TELL FERN stories sometimes. Stories I grew up with. From our home in the Wilderness.

I tell a story I made up, and at the end she asks what I call it.

"What I call it?"

"Yes, you have to name the story. My mom always named her stories. The Tale of the Wolf and the Weasel, for example."

"Got it."

"So what is the name of your story?"

"It's the Ballad of Fern."

Fern blushes. "Oh, no," she says bashfully. "That story's not as good as the others."

"It will be," I say.

I'll tell her this story and the others with all their complications and confusions because those complications and confusions are what make them true. It feels at times like the only instinct left in me. It's the only way I know to raise a daughter. It's how my mother raised me.

*   *   *

A FEW MONTHS after returning to the City, I walked into a hardware store. The clerk eyed me. I could not possibly be rich enough to buy anything, dressed in my Resettlement stripes. I went to the paint swatches and I picked out all the colors I remembered from my old life, my wilder life. I took those swatches, the generous rectangles of color, a code and a name in their corners. I took them all and slipped them into my bag and ran from the store well ahead of the clerk.

Back home I spent a sleepless night taping each square to the wall in a mosaic, placing patches and lines of color how I remembered them. Looking out from the height of land over a patch of verdant grasses toward the smudge of mountains on the horizon. Perhaps on a rainy day when all the colors would seem to have blurred their boundaries. It was a pretty and quiet and private place. A place you wouldn't want to leave.

When Fern awoke, she rubbed her eyes twice and said, "I know that place," a serene smile on her face, her voice thick with sleep and with wonder.

LAND ACKNOWLEDGMENT
AND AUTHOR'S NOTE

THIS IS A work of fiction set in the future, and any connection to the real world or real people is coincidental. However, I visited real places and environments, researched real traditions, foodways, and skills of tribal populations, as well as of earlier primitive cultures, looking for materials with which to build this fictional world. I would like to acknowledge the Northern Paiute, Shoshone, Ute, Klamath, Modoc, Molala, Bannock, and Washoe tribes, whose ancestral lands provided inspiration for where these characters lived and walked.

Further Acknowledgments

THANK YOU: Josie Sigler Sibara for accountability. Hilary Leichter, Amanda Goldblatt, and Jorge Just for above-and-beyond reads. Aric Knuth, Jessamine Chan, Heather Monley, Xuan Juliana Wang, Dennis Norris, and John McManus for engaging with part or all and having excellent thoughts. Aziza Murray, Ben Parzybok, and Kat Rondina for playa shenanigans. Berkley Carnine for a helpful question. Seth Fishman and Terry Karten for many, many thoughtful reads and boundless support. NELP for so much, but especially for the mail table. A special nod to the Summer Lake Hot Springs, where, in reality, the water is not too hot.

I am grateful to the National Endowment for the Arts, PLAYA Summer Lake, the Sitka Center for Art and Ecology, Grass Mountain and Frank and Jane Boyden, Ucross Foundation, Caldera Arts Center,

Sewanee Writers' Conference, Yaddo, and the MacDowell Colony for their supportive funding, time, and space.

Research for this book was general and wide-ranging, but early igniting inspiration came from *Oregon Archaeology*, by Melvin C. Aikens, Thomas J. Connolly, and Dennis L. Jenkins. Sarah Green and Fred Swanson, USFS, led the walk that sparked the idea for this book. Alan Weisman's books helped me imagine a future world. And the online trove of primitive-living experts and enthusiasts made researching brain tanning and other wilderness skills surprisingly easy.

© Jorge Just

ABOUT THE AUTHOR

DIANE COOK is the author of the story collection *Man V. Nature*, and was formerly a producer for the radio show *This American Life*. *Man V. Nature* was a finalist for the *Guardian* First Book Award, the *Believer* Book Award, and the *Los Angeles Times* Art Seidenbaum Award for First Fiction. Her stories have appeared in *Harper's*, *Tin House*, *Granta*, and elsewhere and have been anthologized in *The Best American Short Stories* and *The O. Henry Prize Stories*. She is the recipient of a 2016 fellowship from the National Endowment for the Arts, and lives in Brooklyn, New York.

The New Wilderness was shortlisted for the Booker Prize 2020.

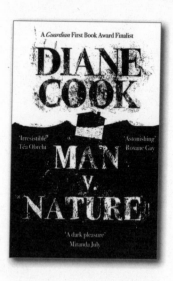

Shortlisted for the *Guardian* First Book Award, 2015
Shortlisted for the *LA Times* Book Prize, 2015
A *Boston Globe* 'Best Fiction of 2014'
One of Roxane Gay's 'Top Ten Books of 2014'
An Amazon Best Short Story Collection, 2014

Perfectly pitched and gorgeously penned, this astonishingly bold debut collection introduces Diane Cook as a major new literary star

Exhilarating and terrifying, *Man V. Nature* pulls the reader into a world where an alpha male is pursued through city streets by murderous rivals; a marooned woman defends her house against a rising flood and hordes of desperate refugees; and a pack of unneeded boys take refuge in a murky forest, forced to compete against one another for food. Wry, transgressive and utterly unique, Cook's wildly inventive debut collection illuminates, with surreal humour and heartbreak, humankind's struggle not only to thrive, but sometimes merely to survive.

'Quirky, often edged with menace... Cook's is a fresh and vivid voice; it's unsurprising the likes of Miranda July and Roxane Gay are fans.'

Observer

'Masterly.'

New York Times